Java
MAN

by
HARRIS GRAY

Java
MAN

[From an editorial in the American Medical Gazette, addressing the tragedy from the recent experimental cancer treatment administered by Dr. Khaled Bhani.]

In 1891 William Coley came across the medical chart of a German immigrant named Stein. Doctors had removed a tumor from Stein's neck, repeatedly, the final time forced to leave behind a portion of the tumor insinuated into parts too important to disturb, along with a gaping ulcerous wound that could not be closed. To boot, Stein caught a raging case of erysipelas as it was known in the day, "St. Anthony's fire", scourge of Civil War battlefields, a strep infection. The bug nearly, but didn't, kill him. Stein was discharged after a months'-long battle.

William Coley found something incredible in the doctor's notes. Over the course of the virulent infection, Stein's wound had healed, and the tumor had disappeared, to the point the dumbfounded doctors could imagine their patient cured.

This was an awe-inspiring clue for Dr. Coley, only a year into his medical career and already on the hunt for an edge against the dread disease after watching (and amputating) impotently as cancer swiftly killed an eighteen year old patient. Through New York City's tenements he searched until he found Stein—bearing an unmistakable, scarred excavation on his throat—and confirmed what the file notes suggested: during the battle with erysipelas, Stein's immune system had seemingly reared up in full force to battle the infection, and in the process obliterated the tumor.

In the following decade the brilliant Coley successfully cured more than 20 cancer patients with an immune response-triggering solution dubbed "Coley's toxins". And thereby revolutionized medicine, saving thousands of lives over the next hundred and twenty years…

That last sentence is fiction, of course. Coley's toxins were not embraced by his peers. For a medical community ready to leave behind the prior era's unregulated, unsophisticated methods, eagerly embracing new technology and establishing rigorous standards of care, Coley's approach was barbaric. Worse, his results could not be repeated by other doctors. Coley continued to publish and present at conferences his purported cures. But with radiation and then chemotherapy galvanizing the medical community, he and his toxins were written off, relegated to a status only slightly better than the traveling peddler of magical elixirs.

So how much of Coley's results were fact, and how much fiction? Read Stephen Hall's account in his fabulous book, A Commotion in the Blood, and you'll come away a believer. Yet after Coley's death, it took the better part of a century for researchers to resume efforts to harness the immune system to defeat disease, and cancer in particular. To this day their results are decidedly mixed. With a growing list of afflictions assigned to the category "auto-immune diseases", the immune system receives less press for healing than for the ravaging damage it can do to us.

And for good cause. No biological force is more fearful than the immune system tricked, triggered and baited to wage war within the body it was designed to defend. Little was known of the mechanics of our immune system back in Coley's day; but perhaps his peers appreciated the threat to the physician's essential obligation, "first, do no harm". Cancer is a horrible scourge, yes; but woe to he who indiscriminately wields our most terrible sword.

I'M AT a good place right now, so I'd like to tell you my story, starting nine months ago. I'm telling it like a NASA countdown, T minus twenty, T minus nineteen, because after all the missteps, faulty parts and deteriorating conditions, I'm finally ready to lift off. I won't blame you if this reads more like a time bomb counting down to detonation.

T-20

PEOPLE TELL me things. People love to talk, and I live to listen. I know when to nod my head in agreement, groan in dismay, lend a subtle suggestion or just stay quiet.

People tell me things. Why, I don't know, because everyone knows I give as good as I get. I don't believe in secrets, other than as conversation pieces.

What I hear from you, about your job or wife or golf game, could very well be passed along to the next guy, embellished as necessary. I'm a storyteller, but I can't just make this stuff up. I have to get my stories somewhere.

So here goes.

This young guy in a business suit had been coming into my coffeeshop for the past couple days. Nice guy, easy smile, introverted in a way that invites conversation. Blushed whenever my assistant manager Charlotte asked him something more personal than How's your day going? He would give her a polite and short answer and then promptly ask a return question, to deflect attention back to her.

Charlotte knew she made this gentleman—all gentlemen—nervous, and not so secretly she enjoyed it. I'd like to think she kept the banter flying and their nerves firing as a sales technique, to build our customer base. But it was for the tips. Nervous sexual tension equals tips. So the banter flew and the tip jar grew.

Even though I'm right there pulling shots and frothing milk, you would never know I'm listening to these conversations, because all the while I'm humming or singing or letting the customer know that her tall white chocolate mocha is ready. But I know the best way to keep 'em coming back—besides hiring cute underdressed employees—is to personalize a dig, a gentle flattering dig. And this sort of tailored teasing can only be achieved by listening.

So when this well-dressed young man came in for the third day in a row, I was prepared. Charlotte said, "Hi there, what can I get for you?"

Speaking for this gentleman, I said, "Your phone number?" He blushed like a fire engine. Charlotte told me to shut up with a suffering sigh. And the next thing you know, with Charlotte off washing dishes and me lounging on the counter with a little time on my hands, he's telling me about a girl.

Kevin was his name, from San Francisco, and he was supposedly in town to audit the local Wells Fargo branch. His real mission, though, was to make time with a woman named Andrea. How this came to be, how he received this golden opportunity, well, I will never cease to be amazed how well life can work out, at least for some people.

Kevin met Andrea at Colorado State University. Kevin was the caring, stable shoulder that Andrea cried on whenever she and her college sweetheart had a fight, which was often, often enough that Kevin fell in love. A month before graduation three years ago, Andrea accepted a marriage proposal from her cyclical boyfriend during one of their reconciliations. Her fiancé had it goin' on, earning a degree in mechanical engineering and going to work for one of Denver's top construction firms, with the knowledge that he would eventually open a Denver branch for his father's successful North Dakota construction company. And so the crestfallen accountant Kevin took an internal auditor job with Wells Fargo in San Fran, resigned to never again set eyes or hands upon his old flame.

"Wow, a mechanical engineer," I said to Kevin. "Sounds like she made the right choice." I can be a smart ass. Not sarcastic, because I actually like people. But a smart ass. Which is a decent segue to tell you about this woman named Francesca who walked into my shop the next day.

"Hey there," I greeted her. "What can I get for you?"

"You have a sandwich board on your sidewalk," said Francesca, a pointy-chinned lady with puffy hair, a dingy scoop of ice cream on a pale sugar cone.

"We don't serve sandwiches, sorry."

"No," she said, instantly exasperated, "your sandwich board."

"I don't know what you want," I said.

"On your sidewalk," Francesca snapped. "You have a sandwich board advertising your store."

My only real customer perked up his ears behind the screen of his laptop. Terrence is a wannabe author who writes his novels for two hours darn near every day of the five years I've owned the shop. He's the best unpublished writer I know.

I like having an audience during times like this, especially one with an ear for snappy dialogue. "A sign board. Yes I do."

"It's called a sandwich board," Francesca corrected. "And it's against town regulations. We have an ordinance against it."

"Well not really."

"Yes. Really."

Among the downtown merchants, Francesca is affectionately known as the sign nazi, which gives you a feel for the not-so-affectionate labels. Signage infractions are her specialty, but she also excels at badgering the police to enforce wintertime parking violations, and keeping the county health department current on potential health code offenses.

Francesca wouldn't approach the counter. She dug through her satchel. "Here's the relevant section of the ordinance." She put the photocopy on the nearest table.

"I'm familiar with it. It's Sally, right?"

Francesca glared. "It's Francesca."

"Frannie, this is a waste of your time. And of course mine. The town has never enforced that statute."

"We have no choice. We've had a complaint."

"Really? Someone complained? Gimme a break. Who?"

After a long internal debate, Francesca decided to make this into a fun guessing game. "A fellow retailer."

Wouldn't have been fun in any case, but I already knew the answer. "Would this retailer sell bad coffee, by any chance?"

Charlotte entered through the back hallway, lugging two five-gallon pails of beans from our roaster across the alley. "What's going on?"

"I'm being busted for an illegal sign board."

"Oh that's crap." She dropped the pails with a bang and opened the freezer door.

Francesca looked over my shoulder toward the kitchen, hoping to score a couple more obvious violations. "Compliance is serious, Mr. Lawson."

"Frannie, a week from now we'll be ten below zero and under two feet of snow." It was late October and beautiful outside, Indian summer they called it. But winter was coming, and always with a vengeance. That knowledge—and because the golf courses were closed—made it hard to enjoy the nice weather. "People will be dying on the sidewalks if they can't find the place with the hot coffee. It's not just serious, Frannie. It's life and death."

"You have one week to comply, Mr. Lawson."

"Or what?" I asked.

"Or what, what?" she said.

Before getting into a bad Abbott & Costello routine, I answered, "What's the fine? What's the penalty if I don't comply?"

She put her weight on one leg and a hand on her hip. "The maximum penalty is thirty days in jail."

"What's the minimum?"

"I surely don't know, Mr. Lawson."

"I'll take the minimum." This got a chuckle from Terrence, pretending not to be listening.

"Mr. Lawson," said Francesca, "you have a week to comply or respond."

"I'll take your 'respond' option. And I don't even need a week. No."

"What's that?"

"My response. No."

Terrence chortled, and quickly put his cup to his lips. Maybe that little exchange would make it in his novel.

Francesca puffed out her itty-bitty chest. "You have one week. Good day."

"You're not going to tell me who it was?"

Francesca raised her eyebrows and lowered her eyes, which isn't the most difficult maneuver in the world, but does take practice. "You may come down to the city administration building if you wish to see a copy of the complaint." With a last glance at the overflowing garbage can, Francesca walked out, stopping on the sidewalk to make record in her notebook.

I cleaned, whistled, seethed. Terrence sauntered to the table where a copy of the ordinance lay. "You want to see this?"

"I already know what it says. Our economic development committee voted to recommend to city council that they do away with it. Outlawing sign boards doesn't make sense, because the town won't let us alter the building signage above the first floor. Historical preservation."

"We have historic buildings?" Charlotte was dubious, on hands and knees to access the freezer's bottom shelf.

"It's all relative. So since the downtown businesses might actually need to announce our presence to the occasional out-of-towner who's running out of gas and accidentally takes the business loop instead of the exit with all the gas stations and fast food shops and great big neon blinking signs, the city council agreed that the sandwich board ordinance is a non-issue. They couldn't bring themselves to get rid of it, but they won't vote to enforce it."

Charlotte pouted. "Why would anyone complain about our sign?"

"Charlotte designed it," I told Terrence.

"It's a beautiful sign," he said.

"Thank you." Charlotte continued to pout as she consolidated beans to save freezer space. "Hey," she exclaimed, suddenly all excited, slapping me on the leg to prove it. "Did you hear Edna Applejack might be getting out?"

"Is that a new cereal?" I asked.

"Her appeal was successful?" Terrence is a mild-mannered chrome-domed six-foot-two jock-turned-engineer-turning-turning-ever-so-slowly-turning-into-a-writer, so I was sure I hadn't heard the squeak of excitement in his voice.

"My friend Tonya's dad is a judge, so this might be confidential," said Charlotte. During my year in college, this was the breathless tone women used when they discussed the latest developments in their favorite soaps. "It sounds like the conviction will be reduced from second degree to third degree, or something like that. But the judge isn't going to rule until spring."

"Second degree what?" I asked. "Burns?"

"Murder," said Charlotte. Still kneeling, she put her hands on her hips. "You honestly haven't heard the story of Edna Applejack?"

"What kind of coffeeshop owner are you?" Terrence piled on.

At the time I got a little defensive, my pride wounded. In retrospect they were right. How did I not see Edna coming?

"Edna is a North Dakota legend," said Terrence.

"How long ago did they put her away?"

"I don't know, what was it?" Terrence pondered.

"Ten and a half years ago," said Charlotte.

"Old news," I told them.

"Not if she gets out," said Terrence.

"Whatever," I said, heading for my office. "I gotta run."

"Brian."

"Hm?"

Charlotte stood there with her arms crossed. "Nurse Nancy was in here earlier today, looking for you. Tell me you're not going to see her."

"I don't need a nurse, Charlotte. I'm not sick." Charlotte had a way of getting me to crack even when I wasn't fibbing, so I turned my back and continued on my way. "That was very thoughtful of her to check in, though."

"You better be telling the truth. But if you're not, promise me you'll shower before you come back."

"Who showers after medical checkups?" I wondered aloud, making Charlotte growl.

"I'm betting Brian is going to Town Hall to see who complained about his sign," said Terrence.

"That's a better guess," I called back. "But I already know."

"Is it the guy who owns the campus coffeeshop?"

I leaned out of my office. "Would you say Hernandes's shop is by the campus? I wouldn't. He's a good mile from the bridge. The way the streets run along the river, his place is no closer to campus than we are."

"Sounds like you pulled out a yardstick and measured it," Terrence joked.

"I'm going by my odometer."

I was hot to open another shop on the Jamestown College campus, but the private school was aware that its well-to-do students were a retailing gold mine. And so the College owned and operated every convenience store, hamburger grill and vending machine on campus. And regularly reminded the city council to keep the surrounding square mile zoned strictly residential, or else. Nobody wanted to contemplate the 'or else'. This is a college town, Jamestown College-town. The billboard off Interstate 94 proclaims us the "Home of the Big Buffalo", but the gargantuan bison statue on the hill is a figurehead. The College operates all the levers of power. My downtown location is about as close as any business can get to the campus.

I was hot to open a second shop, period. Here, there, anywhere. A second, and a third. A whole chain of coffeeshops. Unfortunately, this was impossible.

At the moment I was pissed off that other people were opening coffeeshops. Why is it that no one would think of becoming a golf pro without a stellar short game, yet the only prerequisite to opening a coffeeshop is a failed career and a caffeine addiction? I can't count how many times customers have come in and admired my establishment, with dollar signs in their eyes.

"I love coffee," they say. "I should do a coffee shop."

I try to smile. My head almost explodes. Then I envision this potential competitor swimming and finally drowning in debt. "Yeah, you'd be good at it," I say, as sincere as I can muster.

Hernandes was the perfect example. He was doing everything wrong, and sooner or later he was going to have to call it quits. But in the meantime he was taking business away from me. The timing couldn't have been worse.

But back to Kevin the auditor, the San Francisco cheat, a bit player in this tale, but responsible for so much that follows. He was almost gleeful over his good fortune. Of Wells Fargo's thousands of branches, he managed to get himself staffed on an audit in the little North Dakota town where his old flame lived. At a time when her marriage was falling apart. Is life amazing or what?

Granted Kevin didn't know me well enough to worry about my loose storyteller's lips. But auditors are known for their critical thinking skills, the ability to connect the dots and recognize a problem, right? So how do you figure him regaling me with poorly told tales of how he mooned over this Andrea girl in college, always there to comfort her but never really getting any; and how he e-mailed her the week before this audit started and learned that, just like old times, she was having serious trouble with her man; and how, just like the old blue-ball days, they had gone out drinking, and even spent a couple hours in his hotel room, where nothing had really happened; and how Andrea and her husband, whose name is Rick, Kevin tells me, moved here a year ago from Denver to help out with his family's construction business while his brother underwent chemo treatment—I mean, being a coffeeshop owner in a town this size, wouldn't you figure that I might know this Rick guy? Because I do.

T-19

I WALKED to Town Hall, two blocks away. That's where I park. There are a limited number of spaces behind my shop, and I like them available for the morning commuters. The Chamber of Commerce forgot to confiscate my parking permit after I rotated off the board, so I helped myself to the Town Hall employee lot. Given that I did Taekwondo once a week, and played on a city-league basketball team for a few weeks in the winter, I didn't need the exercise—the four-block roundtrip walk was probably fitness overkill. But I never complained.

Mark Andersen the town manager had received many, many complaints about Frannie. He freely admitted it. How many complaints do you have to hear about an employee before you let her go? Ten? Fifty? A hundred? Charlotte was an amazing employee, but I would still have to let her go on her 50th complaint. Tops.

The last time I called, I had to pause in mid-complaint for all the sighing from Mark. When he quieted down, I had continued. "I'm not accusing Frannie of puncturing my inflatable coffee cup, but she did draw a chalk circle around it. I had customers wondering if someone died on my sidewalk."

"Duly noted. I'm glad you called. Thank you for your concern and input."

Was that a recorded message? What does Frannie have over the city? Photos? Sex tapes? Was Mark in her will? Someone this ill-equipped to deal with the public should be mowing ditches and emptying wastebaskets at midnight. Must be nice to work for a city that has no balls.

So instead of beating my head against Mark Andersen, Town Wall, I got in my van and drove straight to the source.

South from my shop on Main Street, Jamestown's main drag, I turned left at the Hardees, drove three blocks past a string of warehouses fronted by tall security fences, turned left again into a sixty-year-old collection of single-story ramblers housing very little disposable income, and then made a final right onto a street the width of a four-lane highway. Here sat Uncommon Grounds.

"Uncommon Grounds". The name screamed coffee, but no imagination. There are over two hundred Uncommon Grounds in the country, none of them affiliated. Uncommon Grounds, Common Grounds, Muddy Waters, House That Brews, The Beanery, Java Hut…I could go on. I would be embarrassed to use any of these names. Sure, James River Valley Coffee isn't the most creative name in the world. But as far as I know, I didn't rip anyone off.

The building formerly housed a printing shop. Now it was a retail strip, Beads!, Calvert's Tax & Accounting, Replay Sports, and a couple businesses still To Be Determined. Hernandes thought he scored a real coup landing an endcap in a redeveloped commercial strip overlooking the James River, with the campus only a hundred yards away on the opposite bank. But it was a mile down to the nearest bridge, so the students without rowboats stayed on campus and drank terrible coffee made from bulk foodservice beans brewed by ladies in hairnets.

Which was also a fair description of Hernandes's coffee.

As for all the shoppers working up powerful thirsts as they combed strip malls for outrageous deals, somebody should have told Hernandes that while coffee is certainly consumed twenty-four hours a day by rich college kids, for the rest of us it's mostly in the morning on the way to work. If you aren't a convenient stop on the way to the office, you're wasting your time.

The heavy door went unwillingly, the plate glass shuddering and chattering. Every head, all six of them, swiveled to check me out, then returned to reading, conversing, or for one elderly gent in a backwards ballcap, staring at the east wall and picturing the river sparkling in the mid-afternoon sun as if through a window.

The room was long and narrow, fifty feet to the counter at the back. The only light was from shaded lamps perched on rickety end tables, and a fluorescent strip above the kitchen. Fluorescent lights, a staple of a classy coffeeshop. The walls were painted in swirling coffee gradients, a band of French roast at the bottom, cream and sugar across the middle, café au lait at the top. It did make me think of coffee—first time I've ever feared drowning in it.

"Hey Charlie," I greeted one of my customers, nose buried in a book.

"Oh, hey, Brian. I was just trying to get a little peace and quiet," he struggled to explain. "Your store is always so busy…"

I patted him on the shoulder like a disappointed parent. I took his book and checked the cover. "Harry Potter. I've heard it's good." I slammed it shut. "Oops. I think I lost your place."

"Hey, no problem," said Charlie, eager to suffer any penance I dished out. "So what brings you all the way over here…"

I continued the trek to the counter, snaking through beat-up couches and sagging easy chairs, spindly end tables and small mangers filled with highbrow magazines. The man behind the counter pretended not to see me coming, Adam's apple elevated as he hummed along to the house sitar music. He was slim and effeminate, dressed in earth tones. His glossy black hair lay tight to his head, accentuating bulging eyeballs. For someone who had supposedly spent thirty years in the cutthroat Manhattan investment banking scene, his brown skin was unnaturally smooth. Jamestown was founded by men who priced pelts like that by the pallet. "Brian Lawson," I introduced myself. "Welcome to the neighborhood."

"Bill Hernandes." He felt obligated to reach across the counter. "Hernandes with an 's'. It's Portuguese."

I shook his hand. Thought about pulling him off his feet and across the clutter of cute clipstand menus, folk band flyers, coffee-themed knickknacks, and jars, for tips, pens, biscotti, and suggestions, to slap him awake from the nightmare he was putting me through.

You might look at the competition Hernandes was bringing to town and say, hey, it's capitalism, good for America, good for Jamestown. I say guys like Hernandes are the suicide bombers of the retail world—they have no chance to survive, no apparent love for their own financial lives, and they're eager to take everyone else down with them. The only difference being there's no need for a whack-job imam to implant the delusions of financial grandeur—these guys are spiritually self-guided, hanging out at coffeeshops until they're convinced all they have to do is open their own shop, and that mansion and all those virgins will be theirs in a few short years.

Hernandes eyed me warily. "Are you here for, or what do you…can I get you something?"

"Americano would be great. So how's business all the way out here? Slow like now?"

"No, no. This is the first time today the line isn't out the door." He was a terrible liar. Unless he was talking about his line of angry creditors, I hoped. "People are loving us. Feel free to look around."

"Thanks. Love what you've done with the place." I strolled amongst his few customers as I talked, bumping the occasional elbow. "And here everybody was certain the city council was wasting the town's money. You know, paying to clean up all the toxic printing chemicals that had soaked through the floor and contaminated the soil."

"No, it was worth it," said Hernandes, coming around the counter. "Not much to clean." He tried to usher me back to the register.

"I kept hearing the words Superfund, Three Mile Island, Chernobyl…" I looked around apprehensively. "Wish I had a Geiger counter…. I heard they did a terrible job."

"No. Top-notch. Drink…?" Hernandes sounded like he was being strangled.

"Americano," I reminded him, completing my tour and returning to the counter. "Have you met Jasper Smith? He's the—"

"City council president." Hernandes finished. "Great guy. And Carol and Tad, and—"

"Doug, John, Jennifer, Dawn. That's all seven, I believe."

"They bent over backward to make me feel welcome." Hernandes fumbled with the tamper, losing half the coffee out of the portafilter. "Cammie, could you come out here and make an Americano?" He spoke slowly; I could tell he was working hard to eliminate his accent. "I want to talk to Brian here."

A plump girl wearing a pink stretch shirt with a lacy sewed-on camisole appeared from the back. "Americano?"

"Thanks Cammie," I said.

She mumbled something unintelligible as she studied the barista instruction manual with a frown.

I pointed at Cammie. "That's one thing I've always prided myself on."

"Hmm?" Hernandes was watching her closely.

"The ability to fix drinks and work the crowd at the same time. I think it's essential to an upbeat, high-energy store."

Hernandes's eyes kept darting to Cammie, who was twisting knobs and punching buttons like I had never seen. "Uh-huh, true," he intoned.

I waited until I had his full attention. "Do you have time to sit down?"

Hernandes thought this over, wide eyes on me, if not really studying me. Maybe it was those eyeballs, too big for their sockets, giving him the wary chinchilla look. Maybe it was the way he kept grooming his smooth shiny hair. "Okay. Yes. Cammie…" He blinked, like he was fighting off a mild aneurysm. "Make two of those, please?" He pointed me to the nearest table, shoved too close against a bookcase filled with old smelly books. Hernandes waited until I was seated before perching his butt in the chair. He folded his hands on the table. "So—"

"So I received a complaint today."

"Oh, yes?"

"My sign board is an issue."

"Well, yes, I understand sandwich boards are a code violation. It's a potential safety issue. It's important to allow free access on the sidewalks—"

"It's just advertising, Billy. You have a nice storefront. If anyone ever finds their way back here, they'll spot you. But the downtown businesses need sign boards, because of signage restrictions on our buildings."

"It would be nice if we were all treated equally, wouldn't it?"

Don't try to match wits, Billy. "Of course that's not possible," I said, and thanked Cammie as she set down our drinks. I looked for eye contact from her, received none.

"Of course that's not possible," Hernandes echoed. "Fairness isn't always possible. But it's important that businesses have a level playing field."

"Those sound like contradictory concepts. Right?" I chuckled, and Hernandes chuckled with me, with no idea why. "You either compete and accept the consequences, or you spend all your time looking for handouts and favors, am I right?" My chuckles faded to a sigh. "So did you file that complaint?"

Hernandes stopped mid-chuckle. "No I did not file that complaint."

"Good." Liar. "Because we have to stick together. This isn't a competition. If we increase the public's coffee knowledge, we all win." One bad lie deserved another.

"Couldn't agree more." Hernandes forced a smile. "How's business?"

"Great." I beamed as I rose, and stuck out my hand. I was furious. "I gotta run. Stop by sometime." And get a good cup of coffee. "You can check out my sign board, see what's on special."

"You're uh, you're not going to pull your sandwich board?"

"Not a chance." I bared my coffee-stained teeth (a must in the industry). "Take care now." I flicked Charlie's book as I passed. "Charlie. Stay focused."

I was all the way to the door when Hernandes said, "Please, uh…please don't disturb my customers."

My cell buzzed as I climbed in the van. "Hey Mike."

Mike McEwen owns Jamestown's biggest construction company. Commercial, residential, they build it all. Mike runs it with his wife and his son—whose name is Rick, by the way. "Brian, how are you? Making any money down there today?"

"A buck or two. I hear you're sending a little my way tomorrow. We're planning on having the coffee ready to go by noon."

"That's why I'm calling. Not about the coffee. The meeting. I want to make sure you're going to attend."

"Hadn't planned on it."

"So change your plans." Mike spoke like a Mafia don with a Scandinavian accent. "We'll be discussing the retail center we're putting up by the new hospital. I want you to have first dibs on the anchor pad."

"The Bluffs, huh?" I stalled. Even with the new hospital nearby, I honestly didn't think it was a prime location. But maybe that was sour grapes, because I couldn't afford it anyway. "I thought you handled construction and left the developing to someone else."

"I never leave the developing to someone else," said Mike.

"Hold on a second." I pulled alongside a car idling at the last intersection before Main Street. The man behind the wheel looked lost and confused. I leaned out the window. "You looking for the campus-area coffeeshop?"

"I am!" He was pleasantly surprised to find a savior.

"Follow me." I waited for him to make a U-turn. "Sorry Mike. Helping out a lost customer. So you were saying about the Bluffs…"

"I'm saying you need to be in there. It's the centerpiece of one of the biggest developments Jamestown has ever seen."

"How about when they painted the big buffalo's balls blue?"

"That was some development," Mike agreed. "So I'll see you tomorrow?"

13

I have no problem saying pretty much anything to pretty much anyone. But telling Mike 'no thanks' was difficult. "I appreciate the offer. But I'm not sure I'm going to be interested."

"Just come and listen to the details—you'll get too excited to stop."

"I hate it when that happens."

"Yeah, well, it doesn't happen to me anymore. Not without those purple pills. Which reminds me…Margie," he called to his secretary, "get me a glass of water, would you?"

"I hope it's not too late," I said.

"Me too," said Mike. "Which also reminds me. I had lunch with Nancy today. You know that Valerie and I, uh…we like to…"

"Sure." Nurse Nancy had been Brent McEwen's personal nurse during his battle with cancer, his miraculous turnaround, and his sudden death to an infection. Every month since, Mike and his wife took Nancy to lunch, to show their appreciation and to remember their son. I talked so Mike could regain his composure. "Everybody's been talking about the new Italian place by the college. I'd bet everything I have that you went there."

"Cracker Barrel," said Mike. "Nancy kept bringing you up. She seems eager to see you."

"Of course she is. It's been three months." I'll explain later.

"You should date her. She's a helluva nurse. And God knows she's cute."

"If The Man Upstairs says so."

Dry chuckle from Mike. "Alright Mr. Coffee, I'll back off. Let's get back to your plans to expand."

"Unfortunately, my finances aren't that flexible, at the moment."

Mike gave an impatient grunt. "I'm not short on cash. Your investment would be intellectual. And some sweat equity to get the place up and running."

"Mike, come on…"

"I've seen the hours you put in, my friend. You're worth the risk. Setting you up would be a community service, for what you do for Jamestown. The people in this city want you to succeed so badly. You've been here fifteen, twenty years now…"

Mike knew better. "Closer to five."

"That's what I mean, it seems like you've been here forever. You fit in so well, people can't imagine you anywhere else. Brian, you could have picked anywhere, but you picked Jamestown, and Jamestown is the better for it."

I felt myself blush a bit, Mike can lay it on thick to close a deal. "Mike, all I'm saying is, I don't know if the Bluffs is the right place. And it doesn't feel like the right time."

"Believe me when I tell you, it never does. JUST DO IT."

I had the ultimate respect for Mike. He started McEwen Construction in college and built it into a regional powerhouse. He just didn't understand what it took to make money in this business. Hell, I didn't. He didn't know I had already been down the road he was trying to take me, a few years back in California. I knew where that road led. Lupus.

I learned coffee from Dougie Fosseton, owner of the Davis Drip in my hometown. Dougie was a legend. On the rare occasion he was in the house, customers came out of the woodwork, lined up out the door, to get a Fosseton latté. He would entertain the crowds with tales from his childhood on the plantations of Sumatra and his kidnapping by pirates of the Celebes Sea.

Not so surprisingly, Dougie could be a raving lunatic. Whenever his employees hacked him off, which was often, he would chew ass like I have never ever seen. But Dougie took a liking to me.

"Java man," that's what Dougie called me, "you remind me of me." This horrified me, Dougie was badly browned and wrinkly. "Java man, I'm going to open up the vault for you."

Dougie showed me what he called his "patented" roasting technique, which, thank goodness, wasn't—it's a great method and I've been using it for free ever since. If I wasn't in school or playing sports, I was with Dougie, learning how to find the best green beans and getting to know his favorite growers and brokers. It wasn't long before he took me off the bar, so he could teach me the business. I was a sponge and he was a river of knowledge. It takes a big sponge, an oversized sponge, to soak up that much knowledge. I owe him so much. God damn him for all eternity for refusing to show me his "patented" latté preparation technique—but whatever, I was clearly his protégé, and I should be eternally grateful for that.

After a stint in Alaska—that's another story, sort of a collection of strange, only-in-Alaska stories—I returned home, enrolled at UC Davis, and went back to work for Dougie. One day, a couple months into my freshman year, a supplier screwed up our order, and we ended up dangerously low on beans. Dougie sent me to Sacramento to beg for a hundred pounds from his competitors. I returned with the hundred pounds, and an extra thousand, with orders to roast them for his competitors. Dougie got excited. I became his wholesale bean salesman, hitting the road every weekend. Whether it's retail customers or fellow retailers, selling coffee comes natural to me. Working two days a week, I was the Central California Whole-Salesman of the Year (Small Business Division). I still remember the Salisbury steak they served at the banquet. Scrumptious.

My future was clear and bright. I couldn't wait to graduate from college. In fact I didn't wait. I wasn't surprised or bothered by Dad's explosion and Mom's tears when I announced that a degree wasn't necessary. I hugged them and promised that I would make them proud. I was in love. While the memory makes me a little sick to my stomach now, I can still feel the giddy exhilaration over the plan to open my own chain of coffeeshops.

The day after my twenty-first birthday, I ended my apprenticeship at the Drip and started my own coffeeshop, Central Valley Coffee, a few blocks away. I bought the building from a dry cleaner, and if anybody knows easy access, if anyone knows parking, it's the drycleaner. Customers got in, they got out. And in between they were greeted warmly, usually by the right name. They caught some singing, not so good that they felt like they were being entertained, like they had to listen, like a compliment was necessary. Serious conversations could take place in my shop, under the cover of my voice, the music—looking back, a little heavy on the REM and the Squeeze—and the hiss and squeal of the frothing wand.

People loved my shop. The service was prompt and courteous, the atmosphere unbeatable. And of course the coffee was topnotch. I was kicking Dougie Fosseton's ass. CVC was on everyone's lips.

"So when are you going to open another shop?"

I heard that one all the time.

"Do you have a shop on the north end of town?"

Variations of that one, on a regular basis.

"I'm from San Fran. When are you going to open a shop there?"

That was one of my favorites. "Someday," I would say, believing it.

Business was great—although I was puzzled at how little money that meant. Quite the mystery, and Sherlock Holmes I am not. I couldn't wait to get bigger. Then I heard the owner of Timbuktu Coffee in Sacramento was looking to sell. I jumped on it. My banker jumped on me, ready to ride that dark-coffee horse all the way to the winner's circle. I was a heavy favorite, at least in my own eyes.

Profits started out small, and never grew from there. For every new customer who swore allegiance to me, one would leave. Dougie Fosseton cleaned up the Davis Drip's act, taught his employees to smile, and started billing himself as a campus coffeehouse. Fucking liar, he was nowhere near the campus.

"Hi Brian," a customer would greet me. "Where were you yesterday?"

I got really tired of hearing that question. "At the other shop," I would say. "I alternate days."

Pretty soon, so did my customers. And when they couldn't remember whether today was Brian day, they just didn't come.

I looked like a success. People see big fat margins in every $1.95 cup of coffee and every $3.80 latté. At the same time everyone recognizes that America is the land of cutthroat competition, and if competition is good at anything, it's squeezing margins down to the pennies. No one seems to see the mutual exclusivity in these two concepts.

Two years after he had sold me his shop, the former owner of Timbuktu Coffee decided to get back in the business. "Coming Soon!" signs were popping up all across Sacramento, "Timbuktoo Coffee!"

I called him. "Joe, I'm not using Timbuktu—with a 'u'. You can have it back."

"No way," said Joe. "Timbuktoo—with two o's—is even better."

I'll tell you what was better. His new location. Location, location, location. Joe was opening his new shop in the spot he should have been in from the start. I knew it was a great corner, but the price had been too steep for me. Joe scored a big coup. He had to outbid a drycleaner for that site.

To top it off, Starbucks was coming. I had to increase my volume and my margins, pronto. I welcomed the challenge. I really did. My business model was unique, and customers raved about my coffee. To get over the hump I just needed more of them, and to become a fixture in their lives.

For two years I was a maniac. To cut costs I had let three employees go, so I worked multiple shifts by day and did all the roasting by night. My free time consisted of dealing with personality clashes among my few remaining employees, and shuttling back and forth between Davis and Sacramento, making the twenty-minute trip five times a day to cover gaps in the work schedule. Not paying salaries is a pretty good way to pad the margins.

But my volume wouldn't budge. New customers would come in—and old ones would leave. I felt like I won their hearts and their business when I was present, then lost them when I wasn't. Same for my employees. They laughed when I was with them, and grumbled when I was at the other shop.

I was slipping. I forgot customers' names, drinks and stories, and both shops suffered for it. Customers and employees alike resented me for not being there every second of the day. My business was a dike that had two leaks, and all I could do was run back and forth, taking turns plugging them. At least that's the dream I kept having.

I was in too deep, and too wigged out to realize it. I was desperate for volume, for name recognition, for cachet.

So when the opportunity to sign on to a neighborhood retail development project in Berkeley dropped in my lap, I took it. The People's Republic of Berkeley, hotbed of anti-capitalism; where disposable income flows like water, grows on trees, and makes millionaires out of second-rate entrepreneurs; where bankers line up to finance construction, inventory, payroll, the new car and the company van. Where I was going to vault over that hump.

And then I got tired. I ran out of gas.

I couldn't get out of bed. Of course I did, but it was hard for those around me to tell. I dreaded the hour drive to my other shops. All that quiet time to contemplate my misery and worry about the newest problem with the landlord or a customer or an employee that I was going to hear about as soon as I stepped in the door.

So I rehired two of my ex-employees and cut my Sacramento time in half. Which was exactly what happened to my revenue. Without me there, my regulars stopped coming. Without regulars laughing and filling seats and creating a vibrant atmosphere, the walk-up customer started walking on by. Luckily the Berkeley financing came in handy to pay off the mounting deficits from the Sacramento shop. Call me Ponzi. I had to lay off one of the very same employees I had already hired, laid off, and hired again. He walked outside and keyed my car and spit on my windshield, and I understood completely.

The Berkeley strip was nearly finished, and I was halfway through the detailing of my space when I pulled the plug. I didn't actually call it quits, I had my accountant call the developer and tell them I had lupus.

And now here was Mike McEwen, pushing me toward another flare-up. I'm honest with people about my problems. For every dilemma they share with me, I probably divulge two of my own. But my inability to be successful in the coffee industry wasn't a problem. It was the defining crisis of my life. I couldn't discuss it with my friends, I couldn't discuss it with my father, and I couldn't discuss it with Mike. I wouldn't discuss it. I just wanted to solve it.

And then there was the North Dakota issue, which can be summed up by noting that Sinatra didn't sing, "North Dakota, if I can make it there, I'll make it anywhere." The dark secret I kept from my Jamestown friends, employees and customers, was that I was increasingly embarrassed to be there. This was my own little psychosis to be sure, but like any other mental illness it was all too real. It was a diagnosis I sure as hell couldn't confide to Mike, the most rabid North Dakota booster I knew.

So I was going to have to disappoint him, with no explanation. The McEwens loved me—because of what I brought to the town, and just because. When their youngest son died, they loved me all the more. The McEwens are a hard-charging, no-nonsense family—a little scary on the outside, fun-loving and fiercely loyal on the inside. They're my kind of family. If I was an orphan or a wandering amnesia victim, I would have asked Mike and Valerie to adopt me. But I already had perfectly good parents.

And did I mention my sweet mobile coffee shop? Last year Mike convinced his plumbing subcontractor it was time to donate his brand new panel truck, to the local school for developmentally disabled adults. Turns out Mike had a nephew in there who was hell on wheels with a blowtorch and arc welder, and after Mike finished brokering a multi-party deal the Palestinians would have been wise to get in on, yours truly wound up with a no-money-down, no-payments-forever, deluxe javamobile. Not scot-free, but you had to really look to find the advertisement for Dr. Kim's Large Animal Veterinary Services.

You'll understand then that I was in the market for a good deed for the McEwens. A notion of positive payback had been percolating for the past twenty-four hours, since my last visit from Kevin the bank auditor. At that moment on the phone with Mike, said notion became a full-fledged idea.

"Mike, I can't make your meeting tomorrow, but why don't you have Rick come down and pick up the coffee. Around eleven."

"Fine. I'll have him fill you in on the Bluffs. The Bluffs," Mike savored. "Nice, huh?"

"It's a good name."

"You bet your butt. I'll have Rick come see you tomorrow. It's a no-brainer, Brian. A sure thing. You'll slay 'em there."

"Don't tell Rick we're going to talk business. Just tell him to go get the coffee. 'Fetch the coffee, boy.'"

"'And bring me a muffin!'" Mike laughed. "It's a plan, Mr. Coffee."

T-18

KEVIN THE bank auditor was sitting at what had become his spot over the course of a few days. My shop sits on the corner of Main Street and Second Avenue in the heart of downtown. There are three tables on the floor and another smaller table on the dais in the front display window, where the former Herberger's department store put their fall, winter and spring collections, which varied only by the thickness of the scarves. A couch and two easy chairs sit against the interior wall...

I hate to interrupt, but now's the perfect time to point out another critical comparison to Hernandes. My couches are comfortable, not old. My colors are rich and subdued, not dark. My place is clean. This is a college town, but it's still North Dakota. Farmers. When they walk in, they're thinking value, not ambiance. They're not convinced that a store devoted solely to coffee is such a great idea, and the sight of a bunch of lounging, lecturing, tea-sipping hippies only confirms their suspicions. Hernandes was trying to recreate Soho, Haight-Ashbury and the Paris Left Bank, all rolled into one. If only I had the luxury to sit back and wait for that sonofabitch to fail.

I have thirty feet of stainless steel tabletop bolted to the wall, the last couple yards running alongside the counter, creating a chute with just enough room to squeeze in a bar chair. Kevin the auditor loved that seat.

"So how do you find the time to come down here for a couple hours every day?" I asked him during a long lull between customers, seconds after Steve from the Jamestown Sun left without selling me an ad, flyer or coupon, a few moments before Rick McEwen walked in.

"For one thing, we schedule too much time for these audits," said Kevin. "Two weeks is ridiculous. I could be done by Tuesday; but I'm budgeted for fieldwork all the way to Friday. I could wrap it up early and show a big positive variance. But auditors live by an unwritten rule: never bust the budget for the next guy."

Kevin had endearing qualities. He smiled a lot, with nice teeth. A little skinnier than I like to see a man. I was a touch heavy those days. I considered myself a really, really good-looking Jack Black, and an athlete who had grown a gut from working all the time. That's where I was coming from.

"Then there's my technique," Kevin continued. "I slam the bank employees in the morning, first thing, before they can book enough meetings to avoid me. I prepare my list of documents and analyses the night before—"

"Unless you're otherwise occupied."

"True." Slight grin. "I slap this To Do list on them, always with double the documents I actually need pulled. Then I come here for a couple hours. You'd be amazed—I can find a great place like this in just about every town I visit."

"I'm flattered you think this is a great place."

"It's true."

"A little less happy to hear I'm a dime a dozen."

"Actually this is the best coffeeshop I've ever been in."

"Go on with your story."

Kevin debated the need for more groveling, deciding it was safe to continue. "When I show up again after lunch, the bank staff is usually only halfway done with my list. I tell them, 'That's good enough, I'll make do'. They are so thankful. They think I'm a wonderful guy. It's a pretty good system."

"I know quite a few of the people who work at that Wells Fargo branch. I should have probably told you."

Kevin's soft hazel eyes widened. "You won't say anything, will you?"

"Naaww." That's when Rick McEwen entered. "Here's somebody I want you to meet."

Rick is tall, with a tall head. When you add it up, I'd say six-three. His hair is thin and flat to his head. Like baby hair. He has piercing eyes and a thin nose. All that being said, understand that he's a pretty good looking man. I don't think it's just my opinion. For a straight man, I consider myself an objective judge of male beauty.

"Rick," I greeted him. "Here for the coffee?"

"So I hear," said Rick.

"'Hey boy,'" I impersonated Mike, "'you don't seem to be too busy. Like usual. Why don't you run fetch us some coffee.'"

"For never having been to our office," said Rick, "you have a pretty good idea of what goes on there."

"I'm sorry to hear that," I sympathized. "Hey, there's somebody you should meet. Rick, Kevin." They shook hands, and I started filling in the blanks for them. "Kevin's from San Fran, but he went to CSU in Fort Collins. Rick, didn't you graduate from CSU?"

"I did." Rick nodded at Kevin. "You do look familiar. San Francisco, huh? What brings you to North Dakota, for crying out loud?"

"Kevin's an auditor for Wells Fargo," I answered for him because I think his mouth was dry.

"Really." Rick took a step closer, which I knew wasn't unusual for him. Kevin probably didn't. Rick is running a lifelong experiment on people's reaction to an invasion of their personal space. "What was your major?" he demanded. As a related study of the human response to social discomfort, Rick's habit is to make questions sound like threats.

"Accounting," said Kevin, softly, almost as an apology, sitting as far back as the corner would allow.

It's worth noting that for all his size and aggressive habits, Rick is the least threatening guy I know. You can't rile him. You know the old saying, silent waters run deep, and often conceal a twenty-foot man-eating shark? That isn't Rick at all. The man just wants to work. He loves construction— loves it from the moment he wakes up until the second he falls asleep, early, maybe eight-thirty, after a big dinner and a couple glasses of wine. Rick found his life's calling, and is at total inner peace with who he is and where he's heading. He wasn't going to hurt Kevin. He's the only guy I know who could actually take Jesus's advice and turn the other cheek, and not feel like a complete wuss.

"What year did you graduate?" Rick demanded. At this point, because of his natural Inquisitional conversational style, I couldn't tell whether Rick was aware that he might have cornered a fox fresh from his henhouse.

"Oh-seven," said Kevin, squirming in his chair with a burnt amber flush on his cheeks, feathers on his lips.

"Rick, didn't your wife graduate in accounting?"

"Business management. She did take a few accounting classes. Maybe you know her," Rick said to Kevin. "She was Andrea Goldine back then."

The skin below Kevin's eyebrows went white. "Yeah. Yeah I do—well, did, I did, back then." Was he guessing I had manipulated this meeting to set him up? No, Kevin was thinking one thing and one thing only, oh God, forgive me my sins and deliver me from the fatal beating I am about to receive. Me, I was feeling pretty good about myself. I was a helper.

Rick was seeing Kevin through slits.

"Hey." Andrea née Goldine now McEwen had entered the shop without my noticing, to stand behind her husband. "So this is where you go when you leave the house." Andrea had a sassy mouth with Rick. They had moved to town a year ago, when younger brother Brent McEwen's oncologist had pronounced his cancer incurable and given him a few months to live. Rick and Andrea arrived just in time to watch Brent make a miraculous recovery, and then suffer a quick, shocking death. I was working from a small sample size—Rick's birthday bash thrown by his folks, a celebration of Brent's recovery, and Testimonial #1 after he passed—but Andrea seemed unable or unwilling to mesh with the McEwens' tight rhythms.

Rick raised his arm to look down at her through the notch of his armpit. "Speak of the devil." He dropped his arm around Andrea's shoulders—a good foot below his—and pulled her forward, further damming up the chute between counter and tabletop, Kevin's only escape route, if you don't count melting into a puddle of goo and seeping between the floorboards. "And no," said Rick, "I don't come here. I go a lot of places. Here isn't one of them."

"Rick is the errand boy this morning," I said, watching the interplay between Kevin and Andrea. This was a little more than I had bargained for.

"My old man thinks he's funny," said Rick. "I'm going to teach him a lesson, though. Set me up with two dozen muffins."

"I can't help you there," I said. "Unless you want those." I tapped the top of the display case, where a couple tipped muffins and a few loose cookies lay in the crumbs of the previous days' pastries. And there was a croissant, which for the life of me I couldn't remember buying. "I don't recommend it."

"I'll pass," said Rick. "How about if you whip up a few lattés and cappuccinos to go? Something pricey."

"Five of each?" I nodded to my employee Sam at the espresso machine, all six-foot-seven and two hundred sixty pounds of him. When he screwed up, we blamed it on his tallness, and when he did something great, we wrote it off to his unfair height advantage.

"I'm on it," said Sam. No contest, he made the best lattés on staff. But so could we all, if we were as tall as him.

"I've never seen you two together outside of family functions," I said to Rick and Andrea. "And in my shop no less."

"And I doubt you'll see it again anytime soon," said Andrea, cute, petite, long in the hair and face, compact in the torso. She was even cuter than usual that day, perhaps thanks to spending a few additional minutes on the makeup. Maybe just the extra cleavage and leg she was showing. "Rick is a workaholic. Unless you're wearing a hardhat and steel-toed boots, Rick won't spend much time with you."

"Put on chaps and spurs, then maybe we can talk," said Rick. "So." He waggled his hand at Kevin, who looked startled to find himself still visible. "This is—"

"I know Kevin," Andrea short-circuited the introduction. She gave Kevin a wry smile, while he stared at the floor and perspired. Nice poker face, Kevin. Andrea crossed her arms in disapproval. "I should have known you two would find each other." She looked up at Rick. "Can't I have a friend all to myself?"

Rick spread his arms as far as the tight quarters would allow and shrugged. "We were getting along pretty well, but if that's the way you're going to be…he's yours." I couldn't get a read on his mental state.

"Yeah, right," said Andrea, whose clipped syntax meshed well with her husband's. "I know how men are. Now you two are buddies, and I'm out of the picture. Fine." Very cool, very calculated. Andrea was determined to hold on to both her men. Dangerous game, I thought to myself.

My goal had been to fire a warning shot across Kevin's bow, before he dropped anchor in the McEwen harbor. I wasn't looking for an in-store exchange of accusations and, God help me, admissions. So far it was all very jokey, but it was banter I couldn't enjoy. Trouble was brewing, and I prayed for thirty customers to stampede through my door. Then again, I always prayed for that.

Terrence and his laptop walked in. Good enough. "Terrence!"

"I got him, Brian," said Sam. I could have tried to elbow that big boy out of the way, but I would have lost. "Hoodilee-hoo, Terrence."

"Hoodilee-hoo, big guy." Terrence ignored me, too polite to interrupt the conversation I appeared to be enjoying in the corner.

"So let me get this straight," Rick grilled Kevin again. "You're just in town for a few days? Where are you staying? The Holiday Inn?"

"At the Buffalo Motel, actually." Kevin looked miserable. "It's a little seedy, but I like to get the local flavor when I travel."

"Our firm built the addition on the Buffalo Motel last year," said Rick.

"I'm pretty sure I'm in the old part," said Kevin. A warm puff of panic wafted across the counter.

"I've heard that when Wells Fargo hires auditors," I spoke to Andrea, "tact isn't a quality they look for. Just a rumor I heard."

"Then Rick should have been an auditor," said Andrea. She looked up at him, her arms still crossed, maintaining her sassy pout. If she felt any guilt, she was hiding it very well. "Tact is definitely not his strong suit."

"If I wasn't tactful," Rick retorted, "I'd be accusing you two of getting busy at the Buffalo Motel."

"Like you would care," said Andrea.

"Just as long as it doesn't interfere with our regular schedule." Rick gave me a wink. "So are those expensive coffee creations ready?"

"Almost done," Sam called out.

"Let me grab the brewed coffee," I volunteered.

"I'll pull around back to load it up," said Rick.

"God," said Andrea. "How much coffee do you people drink?"

"You should be able to carry it out the front door," I told Rick, while I gave myself silent props for mission accomplished. Kevin had been scared shitless; it looked like everyone was going to walk away in one piece; and Rick wasn't going to bring up the new retail center. That was my favorite part.

Sam helped Rick out the door with the drinks and pump pots. Andrea remained behind with Kevin. I could now ignore them in good conscience. I had no doubt Kevin, who may have wet himself, would be wrapping up his audit a few days ahead of schedule, next year's budget be damned. I went about my business, refilling the portafilters, wiping down the bar, flushing hot water through the espresso machine, whistling while I worked.

"That was interesting," said Andrea to Kevin. "I suppose I should have told him you were in town."

"Does he know who I am?" Kevin hissed. "No way. Does he?"

"Only what I told him back then," said Andrea, calm and slightly bored. "That you and I hung out sometimes. That you were always a good friend whenever he was being a dick to me. Don't worry about it—I could have told him you were my hot passionate lover and it wouldn't have mattered. Rick doesn't have a jealous bone in his body."

"That wouldn't have been my read," said Kevin.

Yes, I was eavesdropping.

"He seemed ready to beat the hell out of me," said Kevin.

"He couldn't if he wanted to," said Andrea. "He never works out."

Andrea moved in tight to Kevin, fingers touching his arm. Kevin couldn't take his eyes off the door, waiting for Rick to walk back in, bearing arms. "Just from observation," I joined the conversation, "I'd have to say that if it came down to a battle to the death between Rick and Kevin—say there's only one spot left on the rescue boat before the ship sinks—I'm taking Rick. No offense; but honestly, he'd rip your head off."

"I don't know," said Andrea. "Kevin has some decent muscles under there." She tugged at the sleeve of his polo shirt. "If I remember right."

Like I said, dangerous game. "Were you two an item at CSU?"

"Not really," said Kevin.

"I wouldn't say that." Andrea shook her hair back and fingered it into place for the waiting barrette clenched between her teeth. In this position she highlighted a flexible spine and a sleek throat. Like I said, Andrea wasn't skinny, but she knew how to smokescreen her lack of a waist. That morning she had chosen apparel that revealed a generous stretch of tanned leg and more than a hint of cleavage, all currently on full display.

Kevin was suddenly antsy in a different way. Exuberance barely contained. The possibility that at any second Death could come a-bursting through my front door was a fuzzy memory. He was dying to touch those legs, and plumb that cleavage. He had exchanged fear for lust, right then and there. This guy was in too deep.

When the show was over, I asked Andrea, "What can I get you?"

"Do I have to buy something to stay here?" Andrea teased.

"I'm afraid so."

"Then you're going to have to kick me out."

"I know you're not afraid of me." I'm tall enough, but not imposing. Even though I played sports in school, I never packed on a lot of upper-body muscle. I was content to go with my God-given abilities, a strategy that freed up a generous amount of high school party time while the other guys were in the weight room, and still allowed me to letter four years in basketball. As a teenager my underdeveloped torso created the illusion that my head was too big for my body, when in fact it was exactly the right size. I'm not going to call it the perfect fix, but now that I've added a few pounds around the middle, everything looks more proportionate.

"Are you afraid of me?" I thought I should check, just in case.

"No," Andrea confirmed.

"I don't blame you. But did you get a look at Sam?" On cue my whopper of an employee returned through the front door, filling it with his thick shoulders and round buzz-cut head. "Sam," I called to him, getting the attention of my handful of customers. "I want you to stay calm when you find out what Andrea here just said about you. I can't afford any rough stuff, my liability insurance lapsed last week." This was no joke; certain bills you can stretch, and some you can't. "Sam. Sam. Gently for once. Kick her out gently."

Sam had played this game way too often, for his tastes. He did his best to threaten from long distance, puffing up his chest and sucking in his gut before lumbering into the office.

I stared after him. "You are going to have to work on your focus," I hollered. "What did I tell you to do? Didn't I say to kick her out? You want a paycheck or a pink slip?" Most people had caught my act enough to laugh. Every so often I shocked a customer. Probably drove them to Hernandes's shop, if they could find it.

Andrea was chuckling. "You are too much."

"He is," said Kevin. "I've truly never been in a shop like this, and I've been all over the past few years. You can feel the clock ticking in every other coffeeshop, the employees waiting for you to leave. Here, it's more like I'm being entertained in Brian's living room."

"You still have to leave at some point." I wasn't in the mood for flattery from this guy. "You're seriously not drinking anything?" I harped on Andrea. "Seriously?"

"Brian, I've been here a year and never come into your shop. Obviously I'm not a coffee drinker."

"You're not going to order a single solitary thing?" I pushed.

"Not a thing." She spread her arms wide, a tough-guy pose. "If you want me out, looks like you'll need to do it yourself."

"If you're going to be that way, I guess you can stay. I don't want to see you sipping on Kevin's mocha, though."

Kevin pulled his drink closer.

"Don't worry," said Andrea. "I don't like coffee. Plus," she said as I walked away, "I heard that new coffeeshop close to the campus has the best joe in town."

That almost hurt my feelings. I froze with my back to them, then threw down the coffee-stained towel I had just picked up. "That cuts it." I played a hammy dinner theater actor playing me, pointing at the door. "Out."

T-17

THE NEXT time I saw Andrea was early January, during a blizzard, outside Martin's Restaurant & Bakery. I was picking my way along the sidewalk carrying a to-go bag when she staggered through the bank of plowed snow separating street and sidewalk and fell in next to me. I mean fell. I saw it coming the whole way and caught her arm, holding her upright until she got her feet under her. At no time were my chicken and dumplings in danger of sloshing out of the Styrofoam container. I looked around, waiting for the applause. Never an audience when you need one.

"Thanks," said Andrea. She checked to ensure her bundle of papers remained secured by the rubber band. "Good thing I don't weigh much, or your back would be out."

If she didn't weigh much, then my feat wasn't all that spectacular. And in fact Andrea's weight was not insubstantial. That gal weighed more than she looked. But I held my tongue. Chivalry was a bitter pill to swallow.

Andrea bent over and brushed snow off her fur-lined pointy-toed boots. A car drove by and launched a glop of dirty salted slush over the plow-bank, landing an inch from Andrea's suede boot. She straightened up and sighed. "Nice winter we're having, don't you think?"

"Winter in Jamestown is hell on earth. Only a lot colder." I inched down the sidewalk toward my shop, eager to be on my way. Without knowing what had transpired the past three months, you might assume it was because I was hungry for those dumplings, or because I was wearing shorts. "By the way," I said, "thanks for not coming into my shop anymore. I don't like trouble with non-coffee drinkers."

"Really." Andrea perked up at the challenge, inching along with me. "What if I came in for a pastry? Would you serve me?"

"A, we don't call them pastries. Around here they're baked goods. B, I don't sell baked goods. Not edible ones, anyway. And C, even if I did sell them, not a chance. No coffee, no service. I'm sorry, but that's my policy."

"If that's the way it's going to be..." She clutched the packet to her chest, and checked out my bare legs. "Nice shorts by the way. What is it today, five below zero?"

"I don't wear pants much. Or ever." Not true, I took Christmas or Easter off, one or the other.

"Aren't you the tough guy."

"Just the only one to realize that if you warm the top, the legs will follow. Your top is the key. I'll stop just short of saying your legs are irrelevant."

"You," said Andrea, "are ridiculous. I suppose your legs are too nice to hide."

"If I'm attractive to the opposite sex, if there's anything remotely appealing about me, it's my legs." I was a hoopster with a soccer player's legs. "And my hair, I suppose." I don't ask for glamour hair, just hair I can take for granted, hair that's going to show up for work each and every day and do its job, which is of course to allow me to nonchalantly run my fingers through it and come away looking no worse than before. "And my eyes...well, enough about my body parts."

"No, go on."

"That's probably enough self-affirmation for one day." Gotta say it to myself you know. It's like a never-ending six-step program.

"Like you need it," said Andrea. "You walk on water around here. At least as far as Rick's family is concerned."

A premature end to an already short North Dakota construction season had postponed my day of reckoning on the Bluffs location. "I'd call it thin ice. I need to get to shore before spring arrives."

My muttering was largely drowned out by a snowplow rumbling down the middle of Main Street, leaving an imposing two-foot berm behind the few cars parked in front of my shop. I had asked the city not to do that—was that Frannie the sign nazi driving the plow? A couple came out of my shop and stood in front of their blocked car, shaking their heads. Former customers, I like to call them. I wanted to tell them "it's not my fault, call the city; talk to Frannie". But of course it didn't work that way. If it happened in front of my shop, it was my fault.

"Do I sense some trouble with the McEwens?" said Andrea, perhaps a gleam in her eye. In truth the temperature was twenty degrees warmer than Andrea's estimate; still, we were standing in a blizzard. The snow was piling up on our feet, the wind periodically whipping a frigid reminder up my shorts. Andrea's winter coat was all fashion, no function. We were both shivering, but Andrea was in no hurry to get inside. "If you don't mind my asking," she probed.

"I'd rather not get into it." I shuffled for the door and nodded at her bundle of papers. "You running errands?"

Andrea chuckled humorlessly. "Legal business. Is that lunch?"

"Sophie, one of the owners at Martin's, she gives me the occasional lunch in exchange for free coffee."

"Sounds like a good arrangement."

"For her. Have you tasted our coffee?" I paused for effect. "No, I guess you wouldn't know how good it is. Well then, have you eaten at Martin's?"

"I don't go out to eat," Andrea stated.

"Let's just say that Sophie definitely comes in for an extra-large three-shot caramel latté ten times more often than I ever grab a half-sandwich and cup of soup from her. But hey, whatever. I don't keep track, and that way it doesn't get to me."

"I'll bet you cry like a baby when she walks into your shop."

That was a good one. And true. Sophie was a schoolyard bully following me into the bathroom every day and stealing my lunch money. "My dumplings are getting cold," I announced. "And your papers are wet."

Andrea looked forlornly into the distance. Snowflakes collected on her eyelids. She was so damn tiny. Tiny little feet taking tiny, careful steps. A slippery patch of sidewalk, a gust of wind, and the next thing you know she's under Frannie's blade, to be found in June when the snow berm melted, frozen stiff like an ancient underdressed pygmy cavewoman. If she was parked more than a block away, I honestly didn't think she would make it in this weather.

Honestly, that was the word that part of myself used to justify inviting her into the shop, to the part of me that knew it was a bad idea. "C'mon in, I'll get you a plastic bag for your papers. Hey, check that out. That's some sandwich board, huh?"

Andrea followed my finger to the white hump a few feet away. A soggy cardboard corner poked through the drift. "It's covered with snow. You can't read it."

"I don't care. I know what it says."

Like snow gods riding personal blizzards, we swept into my empty shop.

"You're getting snow on my clean floor," Sam complained from behind the counter.

"This is just a sample of the drift sitting on our sidewalk," I explained.

"You think that's a good excuse?"

"I guess what I'm trying to say is, shovel."

"Some customers like to play in the snow." Sam grew closer and closer, taller and taller. When I hired him he was a six-foot-two senior at Jamestown High, a few pounds shy of being a fat kid. As a Jamestown College junior he had grown another five inches and still managed to maintain the exact same figure, scaled up. Big kid.

"Don't make me tell Charlotte."

If all of my employees came to blows—say I confiscated smiling Sara's switchblade, and made Dana promise not to use her black magic. Say that I then took them to a deserted island and told them I was going to sail away for an hour (I've given this a lot of thought—possibly too much), and that when I returned, the last person standing would get time-and-a-half for the next three weekends. Assuming no alliances sprang up, the giant, the grinning time bomb, the Goth, the Eagle Scout, they'd all be moaning in the sand at Charlotte's feet. Of course I couldn't afford to pay up, but it's the healthy competition that's important.

Sam towered over us. "Why do I always have to go out and shovel?"

"Because the only other job I have is to redo the menu board above the counter. And your handwriting sucks, frankly."

"Good point." Sam's expression turned grim as he eyeballed Andrea. "Hey. Maybe you could make her do it."

"Sure, I'll rewrite the menu," said Andrea.

"Deal," I said.

Sam hung his head in defeat.

I headed for my office. "Shovel Bodiners sidewalk next door, too," I called over my shoulder. "His son's gone today, and I don't want the old man to have a stroke on my sidewalk."

When I reemerged, Sam was talking to Andrea, shifting from foot to foot, wearing a big goofy grin, the skin below his buzz cut a flushed, happy pink. "That sounds like a great job," he was saying. "Andrea's interviewing to be a research assistant at the hospital," I was informed.

"Oh, hey. Good for you. Who with?"

"It's just an interview," said Andrea. "I'm not counting on it. My business degree specialized in biotech startups, and I worked in a genetics lab at CSU. But this would be a lot different. And I've been out of the loop for awhile. I'm sure he's wondering why he should hire me."

"Because you're short enough to reach the supplies in the lower cupboards," I suggested. "So who did you say you interviewed with?"

"I would probably be a shared resource for more than one scientist."

Besides their money, all I ask of my customers is to name names.

"Genetics lab work," said Sam. "Sounds interesting." If he kept looking at Andrea with those puppy love eyes, I was going to have to roll up a newspaper and stab him in the throat with it. Hopefully in all the pain, confusion and fear, he would wet himself, so I could then rub his nose in his own urine. It takes that sort of firm discipline to break a bad habit.

"Here you go." I handed Andrea a big plastic Pamida bag and stared at Sam. "To protect her papers from all the snow."

"Alright, alright," said Sam, "I'm going." He plucked the shovel from beside the door and ventured into the storm. Another couple inches had drifted against the door, and now fell on my floor.

"He seems like a good man to have around," said Andrea.

"He's alright. He's great, actually." I held the bag while Andrea dropped her papers inside. Legal documents. I saw the words "child custody". (I was going to preface that with Before I could look away, but I'm a bit of a snoop.) "I have a really good crew. I'm lucky."

"I could use a little of that," said Andrea. "A little luck would be nice." Her lower lip quivered.

I would have wished her all the luck and send her packing, if not for my professional obligations. Honestly. "So, can I get you anything?"

Andrea gazed at the wall of white outside my big display window. Sam was just visible, carrying a shovelful of snow, looking for someplace to throw it. "Maybe a glass of water."

"I was going to make myself a tea." I never touched the stuff. "Want one?"

"I'm fine."

"It's the best time to drink tea. When you're feeling fine." Actually there is no time that is right for tea, that coffee wouldn't be better. I dangled and dipped tea bags while Andrea slipped out of her iridescent coat and carefully removed her stylish stocking cap. Her long hair was gently curled, a few hairs frizzy from the stocking cap. A full serving of makeup accentuated her doe eyes and cushioned her pointy chin. Her nails were long and manicured. She moved like a Southern belle, slow and deliberate, planned.

I slid the cup of tea across the counter. "Your legal business must have been pretty important to come out on a day like this."

"I might as well have stayed at the apartment, as it turns out." A grunt escaped her lips as she mounted the stool. That's why you don't see any five-foot tall barfly belles. "Rick and I are divorced, you know." When I didn't react, Andrea crossed her arms, cupping her elbows. "I'm sure Rick's family told you all about it."

"Word gets around." Their marriage apparently disintegrated right after the three-way collision at my shop, and you better believe I had received an earful on Andrea from Mike and Valerie (thankfully with no suspicion that her lovers' fateful intersection was anything other than coincidental.) But I'll bet ten customers had brought up Andrea's infidelity, and not all of their information was courtesy the McEwens. "Fifteen thousand people, and it's still a small town at heart."

"I hate it," said Andrea, just above a whisper. "Tyler and I were going to leave as soon as the custody agreement was final…but it hasn't worked out."

And it wouldn't. I knew from a reliable source the McEwens were bringing serious legal resources to bear to keep Tyler with Rick in Jamestown. Andrea didn't have a chance in hell of moving away with that kid.

"Now I'm in an apartment." Andrea struggled to stay composed. "Our house belonged to Rick's family, so I couldn't very well ask him to leave."

"So…you asked Rick for the divorce?" It was only fair that I asked for her side of the story, as I only knew the McEwen party line. Of course I had seen enough with my own eyes to draw a fairly objective conclusion.

She lofted the Pamida bag. "According to this guy, when it comes to custody of the kids, it doesn't really matter who asked who."

"Chalk it up to a mutual decision then."

Andrea shrugged. "Everyone is so sure Rick is a saint. But what would you do if someone constantly…" She stopped and stared. With her heavy lids and a natural dark shading that haunted her eyes, it was a pretty effective stare. "I probably shouldn't say anything that's going to get back to them."

"Probably not."

"Oh, I have to be careful what I say, but they can say anything they want about me, is that right?"

Of course I was initially upset about triggering the divorce. Scaring her straight, that was all I was trying to do. But chances are Andrea wouldn't have been unfaithful without cause. I had always felt, and was now hearing confirmation, that they simply weren't a good pair, weren't meant to be together. Hand of fate, my hand— if the trigger needed pulling, why waste time IDing the fingerprints? "If you need to get something off your chest…. I'm not much for keeping secrets, but maybe that could work to your advantage."

Andrea studied me, read me like a book, before shaking her head with a bitter smile. "You'd never do anything to make the McEwens angry, because then you couldn't get a coffeeshop in the Bluffs."

She forgot to read between the lines. True, the last thing I wanted was for Mike and Valerie to think less of me. But if doing right by Andrea and helping get the truth out prompted him to pull that sweetheart deal off the table and save me from a repeat of my impersonation of a train-wreck in California, it would be for the best.

Because the temptation was there. Bill Hernandes was stealing my customers. He was printing coupons like funny money—everybody in town must have had a stack of them. You simply couldn't make money if every customer was cashing in a two-for-one. He had to be buying low-grade beans and watering down his milk, ensuring each batch of coupons that rolled off the press was worth less than the one before. Hernandes was a two-bit banana republic dictator running a hyperinflationary economy, gambling on winning the people's hearts before they realized they had lost their minds.

And, I'm not one to pass on a dare. "Just when you think you know someone…that's when you get surprised."

"Mm." Andrea considered me while taking the first sip of her tea. "Eeuu. God. Who drinks this?"

"Bad people. I'll swap it for a coffee."

"No thanks. I should go."

"There's no rush." It's my natural reaction to take it personally when a customer leaves on a down note. "I'm open 'til six. But I suppose you're right. Too much longer and you'll never find your car without an avalanche beacon."

"I heard the snow was letting up," Andrea wished upon a star.

"For sure by May. Pretty much for sure."

"You're pessimistic."

"Realistic."

"But I suppose you love it this way."

"Nine months of winter and three months of pre- and post-winter? No, not particularly. I'm a California boy."

"Then why are you here?"

I started to answer, and hesitated, and then told her why. "Believe it or not, I moved here to start my coffee empire."

Andrea cackled. "Yeah, right. In North Dakota? Really. And?"

"Not so good."

"And now you hate North Dakota. I can tell."

"No. I don't hate it here. I love the people. I have a lot of great friends and customers. And there's a lot to be said for doing business in North Dakota."

"Name one."

"Okay. I won't get sued if someone gets hurt in my shop or spills hot coffee on her baby's head. I had a teenage customer break her ankle—five hundred pounds of poorly-stacked beans fell on her. Her dad came in the next day and called her a clumsy bastard for not getting out of the way in time. You won't find that philosophy of personal responsibility in California."

Andrea grimaced. "I'd say it's a lack of self-worth. People here would never sue you because they don't think they deserve any compensation. They don't think their lives are worth it."

"Thanks for knocking off my rose-colored glasses."

"My pleasure." Andrea was smug. "If you love it here so much, why did you escape to California for the holidays?"

"I wouldn't call it an escape." I would have let furloughed go. "How do you know where I was?"

"I probably heard five times how the McEwens were so disappointed you left town. I guess you've spent Christmas with them before? Of course they could care less that I spent it alone in my apartment."

"Sorry about that. I hadn't been home to see my folks for a year. I actually cut the trip short by a week. Every time I tried to relax and hang out with Mom and Dad, all I could hear was the cash register not ringing here in my shop."

"One more week wouldn't have killed you," said Andrea.

"Another week and I might as well have stayed there for good, because there wouldn't be any customers waiting for me when I returned."

"You honestly don't think your staff can handle things without you?"

"No offense to my staff, they're hardworking kids. But they're kids. And kids attract other kids. Without an adult in charge, the next thing you know you got yourself a hangout full of kids with empty pockets, and not a paying customer in sight."

"You can include me in that category." Andrea slid forward and dropped the last couple inches to the floor. "The non-paying customers. Thanks for the tea."

My cell rang—Charlotte, reporting a successful coffee delivery to the county commissioners meeting, and promising to be back in the shop for the last hour of the day. Charlotte was salaried, but lived on a tight budget and operated under the suspicion that I would dock her pay if she ever went home early. I saw no reason to correct this misperception.

Andrea was going out the door. "Let me get my coat," I called after her.

"I didn't figure you wore coats," she referred to my shorts and loafers.

"I'm not crazy."

"Why are you coming with me?" Andrea demanded.

"I'll scrape your windows for you."

"I'll get your employee to do it. Looks like he's done shoveling."

"Just because Sam can stand on one side of the car and scrape the entire windshield, doesn't mean he'll do a quality job."

"Bye Brian." Andrea stepped into the blizzard, threw a quick look in Sam's direction, and hurried the other way out of sight.

THE SNOW picked up, so I sent Sam home and called off Charlotte's approach. I planned on sitting in my tiny office and worrying over the three-year revenue numbers Charlotte prepared for me, as if it was more data analysis

I needed, rather than more customers. I resolved to work fast and get out of there early, before the temperature plummeted. Maybe call Terrence and Amber, see if they wanted to go bowling.

Instead I sat in the front display window, safe from the whirling snow attacking the glass inches from my nose, and went back a little further in time. Andrea wasn't the only one having difficulty understanding my decision to move to North Dakota.

At my lowest point in California, when I laid awake in bed at night, I wasn't dreaming of greener pastures, of going back to college, of changing careers. I was reading coffee—journals and entrepreneurial how-to's and global field reports—and thinking coffee. I didn't know anything else—and didn't want to. If I was going to make money in this life, it would be in coffee. I was obsessed with discovering a new concept or product that would turn things around.

So when I received the last-chance it's-still-not-too-late reminder for the coffee retailers trade show to be held in Fargo—Cool Trends in a Hot Market! the postcard screamed the theme at me—I jumped on it.

I can't convey to you the excitement I felt. Like sly Fate had convinced the organizers to hold the conference in the great white no-man's land, hidden the Next Big Thing there amidst the booths and presentations, out on the frozen tundra where only the most committed or desperate would find it.

Which described me perfectly.

North Dakota in late October. Colder than I had anticipated. Cold drinks, said the speaker at the first session. Cold drinks are the future. And sandwiches. Everyone was gung-ho for cold drinks and sandwiches. The tone was infectiously upbeat, and why not? Three days to dream big and ignore the fact that most of the coffeeshop owners (and speakers) would be out of business in eighteen months.

The first night I found a bar with an acoustic guitarist on a small stage in the dusky backend, and conducted a one-man brainstorming session at a table halfway back. No ideas had come, just lots of questions, when a stocky blond in a polo shirt and loose-fitting khakis stopped in front of me and said:

"I don't usually go for guys with high foreheads, but, I just had to say hi."

"There must be some mistake." I pulled my mop of hair back. "See?"

"Solid hairline," she admitted. "Then it must be your eyes. You have the sexiest eyes I've ever seen."

"Sexy," I said, like a parrot.

"I'm interrupting your work," she said. "I just wanted to say hi. I would have kicked myself otherwise." Before I could say "kicked", or ask her for a cracker, she marched off and disappeared into the crowd.

I was flattered of course—she was a pretty girl, in spite of the drab clothes—but actually didn't give her more than a couple fond thoughts over the next hour as I drank vodka tonics and continued to struggle between the need to expand my menu offerings, and my intense dislike for anyone who came into my shop and ordered something other than a coffee-based drink.

I will admit that I scanned the crowd as I headed for the door. Not to worry, she had the entrance staked out. We talked there, and then in the parking lot, huddling and using her car as a break against the icy wind.

Nancy was a nurse from Jamestown, a quarter Fargo's size but still one of the state's big cities. She was there for a two-day nursing seminar.

"So tell me about you," Nurse Nancy said.

"I own three coffeeshops," I said.

"I'd like to get to know you," she said, like I was some kind of mogul, or solvent.

"I'm also here for a seminar," I disclosed. "I'm from California."

"I've heard that the world is shrinking, right? Geography is irrelevant." Nurse Nancy winked. "Brian Lawson, there is something special about you."

"It's probably my personality. I'm what you call an extra-introvert."

"I don't think that's a category."

"Either I'm special or I'm not."

Nurse Nancy had smiled. "Whatever you are, it's something I've never seen before. Fate brought you here, and I'm not going to let you go that easily."

We met for trick-or-treating the next evening. Nancy was saddled with her nephew for the night while her sister traveled to Minneapolis on business. Instead of his neighborhood, little Benji wanted to hit the strip mall. Not the indoor kind. With the temperature in the teens and a thirty-mile-an-hour wind out of the north, Benji and maybe fifteen other kids pounded the pavement in costumes masked with scarves, hats, mittens and heavy winter coats.

As we stood in line for bite-sized Bit-O-Honeys at Play It For Me Over And Over Again Sports, a tremor coursed through my shoulders. And then again, enough to make my teeth chatter. "Wow. What's happening to me?"

"You're shivering," said Nancy.

"I find that hard to believe."

"You're wearing shorts," said six-year-old Benji, with a judgmental tone.

"It's my California costume. At least people can see my costume."

The kid stuck out his tongue at me.

"Your lips are turning blue," said Nancy. She crouched to rub life back into my bare legs. "I have an old coat in my trunk. We can cut off the sleeves and you can use them for leg warmers."

"I'm not that cold, honestly. I'll be fine, once this wind dies down."

Nurse Nancy stood and looked me in the eye, deadly serious. "This is North Dakota, Brian. That never happens."

Little Benji couldn't have cared less about my suffering. The kid was focused on filling his candy bag, forcing us to make three passes up and down the row of retailers. Benji was also not concerned in the least about this stranger sniffing around his auntie's skirts, or in this case, heavy woolen pants.

One of the participating businesses was a coffeeshop, The Java Hut, with red-checkered tablecloths and ruffled curtains. The place was packed, people at each of the five tables and another six customers in line. The matronly woman behind the counter greeted us with a smile. "Welcome to The Java Hut. I'll be right with you."

The distinct stench of burnt coffee hung in the air. The woman worked the till and the bar, making one drink at a time. Slowly. I watched her scorch milk and consistently go long on her espresso pulls. Sure enough, my macchiato was watery and flavorless, except for the hint of boiled milk.

"You're smiling," said Nancy. "Must be good."

Not only wasn't it good, it was barely coffee. "I'm pleased," I said.

"This is the best coffeeshop in town," she said, dunking a gingersnap cookie.

"No kidding." My mind was whirling.

We said a brief goodbye—Nurse Nancy was clearly into me, but unwilling to invite me back to her sister's house. In retrospect she really wasn't in the running for a chastity trophy, but at the time I was impressed by her self-control and her respect for her sister.

We agreed to meet the next night for dinner. As I drifted off to sleep, I realized Nancy was right. I swear I could feel the hand of fate, reached down from its ghostly shell between Earth and Heaven, patting me on the back to let me know life-changing events were in process.

Now, that next night when Nurse Nancy told me she was a lapsed lesbian and then stuck her tongue up my rectum and jacked me off, I did have a Hold on there! What am I getting myself into? moment. But it passed—doubt had no chance to take root, after another big-tent coffee revival at the conference, and after all the excited talk earlier at dinner, about starting what would be the only coffeeshop in Jamestown. Maybe the only real coffeeshop in North Dakota. Sounded like a no-brainer.

Six winters later and there I was, alone in a blizzard, my business's lights invisible to would-be customers as they passed by. Felt that way.

T-16

I INTENDED to show up early for Testimonial #3 for the McEwens' deceased son Brent. Because for one thing, like my dad taught me, it's just as easy to be early as it is to be late. For another, I was hoping Mike would put me behind the bar. Not for the tips. It's where I'm most comfortable. An extra-introvert? That's not just a stupid phrase I made up to irk Nurse Nancy. It's the truth. I love being around hordes of people, as long as we're separated by a couple feet of stainless steel or solid mahogany. I'm at home as the center of attention, but I don't like to be exposed. I think of it as my presidential complex; whenever I have to leave the shop mid-morning, when the place is full, I make Charlotte take me by the elbow and whisk me out the door.

En route to the McEwens I saw Terrence making a left off Main in front of Hardees. Pull into Hardees, I tele-mentally commanded him. Be hungry for a Thickburger, damn you. But he kept on driving. My heart sank. Terrence didn't know anyone in this part of town (I was sure). There could be only one reason for his presence here. Dreading what I was about to see, I followed him.

Terrence parked across the street from the strip mall where Bill Hernandes preyed upon the innocent. He sprang from his car, a spring in his step that I had never witnessed, and marched into the Beads! shop. Just

43

around the corner, idling in someone's driveway, I waited. For quite some time. Terrence finally emerged, a big bag of beads in his hand, that spring still in his step. He jumped in his car and drove away. This was clearly misdirection, to dupe whoever might be surveilling him. I decided to wait for him in Hernandes' lot. Although Terrence never did show, my time wasn't wasted, I recognized two other customers' vehicles and wrote Swill lover! in the late-May grime encrusting their doors.

So of course in the end I was right on time for Testimonial #3.

"Right on time as usual," Mike welcomed me at the door wearing a dark blue sportcoat over a slightly lighter blue pullover. "That's one of the many things I love about you, Brian. Swear to God."

"I love the way you love me, Mike."

"Nice job today," said Mike. "Great warm-up for the real thing."

Although the foundation for Mike's retail center, the Bluffs, had been laid before winter set in, the groundbreaking ceremony had been put off until spring. I served the crowd in my javamobile. Have I fully described my coffeeshop on wheels? It was a honey, retro-fitted by Mike's special needs nephew with a generator, water tanks for brewing, a coffee machine, and a swing-out counter, so we could serve our customers at ground level instead of looking down on them like from a county fair concession stand.

Charlotte told me I was too proud of that sweet ride. Maybe she was right, maybe it was another vanity, like renting an apartment instead of living out of the storage room behind the shop. As my credit card balances grew and the past-due notices piled up, fiscal prudence no doubt dictated that I sell the javamobile before firing employees. Luckily Craig hadn't drawn that comparison when I let him go, two months prior. What can I say, Craig did things I could do myself, like roasting coffee and delivering beans to wholesale accounts. And the javamobile treated my customers a lot better than Craig did.

Mike gave me a strong hug. "I'm glad you're here. I've got a surprise," he said in a husky voice while rocking me to and fro. "Guess who else is here? Nancy."

Oh I knew that. I had received a text from her that morning. Honestly I would have gone to the testimonial anyway, but, it had been three months.

"Pretty special gal, huh?" said Valerie McEwen, patting her husband's shoulder as he turned away to dry his tears.

I nodded, at her black dress. "I guess I'm not dressed appropriately."

"Floral shirts and shorts are never inappropriate for you, Brian," said Valerie. "It's not what you wear that counts. It's that you're here."

"Thanks Mrs. McEwen."

"Listen to him," said Valerie, owner of one sexy senior neck, smooth skin and ropy muscles feeding into a velvety crescent of collarbone exposed by the broad necklines she favored. I fantasized about that neck. Her bobbed brown hair was thin; her eyes and mouth heavily creased; her breasts, until proven otherwise, presumed wrinkled. So, just the neck. She kissed my cheek. "Brian's not even a local and he's one of the few people in this town who pronounces our name right."

They pronounced it "McCune". I wanted to call her Val or V or even Mrs. Robinson, but Valerie just loved it when I called her Mrs. McEwen. "I'm just one of the few who's willing to mispronounce it the way you like," I said.

Valerie beamed. "Oh you."

"It shows respect," said Mike. "A rare commodity these days."

Made me feel guilty for the Mrs. Robinson thing.

Speaking of uncommon romance, time is running short to tell you a little more about Nurse Nancy, so that you're not caught completely off-guard by what was about to transpire. You see, I was taking great pains not to become emotionally tied to any local girls, on the assumption that prosperous or penniless, I would ultimately inevitably be heading back to California. Aware that I had a delicate balancing act on my hands, I was simultaneously on the lookout for a woman who wanted to periodically get together for some sex. What comes immediately to mind is a rural lesbian who's certain she will at some point go hetero and settle down with a nice rural boy, in the meantime needing to keep her feet wet, say once a quarter. How fortunate I was to find that someone in Nurse Nancy.

Once a quarter? I hear you snickering, and yes, normally I would agree, but three months was the recovery time, with Nurse Nancy. I nodded to her now, as she waited by the mahogany bar in the main room.

We were in the foyer, curved frescoed walls sporting tall unframed paintings of Italian vineyards and Euro-countryside, spindly trees in the corners, and Mike's collection of medieval pikes displayed vertically over the fireplace mantel. The foyer created the sensation of soaring open spaces, as if you might catch a summer's breeze and go floating about the house, free and unfettered.

Then you realized the air was a little stale, the ceilings weren't all that high, and there was only one way forward, through a narrow gap between the wall and the top of the basement stairs. Mike liked to stand at this pinch point.

He had designed the house himself. The foyer was his containment area, an attractive holding pen for milling and chatting while Mike debated whether to send you packing. If you passed his muster, it was on to a cozy lounge with a generous wet bar, currently unmanned, and the huge deck beyond.

"Come on in," Mike ushered me forward. "I know it's a little chilly, but we're gathering on the deck. The heat lamps should keep us warm."

Like the Bluffs, the McEwen house sat at the edge of the modest James River valley. Their bluff sloped in a series of small earthen cliffs a quarter-mile to the river, which was mostly obstructed by cottonwoods. The long-range vista had a Lewis and Clark feel to it. Rolling prairie grass hills bordered the east bank of the river—after a string of unseasonable days in the fifties, only their northern sides had snow. A couple hundred yards further east the land flattened, and so of course it was farmed. Stubble fields not yet dry enough for the plow were the rule as far as the eye could see, making it more difficult to imagine roaming buffalo and camping Indians. But being the son of a crop insurance adjustor, I appreciate the hard work and economic impact that large-scale farming represents. Too bad for the Indians they didn't think of it first.

We added Nancy to our entourage and continued through the sliding glass doors onto the deck. Five folks dressed in their funeral best were gathered around Rick at the railing. Rick knifed through them, extending his hand. The shake was firm and brief. "Thanks for coming, man."

"No problem, homey."

"Let me introduce you."

Thirty or so friends and family came to pay their respects over the next two hours. I suppose I knew half. To the others I was introduced as the local coffeeshop owner. Three of them told me how they almost opened their own coffeeshop, and another two let me know they were currently considering it. That's about the usual percentage.

Some of the stories were about Brent. I told the one about the woman, a recent transplant to Jamestown, who saw Brent walk into my shop and whispered to her friend how she would be all over that guy if she wasn't married, with no clue her friend was Brent's mom. Nurse Nancy described finding Brent hanging from the ceiling in a pair of gravity boots, insisting she hook up his chemo IV bat-style, kidding her that with his world turned upside down, this was the only way of seeing things right.

A few of the guests seemed intent on ensuring we had ample tales to tell at their testimonials. More than once, Travis Hafner's name came up. Twice I had to listen to the story I had already heard a thousand times: small-town boy makes it to the big leagues, now with the Yankees. The details always changed, but the escape theme was constant. Considering my life had played out in exactly the opposite direction, I didn't care for the story.

Testimonial #3 did its job, fixing a little more permanently the distilled memory of Brent's goodness and popularity. And then it was just the five of us, lounging at the wet bar. The McEwens stood between us. Nurse Nancy focused on peeling an apple. Our quarterly courtship was at fever peak. Valerie beamed at me and then said, "I can't believe Andrea didn't show up."

Thanks to shop talk, I had a good idea of the current friction between them. On Friday the judge had turned down Andrea's request to move Tyler back to Colorado. I'm sure the judge was impartial, but I also knew that McEwen Construction had built his house, two doors down from Mike and Valerie. I guess Andrea had freaked out in court, going off on Rick, Mike, the judge, and the state, in that order, before breaking down sobbing. She had to be escorted from the judge's chambers.

Meanwhile, the McEwens' lawsuit against the hospital and the doctor was still in process. Mike had offered to drop the suit in exchange for a ruling forcing Dr. Bhani to cease all research and experimentation on the "miracle" cure he had used on Brent. But the judge refused to grant the injunction. Coincidentally, Mike had to be escorted howling and cursing from the judge's chambers. I don't believe that judge owned a McEwen home.

"Little Tyler should have been here to hear all the stories people were telling about his uncle," said Mike.

"Except the one about shotgunning Red Bull and vodka," I pointed out.

"True," said Mike.

"And the part about peeping at the cheerleaders through the slit in the locker room window."

"Yes," said Valerie. Nurse Nancy shrugged.

Normally in scrubs or something scrub-like, today Nancy was in a hip-hugging charcoal gray dress. She would rub the apple, small circles with her thumb, until the skin released. One small circle at a time, slipping the skin into her mouth, leaving the bared, perfectly contoured fruit in her hand. This was for my benefit. She was peeling the apple the way I guarantee you it liked to be peeled. Nancy is a caretaker. I don't know how she feels about men in general, but she has this thing about taking care of me. I don't see myself as needy—I think I come across as just the opposite. But Nancy wasn't the first woman to go out of her way to look after me—Mom of course, friends' moms, teachers, customers. I don't need it, but I sure do like it.

"Tyler was probably napping," said Rick, watering down the tinder fueling the flames crackling in his parents' eyes. "He's tough to get ready and out the door. They'll be here."

"What does she do all day?" Mike demanded. "People tell me she never leaves her apartment." 'People tell me' was a little passive. I'm sure Mike had her watched. "A person can't sit at home all day," he stated emphatically. "A person can't live that way. It's a terrible environment for Tyler. What the hell is she thinking? Does she have any clue how to be a good mother?" He worked himself into a lather. Before Brent's tragic ending, Mike's devotion to his family was fierce. Now it was maniacal.

Rick put up a lukewarm defense. "Andrea doesn't have any close friends here. She's feeling isolated."

"Of course she's isolated!" Mike erupted. "She's sitting home all day!"

"She might be depressed," I offered. "It can be debilitating."

"So are my hemorrhoids," Mike grumbled. "I don't let it stop me."

"I've been pretty worried about her," Rick confessed. "She's not the same person she was."

"I introduced her to some of my friends," said Nancy. She had moved to my side, publicly announcing our togetherness by reaching across her body to hold my left hand with hers. With her right hand, her private hand, she probed my armpit, pushing tendons aside, slipping between the muscle fibers. A little deeper all the time. Shouldn't have been erotic but it was. If she smelled her fingers, I'd probably cum in my pants. "They said she refuses to participate in anything they invite her to," Nancy reported.

"We've done all we can," said Valerie, exasperated.

"I'm worried about our grandson," said Mike. "That's a terrible environment."

"He's doing fine," said Rick, looking around the room, searching for some distraction, anything, maybe a grease fire. "Jamestown's not the easiest place in the world for an outsider to fit in."

"There are so many wonderful people here, son," Valerie corrected him. "You're being nice, which is admirable. But Andrea really has no excuse."

"You damn right," said Mike. "This town has a lot on the ball. Speaking of which, Brian, Kip is ready to map your store's interior. Let's get it done."

"Mike—uh," I grunted as Nancy hit a nerve. She pushed it aside and plunged further into the interior. Was anyone else seeing this? I cleared my throat. "I'm sorry. I don't know if I'm ready to move forward on this. Timing's pretty terrible."

"Timing's not optional, Brian. The Bluffs will open in less than two months. They can't have a vacancy—especially not the anchor. Gotta have someone in there. If not you…" Mike winked, making clear this wasn't a threat.

"I simply can't understand people like Andrea," Valerie was saying. "Letting life pass her by."

"She got a job as a secretary at the hospital," said Rick. "That's a start anyway."

"Someone with her attitude cannot make a good secretary," said Nancy.

"Research assistant, isn't it?" I recalled.

"Listen, Brian." Mike held my elbow and lowered his voice. Hand, elbow and pit. The three points of contact were unnerving. "We talked about your startup costs. We'll make them manageable."

"That's very generous of you. Way too generous."

"You deserve success," Mike said earnestly. "You're a hard worker."

Valerie was frowning. "I didn't know they did research at the hospital, other than…"

That's when Andrea and Tyler walked through the door. Tyler ran forward to hug Rick's leg and receive an affectionate hair tousling. "Sorry I'm late," said Andrea. "I didn't want to miss this, but, you know how it goes." Oblivious to my presence and the stoneface statues that were the McEwens, she unshouldered a backpack bigger than her torso and dropped it against the wall with a groan. She unzipped it to peek inside. "Tyler, did you bring in your toys and your books?" She looked up and saw me and pursed her lips. "Oh. Hi. How are you?"

"I'm good."

"Andrea." Valerie put her hand to her mouth. "Are you working for Dr. Bhani?"

Nancy's hand fell out of my armpit. Mike's eyes bulged. The scientist's name sent a shockwave through the McEwen family.

Rick wiped a bad-looking taste from his mouth and followed his son downstairs to the playroom. Andrea was on her own. Oblivious to the bomb that was about to go off, she focused on Nancy's and my interlaced fingers.

"Brian said you're working for a researcher at the hospital," said Valerie. "We don't know of any other researchers in Jamestown."

"Oh, that's what Brian said." Andrea crossed her arms and gave me an ice-cold glare. "That's right. I took a job with Dr. Bhani."

I can't even begin to tell you what a bad idea that was. Bhani was indeed the only federally-funded researcher in town, a fact trumpeted in a glowing article published in the Sun a few months before Brent died, an article that had made Bhani a local celebrity. Bhani was a Bangladeshi doc who had started his career as a North Dakota physician. Ten years ago he hit upon a potential cure for cancer, and was inspired to devote his life to research, moving to a lab at the University of Minnesota, his alma mater, and eventually relocating to Jamestown, putting the local hospital at the cutting edge of cancer research.

The day Brent died, Bhani went from the toast of the town, to toast in that town. He used to come into my shop regularly, probably just to soak up the rock star treatment. But after Mike tried to beat his face in at the Safeway store a month after Brent's death, Bhani went underground. If it weren't for Andrea's bombshell, I wouldn't have known he was still in town.

"You took a job with Dr. Bhani," Valerie mumbled, dumbfounded. "But why? Honey, we could have found you a job at Richford Homes or Madison Electric, or the Tool Crib…"

"Yeah, well," Andrea chuckled bitterly. "This was a little better match for my background. I had just started my dream job at a genetics lab in Denver when Rick made us move here, you know."

Wrong time to grind that ax, I thought to myself.

"Honey," Valerie pleaded. "Dr. Bhani…?"

"For Pete's sake, Andrea," said Mike. "That quack killed our son!"

"No." Andrea vehemently shook her head. "Dr. Bhani saved Brent. If you recall, Brent's oncologist told him his cancer was incurable. Dr. Bhani's treatment saved Brent. An infection killed him."

"An infection your boss gave him!" Red-faced, Mike stabbed his finger in the general direction of the hospital. "He gave it to our son! On purpose!"

Andrea trembled as she knelt again to rummage through the backpack.

"He gave Brent an infection!" Mike croaked. "That's what killed our son! You can't deny it!"

"I'm not going to," said Andrea, digging vigorously in the backpack. "I could tell you why you're wrong, but you wouldn't listen anyway."

"I'm listening!" Mike's voice cracked. "I'm listening!"

Valerie put her arms around Mike and rubbed his neck. "Andrea," she said condescendingly, "we're listening."

Andrea talked into the backpack. "I don't want to talk about it."

Rick returned to stand beside his sobbing mother. "Andrea," he appealed.

"You know Dr. Bhani feels bad about what happened," Andrea countered.

"He feels bad?" Mike exclaimed. He took a step forward. "That sonofabitch feels bad? How do you think we feel? After everything we went through, only to have Brent get sick and die from your doctor's bug."

"It wasn't his bug."

"Oh!" Valerie and Mike exploded together. "Bhani gave Brent strep," Mike wailed, "and according to the coroner, Brent died of strep!"

That strep could kill you was news to me, but this wasn't the time to ask for clarification.

Rick stood in front of his ex, shielding her from his family's venom. "That's enough for tonight," he said, like he was accustomed to people listening when he took charge. "We'll discuss this another time."

"There's no discussion," said Andrea, shaking her head when Rick fluttered a shushing hand in her face. "I'm not quitting."

"You sure as hell will!" Mike shouted, stretching his neck to look around Rick, who shook his head in resignation and backed off.

"You have to, honey," said Valerie sharply. "For Tyler."

"How can you work for that evil bastard?" Mike demanded.

"I'd like to think I'm helping him make a difference—"

"You are disgracing this family!" Mike thundered. "You are disgracing this family by working for him!"

Andrea marched to the door. "Say goodbye to Tyler for me."

Instead of goodbye, Nancy said, "You are a selfish bitch."

Andrea turned around and shot a stunned, hurt look not at Nancy but at me, before slipping out the door.

I was a little stunned myself. Why did I get the look? I was at worst a negligent bystander to the verbal beating Andrea had taken. Nancy did have a husky voice—had Andrea mistaken hers for mine?

"Nancy," Valerie scolded, "you know I don't like that word."

"If the shoe fits," said Mike.

I was upset. "Did you see her look at me? I think she thought I said it."

"Don't be silly," said Nancy. "You're standing next to me, it just looked like she was looking at you."

"No. She looked directly at me."

"Maybe she mis-looked," said Valerie. "That happens."

"It's not like an errant golf shot, Val," said Mike. "Andrea understands that Brian is a member of the family. No, I think that look was no accident."

"You did the right thing to tell us about her job," Valerie assured me.

"It wasn't a secret," I noted. "You would have found out sooner or later. I really don't want to be in the middle of this."

Valerie nodded. "It's hard to fathom what that girl is thinking, isn't it?"

"Brian and I are going to take a drive together," said Nancy, plucking a sweat jacket off the coat hook and slipping it on. "I'll pick up my car later."

"We're so glad you shared this time with us," said Valerie, forming a V with her hands, putting my face into that V, and kissing me, our first lip kiss.

Rick invaded my personal space to grip my hand. "Thanks for coming, man."

Mike was holding his arms apart, waiting for me to come get some. Then he hopped forward with alarming speed and hugged me good. "We'll talk tomorrow." This was an order, not a request.

Outside, Nancy said "brr" and "Wasn't that interesting?" and towed me to my van. The wind had picked up and the temperature had fallen, after what had been a fabulous spring day. I held the passenger door for her and then ran around the back of the van and jumped in the driver's seat. "Speaking of interesting...actually, there's no good segue for this. What exactly were you doing to me in there? I've been, you know, interested, ever since. Is that weird? That doesn't seem right, does it? I mean, you were in my armpit."

"Sounds a little twisted, I agree," said Nancy.

"You wouldn't want to keep doing that, would you?"

"So bad I can taste it."

An inappropriate figure of speech for a discussion about the armpit; with Nancy, it was no figure of speech. "I'm going to drive very fast now, so hang on."

"Drive around the block," Nancy instructed. She had me switch off the headlights when we came back around the McEwens' corner, and park in front of a rugged strip of no-man's land that drained the neighborhood down to the James. Nancy jumped out. "Follow me."

We picked our way across the mucky open space before curling left toward the bluff. At the blunt edge of the cliff Nancy found a graveled gap through the ice-clotted weeds. We slide-stepped down and picked our way along a skinny catwalk that gradually descended until our heads were below the top of the bluff. We continued shuffling along.

"I think this is it," Nancy whispered. She mounted an assault on the ten feet of embankment above us, struggling and grunting up the muddy gravel slope, the shushing of her filmy dress and the glimpse of black lace high up her thigh compensating for her lack of grace. She scrambled over the edge before I could reach up to give her a boost. Stepping on upright clumps of grass and kicking in a toehold here and there, I followed.

We were behind the playhouse that Mike's construction team built for his grandson. "Here?" I hissed. "Won't Tyler come out here?"

"Too cold," Nancy whispered. "Brent spent a lot of time out here, whenever he was hurting and didn't want his folks to see him. He gave me a key." She peeked around the corner, then held out her hand. Feeling as though I should be the mission leader, I swallowed my pride and allowed her to lead me to the front door. She keyed the lock and pulled me inside.

I pushed the door shut. "Hey, how convenient, a bed—"

Nancy was on me, kissing me, hands all over me, tongue way down my throat, pants unzipped, my schlong in both her hands, pulling hard enough to uproot it.

"What about the armpit?" I mumbled. "Do that armpit thing."

"Pull up your shirt," she ordered.

I grabbed my shirt down low with crossed hands the way I always practiced at home, and pulled up. When my shirt was over my head and my arms were at full extension, Nancy clamped her mouth on my left pit. "Whug," I groaned. I maintained this position, trying not to move a muscle, in no way wanting to dislodge her.

First her lips worked me over. She could have been a lip masseuse, such strength and multi-directional control.

Then the tongue. With every deep probe, concentric waves of delight fanned out across my chest, making my heart and lungs ripple.

Finally the teeth. Nurse Nancy was chewing my pit. I was crying out, something like, "Oh Goddie—mommy—ho-ho, oh my lordie—no—"

Nancy finished pulling off my shirt so she could put her fingers to my lips. She tossed the shirt onto the kiddie desk against the wall of the ten-by-ten playhouse, and went back to work. I wheezed, I giggled, I wept, I bestowed blessings upon her as best a layman could.

"You're hyperventilating," she approved.

"Sweet Song of the South, what have you done to me?"

"What you're experiencing is a flood of toxins into your system."

"That's what it feels like to be poisoned?" I gasped. "I always wondered."

"Sometimes hormones will be flushed along with the toxins," Nancy purred. "Your lymph nodes are filled with all kinds of goodies."

"You're diddling my lymph nodes." Uncontrollable quivers coursed through my private parts.

"We need to finish the flush," said Nancy. "Roll over."

"Roll over, roll over…and then the porcupine fell out." High on lymph goodies, I babbled nursery rhymes while Nancy flipped me over and worked my shorts off. "Ten in the bed and the little one said—holy shit!"

In a highly coordinate attack, Nancy fingered me in three places, under each butt cheek and in that soft spot below the scrotum. I bucked as she fingered. Nancy saddled up and rode me backwards, hot breath on my ass. Thighs clamped on the sides of my head, she buried her face in my crack, fingers fingering all the while. I grabbed her thighs and screamed into the pillow. My body spasmed and flopped as the demons of the immune system howled through my bloodstream.

For all that, my ejaculation was short and unnoticeable. I only knew it happened because my body went instantly to jelly. I lay underneath her, unable to breathe, unwilling to even try. Through my delirium I had a notion to somehow attempt to return the favor. I threw a couple lame licks at her sweaty thighs.

"Shh," Nancy stopped me. She sat up and kneaded my butt and hamstrings. After working me over for awhile she said, "That was a fairly extreme reaction you had. I'm expecting the police in a few minutes." She slid down a little further and massaged my calves. It would have felt nice if I had had any muscle tone left. It must have been like massaging a bag of gel.

"That was the longest I've ever been insane," I mumbled into the pillow. "I touched the void, I'm sure of it." I struggled to rise, to breathe. Nancy dismounted and knelt beside me on the floor. I laid on my side, my head propped on the pillow, and blinked at her. "It was probably the best two hours I've ever had."

"Five minutes, tops."

"Promise you won't do that to me more than once every couple years."

"That seems about right." Nancy drew spirals in the pubic hair that grew like ivy up my belly. And let me just say that if ivy looked like pubic hair, the Cubs wouldn't have nearly as many fans.

My belly was way too big. Nancy didn't seem to care, but I vowed then and there to start going to Taekwondo class more than once a week.

"Will I feel a difference now?" I asked my personal lymph system guru.

"Eventually. You might feel like you have a touch of the flu for a day or two. But once the toxins clear your system, you should feel the difference."

"Wow. This is great." I cocked my head and listened like a dog. "And no sirens. So, can I do the same for you? As soon as I can lift my head for more than a couple seconds at a time."

Nancy petted my face. Her hand smelled like my butt. "We each have roles to play in this relationship. You help me in other ways."

"Good point." I rolled onto my back, sighing into the thin mattress. "I don't think I've ever felt this peaceful."

"I'm glad." Nancy stroked my stomach. I tried not to be self-conscious about the extra pounds. The muscles in my hips and lower back weren't worried about it; they sagged in blissful contentment. I became one with the mattress. I couldn't get any more relaxed. Nurse Nancy had the magic touch.

She cleared her throat. "I did notice a lump on the back of your thigh, right where it meets the buttocks."

"A lump?" I said dreamily. "What kind of lump?"

"Mm, I don't know. You should get it checked."

"Geez. Okay. I guess I could…"

"Tomorrow. I'd feel better if you went to the doctor tomorrow."

T-15

THE NEXT day was crazy. Like usual I was at the shop by five, to open at six. We were busy, just not as busy as I would have liked. By eleven o'clock when Charlotte's shift ended, we had made five hundred twelve dollars.

I used to round to the nearest fifty or so. Nowadays that wasn't precise enough. "Around five hundred" didn't tell me whether I had covered Charlotte's salary with enough left to pay Dan the muffin man when he made his third and what I'm sure he hoped would be his final trip to collect the prior quarter's outstanding balance.

"We cleared sixty bucks in tips," Charlotte reported. She raked one of the divvied piles off the counter into her hand. "Not bad."

"Sixty even?" I prodded casually for more information.

"Fifty-eight, actually," Charlotte clarified.

"Oh," I said, trying not to sound too disappointed. "Why don't you take it all today." This was difficult to say. I make it a policy not to understand my employees' financial situations, or pretty soon I would be subconsciously favoring the poorer kid over the richer one, giving her more hours, better shifts, quicker raises. I preferred my discrimination to be conscious.

But I do hear things. Charlotte needed the money even more than I did.

"Nonsense," said Charlotte. "I know Dan's coming back again today. You have to pay him. I do not want to see him again this month. Eeu."

56

She shivered. "He gives me the creeps. He leers at me." Most of our male customers did, some were just better at it. She leaned on the counter, looking down into the pastry case. "I don't know why we even bother with pastries. This case. Ugh."

Muffins and cookies were piled on one side of the far-from-spotless shelf, amidst crumbs and a few larger chunks from days gone by.

"I've been meaning to get to that."

"Brian, you hate selling pastries."

"But I really hate watching people leave Martin's Bakery with a coffee." I pointed to the pile of dollars and coin. "Go ahead," I told Charlotte. "Take it."

"No, you're gonna need it to go get drunk after putting in a double shift. Sam called a few minutes ago. He can't make it in."

"What? When? Awww…. What about Sara? Can she come in early?"

"Nope. She has class until five. So it'll be five-fifteen at the earliest."

"Dana?"

"Out of town until Thursday."

"That's right. Crap. Did I know that?"

"Yes you did. I was standing right there when she told you."

"I have a lot on my mind," I complained. "She should know better than to tell me things and expect me to remember."

"Fire her. Wouldn't break my heart."

"And I need to run to Sam's Club. We're out of—"

"Just about everything?" said Charlotte. She sighed. "I can come back for an hour between three and four, so you can go shopping."

"You don't mind?"

Charlotte put her hands on her hips and stared at me.

"Stupid question. I appreciate it. Alright, get out of here."

Nurse Nancy called late in the afternoon, to chew me out for not going to the doctor. That night, I wished I had. I lay in bed touching the lump and telling myself not to. This wasn't the first time I had touched it, of course. I had been feeling it all day. Every time as my fingers approached the site, I prayed the lump would feel smaller or softer.

Exhaustion from the playhouse romp had ensured a peaceful sleep the night before. But not now. I laid there for a couple hours, my hands all over that lump, worrying about what it might be, worrying about being exhausted when the alarm went off at four-forty-five, worrying that worrying was exactly the sort of negative energy a malignant lump would feed on. I was desperate to fall asleep.

Hey, I thought, a good self-servicing always does the trick.

I laughed at the ridiculous assumption that Nancy had left anything in my tank—and then went pale with the fear that the cancer might perk up its ears at the rustling in my 'nads, and go have a look-see. Everyone needed to remain still and quiet and give the cancer no cause to leave the back of my leg.

I was sure that's what it was. I've always feared death, and cancer seemed the best bet. Nothing violent, like a car crash or terrorist attack where I would have a decent shot at cheating death with quick thinking or my cat-like reflexes. Instead, Death would be silent and sneaky and immune to my knack for landing on my feet.

I only thought it would be more patient, waiting until the worst possible time to gun me down—waiting until I was at my highest point, with stores in fifteen states, married to a wonderful wife, proud father to a newborn baby.

But when I thought about it, this was even sadder. Taking me before I had achieved any success whatsoever.

In the end, the only thing that allowed me to get a couple hours' sleep was to stop agonizing and accept as fact that I had cancer. I definitely had cancer. Let the battle begin. Being stalked by some anonymous killer was scary. A battle against a known enemy, on the other hand, was something I could handle. And what was one of the most powerful weapons in any battle? A good night's sleep. With one last shuddering sigh, I fell into a dreamless slumber.

THE NEXT morning I called Jackie, receptionist at the hospital and a customer of mine.

"Who's your doctor?" Jackie asked.

"You choose. General practitioner, I suppose. To start with anyway."

"How long have you lived here, Brian?"

"Five years. Sixish."

"And you haven't ever been to a doctor?"

"I was in the emergency room for a racing heart last year."

"A lot of people think regular checkups are a good idea," said Jackie.

"I thought that was for old people."

"Old people don't need checkups," said Jackie. "They pop in regularly and always bring a list." We shared a laugh on the elderly. "So why see a doctor now, after all these years?"

"I have a lump."

Joke time was over. "I'll make you an appointment with Dr. Bonilla. He has a strong background in, in things like that. Be at the hospital by nine."

I called my mom and dad on the way to the hospital. I haven't told you much about my parents. They haven't impacted this story, yet they're everything I am. If I differ from them in any way, it's only by conscious effort.

I hung up before they could wake up and answer. No need worrying them before the doctor took a look at me. Although I already knew I had it. Nancy was a caretaker, but she wasn't a worrywart. If she was concerned, it was time to start shopping for wigs.

SITTING IN the waiting room I couldn't get over the fact that the timing wasn't right. Death was supposed to strike later, after I had become the person I wanted to be, after I had seized the good life. For maximum effect, Death should arrive a split-second before I was ready to rest on my laurels, just as I prepared to sit back and survey my thriving business empire and enjoy my beautiful family. Death was patient; Death wrote the book on heartbreaking tragedy. Death was forfeiting the opportunity to drop a doozy of a bombshell twenty years down the road.

But of course the cancer had perfect timing. What's more tragic than a thirty-two year old with cancer? It wasn't the cancer's fault that after fifteen years in the biz, here I was in North Dakota, coupling quarterly with a lesbian and running one rinky-dink shop. Couldn't blame the cancer for assuming I was a guy with low expectations who had already achieved his mediocre goals. No matter what I was about to find out, I couldn't whine that life was unfair. It is fair. It was my own damn fault.

BEING MY parents' child worried me, as the nurse sampled my blood. If I reacted to a bad diagnosis like my mother, I was going to say "oh well" and go about my business, no less kind or gentle. La-la, what are you going to do. I would cry myself to sleep most nights, but then get up the next morning as chipper as ever. La-la, don't you worry about me. "I'll say this for Brian," people would say after I died, "he sure dealt with his cancer well." La-la.

If on the other hand I took it like the old man, a fatalistic numbness was going to come over me. I would detach from myself, step back and watch, closely, the cancer's every inroad and progression. Take it like a man. I would neither say it was fine by me, nor would I complain. A man doesn't complain, and he doesn't struggle. He accepts his fate. He doesn't alter his routine, except to forfeit all the joy that life used to bring him. He doesn't miss a day of work. Never. Never ever.

After I died people would say, "That Brian sure didn't let cancer slow him down."

I flipped onto my stomach so the physician's assistant could deaden my backside for the biopsy. I decided right then and there to fight my genes and do things my way. I couldn't go la-la, and I couldn't go numb. I had to be fully in every moment. Ask a lot of questions, listen very carefully, record everything. Find somebody with a computer and go on-line and research every facet of my cancer. Get angry, get upset, get better. Laugh when I needed to, cry when appropriate.

I would take my healthcare into my own hands. A proactive ownership mentality—I would need to become the general contractor, subcontracting each research avenue and procedure to various surgeons and specialists, coordinating them, holding them accountable, never worshipping them and by no means putting my life in their hands. I would listen, research, ask questions and question everything.

"Your shin looks pretty tough," said Cindy the physician's assistant. "What's going on here?"

"Taekwondo." I was working toward my black belt in Taekwondo. I had always wanted to become a deadly assassin, and figured I had the legs for it. "I assume you're talking about the bruises, on top of the bruises."

"Ouch," said Cindy. "Is that normal?"

"I hope not. Hopefully I'm doing something wrong, something that I can correct. I'm looking forward to not shrieking every time I kick somebody."

"You could stop kicking people," said Cindy.

"No thanks." I like to kick people.

Even as Cindy and the nurse, Anna, quizzed me on my lifestyle and family history, my mind wandered. I was trying to figure out why Dad is who he is, so I could choose to be as different as necessary, so I could recognize that crucial moment when to make a conscious break from my genes.

I remembered him coming into my room late one night when I was twelve, in his hand one of the military history books he loved to read. Every year or so Dad would tuck me in, when he had something important to tell me.

"The key to being an effective soldier"—man and soldier were interchangeable as far as my dad was concerned—"the key to getting out of your foxhole as the shells scream overhead, the key to marching forward as men scream and fall ahead of you, is to assume you're already dead."

This was meant to steady my nerves for the MathCounts competition. Looking back, it was a tough sell for a kid who thought he was special, a chosen one, a little more self-aware and suffused with destiny than the next guy, and therefore too extraordinary to die, too valuable to lose.

Now the times when I felt that heroic certainty of a happy ending were fleeting and usually alcohol-related. I couldn't afford to buy enough comic books and booze to maintain that mindset. I was going to need a new outlook.

Recalling that "I'm a dead soldier" crap lying on the gurney brought me close to tears. I believed in God until that very moment. Suddenly I couldn't envision an afterlife, only a void, a whole mess of nothingness, and it scared me senseless. I wanted nothing more than to be a firm believer. I craved Heaven's comfort; I labored to convince myself God was there and waiting to embrace me.

Maybe if I'd had a traditional religious upbringing. Dad grew up Methodist, but by the time I came along he was disillusioned with the dogma and what he called "religious people". "I'll worship my own way in the privacy of my house," Dad would say. As far as I knew he did, but I never saw him with a Bible in hand.

With Mom, any religious discussion invariably, somehow, turns to music. She would drive to the parsonage Saturday afternoon and pick up the playlist, and then spend the intervening waking hours on the piano, practicing. Mom's specialty was harmony. She knows the harmony part for at least a thousand church songs. The minister loved the way Mom filled out the congregation's sound. Fine for him, he didn't have to stand next to her and struggle to stay on melody.

Faith-based or otherwise, there had to be a way to deal with my cancer that wouldn't result in false bravado, stoic acceptance, or paralyzing fear. I wouldn't find it in Mom and Dad's brains—I was getting dizzy and melancholy in there, in too deep to step back and figure things out. I am them, they are in me. I tried to escape the biochemical entanglement, struggling through the jungle of my own mental fibers, glistening, pulsing, fated, fibrous…

I played word association against my will, moving at high speed from a network of neurons to a black writhing snarl of tumor. I threw up on the end of the gurney, soaking the crisp white paper and splattering Nurse Anna's legs.

"Geez, I'm sorry."

Cindy and Nurse Anna told me that puking all over their gurney, floor, clothes, and sterile instruments was no big deal, while simultaneously looking more shook up than medical personnel should at the sight of a patient's internal fluids.

I collapsed into a chair, embarrassed. "That really took me by surprise."

"It's okay," said Nurse Anna, body shaped like a question mark, with wide fluttering eyes.

"Not a problem at all," said Cindy, an elderly woman with mannish hands that stripped the paper roll so the arriving orderly could clean the gurney. "Really. You wouldn't believe how often that happens."

"When kids throw up in my shop, I always wish the parents would give them a good spanking," I said.

"That's funny," said Cindy. "Anna honey, run down and order up an MRI and a CAT scan for us, would you please, dear?"

Nurse Anna practically ran out of the room.

"CAT scans are for the brain, right?" I asked.

"Sometimes throwing up can be a symptom of broader issues." Cindy looked as though she may have said too much.

"It's all in my head. Thoughts, I mean. Not a tumor. Sometimes my mind gets a little carried away. I make mountains out of molehills. You know the type," I babbled, waiting for her to soothe me with something like, "Sugar, don't you fret, we're just going through the motions to keep our insurance company happy."

Cindy was washing her hands. "The best thing is to let us do the work and not worry about this."

Would have been easier without the worried look on her face. Please just cure me. "Can I put my clothes on?"

"Sure. You're going to need a clean gown anyway." Cindy put her man hand on my shoulder. "Your leg is probably a little numb—would you like some help with your underwear?"

—

I WAS doing a poor job hiding my humiliation and black thoughts when Andrea spotted me in the hospital hallway. "There he is," she said.

"How are you, lady?"

"Let's see," Andrea mulled it over. "What would I like the McEwens to know?" She looked for the sting of her rapier wit, but I think my eyes remained dull. "What are you doing here?"

"Waiting to see an oncologist."

"Oh. I'm sorry. You have someone here? Someone with…" She lowered her voice for the C word. "…cancer?"

"Yeah. Me."

"You?" Andrea glanced at my street clothes. "No you don't."

"I just had an MRI and a CAT scan."

Andrea flinched. "I can't believe that."

"They let me wait out here as long as I promised not to sit on my biopsy hole. I can't stand being cooped up in the exam room."

"Well that's terrible."

"I don't think it's in my brain. I don't even know whether I have it. That's not true—I'm sure I do. It's in my leg. Nurse Nancy found a lump."

I thought she was going to console me with a hug. Then the cool detachment returned. "Do you have someone here waiting with you? I'm sure you do. Where's Nancy?" She made a production out of looking up and down the hallway. "I'm sure she'll be along here any moment," said Andrea, snotty. "I'd like to avoid any more awkward moments like Sunday night."

"I don't know if awkward is the right word to describe an attempted lynching."

"You should know." She tossed her hair and struggled with a quivering lip. "You were part of the lynch mob."

"I wished I hadn't been, if that's any consolation."

"Not really," Andrea said softly, close to losing it. "I'm going to go now." She wanted me to stop her, I could tell.

But I had no capacity for sympathy. "Okay lady. We'll see you."

Andrea shook her head and hurried down the hallway.

T-14

A **PLEASING** hubbub came from the other side of the bar that Sunday morning. Men's voices bubbled below random shrieks from toddlers and a chorus of women, seemingly competing with each other, one at a time ratcheting up the volume and sharpening the timbre until everyone was on the verge of yelling, a brassy crescendo climaxing in howls of laughter. Rising and falling, rising and falling, slight variations on a standard theme. Music to my ears.

Except the kids. I know a world without children would soon be nothing but vacant buildings overgrown with Canadian thistle and prowled by scavenging terriers. But still…. Children are generally rude. They spill more than they buy. After little Jeffy knocks his drink over, his mother cuts to the front of the line, demanding the mess be immediately cleaned up, and assuming that a free replacement drink is on the way, something else for Jeffy to spill. When a kid walks into my shop, it's basically a two-for-one. "Make sure you put extra whipped cream on that," the mother says as I'm putting the lid on the free refill. "And sprinkles. My little Jeffy loves the sprinkles."

"Yeah," I try to be sweet, sure that without sprinkles' temptation the lid would stay on and the drink wouldn't spill, for the third time. "Now be careful," I remind them, getting a look from little Jeffy and his mother, as if it was comments like this that made them spill the Ghirardelli hot chocolate in the first place.

Ghirardelli chocolate for a three-year-old. A three-year-old doesn't appreciate Ghirardelli. I needed two cans of Ghirardelli, one filled with Nesquick for the children. The margins would be better and I wouldn't cry as much when it spilled.

"More milk!" Charlotte called to Sara, on the till and serving as our runner. Charlotte and I ran the bar, me on cup prep, Charlotte on the wand, the two of us taking turns pulling shots.

"Kenny," I greeted the manager of the Wells Fargo branch where Kevin the auditor had planned his trysts with the former Mrs. Rick McEwen. "Lady," I greeted Kenny's wife, Laurie. They stood at the back of the four-deep line. They came in four or five times a week. Good, loyal customers.

"Brian, how's it hanging?" Laurie greeted me. For the wife of a bank manager who was also head of the Chamber of Commerce, she's a little rough around the edges. But for Jamestown, just right.

"So far so good," I responded. "I'm not sure how long that will last, though." I was to start chemo and radiation the next day. The biopsy had confirmed cancer.

Kenny and Laurie chortled. "Medium nonfat vanilla cappuccino and a caramel macchiato?" I verified.

"Yes sir," said Kenny, smiling that I remembered their drinks. Customers think I remember only their drinks, only their kids' names, only their latest golf score, only their hard amber durum yield. In fact, I know over three hundred drinks by heart, probably a thousand kids' names, ages and activities, a season's worth of golf scores, handicaps and memorable shots, a bushelful of crop yields. I don't have an exceptional memory. Just the will to memorize everything about my good customers. I hate nothing more than the customer service dogma that you have to treat every customer like a king. If I gave every customer the royal treatment, no matter whether they had just told me how much they love my coffee or how stupid I am for not selling Tazo berry cream frappuccinos like Starbucks, then I've lessened the experience for my good customers. If I treated every customer the same, how would the good ones know how much I appreciated them?

"We should probably be a little more spontaneous," said Laurie, "but we're too old to change now."

"We're in a rut," Kenny confessed.

I smiled. "Looks like a groove to me. Of course," I said to Laurie, "when you're not here, Kenny orders a chocolate espresso smoothie."

"He doesn't!" Laurie cackled, poking Kenny in the ribs. "Do you?"

"That Brian is such a joker," said Kenny, looking flushed.

"Okay, I guess he doesn't," I said, eyebrows raised.

"Sugar-free hazelnut latté," Sara relayed an order, for Genevieve from Taekwondo.

Genevieve caught my eye. "Great workout the other night, wasn't it?"

Thursday night, unable to stand the thought of sitting home alone, waiting for daybreak when I could start calling the hospital to learn the results of my tests, I had gone to Taekwondo class. I doubt it was on the list of approved post-biopsy activities.

Should be. Taekwondo was all about conquering fear. Walk in the place and hear the kihaps, those peculiar shouts we were taught to belt out with every kick, meant to briefly disorient and frighten your opponent. But the kihaps were also a way to manage your own fear. Kihap-triggered adrenaline hung like fog, secreted from one class to be reabsorbed by the next. Adrenaline to replace the fear, the fear of pulling a muscle, of getting kicked in the face.

"Best yet."

"Why is that?" Charlotte asked.

"Master Kwan kicked one of his students so hard, his lung popped," I said. "Sounded like a balloon."

"Who was it?" Charlotte was dying to hear. She really liked the idea of hurting people. Preferably by her own hand.

"That didn't happen," said Genevieve. She sighed. "I don't know if I'm going to make it to the end. I don't know if I want to. I don't think I want to be known as 'that black belt with a fat ass'."

Charlotte gasped. "You do not have that. You are so hard on yourself."

"Charlotte, you don't understand," said Genevieve, crestfallen. "I used to be really good looking. I'm ashamed you have to see me like this."

Sara and I could only laugh. "Just because you don't spend five hours a day working out like some people," Charlotte griped. "Some of us actually have a life. Unfortunately, our butts reflect that."

"You have a great body, Charlotte," said Genevieve.

"Fabulous body," I agreed. "It's incredible."

Charlotte whacked my shoulder. "Shut up."

That may bruise, I thought to myself. Can't have my body working on healing a bruise. Only the cancer.

"It's true," said Genevieve. "I always used to think I was too fat. Now I look back at pictures. I had a knockout body. I should have been wearing bikinis twenty-four hours a day. I was an idiot. Whatever you do," she told me, "don't stop Charlotte from wearing tanktops and short skirts. This is her time to shine."

"It's in her contract," I said.

This earned me another backhand, another bruise. Charlotte sighed as she checked out her own figure. "If this is as good as it gets, that's depressing." It was an act. She knew what she had.

"Have a couple kids, get a full-time job. It's all downhill," said Genevieve.

My ex-employee Craig came through the front door pushing a cart, a three-decker filled with pastries.

"Hey," I called to him. This was his first time in since I had let him go. "What's going on?"

Craig stared at me. Craig is a smoker. Smokers get a lot of practice staring while they drag on their sticks and wait for the nicotine to sink in. And beyond these mechanics of the addiction, smokers seem to have a natural soap opera style. Plus he had a mustache. I had time to pour mocha syrup in two cups and write "Jimmy" on a third and then look up to catch the tail end of Craig's stare.

"I'm working for Dan now," he said, referring to our pastry supplier.

I exchanged a look with Charlotte. "That's great," she said. "But delivery isn't until tomorrow morning."

He initiated a fresh stare, this time accompanied by a slow nod, so I knew he had more to say. I knocked spent grounds out of the portafilter bucket, refilled it with fresh ground espresso roast, re-holstered the portafilter and hit the shot button, and then made eye contact again as he said, "Dan thought we could boost sales by selling direct." Craig trundled his cart forward, tapped one of my customers on the shoulder and said, "Would you like to buy a baked good?"

I exchanged another look with Charlotte. "Craig, no," said Charlotte, "that's not going to work…"

"I've got donuts here," Craig called out from under his mustache, drawing nearer in fits and starts as customers scooted chairs and scooped up their children to make way for his cart. "Bearclaws, Bismarcks, kuchen…" He paused to look at me. "I took a job at Uncommon Grounds, too. You know, the shop by the campus."

"It's nowhere near the campus…" Now's not the time, I counseled myself, as Sara relayed three more drink orders. Kenny and Laurie were in front of me by this point, awaiting their drinks. I had six cups in front of me, in varying stages of completion. I use a mnemonic, a train with different cars—for instance, caramel macchiato was a boxcar full of cellophane-wrapped caramels; for a regular macchiato, there's nothing in that boxcar but the wrappers. While Craig had been talking, the espresso train seemed to have left the rails and disappeared into a deep black gorge. I picked up two cups at random, tried to read my own writing, resisted giving them a sniff.

"So what's the weekend have in store for you?" Kenny asked.

"I figure I have two options." Charlotte had already heard through the grapevine, but I planned on a more formal announcement for my customers. Now I decided I didn't have the time. I don't have time for cancer, I had decided. Life wasn't going to slow down for me, stop pummeling me while I felt sorry for myself, while I got rid of this tumor. I had already kicked my own ass at home for wallowing in self-pity. My customers were busy people too. I wasn't going to ask them to start dwelling on it. "I can start fasting now to get in the swing of things before my chemo tomorrow, or gorge myself all day, one last binge."

"Your what?"

"My chemo."

"Your what? Your chemo?"

"Yeah, I've got cancer."

"No you don't," said Laurie.

"Bone." I pulled shots while giving them the news. "They found it last week." While trying to catch Craig's eye and give him the cease-and-desist head shake, I let the espresso shot go too long; had to toss it and start over. I muttered something about Dan the muffin man owing me thirty-three cents.

Kenny and Laurie were horrified by my news. People in line gaped. Activity around me came to a halt. I kept talking, glancing up from time to time, making no solid eye contact. "I was so sure it was high up my leg, right under my butt. Turns out it's in my shin. Which probably doesn't

matter either way, but at least it doesn't creep me out quite as much."
An urgent murmur traveled around the room. Brian has to be joking,
most of them thought. Brian's such a kidder. Any second now he'll come
clean. Any second.

"The tibia or the fibula?" Laurie wanted to know.

I had to chuckle at that one. "That was my first question too. I guess it
doesn't really matter, since they won't amputate one without the other."

Kenny's eyes were huge. "You, uh, you must uh…how are you doing?"

"Oh I'm pretty upset."

"You wouldn't know it though, would you?" Charlotte shook her head as
she ladled foam into Laurie's cup. "Same old Brian, joking about it. Pretending
it's no big deal." She froze in mid-pour, then set the pitcher down.

"Keep it together, lady," I growled.

Charlotte lowered her head and breathed deep. "Brian, you're such an idiot."
Waving an apology she backed away from the bar, wiping her eyes with her
wrists. Genevieve came around the end of the counter, sobbing and opening
her arms. Charlotte went to her for a hug. Sara was right behind her.

Now Laurie was crying, and Kenny's eyes were watery. "Come on," I
complained. "You people are really making me angry."

The line stagnated. Two prospective customers turned around and
walked out.

Laurie suggested the last thing I needed, a hug, as she squeezed past
the cluster of grappling women. I reluctantly abandoned my post to
meet her at the blender. Questions bounced around the shop, joyful
hubbub reduced to a sea of nervous chirping. Some moans. More
crying. Everyone studying me. Laurie didn't want to let go, finally did
when I gave her a thanks-for-caring pinch, heading for the bathroom
to compose herself.

Mark Knutter breezed through the front door. "Knutter boy!" I greeted
him. Knutter Brothers Dairy is big in these parts.

"Mr. B," Mark responded. "What's shakin'?"

"Oh you know." I jumped to the espresso machine and revved up the
pressure for another shot. "Mocha?"

Mark gave me the pistol finger and pulled the trigger.

I turned to Sara and nodded at the cups lined up in front of me. "What
do we got?"

Sara seemed disoriented, to the point she wasn't smiling. My impatience fell just shy of snapping my fingers. "That's a skinny mocha," she finally said, pointing. "That's a cappuccino, that's a three-shot latté, and that's a caramel macchiato."

"Craig," I chirped, sharp enough to get the attention of most everyone in the now-subdued joint. I nodded at my pastry case. "Every pastry you sell is one you're going to buy back from me."

Two older ladies, Reva and Abby, reached across the bar to grip my hand.

I gave them each a good squeeze. "I'd be afraid to shake a cancer patient's hand. You're not worried about snapping a decayed bone or dislodging a chunk of withered muscle?"

"If you're willing to take the chance with us, we'll take it with you," said Reva.

Craig wheeled on by and said, "You'll have to take your issue up with Dan."

"Don't sell any more," I told him.

"Brian," Charlotte called from the back storage area, "we're almost out of two percent. I need to run to the store, but Sara's off in ten minutes, and I don't want to leave you here alone."

"Are you kidding? I got this."

"I can stay," said Sara. "I'll call Jerilyn and let her know I'll be a little late." Sara worked a second job at the garden center.

"Jerilyn might understand, but those tender seedlings won't. You go."

"You're taking the right approach," said Reva. "Work will keep you alive. Don't you slow down. I'm eighty-five and I'm going home now to finish shoring up my retaining wall that collapsed over the winter."

"You got cancer?" Mark Knutter confirmed. "My uncle had prostate cancer."

"I'm sorry to hear that. Hey, Craig, what did I tell you?"

He was selling to Kip Carlson, owner of the sporting goods store down the block.

"My uncle beat it," said Mark, as I left the espresso machine and rounded the corner of the bar. "You'll be fine."

"That's what I keep telling everyone." I brushed by Craig and his unauthorized transaction in progress. Kip froze in mid-payment, a fiver hanging limp in his hand.

"Brian, you want me to handle the drinks?" Sara asked.

"I need you to hand me a few pastries from the case."

Reva followed me. "I don't know if you've ever had to build a retaining wall..."

"I live in an apartment."

"…but you basically have to approach it like a surveyor. My husband, he died you know, had all the right equipment. Of course I never felt like I needed to learn how to use them…"

"How many is that, Craig? Five? Ten?" I rapped the scratched, age-fogged plexiglass that mercifully softened the customer's aerial view of the pastry case. "Let's call it a baker's dozen," I told Sara. "Ring Craig up."

Some customers were following along and laughing at my hijinks. Most had returned to their conversations—after plummeting from soprano to baritone, the shop's ambient chorus had climbed back to alto. If asked at that moment I'm sure I would have said, Great, glad to see they're not fawning all over me. Business as usual is exactly what I need.

"You want it?" Craig was saying behind me. "Take it."

I turned around with a platter full of pastries and the cart slammed into my shin. I could barely see Craig's mustache through the starburst explosions across my eyes. Pain shot up through my groin and lanced my heart. I crumpled to the floor and screamed, some horrible animal-in-a-bear trap wail.

"Brian!" Charlotte ran to me. "Are you alright?"

"I have cancer!" I cried out. "He hit me in the cancer!"

WHAT CAME over me to cry out like that? In a heartbeat I went from a martial arts warrior—a warrior, period, who had played the second half of a JV football game with a separated shoulder; who had fallen fifteen feet off the side of a boulder while race-climbing his best friend, landed on his back, got up and still beat his buddy to the top; who had elk hunted in Montana with a few customers, illegally shot a timber wolf, and carried the carcass on his back on a five-mile detour to avoid the ranger; who had played poker at Terrence's house till five a.m., gone directly to the shop to open, put in a ten-hour shift, broke the roaster and spent all night with Craig fixing it, just in time to open the shop again—to an object of pity, and probably disgust. I had been proud of my ability to suffer, to persevere. Now I had thrown away all that Spartan history in one pathetic moment of irrational hysteria.

A few kids had been in the shop, standing back while their parents rushed to my aid. From their expressions I could see their worldview had been shattered. They realized now that there was no one out there to protect them, that adults were just as weak and scared as they were. Yeah kids, you're all gonna die someday.

I get that my customers couldn't laugh at me, but why couldn't they have at least shunned me, turned their backs on me and walked away whispering to each other, "I thought Brian was a bad ass, guess I was mistaken." The last thing my subconscious needed was to be coddled, to have my self-pitying behavior condoned. But they had huddled around me making clucking sounds, tissues at the ready to wipe my nose and dry my tears.

I vowed this would be the last time anyone would see that kind of weakness from me, regardless how bad things were going to get.

…and then immediately realized this was my dad talking; or maybe it was my mom. Either way, I retreated from the vow as quickly as I had made it, and was left with no clue how to feel, what to think, or where to go from there.

That night I sat in the dark and cursed myself, envisioning improbable scenarios that would allow me the opportunity to publicly display my fearless manhood and prove this shameful episode was a fluke.

It didn't take long before my rage turned against the cancer that wanted me dead. I screamed for an hour. I cursed my folks and North Dakota, Bill Hernandes and Starbucks. I flung couch pillows, punched the walls, and threw a tantrum in every room until I was spent, lying on the floor, chest heaving, with not an ounce of feeling or humanity left in me.

And then a really big wave of emotion hit, and I broke down, weeping and wailing and begging God to give me a second chance. Now it was everybody and everything I loved, parading through my mind. I had never felt such intense love, and I was desperate to hold onto them, Mom, Dad, my friends, my business. My life. Oh God, I prayed, let me keep my life.

It was no longer a mystery why I had lost it at the shop. I was beyond scared. I had never even wondered how I might react to a bad diagnosis. Poorly, as it turned out.

I fell into bed with my brain empty, full of hopelessness. My last conscious thought was how badly I didn't want to die.

T-13

"*MR. LAWSON.* Mr. Lawson. Brian, I need you to wake up."

For a time the doctor's office and my head were on different coordinate planes. I wasn't sure how to bridge this gap. Finally with a little click the two planes joined together as one. Nurse Anna stood before me.

"I think I dozed off."

"I think you fainted, honey." Nurse Anna had a very white face. Her hair was pulled back into a thick yellow-blonde wad. I wanted Nurse Nancy's sparkling eyes and sweet cheeks and cropped hair that looked so good under a nurse's cap, but they wouldn't assign nurses by special request. "I came in and you were slumped forward in the chair with your face blue," Nurse Anna said. "Gave me a little shock."

"Maybe you overdosed me."

"Mm, no." She was taking my pulse. "We give small doses of the chemo drugs these days, fractions of what we used to. Smaller doses, but more often. It helps with the side effects."

I was oh-so-woozy and having difficulty breathing, like waking up too quickly from a deep sleep induced by strangulation. "Maybe I have a really low tolerance for chemo drugs."

"I don't think that's the problem." Nurse Anna walked me to the exam bed. She helped me up and laid me down.

"You're saying I fainted."

"It happens. It doesn't mean you're afraid."

"I'm scared to death. I wish I wasn't."

She patted my foot. "We'll find someone for you to talk to. There are plenty of counselors here at the hospital to help with the process."

"What process?" Without lifting my head I could only see her nurse's cap as she rummaged through the supply cabinet. I wasn't in the mood to move my head. But it would be informative to see her face when she answered.

Who was I kidding, she wasn't going anywhere near that one. "Dr. Bonilla will be in to see you very soon," she said. "Will you be okay here? Not feeling nauseous?"

I hadn't been sure she remembered me from my last visit. "I'm fine."

I was exhausted, but I forced my eyes open, fixed on the ceiling vent, afraid to doze off, terrified of not waking up.

Not waking up. That was the world's most frightening phrase. Now I lay me down to sleep... I could never say that prayer, which I've heard is meant to comfort children before they fall asleep. Other children must see a gentle Lord carrying them up to the playgrounds of Heaven, now that they had died before they waked. I only saw a gray-black void, and the world going on without me.

But of course that was the kicker. There would be no void, no world to see, because there would be no Brian to see it. How could I suddenly cease to exist? How could the world go on without me? (And with barely a record of me, which was a related but separate despair that would resume its mental assault later.) The idea terrorized and confused me. I didn't want to contemplate it. I was trapped in the adult version of one of Piaget's developmental stages, a man-baby who wants people and objects to cease to exist when he leaves the room. I've even had a hard time coming to grips with the idea that things happened here on earth before I came along. I think that's the reason I love history books. To become so familiar with the details of centuries past that I could almost believe I had played a part.

The incredible sadness of the nonexistence of Brian Lawson. That was the state Dr. Bonilla found me in.

"Hi Brian. Don't get up." When I remained on my back, Dr. Bonilla crossed the room to shake my hand. Bonilla rhymed with vanilla. Tall and thin with light brown close-cropped mildly curly hair. Very intelligent looking, the way I liked my doctors. "So we've worked you over already this morning. Radiation, chemo, the works."

"Ain't so bad." Didn't remember much of it.

"Don't get cocky, that's not all we've got." Dr. Bonilla looked at my shin, lightly probing the skin. "So do you have any questions for me?"

"Pretty much every question on the list. It might be easier to refer me to the FAQ section of your website."

Dr. Bonilla put aside his clipboard and sat on the roller stool. Our heads were at the same height. "Let me give you the lowdown on what we know, and what I think we should do. Then you can fire away. A lot depends on what you want to do."

"Fair enough. Begin," I said like a game-show host.

Dr. Bonilla initially came off as a soft-spoken, cerebral, caring sort of guy. Now that we were going to talk cancer, he worked extra hard not to seem chatty, which probably wouldn't have been possible for him anyway. The result was a voice like a robot with the volume turned way down.

"You have a sarcoma, which is a cancer of the connective tissue, including bone. It appears you have bone cancer. I say 'appears' because it's rare for cancer to start in the bone. Usually it spreads there, from somewhere else. The lung, the prostate."

"I know you told me to hold my questions to the end."

"No, please, ask away."

I sat up and slid off the table and returned to the chair where I had fainted. I didn't really have a question, but Dr. Bonilla's robo-monologue was killing me. "Did I catch it at Taekwondo? I feel like I bruised my shin so many times during sparring, that cancer was inevitable. In retrospect, anyway."

"That a common misperception," said Dr. Bonilla. "Someone bangs his elbow, it heals real slowly if at all, hurts more than it should, and turns out to be cancerous. Did the bruise cause the cancer? Probably not. Most likely a coincidence. A person bumps into things all the time, okay? Doesn't usually result in cancer. More likely, the bruise simply calls attention to the cancer."

"The lump under my ass cheek seems to be calling for attention too."

Dr. Bonilla gave me a polite smile. "As you know, we took a number of pictures. MRI, CAT scans, X-rays. We looked you over from top to bottom. You look clean everywhere else. The swelling back there may have been a reaction to the cancer. Or to an infection. Or just because. Lymph nodes will do that. If it was the lymph system reacting to the cancer, I would take it as an encouraging sign—it probably means we caught the cancer about the same time your body did."

That Nurse Nancy was a heterosexual quarterly and not semi-annually had probably saved my life. Every time she stuck her tongue up my rear I sent her a box of breath mints; this time called for something extra.

"So what do we do next," Dr. Bonilla asked himself. "I propose to continue chemotherapy, in two- or three-week sessions, to stop the growth and the potential spread of any remaining cancer cells. A couple rounds could very well do the trick. But I don't like the wait-and-see approach. I want to take an aggressive stance with your cancer."

Boys are hypnotized as babies and told to act like rabid chipmunks whenever someone says aggressive. I slapped the arm of the chair and wiped foamy spittle off my lips. "You're talking amputation. I'm in. Let's do it."

"Not quite so extreme," said Dr. Bonilla without batting an eye. "I was thinking minor surgery to remove the tumor." He winked. "But I'm glad you're game for whatever I have in mind."

"Believe me, I'll take 'we have to amputate' over 'I'm afraid your cancer has spread', every time."

"My goal is to never have to deliver that line to you," said Dr. Bonilla. "So throughout the process we'll also be hitting the tumor with a couple different types of radiation therapy."

"That makes me nervous. I haven't gone forth and multiplied yet."

The doc smiled. "We'll target the tumor with a precise beam of radiation. The technology at our disposal these days allows us to pinpoint our attack."

"Still, I'm glad it's the shin, miles away from my life-giver. It is just the shin," I verified.

"Correct."

"Tibia or fibia?"

"It's fibula. But it's the tibia."

"The cancer?"

"Yes," said Dr. Bonilla.

"Which one?"

"Bone cancer."

"No, I mean which bone?"

"I told you." He sounded a little irritated. "The tibia."

"Not the fibia?"

"It's the fibula."

"Oh man, is it in both?"

"No, just the fibula. Dammit, I mean the tibia."

"Whichever," I said, done messing with him. I love Abbott & Costello. "So, Jared Caldwell." Caldwell was my radiologist and father of Sam my employee. "What do you think of his abilities?"

Dr. Bonilla frowned. I think he had a headache now.

"I'm just wondering if I shouldn't go to the Mayo Clinic, or Mt. Sinai. Or maybe to a hospital in a town of more than fifteen thousand people."

"Dr. Caldwell has been running radiology for us for the past decade," said Dr. Bonilla. "He's had something like two thousand patients. This isn't a statistic that's available to patients, but when you compare Dr. Caldwell's success rate to the rest of the U.S., he's quite a bit better than the average."

"What about Canada?" I challenged, to loosen him up. "I've heard a lot of good things about Canada's healthcare system. And it's just up the road."

Dr. Bonilla pretended to take my request seriously. "Canada. Hm. Well, I think we could get you in for treatments sometime in the year 2016."

"Must be a quality product, with a waiting list that long."

Dr. Bonilla chuckled. He straightened up on his stool and slapped his knee and outright laughed. "I can tell you this, Dr. Caldwell has worked on quite a few Canadians in his career."

I could have cared less about his international success rate. I just wanted doctors who liked me enough to bust their asses to save my life. I had to believe that a doctor who cared, I mean really cared, would work harder for me. Put in extra hours, lose sleep—but not too much sleep. I wanted a doctor who was clear-headed. And single-minded. A doctor who focused on me at the expense of all else, other patients, dictation, family, everything. That was the doctor I wanted.

"Okay," I said, "let's stick with Jared."

"Good choice," said Dr. Bonilla. "Brian, you look like you're feeling pretty good so far."

"No. Not really."

Dr. Bonilla gave me a tight smile. "It's going to get worse. We soften the effects of the chemo drugs the best we can. But they're designed to do damage to your cancer, so the rest of you is going to take a beating, too."

"So long as my hair doesn't fall out."

"I'll note that." Dr. Bonilla pretended to scribble a note. "'Patient desires to keep his hair. Or at the very least, to grow it back later.'"

"Later? Doc, I don't know how this is going to work if you don't listen more carefully to my demands."

"Brian, with what we're going to give you, maybe one in a thousand patients doesn't lose a good deal of hair."

"Keep in mind that since most people have mediocre hair, they don't make it a priority. I have nice hair. I have to like my odds."

"We'll do what we can," said Dr. Bonilla, looking a little tired of my act. I thought he was going to stand up and bring our talk to a close. Instead he clasped a knee and leaned back on the stool. "Let's talk about anything else you have on your mind. How's your mental state?"

I would have said "fine" and let him be on his way, but Dr. Bonilla seemed like he truly wanted to know. And I was truly ready to tell somebody. "Terrible. I'm really afraid of dying. I mean really afraid. I've always believed in God—didn't really understand Him, you know, the mechanics of Heaven and souls and that whole thing. But I believed He existed. Until a week or so ago. Now, now that I'm trying to visualize it, for the first time, really, it sounds a little farfetched. I really want to believe—that's my number two prayer. 'Help me believe.' Right after 'Save me.'"

Hunched on the stool and staring into the floor, Dr. Bonilla rubbed a knuckle across his lips.

"I know this isn't your area of expertise," I said. "But you did ask."

He broke out of his reverie. "I can tell you what I know, from my experience with similar situations."

"That would be great."

"I've seen people lose their faith, and go kicking and screaming. Their last days are filled with anger and a sense of betrayal. By the end, they're exhausted, depressed, nothing like the people they used to be. It's a terrible last few days. Or weeks, or months."

This rattled me. "If you're not comfortable talking about the deaths of your past patients, I completely understand."

"Are you comfortable hearing what I have to say?"

My feet lost contact with the floor. All the ambient sounds were vacuumed from the room and the halls beyond. The future, the past, all gone. Dr. Bonilla's prominent cheekbones stood out in sharp definition against a blurry background. It was clear to me that nothing mattered but what he was about to say. It was crucial that I understand.

"I want to know."

Dr. Bonilla squeezed the blood out of his lips. "I've seen people who were at peace with their faith, who went much faster than I thought they should have. Circumstances where I thought his or her prognosis was good. And then they passed away."

His voice was soft and rich and touched with heavenly reverberation, filling the room and enveloping my brain. A vise tightened around my chest. I could only nod.

"And then I've seen people who believed life was special. Maybe I read too much into it, but I'm pretty sure they thought they were special too. They were the patients our staff fell in love with. They had a glow."

Dr. Bonilla rolled closer. "And I don't know how they achieved it, but they had a balance. A certainty there was life after death. And a certainty they weren't going to need it quite yet. Even as the cancer progressed and they had setbacks, and all sorts of painful treatments and humiliating side effects, and reactions to the disease…they remained focused on getting better, and on going about their lives. These were the people, no matter how bleak things got, you knew they were going to make it."

"Wow," I croaked. "That's how I want to be. I think, I hope, that maybe that's how I am."

Dr. Bonilla nodded. "They're the hardest to lose. Heartbreaking for everyone."

We nodded together for a time, while my bowels loosened.

"Anything else you're unsure of?" he asked. "Any other questions?"

Any way I could get you to be a lot less candid going forward? "I'm ready to go home now."

"So the plan is chemo and radiation, then surgery to remove any remaining tumor. Then another round of treatments. Sound good?"

I nodded. Dr. Bonilla shook my hand and excused himself. I ducked into the bathroom and threw up.

No, it wasn't the cancer.

But of course it was the cancer.

I do have a nervous stomach. Back in high school I always had to take a dump minutes before the basketball game started, but that was a treat, a cleansing relief. This was a trip to the woodshed. I vomited again, whatever was left of the chicken cacciatore Valerie McEwen had brought by, and picked my head out of the bowl, thankful I had followed directions and fasted for the last twelve hours. This thankfulness lasted no more than thirty seconds, when my empty gut began to twist—fear wasn't done with me, treating my stomach like a wet towel and wringing out every last drop.

My legs were wobbly as I pulled on my shorts, pulled off the gown, mopped up cold sweat, and put on my shirt. I was two for two here. My new MO. "Remember Brian?" the hospital staff would recall me fondly. "The way he threw up every time he came into the hospital, it was so cute."

Needing to give body and brain time to recover before getting behind the wheel, I decided to find Andrea. I asked at the nurses' station for directions to Bhani's lab. The nurse frowned, wanted to know why. I wasn't sure whether she was shielding him from an agent of the McEwens, or protecting unsuspecting patients from his diabolical chamber of horrors.

"A friend of mine works for him," I told them.

"Oh. Andrea. Lower level three."

I waited at the service elevator with an orderly and a corpse on a gurney. When the door opened the orderly waved me in. "After you," he said.

"I'll catch the next one, thanks."

The orderly grunted something derogatory as he wheeled the corpse into the elevator. I watched the indicator lights track to the bottom, to lower level three. I hit the Down button; the same car came to get me, smelling of formaldehyde. "I'll wait," I said to myself and punched the button again. This time the other car arrived, and I descended into the belly of the beast.

The hallway was wide with a cement floor, painted cinderblock walls, and asbestos ceiling. The lights swear-to-God flickered overhead. No sign of the corpse, no sound except the elevator as it left me. I walked the length of the long hall. Doors were staggered every ten yards, most unmarked. A few had misleading labels like Waste & Offal and Bacterial Contaminants, obviously intended to scare off the curious. I had no doubt there were Robin Cook-style atrocities taking place behind these doors, and I was content to let them continue.

Dr. Bhani's office was one door down from the elevator, in the opposite direction. I knocked and entered.

The lab was the size and shape of a boxcar, much smaller than I would have guessed, given the monumental research supposedly taking place. Andrea sat behind a desk stuffed into the corner to my right, facing me. "Hey there," she greeted me. "I'll be with you in a second."

The woman across from her didn't turn around to look at me, which I thought was strange. In this basement, with the morgue a few doors down? I'd be curious who just came in.

The lab reminded me of my barebones high school science classroom, the lab bench equipped with a sink and a microscope, and a piece of equipment that looked like a bread machine. No moaning delirious patients, no tanks bubbling with green goo, no Dr. Bhani—none of the stuff I expected to see.

I hummed Squeeze's Black Coffee In Bed so as not to eavesdrop on privileged doctor-patient or experimenter-experimentee communications. With the woman's back to me, I could only hear Andrea's side of the conversation. Here's a snotty sample: "These are all the records we have to show you. It's difficult to prove that we haven't received something. You're asking the impossible. How do we prove a negative? Hm?"

I finished Coffee In Bed and moved on to Tempted, feeling a little self-conscious, in need of a better way to kill time. But it didn't seem proper to browse a scientist's lab bench, even a mad scientist's lab bench. Especially a mad scientist's lab bench.

"That's something you'll have to ask Dr. Bhani when he returns," Andrea snapped at the woman.

I should go, I thought. Politely wave goodbye and go home. Or to the shop. I was behind on my paperwork. I was overdue prioritizing the nonpayment schedule of my past-due bills. But a catfight was coming. I would stick around to watch tiny Andrea claw this woman's eyes out.

In the meantime I felt stupid hovering and humming over the woman's shoulder. So I browsed the lab bench. A light layer of dust covered the black slate surface. How long had Dr. Bhani been gone? Was Andrea employed not as a research assistant but a smokescreen, to give Bhani time to elude the authorities? Or at least the McEwens' lawyers.

Next to the microscope stood a laminated placard titled Nonspecific Immune Response, a cartoonish rendition of our immune system doing its thing. Arrows led from one group of squiggly cells to a different group of squiggly cells. In the next frame the second group now bristled with antennae. A third species of amoeba-like cells lurked in the margins, looking as threatening as amoeba can. Judging by the zigzag urgency of their short bold-faced arrows, they had locked onto the frequency emitted by the antenna-sprouting squigglies, and were itching to descend upon them for some serious butt kicking. I put my eye to the microscope, hoping to see the bad-ass amoeba in action, but it was dark in there. I didn't have the guts to lift the lid on the bread machine.

"I've given you people everything we have," Andrea snarled at the woman. "This is a big waste of time."

The woman said something inaudible and looked to her left, when clearly she should have been contemplating the exit to her right. That's when I realized the wall facing me was a cheap partition, and that the woman was interested in what was happening on the other side.

"Ma'am, I have work to do," said Andrea. "You're going to have to leave. Come back with a warrant." She came briskly around the desk, her hip bumping the woman's head as she bent to grab her briefcase.

"Bitch," said the woman.

"Now that I heard," I said.

Andrea kept walking, shaking her head. I retreated with her, as far as that boxcar of a room allowed. We waited until the woman stomped out.

"I'm not really sure what was going on there," I told Andrea. "But if you had decided to kill her, the clean-up would have been a cinch." I pointed. "The morgue is right down the hall."

Tears sprang to Andrea's eyes. She wiped them away, careful not to smudge her mascara. "I'm sorry. She makes me so mad."

"I shouldn't joke about wanting to kill her. Unless you want to? We could probably still catch her."

"No. Well, maybe."

We remained tucked together in the corner, standing so close to each other that Andrea was more underneath than beside me. I fidgeted, paced in place like a tiger in a pet carrier. Andrea didn't notice my discomfort, preoccupied with using each finger in turn to ferry tears off her lashes.

"Who was she?" I asked. "If you're ready to talk about it."

Andrea tugged her oversized sweatshirt past her hips and shuddered as the frustration left her body. Her petiteness was on full display, hair pulled back and piled up on her head, exposing a thin neck and allowing a clear measurement of her small cranium. Smallness should have been irrelevant, but it was a factor, making her appear childlike and helpless against the adversity that swirled about her. Frail little Andrea obviously needed a hug, any gentleman could see it, and she was standing close enough to make it a simple act, just stretch out my arms and pull that little body to me. I could envelop her. It would be very comforting, maybe for both of us.

"She was from the state health department," Andrea told me. "They want proof we're not going to infect anyone else."

"Because of Brent? But I thought you said Bhani didn't give Brent that infection."

"He didn't."

"So you shouldn't say 'anyone else'. Leave off the 'else'."

"Her words, not mine," said Andrea. "You look terrible by the way."

"I threw up. A couple few times."

Her eyes darted to my shirt.

"Not on myself. I was pretty much naked."

"How convenient," she said, as if I had been doing a nurse at the time. Which, if the nursing coordinator had assigned me Nurse Nancy like I asked…. "I'm going to close shop early. Did you need a ride?"

"No. Just wanted to say hi."

"Just a hi, or do you have time for a coffee?"

"You're a coffee drinker now? I knew there was something different about you. Smarter, better looking, taller."

"Let's say I can stomach it," said Andrea, "with a lot of cream and sugar."

"Whatever it takes to get it in you." I needed an excuse to postpone going into the shop. Everyone knew I had gone in for my first treatment. They would be looking for an upbeat report and a confident pronouncement of my invincibility, things I wasn't able to give. And returning to my apartment midmorning sounded depressing. I had never been in my apartment between the hours of seven a.m. and three p.m. I should have sublet it to a nightshift worker. "But you have to drink coffee, or I get up and walk out."

"Fine."

"So were you lying to the state health woman, or is Bhani really gone?"

"He's out of town," said Andrea.

"Do you mean out of the country?"

"Not as far as I know."

"The real lab is on the other side of the wall, right?"

Andrea nodded. "This room is for small demos, and interviews. This is where we discover whether the patient is serious about treatment—or really a health inspector pretending to have cancer."

"No way. That's happened?"

"We're pretty sure. Do you have time for a tour?"

Andrea hadn't budged during our conversation, and I had given up trying to escape, leaning back against the wall to create a small buffer between us. It struck me then how all alone we were, in that room and probably on the floor. Us and the corpses. Imagine if the McEwens could see us cozy in the corner like this. Yesterday Mike and Valerie had showed up at my door with a month's worth of prepared meals. They had tried to be strong for me, but the memories of Brent's passing were way too fresh, I ended up doing most of the consoling. I couldn't imagine what it would do to them to see me here with Andrea. I should have followed the state health woman out the door. Shouldn't have gone down there in the first place.

Yet now that I had, I felt guilty for not showing up sooner. It wasn't right for Dr. Bhani to leave Andrea alone down there. Righteous health department employees, sex-starved orderlies not quite ready to try necrophilia, the McEwens—Andrea was ill-equipped to defend herself against any of them. At the same time I acknowledged—most likely Mike McEwen's voice echoing in my head—that Andrea was an adult and a parent, a woman who had survived many nights alone since the divorce, obviously more resilient than I was giving her credit for. The need to protect her was an irrational impulse.

Andrea's eyes were on my purple and green bruised shin, probably wondering how she ended up with a cancer victim for a guardian angel. "I want to show you why you should consider talking to Dr. Bhani."

"True story, there's an acupuncturist in town who swears he can cure me. We call him Asian Vince. You know him? He's equal parts wannabe Confucius, wannabe Bruce Lee, and wannabe ancient mystic healer. In addition to the obvious stuff like backache, impotence and male pattern baldness, Asian Vince is sure he can cure Lou Gehrig's disease, Alzheimer's, and scurvy. And now cancer, if only I'd give his needles and herbs the chance."

"What does that have to do with Dr. Bhani?"

"I've decided to go with Western medicine."

Andrea sighed. "That's fine. Fine, fine. Thanks to the McEwens," she mispronounced their name on purpose, "you're going to just turn your back on your best chance for a cure."

"Should we go get that sweet creamy coffee now?"

"Fine. I'm sure the hospital cafeteria coffee will be right up your alley."

"I actually had another place in mind. I'll drive."

EVEN THROUGH the sleet we could see Hernandes's big blinking portable electronic sign from a block away.

Twofer Tuesdays!

On the other side of the entrance to the parking lot, a bigger sign with Vegas-style running lights announced No Sleep Sundays! This was the cheesiest shit I had seen in quite a while.

"No Monday Madness?" I wondered. I pulled a u-turn in the parking lot and parked on the curb in front of the Twofer sign, completely obstructing it.

"I can't get out," Andrea notified me. "The sign is blocking my door."

"Throw your door open. Maybe you can knock it over."

"No. You pull up."

"I really like this spot. Come out my side."

Andrea made unhappy sounds as she clambered over the console and dropped to the street beside me. "Happy?"

"Not until that sign says Going Out of Business."

"You have sign envy," Andrea cooed. "Get one of those for your shop."

I thought about it. "Maybe I will." Leaving my sign board out in the snow had ruined it, and Charlotte still hadn't made me a replacement. I couldn't stand Frannie the sign nazi thinking for even a day that she had won.

We slopped along the sidewalk. Andrea stopped to study the new sign above the door. "Was this place always called the Campus Coffeehouse?"

"No." All I could think was, Billy, what took you so long?

The place was grungier than before. More dusty sofas, more crap hung on the walls—bad artwork, shelves of books no one in North Dakota was pretentious enough to read, and pictures. Three blue-haired ladies crowded around a tiny table underneath a print of Kerouac, and an old farmer in bib overalls drank coffee beneath a poster of Johnny Depp as Hunter S. Thompson.

Kenny the Wells Fargo bank manager sat with his wife Laurie in easy chairs on either side of a lamp stand illuminating a framed enlarged photo of rough-looking Central American coffee pickers slouching around a pile of empty burlap coffee bean bags. "Hey you two," I greeted them in passing.

"Brian! Hey!" Kenny yelped and jumped up to shake my hand. "We were on our way to the college to drop off some student loan applications."

"Ah." I felt like pointing out that only one coffeeshop sat on a direct line between his bank and the college, and it wasn't this one.

"Brian, how are you?" Laurie used a caring tone reserved for those who gave a shit about me, which she obviously didn't, keeping Billy afloat another day to torment me and wean a few more customers off the taste of coffee.

"I had my first round of treatments this morning, so I've been better. Do you two know Andrea? Kenny and Laurie. They're customers of mine."

"Andrea," said Laurie. "You're Rick's ex-wife, right?"

"That's right," said Andrea, less than overjoyed to be identified as such.

Kenny fidgeted, wild-eyed. "So Brian, checking out the competition?"

"Andrea doesn't like coffee, so we came here."

"Oh, ha-ha-ha," Laurie laughed. She threw a quick look toward the counter. "Your coffee is so much better," she whispered.

"Speak up, I can't hear you," I urged.

They laughed nervously. "It's true," Laurie said, still whispering.

"Obviously not everyone thinks so," said Andrea.

"It's the free refills," said Kenny. He lowered his voice. "It attracts the older-than-average crowd."

"My refills are only a quarter." I tried not to sound defensive.

Kenny waved us forward until we huddled like a football team. "Old folks won't bank with us unless we give them free stuff," he whispered. "Even if it's only a balloon. I'm serious. If I put a 'Free Hard Candies!' sign in the window, senior citizens show up in droves. They're not the most rational folks."

"I guess I'll have to consider free refills to win you two back."

"Oh not us," Laurie heehawed. "You still have us! But yes," she dropped her voice to a loud hiss, "do it for the senior citizens."

"I would, except we're not a Denny's. We'll let you two get back to your drinks." I wasn't in the mood to beat them up over their defection. Kenny and Laurie are good people; if they liked Hernandes's shop better, there wasn't much I could do about it. What worried me was the possibility they were staying away because of my cancer. If it was going to be bad for business, I'd rather it just kill me quick.

"We were leaving anyway," Kenny assured me. "You can have our table. Come on, honey, let's get those applications over to the campus."

"We'll see you down at your shop, Brian," said Laurie.

"Okay lady. Bye-bye." I turned to Andrea. "Do you want to get me a brevé Americano? I don't feel like going up there."

"Okay…." She looked put out. "What's a…whatever you asked for?"

"Brevé Americano. They won't know what it is either, but order it anyway." Kenny and Laurie hadn't yet vacated their spot so I sat down heavily at a spindly-legged table in the middle of the floor. My bones ached. All of them, not just the shin. I knew chemo was rough on the body, but this seemed too soon. I had an awful feeling it was the cancer, everywhere. But it couldn't be, they had x-rayed me, MRI'd me, pumped me full of iodine and scanned me, and found nothing.

I was worried, and my customers weren't helping. Some tried to be supportive, some just wanted to show off their medical knowledge. Mary Kazler told me that swollen lymph glands could indeed mean my immune system was mounting a defense. Or, she said, it could be lymphoma. That's a bad cancer. If there was such a thing as a good cancer, lymphoma was definitely a bad one. I decided I wanted another CAT scan.

Andrea returned and plunked down a cup of milky-brown fluid topped with big bubble foam.

A bubble popped in my cup. "What is this?" I asked.

"Hell if I know."

"What did you get?"

"Hot chocolate."

"Didn't I tell you I was going to leave if you didn't drink coffee? Come on," I complained. "You're putting me in an awkward position here. How are you ever going to take my threats seriously if I don't get up this second and walk out of here?" I faked a move to get up and leave.

Andrea smirked. "You can't leave such wonderful ambiance."

Instead of piped-in music, Hernandes had piped in poetry. Beat poetry, judging by the reader's outraged tone. The quality of the recording and the shop's acoustics were both poor, so it actually made for a mellow, inoffensive background babble. It irritated the hell out of me.

"Or such wonderful company," Andrea added, unable to muster a smile to go along with her sense of humor. Felt like we both had cancer.

Neither of us spoke, misery loving company. Andrea stared at me with a sour, suffering look. "This lady from the state really has you down, huh?"

"I shouldn't care what she thinks." Andrea pulled a clip off her head and her hair dropped to her shoulders. Not thick hair, but nice enough. "As long as we don't have any obvious health code violations, Dr. Bhani is sure they don't have jurisdiction. I guess I'm just not equipped to handle adversity any more."

"Good thing you took a job with a mad scientist then."

"First of all, Dr. Bhani was basically my only choice," said Andrea. "And secondly, he's doing unbelievable things. Honestly. The immune system is the key to fighting cancer. Your immune system doesn't think of cancer as an invader, for some reason. Some scientists are trying to figure out why. Dr. Bhani has found a way to make your white blood cells attack the cancer."

"By giving you a deadly infection."

Andrea gave an exasperated chirp. "It wasn't Dr. Bhani's infection that killed Brent. Do you have to believe everything the McEwens tell you?"

I shrugged. "I'd rather take my chances with the standard treatments."

"Chemo and radiation shouldn't be standards," Andrea said hotly. "They don't work."

"My doctor practically guaranteed me they would shrink my tumor."

"Shrinking isn't curing."

"I'll take what I can get."

"So it shrinks. Yeah, that's fine. But I'll bet they won't promise you the tumor won't come back."

"Promises are for suckers. There are no guarantees in life. Believe me. I've seen too many sure things go south overnight."

Andrea chuckled humorlessly. "You don't have to teach me that lesson."

One-upping each other's tales of woe and hardship didn't appeal to me. I took a sip and regretted it. Did brevé mean burned in Portuguese?

"I won't bug you anymore about your treatment," said Andrea. "But there's a book I want you to read. I have it in my car back at the hospital."

"Sounds good."

"You don't want to know what it's about?"

I doubted we shared the same literary tastes. And I couldn't imagine picking up another book until the cancer was gone. So I didn't pretend to be curious. "Sure."

Andrea's lips twisted into a disgusted configuration. "It's about a guy with cancer who didn't accept the standard treatment."

"What kind of cancer did he have?"

"Lymphoma."

My temperature plummeted. "Do you, uh, you think that's what I have?"

"The type of cancer isn't the point," said Andrea. "The point is that he went searching for alternative treatments, and found a cure."

"You're telling me I should go talk to Asian Vince."

"I'm telling you doctors aren't always open to the possibilities. And just because your doctor doesn't know any better than to pump you full of chemo and hope for the best, doesn't mean you should accept it."

"Okay, whatever, I'll read it."

"For having a fatal disease, you're not taking this very seriously."

"Let me tell you about a dream I had last night. I was floating up into the air. I kept rising, higher and higher. In my dream I realized I had died. I was in spirit form. And for some amazing reason, I wasn't too upset about it.

"I keep rising, and now I'm in space. I can see the Earth below me. It's nice. Now I'm looking out into space, and I see a white light, way out there. I'm heading toward it, this bright white light. I'm flying faster and faster, eager to see what's out there, pretty sure I know what it is. But the light starts to dim. The closer I get, the dimmer the light gets. I'm hurtling toward it faster and faster, the light's getting dimmer and dimmer, and then wham! it's a black hole. That's when I woke up."

"Geez." Andrea blinked a few times. "That's a bad dream."

My heart pounded, reliving the black hole moment. That was the most positive dream I'd had in a week. "I take death seriously."

Hernandes popped out of his office for the second time to stare at me with a troubled expression.

"Maybe it's this place getting you down," Andrea suggested. "I know I need a vacation from this town. A permanent vacation."

"Things haven't improved, even now that you're working?"

Andrea's jaw dropped. "Do you like living here? My God, you're from California. Don't you miss it?" She came alive, lifting off her chair with each burst of emotion. "I've been to Davis. I love that town. The weather is fabulous. You're close to Napa Valley and San Francisco and Tahoe. The only thing we're close to here is freezing to death. How can you stand living here?"

"Is it the winters getting you down?" I deflected her. If she wanted to vent, fine, I expected as much. But it wasn't going to be about me. I had my own issues with North Dakota, always simmering under the surface. I didn't need Andrea fanning the flames.

"Sure, yes, it's the winters," Andrea was sarcastic. And loud. "Everybody here thinks they're so tough. No one else in the world can survive their winters. If you don't like living here, it's because you're too soft to survive the winter. I can't tell you how many times I've heard someone say, 'Keeps the riffraff out.' Or 'Winters here aren't for the faint-hearted.' The next person who says that to me is going to get their eyes clawed out." She crossed her arms, blood-red nails digging into her sleeves, oblivious to our attentive audience. "It's not the weather. If the weather in Davis or Denver suddenly changed, no one would leave, because there's actually something to do in those places. Why does Jamestown even exist? I can't figure it out. It's for people who don't have any goals, who couldn't get a job anywhere else. It's not a place to live. It's a place to hide."

Andrea had jacked my eyebrows halfway up my forehead, and I couldn't get them to return to their resting position. The old ladies at the Kerouac table glared at us. "Maybe you should consider moving."

"Oh, yeah, I'll tell the judge—who's a native, by the way—'Mr. Judge, I know you said Tyler couldn't be moved from Jamestown. But I respectfully disagree. Tyler and I are moving back to Colorado.'"

"I meant without Tyler."

"I've considered it, believe me."

"Tyler seems pretty happy here, from what the McEwens tell me."

"What exactly have they told you?" Andrea demanded.

"In passing. In conversation. Nothing really." Except that you're a horrible mom, person and wife, and your existence in Jamestown, any town, is an abomination. "Nothing in particular."

"Do they say he's happier with Rick than he is with me?"

Of course they did. "No." All the time.

"Because if they're saying things about me, and about the way I'm raising Tyler..." Andrea's little body trembled.

"You know what," I said, trying not to lie, or say anything that would find its way back to the McEwens, "they're worried about Tyler growing up with divorced parents. And they're worried about you, because they know you don't like it here."

I must have walked the tightrope effectively, because Andrea slumped back in her chair. "I've thought about leaving," she said. "But I can't. Every time I consider it, my heart breaks. I couldn't live without Tyler. I'd go crazy."

She didn't break down and weep. But it was obvious she was speaking from the heart. "You just seem so unhappy."

"How would you feel?" Andrea demanded. "I never agreed to this. I thought we were going to live in Colorado. The three of us. The next thing I know, we're here. I was told it's just temporary. But then it's not, it's permanent." Her voice cracked and warbled, but she pressed on. "And it was never the three of us. We basically lived with Rick's family. His family, his job, everything comes before me. And then he divorces me. Now I'm single, surrounded by people who hate me. All my friends and family are back in Colorado, and I'm living in the last place on earth I would have picked. Trapped here, for the next fifteen years."

Andrea was breathing hard and wiping away tears before they left her eyes. I saw a napkin on the next table and swiped it for her. "I'm sorry," I said. "I never really thought about it that way."

"How could you not?"

"I spend most of my time wallowing in my own self-pity."

Hernandes approached our table, his pear head bobbing, black hair shiny even in the dingy lighting, his tiny bulging eyeballs watering like a Chihuahua's. Then, like he had just noticed me, "Brian Lawson! This is your second visit to my humble shop! To what do I owe the pleasure?" He hesitated. "This is only twice, right?"

As if I hung out in his shop whenever he wasn't there, hoping to steal his coffee secrets. "I don't have the time to drive all the way out here very often."

"We got a great location," said Hernandes. "You love the décor? It's my son's idea. He fell in love with the West Coast coffeehouses."

"I'm from the coast, and they don't look like this." Not the good ones, anyway.

"I thought the incense-scented floor wax was a little much." Hernandes bent down and sniffed deeply. "But my son said it's what people expect from a coffeehouse. Especially college kids. And he's right. We've been going gangbusters. And now you're closing. Very sorry to hear that," Hernandes said solemnly, hands clasped at his waist.

"Closing what?"

"Your shop," said Hernandes. "At least until your cancer is cured."

Andrea sniffed. "Unfortunately Brian isn't looking for a cure."

She argued the wrong point, but it did give me couple extra seconds to reconsider the profanity-laced tirade yearning to be unleashed. "I'm not closing, Billy."

"You're not closing?" Hernandes did a great job pretending to be shocked. "I'm sure I heard that."

I drummed the tabletop. I wanted to shake him until he gurgled I am a rumormonger, and a liar. I shot Kennedy, and J.R. And I hate the taste of coffee.

Hernandes wiggled his fingers at the Kerouac ladies. "Martha, your drink is okay?"

"It's delicious," said Martha, glaring at Andrea.

Delicious, my ass. I couldn't choke mine down. Martha must have no fucking taste buds. I was raging inside.

"We aim to please," said Hernandes, spunky and in command. He gave our table a slap, and then had to steady the rickety piece of crap before it toppled, onto my fragile body. "I'll have to have Craig fix that. Speaking of former James River Valley Coffee folks, thanks for sending him my way. He's been a godsend. That kid knows his coffee."

"I didn't send him your way, I fired him. And the kid is thirty-one."

"He's a natural for the coffee business, at any age."

"A coffeeshop only needs one expert. But you're right, it does need at least one."

"You can never have enough expertise on board." The color had left the skin around Hernandes' thin stretched smile. I was getting to him. "That's something I learned in the business world."

"And of course the margins are so huge," I said with heavy sarcasm, "paying for that expertise is no problem."

"Oh I think I had a realistic understanding of the margins," said Hernandes. "I knew my business expertise was going to mean the difference between scraping by, and making a very comfortable living. I had responsibility for purchasing, you know. For a big company."

"You told people you were a broker for a hotshot Wall Street firm."

"My company did have business on Wall Street, it's true. I'm really glad I wasn't a broker, with the market and all. It's almost like fate, how my purchasing background has helped me negotiate steep discounts and favorable terms with my suppliers."

"Of course it's long-term relationships and coffee knowledge that make all the difference," I said, as if this was nothing new to him. "Without the coffee knowledge, the bean brokers will have you paying a twenty percent premium for low-grade peaberries. And unless you're Starbucks, purchasing discounts get nickled and dimed in the handling fees. Isn't it amazing how coffee is such a unique industry?"

"Mm…" Hernandes scribbled mental notes. "Which reminds me…when you sell your shop, I want your inventory. And maybe your location."

"I'm not selling." I was now officially staying open forever, or until Hernandes went out of business, or I died. Whichever came first.

"You should sell," said Andrea. "Move back to Davis."

"Is that where you're from?" said Hernandes. "Davis—California, right? Quite a change. The winters had to be a shock. Not for the faint of heart."

I looked at Andrea and then nodded toward Hernandes. "Go ahead."

She pretended not to understand.

I gave her a disappointed look. "I had a feeling it might be cold here," I told Hernandes. "I own a globe." I stood and was immediately impatient for Andrea to do likewise.

"Thanks for stopping in, folks," Hernandes brayed. "Brian, we're pulling for you. This community wants you back on your feet."

"I've never been off my feet, Billy." I pulled Andrea to hers and propelled her toward the door.

"Whatever I can do, let me know," Hernandes called after me.

"Get a deadly cancer," I answered as we exited, probably out of earshot. I stalked a few paces down the sidewalk. "I think I really shook him up in there. Don't you think?"

"I wasn't really paying attention," Andrea said with perfect boredom.

"He's rattled." We reached the van. "Is that the word on the street? That I'm quitting? Have you heard anyone say that?"

Andrea shrugged.

"Why am I asking you? You don't talk to anybody. I need to call Mike." Wheels were turning. "I need some exposure. It's time to get the Bluffs shop moving forward." My mind was suddenly made up—Hernandes was going down. It felt great to have a plan, to have a goal. I helped Andrea into the driver's-side door. "Thanks for nothing, by the way. You were going to claw the eyes out of the next person who told you the winters are too harsh."

"He said it to you, not to me."

"But I chew my fingernails." I held them up for inspection. "How am I supposed to claw anyone's eyes out?"

"Kick him in the balls," Andrea suggested.

"I am a good kicker," I mused.

"You shouldn't chew your nails. Chemo drugs settle in your nails."

"Thanks for giving me one more thing to worry about."

"No problem," said Andrea. She forgot to enjoy being a smart ass. I think her own wheels had started turning.

T-12

CHARLOTTE SENT me home early on Day Eighteen, my last day of the first of two chemo cycles. Told me to get some rest before my appointment with Dr. Bonilla. No doubt she thought she was doing me a favor—in the event of a stealth alien or Stepford infestation, we had test scenarios for everyone on staff, questions designed to smoke out imposters, and I had failed mine twice that morning, serving decaf without complaint. But I think she was more nervous than I was about what the doc would report, and getting me out of sight helped.

In fact, I knew the cancer had to have been halted, because everything in my body seemed to have stopped growing. I had lost fifteen pounds, and a similar percentage of hair. My innards felt numb. Everything in my belly and my brain had fallen silent, the gears and wiring melted by the chemo poisons.

My self image: a collection of inert organs, no pumping, no processing. I laid in bed at night, perfectly still, waiting to sense movement inside. Focus on it long enough and even your heartbeat seems to stop. Except for the constant stomach ache and the frequent sweating, I felt dead.

Everyone was counseling rest, but I was conflicted on the subject. Should I get extra, to give my body the energy to combat the disease? Or is it during the sleeping hours, when my defenses are down, that the cancer makes its move? It was an agonizing debate. Truly a life or death question. Get extra rest and live; or sleep my life away while the cancer ran amok.

Same for working. Should I devote myself to the business, as a stimulant and to take my mind off the cancer? Become a dynamo of activity, taking on all challenges and muscling my way to good health? Or, do workaholics use up all their energy and die? It was all a question of optimizing my defenses.

Probably a moot debate. With any defenses to speak of, I wouldn't have cancer.

As a compromise of sorts I worked, at half-speed. The competitive spark during my visit to Hernandes' shop with Andrea hadn't lit the fire. I hadn't done a thing toward making the Bluffs a reality. I apologized to Mike and he told me not to worry about it, under the circumstances.

That apology was over the phone. I had turned down their invites to dinner, and I suppose I was avoiding them, but I could honestly say I was busy. (I was counting on Mike's network to confirm this for him.) I knew it would be a mistake to spend too much time alone, and so in the past two weeks I had been over to friends' houses three times for dinner. I even convinced Terrence and Amber to let me entertain them.

And yet I had never been lonelier. I had come that close to asking my folks to fly out and stay with me. Mom, Dad, can you visit? For a year or so?

Actually, I hadn't told them about the cancer. Quit college, avoid marriage, move a thousand miles away; and then tell your folks you have cancer? I couldn't be a worse son. Dad couldn't vacation for more than a long weekend, couldn't sit through a whole movie or take a long crap, without worrying the office was falling apart without him. Even if he thought I was dying, he couldn't bring himself to turn his back on his insurance agency. But all the while he worked, the guilt would be killing him.

I couldn't do that to him. At most I would wait until I had some good news, until I had made progress. Otherwise, they were going to have to wait for the obituary.

If this had been twenty years down the road, at a more reasonable age for cancer to strike, with Dad long since retired, maybe I wouldn't have hesitated to ask them to come stay with me. What a nice picture. The fifty-year-old bachelor cared for in his waning days by his elderly parents.

MY SHIN throbbed as Dr. Bonilla sat me in front of a viewing screen in his office. He watched me fidget and grimace. "Are you ready for this?"

"As long as you're not going to say something like, 'We've never seen anything like this before.'"

"Deal."

"Then bring it."

"Here's what your tibia looked like, three weeks ago." Dr. Bonilla punched a button and an image like an x-ray filled the screen. "We're looking at an angle down the tibia, a diagonal cross-section of the interior of the bone. This is marrow." He pointed to a Rorschach blot that for all I knew could have been my pancreas. "And this is the bone. And here…" He indicated a small discolored patch lighter than the surrounding bone, a starburst blob with two extended arms suggesting the ability to creep and infiltrate. It made my skin crawl. "Here was the tumor."

My heart skipped a few beats. "Was. You said 'was'."

Dr. Bonilla smiled. "You're trying to steal my thunder." He produced calipers and measured the tumor in the three-week-old picture. "Diameter about three centimeters. Now, here's the shot from this morning, taken from the same distance and angle."

Caliper measurement—unnecessary. I could see the difference. The tumor was half the size.

"Diameter one centimeter. We did a more sophisticated computer analysis, and the volume has actually decreased about eighty percent."

"Oh boy." Tears came from nowhere. "You did it. You're killing my cancer." The throbbing in my shin was an indication of healing. I was going to live.

"We're killing it," Dr. Bonilla cautioned, "but it's not dead. You see how the tumor is lighter in color than the surrounding tissue." He tapped the screen with the calipers. "That's because it's alive, compared to the bone cells. If we don't continue the treatments, it will come back, badder than ever." He was staring at my shin. "But it's working. We're on the right path."

"So I'll need another round of chemo and radiation?"

Dr. Bonilla nodded. "It'll be rough. And, I still want to run an arthroscopic laser in there to remove any fraction of the tumor that's still viable and accessible." He cocked an eyebrow. "Are you up for it?"

"You'll be amazed how much I can live through."

He patted my good leg and stood. "We'll give you a three-week break before the surgery and the next round of chemotherapy. Give your immune system time to bounce back. I'm putting you on some heavy-duty general purpose antibiotics to provide some backup for your immune system, since it's been fairly well compromised by the chemotherapy. Try to stay away from daycare centers and rock concert crowds in the meantime."

"Shoot, I had tickets to the Massive Metal Homicide festival Saturday."

"I'll tell you all about it Monday," said Dr. Bonilla, grinning.

"Actually I'm a soft pop fan. You know Kenny G? Small audiences with very little hepatitis."

"Perfect." He shook my hand. "Don't overdo it. I want you to rest."

"So rest is good? I should get more rest than usual? Not less?"

He looked a little perplexed. "That's right."

"That is very good to know." I wanted to hug him. One less internal debate to anguish over. I hugged him. "Thanks, Dr. Bonilla."

I trotted down the hall to the service elevator. My leg felt strong. I jumped into the empty car—no corpses, a great omen—and hit the LL3 button. I cocked my bad leg and held it, ready to throw a kick, maintaining my balance in the swaying elevator. A human weapon, that's what I was. Master Kwan ran an afternoon black-belt preparatory class. I was going. Then I would embrace Dr. Bonilla's advice and go home and sleep the clock around.

The door opened and I sprang into the hall. Same flickering halogen lights, but now it was obvious that rather than straining from the power drain of unholy experimental apparatus, they crackled with excess energy. My stride was long and strong.

At the door to Dr. Bhani's greeting room I came face to face with some sort of Muppet man. He was tall with yellow-olive skin, a long thin face, recessed eyes and a mop of messy black acrylic hair.

"Excuse me." Then I realized it was Dr. Khaled Bhani. He had changed, and not for the better. Weight loss, hair loss, sickly skin tone.

"Brian. It's good to see you," said Bhani in his squeaky British accent.

"Same here. I haven't seen you down at the shop for awhile."

Bhani gave me a sad smile. "I've been traveling a lot lately. Are you…"

"I'm here to see Andrea McEwen. We're friends." This sounded really stupid. I couldn't remember the last person who made me nervous. I had been face to face with Bhani many times before; but not when he was Brent's killer.

"It's not McEwen," Andrea called from inside the office, sounding irked. "Did you forget I was divorced?"

"Yes I did," I called back. I heard her sigh.

"So Brian," said Bhani, "you are a cancer patient here?"

I cocked my head. "Did Andrea tell you?"

"No. I can tell. Skin tone. Hairline. Weight loss." Bhani pointed at my cheek, my hair, my waist.

Same to you. "I'm actually feeling good. My hair has been spunkier, I'll give you that. But I'm not exactly emaciated." I pinched an inch for his consideration. "And my skin tone hasn't been good since I moved here."

"Amen," Andrea called out.

Bhani grimaced. "I've been in the business a long time. Some things are apparent, unfortunately."

"Come on. Andrea must have told you I have cancer." Had.

Andrea appeared in the doorway. "Do you think I talk about you all day?" Her wry scratchy voice was growing on me.

"How long have you been in treatment?" asked Bhani.

You tell me, Nostradamus. "Three weeks or so."

"What was the diagnosis?"

"Sarcoma. Bone."

"Primary?"

"Yes."

"I told Brian he should have come to you," said Andrea, "instead of the chemotherapists upstairs."

Bhani looked like an alien race's best attempt at a human. In his recessed eyes I saw huge intelligence looking out at me—I would have bet the shop his IQ was double mine—and a touching compassion for me and my species. "Enrolling anyone new in our trials would be difficult right now," he said. "But Andrea is right. Chemotherapy is not the right approach for you."

"Actually, I just found out my tumor shrunk by eighty percent. One more round and I should be cured."

"No wonder you're in such a good mood," said Andrea. I wouldn't say she sounded disgusted. I wouldn't say she sounded happy for me. Without misery, maybe I'd have no need for her company.

Bhani squinted, compassion gone. "Did your chemotherapist tell you that? That you would be cured?"

"You know how doctors play it close to the vest."

"Your cancer will come back," Bhani pronounced. E.T. the fortune teller.

"Let's hope not, huh?" I touched Andrea's shoulder. "I came down to see if you wanted to celebrate with me. Dinner or a drink. A high-five. Whatever."

"Sure."

I held out my hand. "It was good to see you again, Dr. Bhani. Good luck with your…experiments."

Bhani ignored my hand. "When you're through with chemo and radiation, come see me." His raging case of doctor ego was on full display. "Even if there is nothing I can do for you, I might be able to get you into another protocol. Some scientists are doing exciting things with the immune system."

"I don't think that's going to be necessary. But thank you."

"The key is not to destroy your immune system, like chemotherapy does, but exactly the opposite, to harness it, to boost it. Okay?" He turned to Andrea. "You will have my response to the California board ready for my signature before you leave?"

"I didn't know you wanted it done today," Andrea responded softly, looking back into the office.

"Can you?" Bhani willed her to say yes.

"Sure. It might not be by five o'clock, though."

"I won't be able to look at it until later tonight anyway." Bhani nodded at me and walked briskly down the hall, his soft-soled shoes making not a sound. He unlocked and ducked through the door at the end of the corridor, hopefully returning to his pod for some overdue rejuvenation.

Andrea and I stared at each other. I was grinning, she was looking slightly amused. "So," she said.

"Eighty percent shrinkage. How do you like them apples?"

"That's impressive." She continued to stare up at me, head cocked. Andrea was not uncomfortable with extended stares and drawn-out silences. Her patience was a challenge to perform, to say something interesting. Do a jig. Maybe the robot.

Luckily I am quite the talker. "I was so pumped when Dr. Bonilla gave me the good news. I wanted to share it with someone."

"And you thought of me."

"You were closest."

"Is that the only reason?"

"No. Not at all. I feel like we have a bond. A bond of misery and suffering. It's kind of nice."

"Uh-huh." Andrea checked up and down the hall, a magician's distraction enabling her to move a little closer. "You like misery and suffering?"

"Not usually. You want to get dinner and celebrate with me?"

"Sure. Except it might need to be late." She pouted. "I didn't know Dr. Bhani was going to need me to have his response ready to go today. He thinks it's easy to pull it together. It's not."

"That's fine. There's a lot of paperwork waiting for me at the shop. This will force me to get it done."

"Where should we go?" she asked. "I've heard the Grainery is good. Although I have a hard time believing it."

"It's not my favorite. Bad bread."

"I heard you cook. Why don't you cook me a meal."

"I could do that."

"Can you bring your paperwork here to work on?" Andrea suggested.

"You mean like, doing our homework together?"

"Kind of like that."

"Will Bhani be around, or are you going to be all alone down here?"

"I never know what he's going to do at any given moment."

If no one else was going to be there to protect her, I didn't see how I had any choice. "Why don't you call me if he leaves."

This pleased her. "I will."

"I'll let you get to work now."

Andrea swayed from side to side. I felt like we were teenagers wrapping up a date on her folks' front porch.

There would be no kiss goodnight. "Okay lady. I'll be in touch."

"**HEY,**" I greeted my crew as I hustled into the shop ninety minutes later. I pointed Charlotte toward the office. "Can I see you for a minute?"

"Ooh, Charlotte's in trouble," Sam taunted.

"What did I do now?" Charlotte played it up.

I closed the door after she squeezed into the closet-sized chute with me. "I was just at the dojang and I heard there's an open house at the new retail—"

"At the Bluffs!" Charlotte exploded. "Hernandes is running a stand—"

"Hernandes?" I squeaked.

"I found out about it this morning! I called Mike's assistant Margie and asked her what was going on. You're opening a store over there, and that old fool Hernandes gets to serve the coffee! What kind of deal is that?"

With Charlotte riled up, I was free to calm down. "What did Margie say?"

"She said I should talk to Mike."

"What did he say?"

Charlotte looked sheepish. "I thought you should talk to him. He kind of scares me. I know he shouldn't. He just does."

"I could really care less whether we serve the coffee at the open house," I growled, "except I really hate Hernandes."

"I could send Sam over there to beat him up."

"Would you? That would be nice."

Charlotte's smile faded as she studied me. "You look like…a little tired. Wait a second—you said you were at the doe-whatever."

"The dojang. I hit the black belt prep session this afternoon."

"You didn't."

"Oh yes I did."

"Brian, no," Charlotte protested. "Don't be stupid."

"You can't stop me." I wished she had. Not for the exertion—Instructor Garrett went easy on us in my honor—but the embarrassment. We were supposed to be polishing the thirty-odd kicking and blocking sets learned during our progression through the first ten belt levels. After my clueless performance that afternoon, I was sure Garrett would recommend Master Kwan demote me back to white belt.

Which wouldn't be all bad, after getting a look at our dojang's exotic new super-fox white belt.

"Does it make it alright if I told you my cancer has shrunk to a small, nearly insignificant size?"

"Really?! That's what the doctor said?"

"In so many words."

"Congratulations man," said Terrence from his writing nook on the other side of the wall. My office doesn't have a ceiling.

"Thanks homey."

Charlotte tore off a paper towel and absorbed her tears. "That's still no excuse. You need a wife. To nag you, so I don't have to. Is that going to happen anytime soon?"

I reached past her to open the door. "Not unless I can convince some woman that I'm worth more dead than alive."

"You need a whopping big life insurance policy," Charlotte advised as we joined Sam behind the bar.

"I was holding off until I had a loved one to support. Now it looks like I'll need a policy in order to get a loved one."

"Make me your beneficiary and I'll be your loved one," Charlotte promised.

"What is going on here?" Sam asked, fairly certain he didn't want to know. He ducked under the hanging menu board, docked a pitcherful of ice and smoothie mix in the blender, and punched the button.

"Charlotte's willing to marry me," I shouted over the cacophony of crunching ice and the blender's wailing motor. "Only if I promise to die in the next six months."

"It would be worth it, don't you think?" Charlotte asked Sam. "You should do it. You could handle anything for six months and a million bucks."

Sam grinned and shook his head. "I don't think so."

"Brian's pretty old," Charlotte pointed out, starting to giggle. "Your needs change when you get to be his age. All you'd have to do is read to him and stir up a glass of Metamucil every so often. Sam, the worst thing you'd have to do is give him a sponge bath once a week."

"Promise you'd bathe me more than once a week," I requested.

"I'll hire my brother's scout troop to give the baths," Sam decided. "They're always looking for ways to raise money. Next thing you know, you'll have to earn your sponge bath badge to make Eagle Scout."

"Speaking of sponge-bath candidates, guess who I caught a glimpse of, leaving Taekwondo this afternoon? Tall, blonde," I gave hints. "Homicidal."

"Edna Applejack?" said Charlotte.

"That's what they called her. I hate it when somebody else gets to coin the cool nickname."

"That's not a nickname," said Sam.

"No way. Edna Applejack. Wow."

"She's better looking than that name would imply," said Sam.

"Edna's gorgeous," said Charlotte. "I can't believe I haven't seen her yet." She shuddered with anticipation. To my curious look she responded, "It's not a sexual thing. It's just…Edna."

"The fact she's an ex-con doesn't bother you?"

"Sure," said Charlotte. "Sure it does. But…"

"You really haven't heard the stories about Edna Applejack?" Sam asked me. "The all-time leading high school basketball player in the state? Turned down offers from UConn and Stanford in order to stay in-state? Turned down NDSU and UND when they wouldn't agree to only recruit North Dakota girls? Played for Jamestown College and led them to two national championships? Killed her husband ten years ago, with her bare hands?"

"Whoa. No she didn't."

"And it was a fair fight," said Sam, still in awe after all these years. "Hand to hand combat. She killed him with her bare hands. Edna was in Taekwondo at the time, two weeks away from passing her black belt test. If she had been a black belt, the judge would have had to tack on another ten years."

Jerilyn Givens left her two-year-old at a nearby table to pick up the storyline. "Kyle Micklejohn was her husband. He graduated with my older brother. Kyle was a short nerdy guy. Computer geek. He was already writing programs for a defense contractor in high school. He was talented. Really geeky. It was so cool, how such a huge star stayed in Jamestown and married a nerd. For awhile, we all wanted to date one. It didn't last long." She wrinkled her nose. "Nerds just didn't smell right."

"That's why I won't eat cage-raised beef," I said. "All that sitting around, taints the flavor."

"Amen," said Sam.

"So she killed Kyle with her bare hands," I marveled.

"They say Edna strangled him and tore him up pretty good," Sam reported. "The death blow was a punch to the temple."

"So the warnings are true," I said, gingerly touching my temple.

"Apparently," said Sam.

"So stay away from her," Charlotte advised.

"If she wants to spar, I'll tell her I'm a man of the mind, not the body."

"That will only turn her on all the more," Sam warned.

"What if she hears through the grapevine that I was a chess club champion in high school?" I said.

"You weren't really," Charlotte challenged.

"No, but Edna doesn't need to know that." I exchanged a knuckle knock with Sam. "Make sure that gets to her."

"That's why I bring Nathaniel in here," said Jerilyn with a grin as she walked past the display stand that used to hold the James River Valley golf caps her kid had knocked to the floor. "Great role models."

I was suddenly too sick to my stomach to keep up the banter. The anti-nausea drugs weren't working so well. Sweat ran down the back of my neck and I fought the urge to assume the fetal position on the milk-splattered safety mat. "Okay, I'm out of here. Has it been slow?"

"Not too bad," Sam reported. "A little over a hundred since ten o'clock. Where are you going?"

"The open house at the Bluffs."

"Go bust some butt," said Charlotte.

"Go bust some butt?" Sam pondered. "Don't you mean skulls?"

"That sounds too violent," said Charlotte.

"You bust your own butt, Charlotte," I explained. "You bust other people's skulls. It's just the way it works."

"Well I don't do either," said Charlotte. "But you go do whatever you want to that Hernandes fellow."

"It's true, you don't bust your butt, do you?" Sam asked Charlotte to confirm. Yelling followed me out onto the sidewalk, and through the big front window I saw Sam ducking and weaving to avoid Charlotte's blows.

Now was the perfect time to take Dr. Bonilla's advice and sleep. Lingering effects of the chemo drugs left me pleased but no longer euphoric over the encouraging MRI report. I should lay me down to nap, satisfied with how I had gutted it out at Taekwondo, hopeful about the prospect of a cancer-free future.

But I was way too angry. Hernandes and his coffee freebies were prying away my customers. Cutting Craig's position had only prolonged the inevitable, and what was happening at the Bluffs was no doubt speeding it up.

I should have been completely preoccupied with not dying. That's the way it works, I was told. A serious illness clarifies priorities and renders meaningless all petty grievances and stressful obsessions with career, money, bills, success. Smelling the flowers, laughing with the children, growing old with loved ones—you learn to cherish the gift of life. Being a big fan of living, I definitely don't disagree. But I couldn't stop worrying about my business.

Maybe because in my heart of hearts, even before Dr. Bonilla gave me the good news, I knew I was going to survive. The overall survival rate for bone cancer is seventy percent. Bonilla had rated my cancer Stage II / Substage A / Grade 2—small and contained, with no more than a twenty percent chance of spreading. High marks for a tumor, so I had self-computed my chances at ninety-two-point-five percent (which The Teacher would surely round up to an A based on my participation). Not only that, the cancer was sitting a long way from the heart, the brain, the important stuff, content to nibble away at a fairly minor bone. If the doctors couldn't save it—hey, I still had the fibula after all.

That's what the logical, higher-order layers of my brain were thinking. Dig deeper, where caveman testosterone raged, and maybe there was still a functioning remnant of the childhood self-image of the invincible hero.

So even while wallowing in the injustice of being struck down by cancer in the prime of my life, I inevitably found myself assuming I would soon be cured, and then looking beyond, to the resumption of my former healthy life. That's when my stomach really ached. Cancer and capitalism, what a tag team. The second I decided I was going to beat the disease, I was slugged in the gut by the fearsome certainty my coffeeshop was going under.

I failed in California at my calling, my passion. Now I was failing in North Dakota. A goofball who didn't know a thing about coffee was kicking my ass. We were competing head to head, and he was beating me.

And for some reason Mike McEwen was helping him.

THE BLUFFS retail center was painted in adobe colors, red clay to golden sandstone and a few desert hues in between. The shops were aligned on a gentle curve, so that every storefront was visible at all times. I liked the sales psychology—why leave when everything you need is right there in front of you, lunch, videogames, clothes, tools, liquor, shoes and coffee. I liked having my sign in the shoppers' faces at all times, just in case the first glance at my stylized meadowlark emblem didn't make you uncontrollably thirsty.

I wasn't as crazy about my door opening directly onto the sidewalk. This was the three-season Upper Midwest, winter coming, winter, and winter reluctantly leaving, birthplace of the enclosed mall. I had flashbacks to the miserable trick-or-treating with Nancy's nephew at the Fargo strip mall those many years ago.

"Architects experimented with setting the stores behind a long enclosed fronting hall," Mike had explained. "It was impossible to make the hall feel like anything other than empty space, a moat between the retailers and the customers." Mike's solution was heated awnings that created a hot zone buffer to stop the icy wind in its tracks before it crept up the pant leg and penetrated the window shoppers' longjohns.

"How about a glass-enclosed plaza instead," I had suggested. "With palm trees and a huge fountain."

"How about an extra five hundred a month rent?" Mike had shut me up.

The parking lot was three-quarters full. The same fraction of the tenants were open for business—Herberger's department store, ACE Hardware, Taco John's, Jordie's Drycleaning, Northern Harvest Bread, and J-Town Games & Such. Hernandes' Campus Coffeehouse cart was parked under the awning in front of my future store. A very young girl filled customers' orders and worked the till while Mike McEwen and Billy-boy talked. Mike hurried to intercept me.

"Brian! I didn't know if you could make it. You got my message?"

"My message service is unreliable." I didn't let Mike stop my forward progress. Keep your feet moving, that's the key. "What the hell is Hernandes doing here?"

"Serving it up hot and fresh," Hernandes called out. He did an abbreviated dance step, the hot'n'fresh jig I suppose.

"We had a little glitch in scheduling the coffee service—" Mike tried but couldn't get it all out before we were standing in front of Hernandes. Who now decided to lend a hand to the grade-school girl behind the coffee cart.

"Hello Billy," I said.

"Hey Brian." Hernandes could barely look up to give me a wink, he was suddenly so busy. "How are the treatments coming? Any progress?"

Mike tugged me down the sidewalk before I could respond. "My office wasn't involved in scheduling this," he explained. "The management company handled it. Let me tell you," he griped, "I'm gonna kick some ass."

I took a few steps back and gazed at the vacant endcap storefront, at the sign in the window that Charlotte had made—Coming Soon, James River Valley Coffee! "Did they have to park him in front of my shop?"

Mike finger-combed his thick salt-n-pepper hair. "Criminy I feel terrible. I asked Bill the same thing. He says this is where they put him."

I listened hard for sounds of true remorse. I didn't want to believe he had orchestrated this in retaliation for my foot dragging. "So I should be chewing the management company's ass. Who is it? Steve?"

Mike grimaced. "You don't look like you're ready to chew anyone's ass."

"I chew ass better when I'm dead-dog tired."

Mike put his arm around my shoulder. "Are you okay?"

"Just sick about my future, that's all."

"Nancy tells me you had another MRI."

"My tumor has shrunk quite a bit."

"That's fabulous, Brian! I am so happy to hear that!"

During Mike's hug I tried not to stare at city council president Jasper Smith, in line to buy a cup of Bill's swill, smiling and bantering with the couple behind him—I didn't know their names, but they had been in my shop once or twice. "Next step is surgery, after I get back from San Diego." Jamestown was conducting road shows, sort of a rescue pirate ship cruising the coasts for businesses ready to flee other states' sinking economies. "Unless the Chamber decides to send Billy-boy instead."

Mike tipped his head back. "You're killing me." He held me at arms' length and forced eye contact. "Accept my apology, alright? And trust me, you're the man the Chamber wants in front of a crowd, selling this city." His face tenderized. "Are you physically up for the trip? Because I think it's a great idea for Nancy to go along and keep you well-fed and cared for. A paid nurse. Our gift to you, whenever your birthday is."

"I'm actually looking forward to some alone time."

"You're alone all the time!"

"Maybe by your standards. I'm an extra-introvert."

Mike eyeballed me. "What kind of psychobabble is that?"

Jasper came over, immediately assured me he was drinking Billy's coffee only in his official capacity, and gave me a hug. Jasper wore his long straight hair parted right down the middle. That's not an unusual style around here, but it was still distracting.

In fact, I was becoming obsessed with hair, hairlines, hair thickness. Jasper's hair probably wasn't as thin as it appeared, more fine than thin, I'm sure that's how he would have described it. Did mine look that thin? I wondered. The first round of chemo was surprisingly gentle on my scalp. I didn't notice hair on my pillow or clogging my drain. But it was preying on my mind. I don't comb or brush my hair, ever, not once in all my thirty-two years, yet I kept having visual flashes of a yellow long-handled comb with clumps of my hair clotting the teeth.

Billy joined us. "What a special guy, huh Jasper? Brian, I can't tell you how many people from the community come into my shop, and tell me how they're praying for you. That's the mark of a truly blessed man." He wiped his hands on the towel tucked in his belt, and then he touched me. "You better get better, so you don't disappoint everyone."

In order to kick Billy in the face with my good leg, I would need to take a shuffle step to the left—and maybe stretch out the hamstring a little first. "I was thinking of getting better for myself, actually."

"Bill does have a point there, Brian," said Mike. "Sometimes we need something a little bigger to live for. My son's nurse is crazy about Brian," he shared with Billy. "She would take a leave of absence from the hospital and go to work caring for Brian full time, if he gave the word." He looked at me, waiting, hoping.

"So that's the good-looking lady you were with in my shop the other day," said Billy. He didn't phrase it in the form of a question, so I didn't answer.

"That reminds me," said Jasper. "Denise wanted me to ask you over for dinner tonight. Can you make it?"

"I'm a little whipped today. But I was wondering, you wouldn't happen to have any more of those trout you caught up in Canada this summer?"

"I do have a few filets left from last weekend at Sacagawea."

"Can you spare a couple?"

"I'll have them ready for you tomorrow night. When you come over for dinner."

"Actually I need them for tonight. I have a hankering for trout," I explained. "It's like pregnancy cravings, only that's no baby growing inside me."

Mike winced and I regretted the joke.

"Stop by the house," said Jasper. "I'll have Denise pull them out of the deep freeze. You just need one, right?"

"Two," I said.

"They're big filets," said Jasper.

"I know a lot of people feel differently, but I really like leftover fish." I almost gagged saying it.

Hernandes faced his cart and whistled. "We're already running low on milk, and just look at that line."

"It's not that the line is so long," I said, watching ten-year-old Betsy frowning down at a pile of change sitting in her palm. "It's just not moving. But don't worry, I won't be putting you any further behind."

"I had coffee at home," said Mike. "All coffee'd out."

"Thanks for stopping, Brian," Hernandes called to me as I headed for my van.

"Sorry you're all out of milk," I called back, loudly.

And I'll be darned if people didn't step out of line and head for their vehicles.

T-11

I HAD a foot on the bottom step leading to my second floor apartment, toting the cooler of fish from Jasper and Denise, when the door to apartment #1 opened beside me.

"Hey Brian," Dennis hailed me. Dennis Rearden, short and powerful with a thick neck. He came into my shop most days. I've never figured out what he does for a living, because he's vague when I ask him. "A little here and a little there, a little of this and a little of that" was his standard reply. From listening in on his conversations I knew he was an extreme fighter. I don't believe he fought in a sanctioned league. I do think a lot of money changed hands. Which was at least a partial answer to my question.

"What've you got there?" he asked me.

"Trout."

"Throwing a party?"

"Just a couple filets."

"A couple. Who are you cooking for?"

"It's only a couple trout," I dodged his question. "A lot of ice, though. Getting heavy." I plodded up the stairs, embellishing the effort with grunts. "I'll catch you down at the shop."

"We should get together sometime," Dennis called after me. "Maybe do dinner. Your place or mine. Either way."

"Sounds good."

I ducked into the apartment, aware that I had a problem. Andrea was going to come prancing up that sidewalk and inside the building and up those stairs, under Dennis's watchful eye and keen ear. When she stopped at the first door on the second floor and knocked, I was busted. Dennis was our neighborhood little old lady, sitting at the front window in his rocker, keeping an eye on the comings and goings.

When I first moved in, Dennis knocked on my door with mail in his hand. "Look," he said, "my key opens your box too. Cool, huh?"

"Yeah, cool," I answered, looking at my mail in his hand.

After a couple weeks of this hand-delivery service from my non-government-sanctioned mail carrier, I started to get perturbed. Dennis would call out "Mail!" as he knocked on my door. "Whoops, looks like someone's late with his phone bill!"

Finally I had Vern from the post office stake out our lobby. I didn't know he would bring backup. Dennis was hauled away in handcuffs and spent four hours in a police interrogation room. The cops made me come down to the station, where I declined to press charges. I gave Dennis a ride home, apologizing all the way. He said the worst part was getting his ass chewed by Vern.

Dennis never touched my mail again, but I think the whole episode only heightened his commitment to watch over me.

"James River Valley Coffee," Sara answered the phone. Sara is always smiling, and it came across over the line. It was a good feeling, when Sara answered your call.

"Hey. It's Brian."

"Hi Brian."

"Brian from the coffeeshop."

"I know," said Sara. "Where are you?"

"I'm home, why?"

"No reason," said Sara, cheerfully, always. "What are you doing?"

"Preparing a coffee soy ginger marinade for my two trout filets, why?"

"No reason." And this was true. "What's up?"

"Did Dennis ever fix the drain catch under the sink?"

"You mean that thing that keeps backing up, with all the disgusting stuff?"

"That's the one."

"I don't think so."

"You want to give him a call and ask him to come down and do it?" Dennis was a decent handyman. He helped me out with the little mechanical stuff that drove me crazy. Maybe his handyman skills actually made him some money. Just not from me.

"Right now?" said Sara.

"Yeah, it's really bugging me."

"Okay."

"Don't tell him I asked you to do it. If it comes from you, he'll be down there right away. He likes you."

"Eeeuu."

"Not that way. Like a little sister."

"Eeeuu."

"Not in the West Virginia sister way. Will you do it for me?"

"Of course. Right now?"

"I'd prefer it."

"Okay. Was that it?"

"That's it, lady. I'll see you tomorrow?"

"Sure."

The floor and ceilings and walls weren't so thin that I could hear Dennis's phone ring, but I did hear a door thud shut a few minutes later, and sure enough there was Dennis hustling toward the detached garage with a little skip in his step. I had lied, he liked Sara in the Biblical way. Hopefully I wouldn't burn in hell for that.

That was no longer a throwaway line. The more I thought about it, the more nervous I got.

"James River Valley Coffee," Sara answered cheerfully.

"Hey. It's me again. Brian. From the coffeeshop."

"Brian, what's up?"

"Don't tell Dennis this was your idea. Tell him I told you to call him. Tell him I asked you a week ago, but that you had forgotten to call him until now."

"Why?"

"I don't want him getting the wrong idea."

"Thanks," Sara said with a smile in her voice. She has a smile on her face all the time. I mean, all the time. A customer had come in a few days earlier. "My drink yesterday was cold," the pudgy-faced lady said to Sara.

Sara smiled. "I'll get you a free drink today, and I'll make sure it's hot," she assured the lady. "Vanilla latté?"

"Yes," the lady replied. I was off to the side reading the paper, eavesdropping. Sara finished the drink and handed it to the lady. The lady took a sip.

"Is it okay?" Sara asked, smiling even wider.

The lady winced. "A bit hot," she said. I held back a chuckle. She looked at Sara suspiciously. "Decaf, right?"

Sara smiled. "Oh, I didn't hear you say decaf." That's because she didn't say decaf, I said in my head. "Would you like a new drink?" Sara asked, smile as big as ever.

"Yes. I always get decaf," said the lady, disgusted with Sara.

"I'll remember that," said Sara with a smile. After the lady left, Sara looked at me, smiling. "I could kill that bitch," she said.

I wandered about the apartment looking for something to clean, until there was a light, crisp knock at my door. Small and sharp, Andrea's knuckles.

She greeted me with an impish smile, plump in her puffy iridescent winter jacket. "I'm a little early," she said. "Hope you don't mind."

"As long as you don't mind dinner's not ready. Can I take your coat?" I wanted her out of that coat, pronto. I hated that puffy coat, especially in April.

From the pillowy depths Andrea produced a bottle of white wine. "Something told me you wouldn't have anything to drink around here."

"That's pretty intuitive." I had beer, I had wine, and I had booze, a lot of it, but planned on keeping it hidden. If inviting Andrea over for a cozy quiet dinner for two was a bad idea, and it was, then serving alcohol was downright insane. "I honestly don't even know if I have a corkscrew," I said as I tossed her coat on the floor of the empty spare bedroom.

"I have one in my car."

I couldn't help but be impressed.

"It's my winter emergency survival kit, in its entirety. Should I go get it?"

"No, you stay put." I didn't need her parading back and forth for all eyes to see. I rummaged in the miscellany kitchen drawer. "Here we go. I'll leave it here on the counter, whenever you're ready."

"That would be now." Andrea made short work of the cork. "You're having a glass, aren't you? Of course you are," she said firmly.

I stood staring at the fish filets soaking in my marinade. Flustered or retarded, I couldn't remember what to do next. "I don't know that I should be mixing alcohol and chemo drugs."

"Don't tell me you haven't had a drop to drink the past month."

"No, that would be a lie."

"Don't lie to me anymore. Or any less. Ha ha." Andrea found the cupboard with the wine glasses. And the wine did look good. Every so very often I have a deep parched thirst that only white wine can slake. This was one of those times, unfortunately. "Here you go." Andrea handed me a glass and stood facing me, pretty close. "Should we toast?"

"What would we toast?" My voice croaked. I jumped the gun and took a sip. "Oops, sorry. I blew the toast. Dry throat. Probably catching what will become a fatal cold, with my depleted immune system."

"You don't want to toast, that's fine. I had a good one all ready to go, but..." Andrea turned away. I think she was truly put out. "Aren't the fish getting soggy?"

"Maybe. I've never tried this recipe with trout. I'm a salmon guy originally." I couldn't take her pouting. "Okay, what was your toast?"

"Nope."

I felt like I was back in high school. "Come on. I'm sorry. I should have waited." My throat was cracking again, dried out by the chemo. Possibly the excessive vomiting. I needed more of that sweet nectar in the worst way. "Give me the toast. Quickly."

Andrea cupped the bowl of the glass in both her fine-fingered hands, staring down at the shimmering swaying surface of her chardonnay. "I was going to toast to being stranded together on a frozen, deserted island." She raised her eyes to me. "And to finding a way off."

I let that one sink in.

"Speechless, huh?" Andrea clinked my glass. "I've been doing all kinds of thinking since the last time we were together."

I took a two-swallow drink.

"Did that loosen up your vocal chords? They must have been stuck."

"You just have me worried about the trout, that's all," I lied. "I'm going to throw them on the grill. Be back in a sec."

"On the grill? It's freezing outside."

"If it's worth cooking, it's worth grilling. Even if it really was freezing outside."

"Then you go do that." Andrea savored the toast with another mouthful of wine. "Is that all we're having? Wine and fish?"

"I'm pretty sure I asked you to bring a side dish."

"Nice try. Don't worry about it, I'm fine with a limited menu. So. What did the McEwens say when you told them about this?"

"I'm not planning on telling them."

"Oh is this a secret?" Andrea was positively purring. "Hm, I wonder what Rick would say."

"It's up to you, of course, but I'd rather you didn't tell him."

"Why?" Andrea wondered. "Do you think he would assume there's something going on between us?"

I escaped to the tiny deck and dawdled there, fiddling with the grill, brooding, and not just about Dennis eventually returning home to notice Andrea's car—but that too, because holy crap of course everybody knew everybody in this town of fifteen thousand, as well as what he or she drove, which seemed to be more important than what he or she did for a living.

Andrea had made a terrible toast. Maybe I was stranded in North Dakota. But the island wasn't deserted. Literally hundreds of people in Jamestown had taken me into their hearts—and a substantial number had taken me into their homes. They cared about me, and trusted me; and vice-versa to all of that. I wasn't a huge fan of the town itself, the weather, or the proximity to Canada; and I hated the mood, that seemed to condone aspiring to nothing more than barely scraping by as the owner of one little coffeeshop. But I liked the people. Talking to Andrea was like plotting with a conspirator, against everyone in Jamestown, all their affection, all their trust.

"I guess you were thirsty." Andrea looked askance at my empty glass when I stepped back into the dining room. "Can I refill that for you? We are celebrating, right?" She tried to perk me up. "You're on your way to being cancer free."

"I'm pretty excited about it."

"You look excited," Andrea said sarcastically. "What are you thinking right now? That your fish are soggy and you're embarrassed you can't offer me a salad, and you wish we had gone out to eat?"

"No, that's not it."

The sarcasm left her voice. "So what is it?" she asked softly. "That you don't want me here?"

"That's not it either." I discovered my hand reaching for my head, and stopped it. I was terrified of running my fingers through my hair and coming away with a handful. "Not exactly."

"I won't tell Rick," Andrea assured me, sourly.

"I figure he's going to know sooner or later anyway."

"Oh, do you envision this being a regular thing?"

"No. Maybe. I mean, I do things on a regular basis with a lot of people. I have people over for dinner all the time."

"Single women? You have a lot of single women here? Maybe I should have asked around before I accepted your invitation."

I poured more wine for both of us. "Who are you kidding, you don't know anybody to ask about me."

"Lucky for you."

"Why don't you come down to the shop? Spend some time down there. You'll get to know a lot of people in a hurry."

"Yeah, well, I don't want to know anybody."

"Why would you say that? This is where you live."

"Not really."

"You're here until Tyler graduates. Fourteen years is a long time to be a recluse."

Andrea shrugged. "If you don't belong someplace…. And what do you care whether I fit in? Maybe you'll be my only friend."

"If we're going to be friends, then I want you to get to know a few people and try to fit in, at least a little bit. You can be nicer than people think."

"Gee, thanks." Andrea acted put out, but I could tell I had scored a couple points. She strolled to the deck window. Other than my primo Beefeater grill, it's not a memorable view—more apartment buildings across the street, an empty lot on one corner, a sliver of a neighborhood visible in the other direction, one-story starter homes behind big cottonwood trees. "Maybe," she said, "we'll have to be secret friends."

"I'm no good at secrets. I don't keep other people's secrets. I doubt I can keep my own."

Andrea faced me. "Then I guess it won't be a secret."

"Shouldn't we have something in common? Besides misery, I mean."

Andrea grinned, I think. The sun was backlighting her as it set between the apartment buildings across the street, wiping out her features. "I'll bet we both love sunny beaches."

"There's that, I guess."

"I want you to take me with you."

"With me? To San Diego? With me, to San Diego?"

Andrea chortled. "Don't you think we'd have fun?"

"Uh. I'm sorry. I can't."

"Well I'm going. And then I'm going to follow you, to your hotel." She moved toward me with careful, graceful steps. A bride moving down the aisle cradling a wine glass instead of a bouquet. "I guess you'll have to turn me away at the door."

I stared her down. "If I have to."

"How come I doubt that?" She rubbed my arm, gently enough not to slosh my wine or irritate my chemo skin, and then strolled into the living room. "I've decided I'm going, so you're going to have to deal with it."

"I'm going to clean the cooler," I announced, determined to pretend this conversation hadn't occurred, couldn't occur, not in the world of the rational and the sane.

I cleaned the kitchen and tended to the grill, a little rattled that Andrea gravitated to my favorite band amidst four towers of CDs. Squeeze had a story-song for every major event in my relationship history. It was hard not to like a band who had written your dating soundtrack.

"How's it coming?" Andrea called out while Squeeze sang about that time I cheated on my girlfriend with the state jobs development intern in Sacramento. "Every time you open that door, it smells great. I'm starved. Do we have to eat at the table, or can I stay here on the couch? I'd like to sit in here and soak up the fabulous ambiance you've created."

A fair dig. I spared no expense on my grill. My CD collection was amazing. Otherwise, all my money went to my shop. A secondhand couch, a threadbare recliner with a busted footrest and two bean bag chairs in my living room, that's all. No artwork or framed family pictures on the bare avocado walls. Four place settings and a few pots and pans. A king-size bed from the previous dweller, and all my clothes in neatly stacked milk crates that doubled as packing boxes. My friends, folks and the Salvation Army were going to have it easy if I died suddenly.

"Couch is fine." I presented her filet, all alone on the plate. "Can I get you anything else?"

"More wine. Unless you finished it off already."

"I may have refilled my glass once or twice." I retrieved the bottle and emptied it in Andrea's glass. "I think you bought alcohol-free wine by mistake. It's not doing anything for me."

"Maybe you're an alcoholic."

"I'm really thirsty tonight, for some reason."

"Let me try this fish." Andrea flaked off a wedge of trout and slipped it in her mouth. Her lips weren't big, but the surrounding flesh was, causing her lips to protrude. Her lips were active as she chewed, drawn in to be licked clean, then popping out again to proclaim the fish tasty. As an old lady those lips would be frightening. Her grandkids would be afraid of them, radiating deep wrinkles and bristling with prickly hairs. But for the time being they weren't half bad.

"So you don't need anything else before I sit? Salt, pepper? A side dish?"

"You never told me to bring a side dish," said Andrea.

"You don't have to feel guilty."

"Oh I'm not." She thought for a second while daintily separating another morsel. "Honestly, I don't think I've felt guilty for anything I've ever done."

"I doubt that." I stabbed a bite from my plate and ate it on my way out to the grill. "The fish is good, huh?"

"It's great. Why don't you believe me?"

"It's my own special marinade," I called from the deck.

"Uh-huh. It's wonderful. What do I have to feel guilty about?"

"Didn't you ever steal candy from the grocery store?"

"Yeah. But I didn't feel guilty. What's this?" She referred to the steaming tinfoil pouch of grilled potatoes and veggies in my potholder-protected hand. "A side dish?"

"You didn't strike me as dependable, so I had a backup plan. Didn't you ever get caught lying to your mom and dad?"

Andrea held the glass to her mouth like an oxygen mask. "I'm a really good liar."

"How about your marriage?"

"Aha." She held up her fork and examined a chunk of fish, losing and not replacing a drip of marinade. It made me a little angry. Maybe I was too proud of that marinade. "Well. I'll tell you about my marriage to Rick, if you want to hear."

"I'd be fine sticking with the smart-ass banter."

"Because he treated me bad," she said. "He really did." Andrea must have had the terrible memories at the ready, because she instantly looked miserable. "I had an affair with a college boyfriend. Do you remember the guy who was in your shop the first time I came in?"

"Vaguely."

"I thought it might make Rick jealous enough to want to know why I did it. But his parents convinced him it was inexcusable. End of story. So he divorced me. We'll see."

"We'll see what? Is your auditor boyfriend back in the picture now?"

"He's engaged. And there's no way he'd move here from California. Even for me." Andrea set her plate on the floor and wiped her lips. "I blame him for getting engaged, of course, but not for loving California. I know you love California too." She kicked off her shoes and drew her legs up under her hip, settling deeper into the pillows in the corner of my couch, making herself cozy. What is it about a woman feeling comfortable in your pad? Biggest turn-on I know. "So why did you leave?"

"Because I couldn't make any money. Not that it's been any different here."

"Why? Why you can't make money with your coffeeshop?"

"It's volume. I can't do enough volume with one shop."

"So open another one. What about the Bluffs?"

"It scares me to death. I branched out in California, and it went poorly."

"Why?"

"You don't really want to hear this, do you?"

"Did I ask?"

She actually seemed interested, so I told her. She let me talk uninterrupted.

"...and if customers don't think they're going to see me, they'll go wherever's closest." I wrapped up the Reader's Digest version of my business history, edited for most of the tears, profanity and self-pity. "Just the other day, Genevieve from Taekwondo told me she loves my coffee, that it's the best she's ever tasted—but that she wouldn't go out of her way to come to my shop if she thought she wasn't going to see me. It sounds vain—in fact, it sounds really stupid to say it out loud, but I've come to the conclusion that a lot of my business comes because people like me."

"I don't find that hard to believe," said Andrea.

"A compliment, and the kiss of death."

"So when you open a new store," she summarized nicely, "you put in less time at the first store, and so you start to lose customers. You need someone to run your first store in the meantime, someone everyone likes."

"But I can only afford to pay high school or college kids. They just don't have what it takes to attract customers older than thirty-five. You know, customers with money."

"So get a partner."

"A partner would be nice. Somebody who would work his butt off and get along with the customers as well as I do. And not give me orders. I've been calling the shots for so long now, good or bad, I couldn't let somebody else call them for me."

"Just be clear on the decision-making responsibilities."

"But we'd also be halving the profits. So we'd have to open six stores in order to make any money, and then we'd have the same problem I have now."

"Hm." Andrea was actually working on this. I was flattered. "Why can't you spend a lot of time at both stores? Not really working, but making your customers happy."

"Somebody would have to do the real work, and I don't think I could support the increased payroll."

"But your volume would increase. You said volume is the key."

"It is. It is."

"It seems to me," said Andrea, "the only way you're going to make it is to open lots of branches. Then everybody knows your name, and it becomes a habit for people to go to your shops. You need a strong manager, who can handle the employees and the business side. Then you're free to do customer service."

"I'll be right back." Talking about ways to salvage my business, the ideas Andrea was throwing out, the fact that she was excited about it—my brain was firing with positive energy for the first time in weeks. It was an aphrodisiac, and I didn't want the conversation to end. I crouched at the tall pantry door, ignoring the burning down my shin to reach way back and feel around and pull out a bottle of merlot.

"I thought you didn't have any wine."

"Oh no. I have plenty."

I uncorked it and poured it and aimed my butt for the chair, but Andrea patted the couch, so I sat there. She said her feet were cold, so I let her push them under my leg. She wanted to talk about Rick, so I listened.

Standard marital complaints. He ignored her. His family came first. Every time they went out, it turned into a greater McEwen function. Andrea would often end up driving home alone. She's a sexual creature; Rick would come home exhausted after working late and doze off in the middle of her attempts to rouse his interest.

"Hey." Andrea nudged me with her feet. "Wake up, for crying out loud."

"Whoops." I had fallen asleep. Didn't spill any wine, I was proud to see. "Playing the part of your ex-husband Rick, will be Brian Lawson."

"God. I must be really boring." There was no self-pity in her voice. She was disgusted with me. "Are you awake now?"

"I don't know for how long. It's been a long day. I was up at four-forty-five to open the shop. The final chemo treatment. Taekwondo." I sat up straight and blinked. My head was spinning. "Cooking this big meal for you."

"Yeah, yeah. Wake up." Andrea grabbed my arm and yanked me back and forth. "Come on. Surely you can think of something better to do than sleep."

My mouth tasted like chemical. My throat hurt. "I have to get up early again tomorrow. I need to get some shut-eye."

"Fine." Andrea set her glass on the floor and got to her feet.

"I'm sorry."

"No," she said curtly. "It's no big deal."

"If you're too drunk to drive, you can crash on my couch."

"I'm fine."

I retrieved her puffy coat and caught her at the door. "Thanks for coming."

"Yeah, well." She put on her soap bubble costume and stood there, facing me. She expected me to kiss her goodnight.

If there was going to be a first kiss, it wasn't going to be with chemo breath and dried eau-de-trout spit on my lips. "I'll walk you to your car."

"You don't need to do that. I doubt North Dakota has muggers."

She was being a martyr. I was prepared to let her. "How about a hug?" While Andrea debated whether this would suffice, I hugged her, a solid one, cheek to cheek. I had the door open before it was over. I gave her a final squeeze. "Good night."

She shuffled into the hall. She was so darn tiny. "I'm going to walk you out," I decided.

Andrea followed me, excruciatingly slowly, down the stairs. I waited, holding the front door for her. "Are you parked on the street or in the lot?"

"Maybe I'll let you figure that out."

"That's a fun game."

Andrea didn't like my tone. "Heaven forbid we should have any fun." She hurried to her pickup, parked front and center on the street, and opened the door. "Well," she was snotty, "thanks for a nice evening."

"Sorry I'm such a party pooper. Sorry I'm such a cancer patient."

"Yeah well." She was pausing again, shivering, stamping her feet against the chill, overdoing it a little.

I kissed her on the lips to get it over with.

"There. That wasn't so hard, was it?" she asked. "It didn't take too much out of you, did it?"

"I hope you didn't give me any germs. I have a compromised immune system, you know."

Andrea dropped into the driver's seat. "Just remember, you kissed me."

"I promise not to blame you if I get sick and die."

"Good. Good night." She drove off, looking satisfied.

Things were stranger by the day. A walk to clear my head and collect my thoughts seemed like the right thing to do. Even the romantic thing to do. I admit I was glad Andrea liked me; it was a huge relief to think she was looking forward to spending time with me…anywhere but San Diego.

But imagine if I had a true soul mate, right there in Jamestown, and she happened to see me, the solitary man walking the silent streets as the fateful prairie winds swirled around him. She wouldn't even have to be my soul mate. Just a woman who was good for me, a woman everyone would be glad to see me with, out for a late-night drive, wrestling with her own assorted crises. Her heart would be mine forever.

But without knowing my context—the struggle to achieve my coffeeshop dreams, the battle against cancer, the less-than-storybook relationships— my dream girl wouldn't see the romantic glow about me. She would assume the worst and drive on and we would both go to our graves sooner or later without knowing how close we had been to true love.

Besides I was beat. I trudged up the walk. Dennis waved from his chair by the window.

I was up at five-fifteen and at the shop by five-thirty. Terrence liked to help me open. Put him in the right frame of mind before heading to his traffic engineer job, he said. Said he plotted his novel while he took down chairs and unrolled the floor mats and put out the creamer.

Don't know how that's possible, because I talked to him the entire time. I appreciated the company.

And his baldness. I still had a ton more hair than Terrence.

"Brian," he called from outside the open front door. "I can't put your sign board on the sidewalk."

"Why not?"

"She won't let me." Terrence stood aside to let a woman enter the store.

"We're closed," I told her. "We open at six…oh, hi Frannie."

"It's Francesca," said the sign nazi. She raised her eyebrows and dropped her eyes to the counter, two feet below my face. "I wanted to catch you before you opened. You know you can't put a sandwich board on the sidewalk. It's against the law." Law versus ordinance, an irrelevant distinction for Frannie. She held up a stapled booklet. "I brought you a copy of the municipal code."

"You brought me one last time, Frannie."

"I'll leave it for you." Frannie dusted off her booklet, smoothed it, petted it, and laid it gently on the nearest table. Parting was such sweet sorrow.

"I don't see what's so wrong with having a sign on your sidewalk," said Terrence. Terrence almost always smiled, so you couldn't tell how big he was. He was the son of a former NFL linebacker and a pro prospect himself before participating in a multi-car pileup fifteen years ago. Heading back to college after a weekend visiting his folks in Jamestown, he and his Chrysler K-car were the last to join the accident, on an icy stretch of Minnesota interstate. Terrence hit the brakes and ended up coming in backwards. There were significant injuries, but probably none as costly, from a career earnings perspective, as Terrence's ruptured discs.

Still, he smiled. Rare times like these when he didn't, he was an intimidating presence.

"There's nothing wrong with a little sign on the sidewalk," I said.

"That's not for you to decide," said Frannie. She wisely kept her eyes averted as she moved past Terrence. "Since this is your second warning in the last six months, the next violation will result in a penalty."

"Penalize me now, because it'll be out there all summer long."

From the doorway Frannie pointed her hooked finger at the booklet. "The appeals process is spelled out in there. Page seventeen, I believe."

"Frannie, if Billy-boy Hernandes can call his place Campus Coffee, I can put a little sign on my sidewalk."

"What does that have to do with anything?" Frannie demanded.

"False advertising," I replied. "I'm pretty sure it's against the law."

"Is that who complained?" Terrence demanded. "Bill Hernandes?"

"We're not at liberty to discuss that," said Frannie. "If Mr. Lawson wishes to stop down at our office, we can show him a copy of the complaint."

"Frannie, save yourself another trip and go ahead and fine me."

She paused in the doorway, wringing her hands. "We'd really prefer you didn't put that sign on your sidewalk."

"I'd really prefer you quit letting Bill Hernandes call all the shots."

Frannie fled without responding. I stocked the cash register, stewing, until Terrence spoke. "What do I do with this sign?"

"Put it out there. I'll make Jasper and Carol come collect the fine in person." I knew all the council members and considered Jasper and Carol to be good friends. "If Jasper pushes it, I'll kick his ass on the golf course and take the money right back from him." I slammed the register drawer. "Have you seen the flashing neon billboards Hernandes has in front of his shop? Whether he's breaking any ordinances or not, how about a little common sense? Hernandes must be sleeping with Frannie, that's all I can figure. I gotta talk to Mark the town manager again. I don't want to interfere with Frannie's only way to get nookie, but this is crazy."

"She enjoys this role," said Terrence. "She tried to stop Amber from hosting Longaberger basket parties because our house isn't zoned commercial."

"Did somebody complain?"

Terrence paused before answering. "Amber started selling Longaberger right after another woman in the neighborhood. I'm pretty sure Amber won over some of her customers."

"Poached them. That's what we call it in the commercial world."

"I'll make sure she uses the right terminology going forward."

"Didn't the same thing happen with Amway?"

"Just a coincidence," said Terrence.

I would defend Terrence and Amber to the end. But I doubted it was a coincidence. They had two kids and another on the way, with a big mortgage (for Jamestown). Terrence hated his career choice—he hadn't realized a traffic engineer's job is to frustrate drivers so much that they decide to take the bus—and Amber God bless her wanted to save her man. She was determined to strike it rich, to give Terrence the financial freedom to write full-time. She had tried every pyramid scheme out there, from phone cards to juice pills. If she saw someone making money, she wanted a piece of the action. Talked about opening a coffeeshop once.

"Your family is like the early years' United States. Growing and hungry for more. The Old World doesn't understand that mentality."

Terrence paused again. I waited. Terrence was prone to pauses. I had known him since my first week in Jamestown, and had watched the pauses lengthen. These weren't the smokers' sort. Terrence didn't use the pause to read you or to gauge the effect of his words upon you—if that were the case, his pause length would have decreased as he got to know me better. Instead, it was taking him ever longer to form the next sentence.

The easy correlation to pause length was responsibilities—in the past four years Terrence had married, created three kids, and worked double duty toward a career change, all the while becoming more involved in his church and the business community. The coup de grace was taking up golf. Terrence had a lot on his mind, more every year, so some amount of distraction was understandable.

But my theory was that he was choosing his sentences more and more carefully. Terrence was a smart guy. He could lead a full life and carry on normal-paced conversations, if he wanted to. I think he was gun-shy, with an acquired taste for vague chit-chat. Like a chess master he worked three or four moves ahead, trying out sentences and the likely ensuing conversational give and take before choosing one that didn't lead to trouble.

I had time to fill three pitchers with milk. "Speaking of growing households," Terrence said, "I hear you've expanded yours by one."

"Oh?"

"Andrea McEwen."

"Huh?"

"Or whatever her name is now."

"What are you talking about?"

"You had her over for dinner last night," said Terrence. "Dennis told me." No pauses here. "I saw him at the gas station this morning."

My counter was low enough that I could lean on it with my hands spread wide and my elbows locked. This brought my shoulders up beside my head like a turtle shell.

"We're both early fillers," Terrence explained.

"Huh," I grunted. Repercussions. Repercussions, repercussions….. I wasn't envisioning anything specific, just the word, over and over.

"We both like to keep our tanks topped off," said Mr. Conversationalist.

Oscar George walked in. I usually have a handful of customers before we officially open. Oscar is a retired farmer, two cups of regular and a cup of decaf before heading out to the farm to harass his son. "Gentlemen," he greeted us. Born and raised in North Dakota, and he still had a thick German accent.

"Oscar," said Terrence.

"Oscar." I handed him his first cup.

Oscar frowned at the tall bumblebee-decorated mug in his gnarled chapped hand. "Is my favorite cup dirty already then?"

"Oh, shoot, give me that." I took the bumblebee mug and poured the coffee into his favorite, a deep purple Lake Tahoe mug.

If the bumblebee mug held eleven ounces, then the Tahoe mug held ten. Roughly one ounce of freshly-brewed coffee curled like a surfer's dream wave out of the Tahoe mug and broke over my crotch. The sound of the surf roared in my ears.

"Ouch, oh, man!" I thrust the mugs onto the espresso machine shelf. The Tahoe mug tipped over and splattered my legs with more steaming coffee. "Son of a…" I pulled my corduroy shorts away from my private parts and strutted up and down behind the bar. "Ahhhh…"

"You alright there, Brian?" Oscar leaned over the bar, craning his neck. "Uh-oh. You didn't break my Tahoe cup, did you?"

"I hope so," I groaned.

Terrence moved up for a better look. "What happened back there?"

"Brian's a little clumsy this morning," said Oscar.

"Oscar just has to have his favorite mug," I said, sopping at my shorts with the bar rag. "No matter who gets hurt."

"I hope you didn't break my cup," said Oscar.

"You bring your own mug from home?" Terrence questioned Oscar.

"No-no. It's Brian's. I just love it. Coffee tastes better in it, you know."

I wiped off the Tahoe mug, refilled it with nine or so ounces, and handed it to Oscar. "That'll be a buck-ninety."

"I didn't bring my coffee card today," said Oscar. "Put it on my tab."

I nodded, wincing. My left nut was aflame. "Terrence, watch the bar for me, would you? Charlotte should be here any minute."

"You need a 'Warning: Hot Coffee' label on your cups," Oscar suggested.

"I'll carve it into your fucking Tahoe mug," I threatened.

"No need to do that," said Oscar. "Just be more careful next time. I hope you're not burned too bad," he called out.

"I'm sure Brian has someone who can kiss it and make it all better," I heard Terrence say as I stared at my stained shorts in the bathroom mirror.

"That's not happening," I hollered. "No intimacy until I'm done with my cancer treatments. Doctor's orders."

Oscar hooted and Terrence asked, "Why's that?"

"My sperm's radioactive," I yelled. "Someone could get hurt. That's why Superman never has sex."

"What about Lois Lane?" Terrence asked.

"He always pulls out. Of course now that I've boiled my balls," I called out as I left the bathroom, "my jizm's probably no longer a health threat."

Oscar, an eighty-year-old Korean War vet, was blushing in the deep creases of his weather-beaten face. He directed my attention to the register, where Donna Erlingmayer stood.

"Oh hey Donna. I didn't hear you come in."

"I'm going to sneak in every time now," said Donna, a middle-aged Sun Country flight attendant. "I had a feeling that all the good conversation stops as soon as I show up."

"I try to tailor my stories to the customer," I said.

"I like 'em dirty," said Donna.

"Now I know."

"It isn't every day that Brian spills hot coffee on his lap," said Terrence, accurately.

"Oh no," said Donna. "Oh no," she repeated when she caught sight of my crotch. "Are you alright?"

"Maybe. I'll find out for sure tonight when I take my shorts off."

Oscar hoisted the Tahoe mug. "My cup is fine, you see."

"Good for you, Oscar," said Donna.

"Hey," I said to Terrence, "how about golf this afternoon? It's a beautiful day. Supposed to hit sixty."

Terrence stared at me for five seconds. "You can golf? It's fine for the leg?"

"The leg's fine. My back, though, that's another matter."

Terrence blinked a couple times. "The cancer moved into your back?"

Oscar and Donna froze. Flash-frozen. "No," I said, flash-thawing them. "I just have a sore back."

"Probably from the other night," Terrence said to no one in particular.

"God help me, my back kills me most mornings," Oscar growled as he sat at his favorite table closest to the counter.

"Maybe it's cancer," I said. "You should get it checked."

Oscar shook his head, gazing at the little pine tree on his Lake Tahoe mug. "You can't joke about that kind of thing now."

"I know," I said. "But I still do."

"You have to joke about it," said Donna. "It's all you can do sometimes."

"That's for sure," said Oscar. "My cousin died of cancer when he was thirty-eight."

There was a moment of silence for Oscar's cousin, for cancer patients in general, for me. I turned to Terrence. "Golf?"

He had mapped out a safe, acceptable conversation. "You're jumping the gun. Courses don't open until May."

"Are you serious? Not one? No matter how nice the weather is?"

"How long have you lived here that you don't know that?" Donna asked.

Terrence smiled and shook his head. There was no doubt he intended to speak. So we waited. He cleared his throat. "I go through this with Brian every spring. He forgets he's not in California anymore."

"It was Sacramento, right?" asked Donna.

"Davis," said Charlotte, breezing in from the alley door. "That's all I hear from Brian, how wonderful Davis was."

"Just the weather," I said, moving into high gear, pulling shots and cranking up the frother, matching Charlotte's crisp movements at the cash register as a host of regulars converged on the front door, six o'clock sharp.

"Tom," I greeted the middle school science teacher. His skull was knobby, his hair was long and stringy, his drink was a depth charge.

"Brian, hey there," said Tom, "good morning. I was afraid I was early. Thanks for being open, not making me stand out there in the cold."

"It's beautiful out there, what are you talking about." I held up a shot of espresso in one hand, rearranging milk pitchers with the other; Charlotte held out a large coffee in a to-go cup; I dumped in the shot, the depth charge. I could have poured it without looking, we were such a well-oiled machine. "Golfing weather!"

"Brian's California dreaming," Charlotte told Tom as she fitted on a lid. "That'll be two-forty-five."

"C'mon," I complained. "It's a crime the courses aren't open. A crime! Melissa," I called out to the elementary school principal coming through the door. "Tell them it's a crime!"

"Whatever happened, I think Brian's guilty," Melissa testified.

"That's a pretty good rule of thumb," said Charlotte. "Brian's guilty, guilty until proven innocent. Adam, XL latté?" she verified with the auto mechanic standing quietly in line.

"You know it," said Adam. He already had a grease smudge on his cheek.

"I'm getting crucified here," I announced. "Feel free to step in at any time and defend me," I told Adam.

"Oh I will," he said, eyes on Charlotte's chest.

I banged out the used grounds and refilled and holstered the espresso bucket. I gave Adam a strong look as I handed him his drink. "When you finally get around to defending me, it'll probably be too late. Just so you know."

Adam grinned. "Charlotte, thanks for the drink."

"I'm the one who made the drink," I grumbled. "I make the drink, while getting pounded, and you get the thank you."

Charlotte laughed. "What can I say, Adam likes me better."

"Maybe it's the tanktops," said Tom the hippy science teacher, sitting at the counter.

"I don't have any choice," Charlotte pouted. "It's at least a hundred degrees back here." She turned to the next customer, a new face in the store, and turned on the charm. "What can I get for you?"

"I count on those tanktops to deliver the tips," I told Tom. "Don't make her feel self-conscious."

"Skin equals tips," Tom made an equation out of it.

"Don't go there," said Charlotte, blushing ever-so-slightly. The new face at the till happened to be a handsome one.

"What do you recommend?" asked the new face.

"I personally like our mochas," said Charlotte. "They're not so sweet, but the chocolate flavor is intense. If you're looking for a cold drink, the mocha smoothie is our most popular."

"I'll take a mocha," the young man decided.

"Do you want it hot?"

"I do."

The hooting started and Charlotte turned on me, already in full blush. "Brian, don't you dare."

"Somebody has to ask him if he wants whipped cream on it," I said, powerless to do otherwise. "It's just good customer service."

T-10

OUR TRIP to San Diego would make a great story. There was the unexpected pleasure of paying the hotel desk clerk a reasonable markup over retail for his personal tequila stash, with all the trimmings. The disappointment at finding Canadian-speaking children on the beach. Winning the deed to a Costa Rican coffee plantation in an arm-wrestling match (no words for my emotions).

But by now you've had your fill of my sexual escapades; I could redact the juicy parts, but the holes in the transcript would be jarring. There's the "tasteful references" approach, but that would be like asking Ken and Barbie to be our sexual stunt doubles. Awkward.

So instead of a delightful recounting, you get a highlight reel, one step up from a list of bullet points. Cue:

The Flight

ANDREA DID indeed accompany me. No guilt for her, just regret that we didn't drive to the airport together like a regular couple. Arriving in Denver for our connecting flight, Andrea was so pleased with herself as we climbed down from the little plane and strolled across the tarmac, rhapsodizing to the view of the snow-white mountains shimmering in the west, that I decided to put her on the spot for leaving her kid behind, on a lark, on a junket. I couldn't count on being able to shame her, but I was going to let her know how I felt.

But then she spent most of breakfast talking about Tyler. How he was driven batty with jack-in-the-box tension when she pretended to be the hands of an alarm clock, about to strike the appointed hour. How he loved to go to the playground, even in the winter, forcing his mom to freeze her ass off on a snowy bench while he played on the equipment. How he couldn't sleep until she read him at least three picture books.

I found myself visualizing the two of them cuddled up in an easy chair—I could hear the tone of Andrea's voice, loving and happy, the cynical edge missing. I couldn't stop myself from deciding that she's a good mother. And so I stopped stewing, and I stopped worrying (I was pretty confident no one knew she was with me). I enjoyed her company, to the point where I too regretted not letting her drive me to the airport, especially since it hailed there while we were gone.

The Hotel Room

ACTUALLY THIS is about the call I received while in our hotel room. I just wanted to help you create a mental picture of the backdrop.

"Hi Mom."

"Well hey there," my mom cooed. "We found you."

"Aren't cellphones nice?"

"Where are you?" The way she said it, somehow Mom could tell I wasn't in North Dakota.

I decided to lie; even though I was still a half-continent away, they'd be hurt to hear I was in the state and hadn't bothered to stop by. "Miami."

"No! Why?" With absolutely no basis, Mom was sure I was on the lam. Too many cop shows. She loved Harrison Ford in The Fugitive. Always had an alibi at the ready for me, in case things got dicey.

"A bunch of us from the Chamber are doing road shows, to convince folks that North Dakota ain't so bad."

"You're in the Chamber? Of Commerce?"

"The most prestigious of all the chambers."

"Did we know that?"

"I've been in the Chamber for a few years. I'm pretty sure I told you."

Mom conferred with Dad who always lurked in the background. Dad liked his phone conversations filtered through Mom. "We're proud of you," said Mom. "The Chamber is lucky to have you. Honey, are you feeling okay?"

"I'm great." My self-assessment prompted Andrea to preen with smug satisfaction as she brushed salt off her hand and sucked a lime wedge, so I downgraded myself. "I'm doing okay. How's things?"

"We're doing good. Your father pulled a muscle this morning climbing on a forklift to inspect some frost-damaged avocados." I heard Dad correcting her. "You father says it was a front-end loader and almond trees." Dad added clarification. Mom sighed. "I guess he'll have to tell you himself. But he didn't stretch this morning, that's for sure." More kibitzing from the peanut gallery. "I know your body," Mom told him, ending his heckling. "Brian, I have to tell you it worries me to hear they have you traveling. And to Miami of all places."

After receiving the good news from Dr. Bonilla, I had finally told my folks about the cancer, as an afterthought, painted as a nuisance, like kidney stones or a yard fungus.

Mom had still cried, and I could hear her lips quivering now. "When is your surgery?" she asked, full of dread.

"In two weeks. I'm sure it'll go fine."

"We want you to come home to recuperate."

"To Davis? I'd like to…I just can't, Mom. I really appreciate the offer."

"Brian, I could take care of you."

"Mom, it's a minor surgery. A little clean-up, that's all. There probably won't even be anything left by then." I avoided words like tumor and cancer and stage and disease when I talked to my folks.

"You're not going to be able to walk, are you?" Mom was sure I would be a paraplegic.

"It could be a couple days on crutches, depending how much bone they need to remove. Don't worry, I'll still have the fibula." My new favorite bone, the fibula. Instead of counting sheep I could just say fibula over and over, and drift into pleasant slumber. Fibula. Fib-u-la.

"Let me take care of you," said Mom. "I really want to." She started to cry. Dad took the phone.

"Hi Dad."

"Come home for a few days and let your mother take care of you." Dad's bark was hard on the ear after Mom's honeyed pleadings. "I told her she doesn't have time to take care of two needy men, but she says she does."

"I can't, Dad. I can't afford to take that much time off from work."

"But I hear you're in Miami for a few days," Dad questioned my logic.

"So now I really can't take any more time off."

"So you pay an extra salary for a few days. That won't break you."

"It's more than that. I can't afford to lose any more business right now. Things are pretty tight." I would never tell Dad how dire my financial situation really was. The amount of debt I had rung up on credit cards and past-due payables to suppliers—it would kill him to know. Like everyone else in the world, Dad believed I should be making money hand over fist—hire teenagers at minimum wage to froth ten cents worth of milk, toss in espresso brewed from five cents' worth of beans, and charge three-seventy-five—how could you not make a killing on margins like that? The coffee biz was almost criminal.

And so I was clearly doing something wrong. A decade after launching my so-called coffee career, I was running one single solitary store. Dad never said it out loud, but I was a disappointment.

"I suppose your market is shrinking," he provided me an excuse, to salve my pride and probably his own. "I read something the other day how all those North Dakota farmsteads are being abandoned while everyone moves east to Minneapolis or west to the oil fields. You can't make a living in a dying town."

"Jamestown is actually growing, Dad." No lie, we went from 15,085 to 15,101 last year.

"Growing old, maybe," said Andrea, able to fill in the other side of the conversation. "Your dad's right."

"Who was that?" Dad asked.

"The mayor. I should probably get going."

"Oh, I'm the mayor now?" Andrea cackled. Not loud enough for Dad to make out the words, but I had a feeling she was only going to get louder.

"So why don't you have the surgery here?" said Dad. "We have a great hospital, you know."

"Jamestown has a great hospital too, I'm sure. It'll go fine."

"Huh…. Your mom's saying we're going to fly there then. We'll stay with you for awhile."

"Dad, no. I would love to have you two visit, but that sounds really depressing. Like I'm a queer fifty-year-old bachelor dying of AIDS."

Dad coughed out a serious chuckle. "Bone cancer is nothing to joke around with. A lot of people don't recover too well from it," he said gravely.

"Let's just plan on me driving out for a week this summer, after everything settles down."

"Naw, you gotta fly. It's too far to drive."

"By the way, I've been getting quite a few calls lately. Ryan, Jared, Tammie. And Mrs. Van Rosen. I had to listen for an hour while she cried and prayed for me. I told you not to tell anyone."

"People ask about you," said Dad. "What are we going to do, lie?"

"Don't tell anybody else. I mean it this time. I better run."

Andrea seconded this as she picked through our dinner for another piece of pork.

"Your mom and I have been doing a lot of thinking." Dad wasn't through with me. "And I've been doing some poking around. There are a few opportunities around here that don't look too bad. Stuff you might be interested in."

"I appreciate you exploring the Davis-area employment market for me, but this isn't a good time, with the mayor listening and all. We can talk more later."

Dad reluctantly agreed and I hung up before Mom could take back the phone. I wasted no time catching up on the pork. And the tequila.

The Pain

ANDREA TOOK it poorly when I announced that we were going to have to go back a day early.

"Why?"

"The Chamber was more efficient than anyone could have ever imagined. We're done."

"All the better," said Andrea. "Now you won't be distracted."

"But I am. My business is tanking. And while Mike works to get me into the Bluffs, I'm lying on a beach. With his ex-daughter-in-law. The road show was the only thing holding back the guilt."

"Oh so I'm not enough to keep you here. For one more day."

"The beautiful thing is we can still be together back in Jamestown, and I'll still have a business."

"You won't give up one day of your precious schedule for me."

The tide ate fifteen feet of beach while we took turns repeating ourselves, using the classic debate tactics of scrambled word order and escalating inflections. When every other syllable dripped with passion and reeked of injustice, I was ready to play my hole card.

"My leg is killing me. God I pray it isn't the cancer."

You have to play the hand you're dealt. On rare occasions like this, that's a good thing. We scored the last two standby seats on the next morning's flight to Denver. Andrea pouted until I promised her a trip to my plantation and bluffed us into the frequent flier lounge so we could have more sex during our three-hour layover.

By the time I limped into my apartment that night, my leg really was killing me.

T-9

I REGAINED consciousness in gentle stages, in a big white hall on a cot, one of many cots, one of many patients. Nurses were moving from bed to bed. One came to mine, a big one.

"You're awake a little early," she said. "Is everything okay?"

"Not sure," I croaked.

The hulking nurse pulled up the sheet and appraised my lower half.

"You didn't..." I made a nasty smacking sound, looking for spit to swallow. The nurse let me sip from a straw, from a styrofoam cup of ice water she was carrying around. I nodded my thanks. "Is my leg okay?" Lying in what felt like an Army hospital, sipping from the communal cup, in the hands of a nurse who looked like she'd be equally comfortable wielding a thermometer or a hacksaw, I wouldn't have been shocked to hear I had lost the leg.

"Everything went well," said the nurse. "I'll let the doctor give you all the details. Do you feel like you need to sleep some more?"

"I could." I struggled to free my arms from the bedding or maybe it was restraining straps, in order to sit up to get a look at my leg. That's the last thing I remember from that high-ceilinged hall. When I opened my eyes again I was in a semi-private hospital room and my mother was sitting there looking at me. I mean she was on the edge of the chair, leaning forward, examining me.

"Whoo," Mom said. "You looked so white and peaceful, I thought you might be dead."

My childhood buddy and best friend from Davis moved into view. Things had to be bad, for Ryan to be there. "Hey bud," he said, stepping forward to clasp my hand. "It's good to see you awake."

With my free hand I reached down under the blanket. "Still have both legs. That's a good sign." Flexed some muscles and saw my feet move. "And everything's still connected."

"The doctor stopped by an hour ago," said Ryan. He's a half-breed, Chinese and white. His sisters look Chinese, he looks South American. "Dr. Bianci, or Chinchilla…"

"It was Brillo," Mom corrected him.

"Bonilla," I corrected her. "I hate his name. I feel like a little kid with a lisp who can't say vanilla."

Ryan grinned. "Dr. Vanilla didn't have time for questions. But he said everything looked good."

"Really? He wasn't just saying that?"

"I didn't sense any sugar coating."

Mom stroked my hair, tearing up. "You pulled through."

"It wasn't brain surgery, Mom." Now I could be brave. "How embarrassing would it be if I couldn't survive tibia surgery?"

"You have cancer," Mom scolded me.

I waved my hand in her direction until she snared it, so I could squeeze it. "I'm just acting all tough for Ryan. When did you guys get here?"

"Early this afternoon," said Ryan. "I was surprised how easy it was to get here. Just one connection."

"Now you'll be popping in on a regular basis," I complained. "You two flew together? Dad didn't come, did he?"

"He wanted to." Mom daubed her eyes with a used tissue. "He has a big meeting Monday to prepare for. But he would have come—"

"If I had died on the operating table?" I finished her sentence with a wink.

Mom turned white. "Please don't say that."

"It's funny now that I survived."

"Not for your mother," said Mom.

"I'm pinch-hitting for your dad," said Ryan. "Team Lawson has a great bench."

"You could be a starter on any other team," I said.

"Thanks, bud." Knuckle knock.

I got emotional, knowing my buddy was willing to pay for a ticket and jump on a plane to come see me. "Mom, tissue." My vision was too blurry to see whether she gave me a fresh one. "Salty discharge is a normal post-op event," I explained.

"I've heard that," said Ryan with a wink.

"How do you like Jamestown so far?" I asked while I collected myself.

"I think your father and I should move here," said Mom. "Everyone's heavier here. I fit right in."

Ryan chortled. "Mrs. Lawson, you're not what I would call heavy."

"Are you kidding? I have the biggest white hips in California." She stretched her floral shirt to her thighs and sat on it.

"No way," I said. "Ryan, what about that Eileen Henderson, the girl you dated from Dixon?"

"She was white," Ryan agreed. "And her hips were definitely bigger than yours, Mrs. Lawson."

"And you didn't seem to mind," I said.

Ryan sighed a happy little sigh and gazed dreamily into the distance.

"Alright you two," said Mom. "Time to change the subject."

A big wave of noise and air and finally people swept into the room. "Hey!" council president Jasper Smith bellered, running around Ryan to attack me on the other side of the bed. His wife Denise trailed him. Filing in and crowding behind her were Genevieve and Khalq from Taekwondo, Dennis from downstairs, and a few regulars, Carol, Donna, and Kip and Kelsea Carlson, who owned the sporting goods store at the other end of our block. Andrea too, peeking around the room's dividing curtain.

Jasper pulled me half out of bed to hug me. "You survived!"

"Jasper!" Denise wrestled him off me. "What are you doing? You're going to hurt him! You'll rip out his IV!" She was embarrassed and proud.

"He's in a hospital!" Jasper countered. "They'll put it back in!"

"There's no better place to have a medical emergency," Ryan agreed.

"See?" Jasper demanded an apology from his wife. Denise shook her head, mortified and beaming.

"Jasper, Ryan. Ryan's my best friend from back home. And this is my mom. This is Jasper's wife Denise…alright, there's no way I can handle all these introductions in my weakened state. Can someone else take over?"

Jasper started pointing and naming people, even those he didn't know. Everyone collapsed toward the middle to shake hands.

He missed one. "And behind the curtain," I said, "is Andrea."

The conversational hubbub died on cue. "I have a form for you to sign," said Andrea, emerging. "Will you?"

"Definitely." I positioned the document's signature line over the top of the bed's railing. "Grab me a pen over there, Mom."

Mom hesitated. "What is this form?"

"I have no idea," I said, snapping my fingers for the pen.

Mom clucked disapprovingly as she scooted her chair to the nightstand, intent on retrieving the pen without getting up.

"I have a pen," said Andrea. She held it a few inches beyond my reach. "Dr. Bhani wants permission to use a sample of the bone they removed."

Ryan absorbed the gasps from those native to Jamestown and frowned. "Dr. Bhani? That's not your doctor's name, is it?"

"It's the mad scientist Andrea works for in the basement."

Mom covered her mouth. "Oh my goodness."

I sat up and snatched the pen out of Andrea's hand. "Sure, Bhani can have my leftovers. I'm working on a stool sample for him as we speak."

Andrea crossed her arms. "I don't think that will be necessary."

"Anything for mad research."

"Brian," Mom snapped, panicked. "You don't mean that."

"He's not a mad scientist, Mrs. Lawson," said Andrea, frustrated by the both of us. "Dr. Bhani is a cancer researcher. He could have cured your son by now, if Brian had let him." She yanked the release form away before I could put the final flourish to my signature.

"What's he going to do with your...leftovers?" Mom fretted.

"Clone me."

Andrea folded the form and tucked it in her handbag. "He's going to design a vaccine targeted to your cancer." While her tone was abrupt, she remained hovering over me, perhaps a touch of compassion in her eyes. "Not that you'll ever give him the opportunity to use it."

"Vaccines prevent you from catching a disease," Mom pointed out. "Even I know that. Brian already has cancer."

"Spot on, Mom." I requested that Ryan give her a high five.

"I'll make sure I tell him that," said Andrea, rolling her eyes.

Mom was wiggling her chair forward, creeping closer, wedging her way back in. The metal casters squawked on the tile floor.

"Careful, Mom's going to run you over."

"I see that." Andrea debated whether to dig in like a tick or cut bait and run.

"I hate not being close to Brian," said Mom. "You know how moms get."

"Sure." Andrea didn't. "I better be going."

"Stop by later."

"I'll see you when you get out," Andrea said en route to the door. "That will give you incentive to get better."

"You can't stop me."

"Don't you feel sick to your stomach?" Khalq asked, either making conversation or desperate to know. "I always get viciously sick from the anesthesia."

"No, I feel pretty good."

"I felt pretty good after arthroscopic surgery a couple years ago," said Khalq. "So I ordered a pizza when I got home. I threw up nonstop for the next twenty-four hours."

"You're used to that," I said. "I know they taught you in modeling school to purge before a big shoot. To get that sunken cheek look."

Mom turned around to get a better look at Khalq. "Oh, you're a model? That's wonderful. I didn't know they had models out here."

"I'm not a model, Mrs. Lawson," said Khalq.

"Well you are a very handsome young man," said Mom, looking him up and down. "I love your Arabic features."

"He's a dreamboat," I said.

"When do you come back to Taekwondo?" Khalq asked me politely. "So I can kick your ass."

"That may be a little while," said Dr. Bonilla, squeezing through the crowd. "We had to replace a little bone below the knee, so I'd recommend keeping your kick-fighting to a minimum for a few weeks."

"There's gotta be a way for them to settle the score," said Dennis.

"Anything but a fashion runway walk-off," I said. "Khalq would annihilate me."

"Doctor, do you need to talk to Brian alone?" Mom asked. She was all business, ready to clear the room.

"If that wouldn't be too much trouble," said Dr. Bonilla, and Mom sprang to her feet, shooing my friends away from the bed. "Only for a minute," the doc apologized. "And then everybody can come back in."

"Brian," said Kelsea, backpedaling out of Mom's reach. "Kip and I just wanted to say hi and let you know we're thinking about you. We'll stop back when you're not so busy."

"Sounds good. Thanks for stopping."

"We left some flowers for you," said Kelsea, pointing at the rolling table under the television set, crowded with flower pots.

"I'll plant them as soon as I get home," I promised.

Mom poked my shoulder. "You don't plant them, son."

"No. Okay. I promise not to plant them."

"Thank goodness your mom is here," said Kelsea.

Dennis and Carol begged out in similar fashion. Andrea had lingered, now giving me a long look before disappearing. I obtained a special exemption for Ryan, sparing him from being swept along in Mom's bum rush. He hovered at the edge of the curtain. "So," I said, "shoot me straight, Dr. B."

"I would classify your surgery as successful," said Dr. Bonilla in a quiet voice from his anchorage at the foot of the bed. "Under the kneecap we did find some cancerous growth, high up on the tibia—"

Mom gasped.

"…right under the knee, as well as in the kneecap itself. We replaced a little more bone than we had anticipated, but that part of the procedure went fine. We used a new technique…a lightweight polymer…"

Mom's moaning was distracting.

"…bone mold…injected—"

"What about bone mold?" I interrupted. "Is that bad?"

Dr. Bonilla waited for Mom to settle down. "It's a biodegradable injection molding of your tibia," he explained. "We inject the polymer into this mold, after dissolving the bone that contains the cancerous tissue. As we inject the liquid polymer, the old dissolved material is extruded, replaced by the polymer. When it dries, the polymer is very lightweight and strong. Stronger than the original bone."

"What about the cancer you found in Brian's kneecap?" Mom's voice quavered. "You said there was more cancer than you expected…?"

"We really didn't know what to expect until we got in there," said Dr. Bonilla calmly. "Even the best MRIs and X-rays don't tell you everything. We hoped to find the area completely clean. Because it wasn't—do we do anything different now? No. We still go forward with another round of chemo and radiation, like we planned."

This was terrible news to Mom. "I was hoping it was gone."

"Me too," I said.

"Was that a realistic expectation?" Ryan asked.

"Realistic?" Dr. Bonilla pondered. "Cancers of this type are rare enough that each case is its own animal. We have a standard approach, but we know going in we'll have to tailor it to the specific circumstances."

Mom reached for my hand. I gave it to her. She gripped it in both of hers. "How would you rank Brian's cancer with others you've seen?"

Dr. Bonilla frowned. I looked at Ryan. "What's my weight class?"

Ryan bent to read my chart at the foot of the bed. "One-seventy-two. I believe you're a super-middleweight."

"I'm not sure how cancer rankings work." I looked at Dr. Bonilla. "Do I want to be a contender?"

"Ah, well," Dr. Bonilla fumbled for a way to not answer the question. "That's not the way we normally like to think about disease management. I guess if I had to—"

"I'd actually rather hear about the polymer you used," I said.

Dr. Bonilla patted my foot to show his gratitude. "The polymer serves two nice purposes. Enhanced structure for your leg, and a barrier to the cancer. It's coated in immune blockers to avoid rejection, and it's an inorganic material, so cancer cells can't proliferate any further up or down your leg. Assuming we've excised or killed all the cells in the tibia and the kneecap, we can expect the growth of the cancer to have ended."

"But I'll still need another round of chemo."

"We think it's best."

"I was really hoping to avoid any more chemo."

"I've heard there are a few experimental treatments out there," said Ryan. "Alternatives to chemotherapy."

Dr. Bonilla nodded. "There are quite a few experimental treatments out there." He was ready to let it go at that.

"Do you provide info on the more promising ones?" Ryan persisted.

"We let the institutional review boards or the FDA decide whether any given treatment has promise," said Dr. Bonilla, making notes on his pad. "That saves physicians from having to separate true results from the hype."

Ryan stared at the doc. "I'd like to know whether you recommend Brian look into any particularly promising new treatments."

Dr. Bonilla was oblivious to the bulldog tearing at his pant leg. "Brian could look into getting himself into a protocol, if he felt like it was an avenue he needed to take."

Mom's head was swiveling between Ryan and the doc. She turned to me. "Well, what do you think? Should you?"

"Maybe I should."

"I don't recommend it," said Dr. Bonilla, irritated at being forced to go on record. "These treatments are unproven. They haven't received regulatory approval. They're experimental."

"Experimental," Mom whispered the word. "That sounds dangerous."

"It can be," said Dr. Bonilla ominously.

Mom put a death grip on my hand. "I think you should stick with the traditional approach."

"Okay," I said. I hadn't been seriously debating it. "When do I start my chemo treatments again?"

"As long as we have you here for a couple days," said Dr. Bonilla, "we'll begin tomorrow, if you're feeling up to it. Now that we've had a look inside, I'd rather be too aggressive than not enough." He drifted away from my bedside. "Any other questions? No?" He couldn't get out of there fast enough. "Rest easy. Keep the visitors to a minimum"—he twitched his head in Ryan's direction, but it could have been a muscle spasm—"and give your body a chance to recuperate. Mrs. Lawson, it was good to meet you."

"I'm not going anywhere," said Mom, sniffling.

Dr. Bonilla smiled. "I'm sure Brian appreciates you being here." Ryan the medical gadfly was clearly excluded from this sentiment. "I'll see you tomorrow."

The remnants of my visitors filed back in, Jasper and Denise and the Taekwondo crew. And Charlotte. Mom was wiping a steady stream of tears. "Mom, you're supposed to be cheering me up," I said for everyone's benefit. "Come on lady, lighten up a little!"

Mom swatted at me and excused herself.

"So what'd he say?" Jasper demanded over Mom's honks from the bathroom. "Are you cured?"

I held my hands a foot apart, so that he would picture a medium-sized trout. "Close."

"Your mom didn't seem to think so," said Charlotte. "What's up?"

"More chemo," said Ryan darkly, recruiting conspiracy theorists.

"But, I am now the proud owner of a space-age super-strong tibia," I bragged.

"They had to replace your bone?" Charlotte gagged. "God."

"I told you what they were doing."

"I know but…" Charlotte shuddered. "Eeuu."

Time for another topic change. "How's things?"

Charlotte knew what I meant. She sighed. "It's fine. We ran out of Sumatran yesterday. And of course the next three customers all wanted a pound of Sumatran. We're running low on Colombian, too. Craig thinks we might have a week or so."

Sam had left for Alaska the week prior, and I never made it into the roasting room after San Diego. Ten minutes before they put me under, Charlotte had called to tell me we had a bean crisis on our hands. I held off the gas mask with one hand and called Craig with the other, to ask him to roast for me. He was reluctant, so I had begged. He made me promise not to tell Hernandes. I offered him time-and-a-half, but he wouldn't accept more than his current hourly rate. Which was about fifty percent higher than what I used to pay him.

The conversation lost energy. Jasper and Denise made me promise to let them cook my meals for the next month, and hustled out.

"We should be going, too," said Khalq, including Genevieve.

"Did you two come together?" I insinuated hanky-panky.

"We agreed to drive together after class," said Genevieve. "That's the last time I ride with Khalq. He drives like a madman."

"Did you get to ride in the Viper?" I asked. "That's worth the risk."

"No it's not," said Genevieve. "I'm not one of those floozies who put up with assholes just because they drive a nice car."

"I am," said Ryan. "You have a Viper?"

"It's an unbelievable machine," said Khalq. "Want to take it for a spin?"

I shook my head violently at Khalq, no-no-no, until Ryan turned to look at me. "Sure," I said, smiling and nodding. "Ryan's a great driver."

"I've improved since high school," Ryan defended himself.

"You wrecked three cars in six weeks. You couldn't get any worse."

Ryan turned his back on me. "I promise not to break anything."

"Are you a…you know," said Khalq, "a U.S. citizen?"

"Ryan only looks Nicaraguan," I explained. "He's half-breed grade-A U.S. Chink."

"And damn proud of it," said Ryan.

Genevieve kissed me on the forehead and the three of them walked out. Mom returned from the bathroom in time to say goodbye, and then pulled a chair close to my bedside. "You had quite a crowd in here. You should have seen all the people who came by while you were sleeping."

"I see all the flowers."

"They wouldn't all fit in here. You have flowers in the hallway and at the nurses' station."

"I'm lucky. I have some great friends."

"I liked that blonde girl," said Mom. "I feel small next to her."

"Her size comes in handy."

"Should I let you rest for awhile?"

"You don't have to go. But I might be ready for another nap."

T-8

THE CHEMO didn't beat around the bush this time. It started kicking my butt on Day One. By Day Fifteen my gums were blistered, my joints crackled when I moved, and I pooped blood. Ordinarily pooping blood would have alarmed me. Now red poop in the bowl wasn't a big deal. As long as my eyes opened when the alarm went off, it was a good day.

"How are you feeling today?" Jerilyn Givens asked me at eight-thirty that morning. I had eight customers at the bar and tables and two more in line, maybe forty dollars of revenue. Taking into account the twenty dollar-a-day fine for the sign board on the sidewalk, I was fifty-eight customers from breaking even for the day.

"Crappy. Really crappy. I'm miserable. The good news is that the fake bone in my leg is actually feeling pretty good. I'm not even limping any more. Otherwise, everything feels awful."

Charlotte worked next to me, running the register, pumping brewed coffee, prepping cups, costing me seven-fifty an hour. Whether she was sick of hearing me whine or too emotional to speak, she said nothing.

Jerilyn clucked. "I'm sorry." I wasn't getting the same degree of sympathy during Round Two. No more tears. What did they take me for, a career cancer patient? Brian has cancer, we're reconciled to that. He'll take treatments for a few months and the cancer will go away. In a few years it will probably return, in his liver this time, and he'll go through treatments again. And so on.

A few years' remission with a guaranteed recurrence was a deal I would have taken. I was frightened the cancer had climbed my leg, even after everything they had thrown at it. What was the chance the treatments and the surgery had cleaned out every last cancer cell? And the cells that had outlived the chemo and radiation, wouldn't they be more malignant and resilient than ever? Like germs that survived a round of antibiotics.

This I had asked Dr. Bonilla. "It's possible," he said. I think even my doctor was getting tired of all my downer cancer talk.

I wasn't confident I could survive this second round. The chemo was killing things inside me, useful things, things I was betting I couldn't do without.

And my hair. The fallout began in earnest. I'm not a vain man, but I definitely like to look good. I'll accept a few extra pounds and wrinkles. The slow decay of time I'm comfortable with. But there is no evidence of balding in my family picture album; I've never felt the need to reconcile myself to hair loss. I could—if the doc told me I had recently acquired the male pattern baldness gene, accidentally or by some inappropriate choice, and that beginning today the hair would start melting off my crown, my hairline receding gradually over many years' time, I would be fine with it. I would start cutting it shorter. I would thank God every day for the hair I had left. I would quick get married before the pool of willing candidates thinned in lockstep with my hair.

Out of spite or panic or unrealistic expectations of a Bruce Willis cranium waiting to be unveiled, I had shaved my head two nights before. No such luck, I looked like a cancer patient. Now I wore a ballcap.

"You hang in there," Jerilyn counseled me.

"Queen don't want me to try suicide."

"See you tomorrow," Jerilyn chirped on her way out.

"If I'm still alive." This got a chuckle, like a decent joke, but I would not have been shocked to have died that night. Terribly sad, but not surprised.

Terrence walked in. "Thought you were going to help me open," I chastised.

"I overslept." Terrence was embarrassed. He handed Charlotte his prepaid coffee card. "I don't remember turning off the alarm clock."

"That's your brain saying you need a break," Charlotte comforted him.

"For here?" I held up a wide-mouthed ceramic mug that would match the color of the rich crema that would rise to the surface of his latté. "You're staying to write, right?"

"Better get it to go." Terrence stuffed his hands in his pockets and kicked at the floor.

"Stay. One less roundabout will make the world a better place."

I finished one drink and started two others during the ensuing pause. "Okay I will," said Terrence. When I glanced up to smile at him, he said, "Why are you looking at me like that?"

I peered at him from under the brim of my ballcap. "Like how?"

"Like that. Like a gangsta. You wear your hat too low."

"It's because I don't have a friggin' forehead." I ripped off the cap and chucked it to the floor.

"Whoa," said Charlotte, eyeballing my head and sidestepping away.

"I hate hats," I bitched. "I quit baseball when I was thirteen because our coach made us wear hats. I loved playing the outfield, but because I don't have a forehead I couldn't see out from under my cap well enough to catch fly balls. So he moved me to the infield. When there was a pop-up, I had to rip off my cap like a catcher's helmet." I stifled a curse word and kicked the hat into the storage shelf under the bar.

The rest of my customers waited for a funny follow-up quip. I had nothing. I was feeling slow-witted, as if the chemo was eating my brain right along with the hair.

"Nice kick," said Terrence. "You should have played soccer. No hats," he pointed out, demonstrating a seldom-used quick wit and probably topping my belated I'd love to shove that hat up my baseball coach's ass.

Charlotte was a blur of activity, making change and queuing cups and bagging a muffin all at the same time. "I need a tall caramel macchiato—"

"Tall caramel macchiato, stat!" I yelled. Heads swung my way.

Charlotte shook her head, deafer in the left ear. "And a skinny white mocha—"

"Skinny white mocha, coming up!"

Charlotte sighed and glanced down the line. "Ma'am, what can I get you? Oh, Valerie, hi. It's been awhile. The usual?"

I hadn't seen any of the McEwens since before the San Diego trip. That's not true, a week prior I had seen Rick from a distance at Sam's Club and ducked and scuttled into the pet supplies aisle, pretty sure he didn't own a dog, until the coast was clear.

I wanted a long rehearsed speech at the ready when the inevitable confrontation came, to let them all know how much I cared for them and appreciated what they had done for me, including the Bluffs site, segueing into a vivid description of my loneliness and my needs, which only Andrea seemed both able and willing to tackle. But I hadn't found the energy to write said speech.

Valerie watched me, shaking her head in response to an internal rhetoric that went a little sumthin' like this: Haven't we done everything for this boy? Yes we have. Did we not take him under our wing, provide him with a golden business investment opportunity at very little down, treat him like a son, and serve his coffee at all the meetings and industry symposiums that we host? Yes indeed we did. Then what kind of monster could do this to us? Of all the McEwens, Valerie was the one I least wanted to face, and without a prepared speech.

"Hey lady," I said. "Two percent chai latté with honey, coming up."

"Well that was pleasant for a change," said Charlotte. "What do you know, maybe you don't need to shout."

She was right, I could taste blood in the back of my throat. Out of the corner of my eye I watched Valerie glide forward like an avenging specter, to pay for her drink before taking a bite out of my everlasting soul.

"Hey Terrence." I tried to make eye contact with my big bald buddy as he stood at the bar contemplating his navel. "I forgot to tell you about my latest run-in with the town."

"I want to hear about it, but I better head into work." Terrence dumped his latté in a to-go cup, precariously placed his mug in the heaping dirty dishes bin and made for the door. No doubt Mr. Morality and the rest of Jamestown knew why Valerie was there and approved of what was about to happen, but cared about me too much to stay and watch. "Tell me tomorrow."

"Tomorrow will be too late, but whatever, homey. Whatever." I was casing the crowd for someone in need of a mediocre story.

Valerie floated from the cash register to stand before me. "Hello, Brian."

"Hey lady, how's the McEwen household today?" I talked without looking up, clanking cups and rattling the metal frothing pitcher against the wand, making the sounds of very busy. "Charlotte, what was this?" I nodded at a to-go cup marked SM LW.

Charlotte stopped to stare at me. "The same thing that particular arrangement of symbols always means. Skinny mocha, light whip."

"Oh. Looked like you slipped a couple Chinese characters in there."

Charlotte grabbed the cup. "Where?"

I snatched the cup back. "It was the angle." I glanced over the espresso machine at Valerie. "I'm sorry, I didn't hear your answer."

"I didn't say anything."

"Mike is good? Rick? I haven't seen you guys." I announced the skinny white mocha's presence on the receiving platform like a debutante arriving to the ball. "And you?" I asked Valerie. "You good?"

"I was hoping to speak to you," said Valerie. "Will you have time?"

"Uh, yeah, I should be able to sneak away for a few minutes. As soon as we get through this rush."

"Go," said Charlotte. "You'd probably just mess up the drinks anyway. Since you seem to be having trouble with my handwriting all of a sudden."

"Your penmanship is definitely deteriorating," I said. Valerie drifted to the end of the bar and bobbed there, waiting for me. "Call me if it gets busy. Call me pronto."

"Yes Brian. I will call you." Nothing irritated Charlotte more than pretending we weren't a well-oiled machine able to read each other's thoughts and anticipate each other's next move.

Valerie preceded me into my little office and waited for me to squeeze past before taking a seat, crossing her legs and carefully adjusting her coat over her kneecap. "So."

"I've missed you guys. I feel like we're due for another game night. Or maybe the first ultimate Frisbee game of the season. Are Monica and Gene coming back for a visit any time soon?" Their son-in-law Gene, big ultimate Frisbee fan.

Valerie scowled. "Brian, we're very confused. I was hoping you could shed some light on what you're thinking."

"You mean lately? The past couple weeks? Let's see…I've been focused on trying to keep a meal down. Trying not to think about whether they're going to have to amputate my leg. Wondering whether I need to fire another couple employees to avoid bankruptcy." I hit her with everything I had, to knock her senseless with pity. "Debating moving back to Davis to live with my folks. Just trying to survive."

There was a loosening of the drawstring puckering Valerie's face. "Well…I'm sad to hear all that. We've been worried about you. Mike is beside himself…." Valerie tugged on the drawstring. "Rick said he saw you at Sam's Club the other day."

"Wish I had seen him. I wanted to tell him I'm impressed with the warehouse his team is putting up on the north side of town."

"Mike has been waiting to hear from you on the Bluffs site."

"I know." I started entertaining the glorious impossibility that the McEwens were unaware of my San Diego bunkmate. "Apologize for me. I've been so busy here. And at the hospital."

"You're still planning on going forward with the store?" Valerie pressed.

I started rearranging the stack of bills, shuffling the past-due notices to the bottom. "Sure."

"Brian, if you're not committed to this store, we have to know."

Valerie was Mike's strong arm. Mike had been known to let bad employees run roughshod over him and destroy morale. He would let customers' bad debts ride for months and years and finally fall off the books. I was a case in point. For a construction guy, Mike was a softie. Valerie wasn't.

"The Bluffs will live or die based on that anchor spot," she continued. "We owe the other tenants a quality, committed store. It can't sit idle, and it can't move at half speed." She sat forward and tapped my knee. Her plucked eyebrows were raised for the entire ultimatum. "We feel as though Monday is as long as we can be expected to wait. Do you agree?"

"That would be..." I checked the calendar, for absolutely no reason. "...the thirty-first? If I'm reading it correctly."

Valerie nodded, slowly, until my head started bobbing too. "Okay," I said, and Valerie relaxed. "I feel like I've been roughed up a little bit." In fact I was borderline giddy, to have escaped San Diego scot-free. It was possible the McEwens knew and could care less, just as giddy that Andrea was someone else's problem.

"I'm sorry, honey. I can be a little short." Valerie caressed my cheek. "We're so worried about you. The chemotherapy is harsh, isn't it? I remember Brent at this point."

Charlotte was calling, sounding harried, but I couldn't break away from Valerie's gaze. Her hand found mine and squeezed my fingers, turning the tips white. "You have to hang in there and make it through your treatments. We felt so terrible for Brent..." Valerie's eyes glistened. "We didn't want him to suffer any more. So we took the easy way, with Dr. Bhani. It's hard to forgive ourselves for that."

"I'm sure it seemed like the best option at the time."

"We anguished over it," said Valerie. "You remember. That bastard Bhani was so persuasive. He was so confident." The bitterness tugged at Valerie's skin, adding weight to the bags under her eyes and causing her wonderful throat to sag. "I'll never forgive him for what he did to my son. He experimented on us, when we felt like we had nowhere else to turn."

"Desperate times, I suppose," I said, standing up, a little brusque but feeling like I was the wrong person to sympathize with her son's tragic cancer-related demise.

"We're going to get through this with you, Brian. We'll fight it together. No shortcuts. We'll do things the right way this time." Valerie produced a tissue from her coat pocket. Between soaking up her tears and kissing me on the cheek, she said something, something that threw me for a bit of a loop, said it softly in my ear: "I'd say opening a second store is just too much for you right now. I know Mike has been putting a lot of pressure on you. I want you to know it's okay. Okay? Let's just chalk it up to bad timing, and shoot for the next time around. We love you no matter what, honey."

She walked out of the office—then stopped and put her hand to her chest. "Edna! Edna Applejack!"

Edna Applejack. The murderer was in my shop. I hurried to see.

A little crowd encircled her. I thought she was going to be beaten by a mob of my customers. How many could she kill before they took her down?

Mary Quill the wife of Pastor Brad was shaking her hand. Bart Schock the husband of the local pediatrician was touching her sleeve. Farmers rotated like flower children around a Maypole as people streamed in from the street to join the ring around the tall beautiful ex-con. Valerie plowed through the group and hugged her.

"I thought we had an emergency out here, from the sound of your voice," I said to Charlotte.

"Sort of," said Charlotte, star struck.

"Because she's a killer?" I said below the roomful of excited chatter.

"No because I think I'm going to faint," said Charlotte.

Charlotte was pale, a little wobbly. "Because you're afraid?"

"Because she's a legend," Charlotte hissed. "She's just so…so amazing."

I let loose a blast of air from the frothing wand, claiming everyone's attention for an instant. No reason people couldn't buy drinks while they fawned. "Lady, can I get you something?" I asked Edna.

"It's on the house," Charlotte blurted.

I looked at her.

"I'll pay for it," said Charlotte, heading for her purse.

"No employee discount," I yelled after her, half-joking. "Wow." I punched buttons and shuffled cups, for effect, as Edna moved toward me. "Will I get this treatment too when I get my black belt?"

"Only if you can dunk a basketball in your little karate uniform," Charlotte gushed as she came hurrying back from the office waving a five-dollar bill. She locked eyes with her favorite killer in the world and blushed. "Oh, hi."

Edna smiled. She had luxurious blonde hair, almond-shaped eyes, and a long delicate pointed jaw. "Actually I never quite made black belt. And now Master Kwan demoted me back to white after my extended absence." Sharp chin, mellow voice. "And you can interrupt me for espresso any time."

"And ice cream, don't you think?" I said.

"When are we going to get a Cold Stone here, huh?" Edna was a couple inches taller than me. It was an unusual view, the underside of a woman's chin. The skin was stretched taut, a flying buttress from her chin to the midpoint of her throat. If we got into a fight, I would put a death grip on that buttress and ride her like a bucking bronco.

"I love Cold Stone," Charlotte chirped, eager to be included.

"If we don't get one soon," said Edna, "I'll have to start one myself. Until then, thank the Lord for Ben & Jerry's."

"You love Ben & Jerry's too?" Mary Quill squeaked, desperate to be included. "The Funky Monkey. I love the Funky Monkey."

"It's Chunky Monkey," I said.

"No, it's Chunky Hubby," said Mary, laughing a little too loudly while she hyperventilated. "Chunky Hubby. I should know, believe me."

Edna admired Mary's petite frame. "I doubt you overdo the ice cream."

"No, I mean my husband is fat," said Mary.

"Pastor Brad could stand to shed a few pounds," I said. "I don't know if I'd call him fat. Or even Chubby."

"Well I would," said Mary, staring up at Edna, forgetting all about her porky husband.

"I'd recommend the bone cancer diet for him, but it's expensive. Something like five thousand bucks a pound." No laughs. All the men in the shop, and a few others in attendance, were fantasizing about sleeping with Edna. 'Sleep with Edna' held little allure for me. 'Sleep and wake up' was good enough. "What am I making for you?" I asked Edna's buttress. "Go nuts, Charlotte's buying."

"It's Charlotte?" Edna reached across the bar to shake Charlotte's hand and make her knees wobble. "Edna Applejack."

"Oh I know." Billy Ray Cyrus had stopped in for a coffee on his way to the state fair and hadn't affected Charlotte like this.

"Can Charlotte get the employee discount back if I make the drink myself?" Edna asked me.

"Are you qualified?"

"Eminently."

I turned off the frother, set down the pitcher of milk and wiped my hands on my apron as I stepped away from the espresso machine.

Edna clapped her hands. "Honestly? You'll let me pull a few shots?"

"If you make it yourself, and maybe a couple other drinks, it's on the house."

Edna squealed with pleasure and rounded the counter in four long strides. I retreated to the till as she punched the hot water button to rinse the little metal espresso carafe, pounded the spent grounds from the portafilter, refilled it with fresh ground coffee, and seated it in the machine with authority. She stuck her cute little sorority girl nose in my milk pitchers until she found the one she wanted, then shoved it under the wand and cranked the steam knob.

"The lady's got style, Brian," said Cal Brisbee, owner of the Ford dealership.

I nodded. "I'd say she's done time behind bars. Espresso bars."

I tensed for a palm-strike to the temple, but Edna grinned. "I've never worked in a coffeeshop," she said. "But I was taught how to do this by one of the masters."

"Huh," I said.

"I was at the Junior National All-Star game at UC-Davis, a long time ago," said Edna, to me, to all thirty-some people in the shop. "I scored forty-three points but missed a shot at the buzzer, and we lost. Coach took us to a coffeeshop after the game. Being a North Dakota farm girl, it was the first one I had ever been in."

I touched my fingers to my temples and closed my eyes like a psychic. "Dougie Fosseton. The Davis Drip."

Edna was shocked. "You know him?"

"I used to work there."

"No kidding! You worked for Douglas Fosseton? We learned from the same master?" Edna finished the frothing and kicked off the espresso switch in what seemed like a single move. She selected the bumblebee mug and poured in a shot, at the same time adding the steamed milk, starting and stopping, alternating espresso and milk. This was wrong.

"It looks beautiful," Charlotte gushed, admiring the creamy chocolate butterfly pattern that had risen from the depths of the drink.

"Try it," said Edna.

"Oh I couldn't," said Charlotte.

"I insist." Edna pushed the mug at Charlotte.

Charlotte's eyes fluttered at Edna over the rim of the cup as she sipped. "It's incredible," she breathed.

Edna took a sip. "Mm. That's the way I remember it."

"Brian," Charlotte reprimanded me, "it's better than yours."

"Craig did roast a heckuva batch of beans."

"No." Charlotte shook her head vehemently. "The drink. There's something about it. It's the best I've ever tasted."

"Sipsies," said Bart, motioning for the cup.

"Bart, girl cooties," I warned.

He shook me off and slurped Edna's latté. "Ohmygosh. That's good. What did you put in there? Is that cream?"

"Skim," said Edna.

Had to be half-and-half, I thought. Two percent at the very least.

"Cocaine?" Bart asked.

"Come on, Brian, try this." Charlotte stuck the communal cup in my face.

"I have a cold," I said. "I'll never taste it."

"Brian could catch a bug from one of you and die," said Valerie gravely.

"Thank you," I said.

"But I'd like to try it," said Valerie, sparkly-eyed.

"I'll make you a drink," Edna told Valerie. "Then we can have our chat."

She had taken over the bar. I didn't know where to stand. Charlotte hovered at the cash register, not to run it, just to be close to Edna. I'm pretty sure Valerie and the next five customers got their drinks for free.

Edna finally strolled back out onto the floor, to cheers. I told Charlotte I was feeling ill—this was not a lie—and went home.

—

MY APARTMENT looked like it was for rent, furnished. Mom cleaned before she left, four days' prior, and the place remained immaculate. Cancer didn't make me neat—my van was trashed, stray fries, empty cups, bills, newspapers. I just couldn't stomach cooking for myself. And if I wasn't cooking or eating or cleaning up afterwards, my existence left little trace.

Nothing sounded good. I only agreed to eat if someone else cooked it. I wouldn't even warm leftovers in the microwave. My freezer was still half-full of Valerie's dinners.

I sat in the corner of the couch, desperate for deep sleep. Obviously I was overtired, otherwise getting publicly bitch-slapped by Edna Applejack wouldn't have bothered me so much.

Couldn't force myself to crawl into bed, to disrupt the tight corners Mom left behind, so I had been sleeping on the couch. Despite Dr. Bonilla's assurance that plenty of rest was a good idea, I was afraid to turn my back on the cancer. So I would sit up for the first couple hours, intent on staying awake while I rested.

I hadn't adjusted to being alone again, after Ryan and then Mom left. As I had feared, Mom's visit turned me into a sissy, a bachelor mama's boy. I pictured myself dying alone in a sterile room. Tears stung my eyes—the start of a big weeping meltdown if the entrance buzzer hadn't squawked. I sucked it up and asked who was there.

"It's me," came the electronically garbled reply. I hit the buzzer. It could have been Lizzie Borden and Charles Manson, I would have let them up.

Andrea gaped at me when I opened the door. "Oh my. Your hair. What happened?" Looked like she might turn around and leave.

"It fell out." I drug her inside while hugging her, swinging the door shut behind her. Her body was a nugget in the center of the puffy packing material of her down coat. Made me feel big and strong, a nice counter to my new self-image, a shell. "Glad you're here."

Andrea wandered through the living room and kitchen, eyeing my place like a prospective renter. She picked up a candle Mom had placed on the window ledge, like she was thinking of purchasing it. "Does that mean you're ready to apologize for ruining my trip to San Diego?"

"I didn't know there was anything to apologize for."

"Oh?" Andrea went to the easy chair backed up to the window. She huddled on the edge of the seat. "Well, I spent almost two grand on a plane ticket for a two-night stay. That sounds like a problem, doesn't it? When I was expecting a long weekend?"

"Your room was free," I reminded her. Andrea looked down at the floor and started to cry. "Hey now, I'm sorry. I didn't know it hit you that hard." I retrieved the box of tissues Mom had left behind. "Come on now," I coaxed as she dried her face. "You know I had to get back to work, right?"

"All I know is it hurt," Andrea snapped. "It was like you couldn't wait to get away from me after the first night." She choked out a gurgly sob.

"I was so worried about the shop," I groveled half-heartedly. "Although I guess I could have stayed a couple extra days. Since I'm going to lose business anyway, when word gets out that you were with me."

This cheered her up. "Has anyone said anything? Does Mike know?"

"Not unless he's keeping it on the down-low while he lines up the hit. Which might not be so bad." I groaned as I lowered my withered butt into the couch. "I talked to Valerie today and she never brought you up."

"Hmm. Maybe I need to say something."

I shrugged, bluffing.

"Mm. Well then." Andrea removed her coat, exposing skin in a sleeveless skintight sorta-semi-see-through white shirt. "Have you missed me these last two weeks?"

"I have. Right up there with missing not having cancer. How'd my vaccine sample turn out for your boss?"

"Dr. Bhani hasn't had much time for research. He has three state health labs requesting information and interviews. And of course the McEwens are suing him for malicious negligence."

"To be accused of being mean and sloppy. I don't know if there's a worse combination."

"They're idiots." Andrea looked at my head and clucked. I looked back at her, a coconut with a face. "Would you quit the chemo already and let Dr. Bhani cure you?"

"Has he ever cured anyone?"

Andrea was indignant. "A lot of people. He cured Rick's brother."

"Cured him dead."

"A lot of people catch an infection in the hospital. A lot."

"Most people aren't given an infection to cure their disease," I pointed out. "A lot of doctors frown on it. It's on the list with leeches and bloodletting."

"Fine, wait until you're on your deathbed." Andrea was marginally irked. "Dr. Bhani can probably still cure you, if the McEwens haven't completely ruined him. That's not why I came. I've been thinking a lot about your coffee company since San Diego."

Coffee company. I liked that.

"You said you want to open another shop, but you can't, because you can't be in two places at once. I have a solution that works for both of us."

"If it's cloning, I'm all for it. I would absolutely love another me. Without the cancer."

"Yeah. No. That's not it. It doesn't involve cloning."

"Can your boss do it, though? And I'm not talking about a Baby Brian that I have to raise and wait for him to grow up. For all I know, by the time he becomes an adult he wouldn't even want to run a coffeeshop. And it would be too late by then anyway. I can't hang in there financially for another eighteen years. Two is probably a better estimate. He needs to come out of the cloning tank an adult, with my exact brain."

"Are you done? No. What I'm thinking is, I could be your partner. I could manage the workers, and work a shift here and there. You could just flit back and forth between the stores, working the crowd, doing whatever you do to make the customers happy and keep them coming in the door. We could run three or four stores like that, at least. You're nodding."

Andrea had a way of turning me on—she set my mind alight, which through a questionable wiring pattern lit up my libido. "I'm flattered you've been spending time thinking about my business dilemma. But I don't have the cash, and there's no financing to be had in this economy. Without Mike, the Bluffs never would have been an option."

"I received a nice settlement from Rick. Enough to start at least two more stores."

"But why would you? How would this help you? Other than the thrill of partnering with a coffee kingpin."

"Because…" Here was her ta-da! moment. "…our stores would be in Colorado. Or California."

"You can't leave the state," I reminded her.

"I've done a little research," said Andrea. "I'm pretty sure this would be enough reason for the judge to let me go."

"What about Tyler?"

"We'd have to work out a sharing arrangement. Rick can afford to fly him back and forth. Or, I'd get sole custody."

"What would Rick say?"

"What would Rick say?" Andrea pondered, having fun shooting down one objection after another. "Hm. He should say, 'Gosh, I guess I shouldn't have treated you quite so badly. Then maybe I'd still be married to you, and I could move with you back to Colorado.'"

"I think Mike would hire a team of cutthroat East Coast lawyers to get full custody of Tyler and have you declared mentally incompetent, lobotomized, and tossed in a deep dark hole."

Andrea shook her head. "Rick wouldn't allow it. It's not that he doesn't love Tyler. He does. He just wouldn't fight it if the judge okayed it. I think in the end he would move wherever Tyler and I moved."

"And leave Mike and the business?"

"Mike isn't going to retire for a few years. And they have a new guy working for them that Rick thinks would make a good partner eventually. So he wouldn't be abandoning his dad."

"So you want me to abandon my shop and run away to Colorado."

"We could have a transition phase," said Andrea. "You would stay here, and I would run the shop in Colorado. You'd have to make quite a few trips the first couple months. You'd have to stay with me when you were in Denver. I'm sure you'd hate that." Andrea smoothed her jeans atop her thighs, certain that I couldn't wait to get my filthy paws all over her silky drawers.

She was right. Andrea's faith in my business future and her desire to be included made me professionally horny. And regular horny. Horny begat bravado. I was suddenly horny and confident. Confident I was sexy no matter how hairless and emaciated. I patted the couch. "We could get along for a few days at a time."

Andrea gave me a suspicious smile. "You're feeling lonely over there?"

I rubbed the seat cushion. "Uh-huh."

She joined me, leaning back and turning to face me. "What if you traveled all that way, and then I made you late for work?"

"I'm never late for work. I hate being late. I still remember dad chewing my ass for being late. He told me that being late is disrespectful to the people waiting for you, and to yourself. He laid into me for a good ten minutes. I was never late for dinner again. Or anything else."

"Well." Andrea tapped her fingernails on the teardrop curve of the reduced but still decent muscle framing my bare knee. "We'll see who wins that discussion."

I leaned on her and kissed her. Her shirt was tucked in. I took hold of the lowest exposed button and tugged.

"You, uh, you don't like this shirt?" Andrea wondered.

"It's a beautiful shirt." A gut cramp doubled me over; I went with it, kissing her stomach through the filmy fabric. I felt like shit but very much alive. "Is this a deep tuck?"

"I don't know." Andrea sat back and let her hands fall to her sides. "I guess you'll have to find out."

"I intend to." I tugged and tugged, lifting her hips off the couch. The shirttails cleared her jeans. I popped the bottom button and worked my way up. In very little time her shirt was open, exposing a lacy bra. "You have a beautiful body," I told her. "I've been dreaming about it since San Diego."

"Really." Some heat was brewing beneath her cool demeanor. "Have you." She looked me in the eye while I reached around to unhook her bra. "Do you think this is fair? Hm? Well, goodbye shirt," she bid her garment adieu. I was manhandling her, stripping her, pressing against her, kissing her. "Do you think this is fair?" she repeated, reprimanding me. "Shouldn't your shirt come off about now? Uh, goodbye bra. Are you going to strip me bare and have your way with me?"

"Both. So if we're going to do this…" I traced the curves of her breasts. "…we need to be within shouting distance while you learn the business. Contrary to popular belief, coffee takes some skill. We buy the Bluffs store, you learn the ropes there, and then we have a much more valuable asset to sell when it's time to leave."

"We're not doing it here," said Andrea, eyes drifting closed as my tracings spiraled in. "I don't want to stay in Jamestown one second longer than I have to. Neither do you. You can't make any money here. North Dakotans don't appreciate good coffee."

"Neither do you."

"Ha-ha," she whispered, back arching as I kept one hand up top and started the other on a slow trip south.

"We need to be at the top of our game," I said, under her jeans and exploring the waistband of her underwear. "I know what it's like to try to compete in a sophisticated coffee market."

"That was before you met me."

"Talking smack before you even get behind the bar." I undid her jeans and palmed the lowest reaches of her stomach. "I like that."

Knock-knock.

God help me, I said, "Who's there?"

"It's Nancy," came the reply.

I wanted to holler, "Has it been three months already?" Instead, "Give me a second," while I retrieved Andrea's shirt and bra. "Home nursing visit," I explained in a whisper. Andrea just laid there. "Go-go-go," I hissed.

She arched an eyebrow and smacked gum I hadn't known she was chewing. "Are we done?" She kept her voice down, not quite low enough.

"Can I get you to wait in the bedroom?" I whispered. "I'll take her out for lunch, and then you can leave."

"Or maybe I'll stay." Andrea took her time, strutting her stuff across the apartment. She had a high butt and a short back. "Enjoy your examination lunch," she said.

I put on my baseball cap and waited for Andrea to hide, before opening the door. Nurse Nancy stood like a statue, bags of groceries hung from both hands. She stared into my apartment. She scented the air. "Is someone here?"

I was overcome with relief. It was time to come clean with the McEwens. No excuses, no rationalizing—I simply had to take responsibility for my actions. All the better to have a messenger to absorb a few of Mike and Valerie's bullets.

I peeked at Nancy from under my cap, gangsta style. "Someone's in the bedroom."

The groceries hit the floor, and Nancy raised her trembling hands to her face. "Oh God, I knew it."

"But you don't even know who it is…"

"It doesn't matter who." Nancy's eyes were dry and haunted. "The who is never important." She began narrating the moment. "It's all about life stages, and moments in time. This is that moment. The moment when Brian and Nancy take the next step in their journeys."

"Our incredible journeys," I intoned.

Tone and color were draining from Nancy's cheeks. I had to hold her up while she pinched the bridge of her nose and took a few shallow breaths.

"Sorry to shock you like this."

Nancy shook her head and finished hyperventilating. "I shouldn't be falling to pieces. It had to happen. It's not your fault. You're ready to settle down."

"We're starting slow, of course, but you never know. It's definitely time I gave traditional dating a try."

Nancy wasn't listening. Her knees wobbled as she bent to pick up the groceries. "There are eggs in here," she apologized. "I was going to bake you a cake." She jiggled the bag. "And there's a cake in here too, in case I screwed it up."

I squeezed her shoulder. "I really appreciate the thought."

Nancy took a big resolute breath. "I'm going to be okay. I knew this day would come. I guess I just wanted it to be…later." She gave me a sweet sad smile. "Doesn't always work out that way, does it?"

"No," I agreed, and we shared a moment. "So it's Andrea, by the way."

The grocery bags fell to the floor again, this time after Nancy found the strength to elevate them to shoulder height. "You son of a bitch."

"There weren't a lot of eligible Jamestown bachelors for Andrea to choose from."

Nancy had bug eyes. "Mike's gonna kill you."

"That's why I thought you could explain to him. You know what it's like to be lonely in a town like this."

"If you think I'm going to go to bat for you on this…" Nancy faltered; my words were doing some damage, a time-release truth capsule in her brain. Her voice flattened. "I came here to warn you. Bill Hernandes is taking your spot in the Bluffs. He's partnering with Edna Applejack. Mike is looking forward to Tuesday, when he can finally move forward without you."

I was stunned. "Bill in the Bluffs? With Edna?" I pressed the heels of my palms into my forehead and demanded the ceiling give me answers. "Why didn't Mike tell me? Tuesday? What's so special about Tuesday?"

My whining was interrupting Nancy's soul-searching. She raised her chin and mustered as much snide as could be expected under the circumstances. "Maybe that it's going on a year since he offered you the chance of a lifetime?"

"Yeah, well, the chance of a lifetime, too bad that's a pretty short timeframe for me."

"And so I'm surprised you aren't more concerned with improving your heavenly odds," Nancy listlessly batted away my bid for pity. "Enjoy settling down with that witch. Hope she bakes you a great cake."

We looked down at the groceries. Nancy stomped on one of the bags with just enough force to bust an egg. "Now she won't have to mix the ingredients." She dropped her head and trudged down the stairs.

I put the groceries in the sink and went to my living room window. Nancy had collapsed on the front walk. I was about to go to her when Dennis hurried out of the building and helped her up. He put his arm around her and guided her inside. I felt the door to apartment number one thud shut.

Andrea left the bedroom without authorization. "Is she gone?"

"Took one look at me and decided I didn't need any nursing." I was reeling, picturing Edna behind the bar of Bill's shop, a line stretching around the block, Bill working the crowd selling Edna Applejack t-shirts and jailhouse memorabilia. "Let's get out of here, I need to get something to eat, so I can get some more of that freaking poison in me. Not that it matters, the pills are ignoring the food and eating my stomach instead, judging by the blood in my poop."

"Nice visual." Andrea put her hands on my hips. "I think we better stay here and eat. If I recall, what you had in mind wasn't legal in a restaurant."

I took her hands. "I'm not even capable of the publicly legal stuff right now."

"What happened?"

"Mike's putting Billy-boy in the Bluffs. With Edna." I stayed strong, said it without my voice cracking.

"Who's Edna?"

"Miss North Dakota."

"Let them have it," Andrea scoffed. "They'll be out of business, and we'll be opening our third shop in Denver." She stole a kiss and went to the kitchen. "We don't need to go out. I'll fix you something, you'll recharge your battery, and then…"

She meant to leave the rest to my imagination, or had just seen the inside of my fridge.

"Wow," she said. "This is pathetic. Why do you have all that fruit in here?"

"They were going bad on the countertop."

"Now they're going bad in the refrigerator." Andrea opened and quickly closed one cupboard door after another. "Did your mother leave you with absolutely nothing to eat?"

"Mom's resourceful, I'm sure she could whip up something that involves squishy nectarines, moldy bananas and a variety of condiments. A nice penicillin porridge."

Andrea made a face. "Maybe we can be a little less resourceful. I'll drive. You can sulk until we get there, and then I expect you to straighten up."

"You're not the nurturing type, are you."

"I don't like it when people get sick, no. As far as I'm concerned, the last thing you need is pity. I suppose you're the touchy-feely type."

"Kinda."

"One of each," she said, donning her puffy coat. "We're a perfect team."

T-7

*"I **UNDERSTAND*** you had a little trouble at the new coffeeshop this weekend," said Charlotte as she swapped out an empty pump pot after the Monday morning rush. I called it the morning rush, but it was the rush, no other rush in sight.

That's what I'm pretty sure in retrospect she said. At the time I heard: I understand you had a rough time sleeping this weekend, with that knife sticking in your back and your career going down in flames, thanks to the McEwens royally screwing you over with their secret double-dealing with that poseur putz Hernandes.

"Yeah, it was awful."

"I figured there was a story." Like a mother Charlotte sighed and crossed her arms and waited for the ugly details. "Tell me how Mike broke his tailbone."

"I'm talking about Mike giving the Bluffs to Billy Boy."

"No! Why?"

"Because I kept acting like I couldn't afford it. Which is one hundred percent the case."

"Still," Charlotte was outraged on my behalf, "how could Mike do that to you? With Hernandes?"

To keep Charlotte on my side a little longer, I omitted the fact that Edna was in on it too. "I want to be angry at Mike. I really do. But I'm not. He's just doing what he feels he needs to. But this is going to kill me. I was

167

looking at the Chamber's demographics report last night. I'm probably going to lose twenty percent of my business with Billy parked between me and the north end. I can't survive that."

"Oh Brian."

"You need to go work for Billy."

"Never!"

"I'm glad to hear you say that, but you're still going to have to. It'll help to know you're miserable."

"Well I will be." Charlotte blushed. "I mean, I'm not going there. I'm not leaving here."

"So Mike broke his coccyx?"

Charlotte giggled. "I think it's pronounced cock-six."

"I'm pretty sure it's cock-icks."

She had the giggles. "Brian, I don't think so."

"Let's ask Terrence. Terrence."

He looked up from his journal. Terrence wrote all his novels in journals, typed them into the computer at home, and then returned to my shop to hand-edit the printout. Not the most efficient process. "Eh?" he said.

"C-o-c-c-y-x. Did you get that? The medical term for the tailbone. Is it pronounced cock-six or cock-icks?" I really punched the cock on option two.

"I don't know," said Terrence.

Ordinarily Terrence would have known the answer. I don't think his brain was working too well.

"Terrence got a rejection letter from the agent he was counting on," I informed Charlotte.

"He was all hot to trot for my novel," Terrence picked up the thread. "And then he woke up one morning and decided the market was going in a different direction."

"Seems the market is going away from great stories," I concluded.

Charlotte was indignant. "How could they do that? I'm furious." I still think 'indignant' was more accurate.

"That's my third novel," Terrence addended. "I couldn't even get a nibble on the first two, so this time I got creative and had my first chapter recorded by a professional voice man. You know, like a book on CD. Didn't matter," he said before Charlotte could compliment his marketing savvy. "Got rejected, one after another. But it didn't shake me up, because I had continued to research the market, and knew I had finally found the right agency." He held up the rejection letter. "This one."

"Doesn't seem fair," said Charlotte.

"It's all connections," said Theresa, a short well-postured forty-five year old homemaker and former nurse who had aced three years' worth of hardcore science and math classes, still failed twice to get into pharmacy school, and eavesdropped on our conversation. Twenty minutes ago she had melted down about her inability to pursue her passion, using a whole wad of house tissue to mop up her tears. It was very wasteful. I was going to have Charlotte stuff a few back in the box if they weren't too badly creased.

"Brian," Theresa sniffled, "you had another MRI today, didn't you?"

"I did. It went well. Very well. Looks like it's almost completely gone. This last round of chemo and radiation, and the surgery, seems to have done the trick."

"That is beautiful," said Theresa. "I am so happy to hear that."

"That's beautiful, man," Terrence echoed, making a bit of a production of readdressing his journal, signaling his desire to be left alone. "Is that the end of the chemo?"

I sighed. "Three more days."

"That reminds me," said Charlotte, "they're retiring Edna's number at halftime of the JC game tonight."

"How were you reminded of that?" I wanted to know.

She grabbed my arm. "I didn't have to be reminded," she gushed. "I haven't stopped thinking about it since I heard they were going to do it."

Charlotte made herself a bagel and added little red hearts to an "Edna Rules" banner that stretched from Terrence's corner to Theresa's table. They were both hunched over, slumped over their work, Theresa's posture gone to hell. I was slumped behind the bar, and Jamestown was slumped at the edge of a muddy little river. No one cared whether any of us existed. Terrence was right, it was connections, and if any of us had them, we wouldn't be there.

The world was going to be deprived of our talents and our passion; the world was willing to relegate us to lesser roles and settle for lesser output. It didn't seem right, didn't seem American. No matter how much we knew, no matter how hard we worked, we would not be allowed the chance to realize our dreams. Our finances wouldn't even permit us to fake it much longer.

Over the weekend I had become increasingly obsessed with being in the Bluffs. Only partially out of spite. If Mike successfully forced me out, if Bill Hernandes got a foothold on the north end, backed by Edna Mankiller Applejack, I was going to be wiped out. And Andrea's Colorado proposal was at the very least premature, the easy way out; until and unless I left North Dakota at the top of the heap, it would simply be running away. The Bluffs store was my lifeline, my last chance, the figurative and literal commanding position on the hilltop.

"I thought you had a contract with Mike," Charlotte called over to me, like an English teacher breaking that sentence into clauses with two licks at a dollop of cream cheese at the corner of her mouth.

"No."

"Yes you do. I remember filing it."

Five minutes later I came a-bursting out of the office. "I have to run an errand," I announced, already halfway down the back hallway.

"Dana comes on at noon today," Charlotte called after me. "You know she freaks when she's alone and more than two customers show up."

"I'll be back by two."

ANDREA WAS behind her desk, in the little office separated from the laboratory by the false wall and the mock lab bench marketing the notion this was just another boutique clinic selling laser eye surgery or supervised weight loss, rather than germ warfare on cancer. There should have been HazMat warning signs plastered up and down the hall and next to the LL3 elevator button.

That was my thought as I listened to Andrea argue with the state epidemiologist.

"We don't have any live bacteria here," Andrea was saying, in her condescending way. "You obviously didn't believe me the first time I told you. The s. pyogenes is attenuated. We're only using the immune response-triggering endotoxins, not the entire bacteria."

I whistled. "Attenuated. Endotoxins. Wow."

Andrea had no difficulty ignoring me. "We know the statute," she sassed the state lab. "We are familiar with the biological agent classifications. Dr. Bhani had the state of Minnesota review his work. The CDC is aware of his research. ...hm? That's not relevant. ...no. No. If you want to discuss Dr. Bhani's history, you'll have to talk to him personally. ...no, he's out this week. …no I don't. I'll let him know you called. …that would be fine. …okay. …uh-huh. …fine." She hung up with authority. "What assholes."

I plopped into her guest chair. "Are they ready to quarantine the basement and send in the guys in the white biohazard suits?"

"Practically." Andrea was jotting notes from her conversation. "God I get sick of dealing with these people. They don't have a clue what they're talking about. But does that stop them?"

"Nope. Luckily, I'm here to take you away from all this."

"Oh?" Andrea cocked her head. "Where are you taking me?"

"To the bank. We're going to buy the new store at the Bluffs."

"We? You must have a turd in your pocket."

"No turds. Just you. And me. For fifteen grand, we're going to be partners."

An old lady knocked on the jam and entered the office with a young boy. The lady was haggard, and the kid looked worse. Pale, super skinny, with a few sores on his chin and neck, like zits repeatedly scratched open.

"Hi Mrs. Price," said Andrea. "Hi Thor," she sweetly greeted the boy, who was maybe twelve years old. "How are you today?"

"Fine," he mumbled. The kid was obviously a cancer patient, except that he had all his hair. He had better hair by far than the old lady. Hers was permed into see-through loops and waves. His was long and blonde, in his eyes, snagging on his eyelashes until he flipped it to the side.

"Are you ready to see Dr. Bhani?" Andrea asked Thor. "Your grandma is taking off work to bring you here. That's a pretty good grandma." She received a quick nod. "I don't know if anyone has told you this, but my God," said Andrea. "You have the most beautiful eyes."

Thor fought back a grin while he examined the floor.

"Too bad no one gets to see them anymore," said his grandma. She tried to push Thor's hair out of his eyes but he slipped her swipe with a practiced head turn. Grandma settled for smoothing the shoulder seam of his shirt. "We're a little nervous about our visit today."

"Dr. Bhani is looking forward to seeing you," said Andrea. "He's reviewed all your history and notes. Even though the hospital wasn't exactly forthcoming with your records."

"I'd be glad to break into the records room upstairs," I volunteered.

"We're from Indiana," said the grandma. "We're staying at the Ronald McDonald House for a couple weeks while Dr. Bhani helps Thor."

"All the way from Indiana," I marveled.

"Dr. Bhani is famous in the small circle of bone cancer patients," said Grandma. "And infamous in others. We like what we've heard though, don't we?" She laid a wrinkled hand on top of Thor's head. He didn't have a problem with this. He nodded.

"This is Brian," Andrea introduced me. "He has bone cancer too."

Thor gave me a good look for the first time. The kid had big blue suspicious eyes. "Oh," Grandma exclaimed. "Are you seeing Dr. Bhani too?"

"He's seeing me," said Andrea.

"I have it in my leg," I told Thor. I hiked up my shorts, an unnecessary move, and pointed to my scarred, puffy, discolored shin. "How about you?"

Thor glanced at his grandma. He gave a quick up-and-down flick of his hands. "All over."

My throat closed up. I nodded.

"That's usually when people come to us," said Andrea quietly. "After a lot of chemo and radiation, and the cancer continues to spread. At some point maybe we'll be able to convince doctors to send their patients to us earlier. So they don't have to go through all the misery caused by the chemotherapy. So we can cure them right away." She gave Thor a sweet soft-core flirt face, until he smiled and blushed, apparent on his white cheeks. His grandma's eyes were swimming in tears. I had to look away.

"Dr. Bhani is ready for you," said Andrea. "It's the first door on the right, just past the elevator."

Grandma nodded at me and they shuffled away.

"Phew." I took a couple deep pulls of basement air. Seems I had been holding my breath. "That's gut wrenching."

"I adore that boy." Andrea made notes while she talked. "He's been through every treatment you can imagine, but the cancer keeps spreading."

I can't tell you how thankful I was for that morning's good MRI results.

"There's a writer who wants to follow his story," said Andrea. "He wanted to sit in on their visit with Dr. Bhani today." She stood to access the file cabinet behind her, on her tiptoes peering into the top drawer until she found the right file. "His grandma wouldn't let it happen. I think she doesn't want Thor to know how serious this is."

"But it's pretty bad."

Andrea stared at me for awhile before answering. "Dr. Bhani thinks he has a few months at most."

"Oh." My stomach did a flip. "Jeez."

"You should see his MRIs." Andrea's voice went hoarse. "The cancer is everywhere. It's everywhere, really. But Dr. Bhani will cure him."

"Most doctors don't use the C word," I said.

"Most doctors are too afraid to try to cure their patients," she retorted.

"You were sure nice to Thor," I observed.

She smirked at me. "What, you think I should be that nice to you?"

"You could compliment me on my eyes. Or my hair. That would be nice." I removed my cap and waited.

Andrea raised her eyebrows.

"Make it convincing."

"You've lost more weight."

I put the cap back on. "So let's go. To the bank."

"For one thing," she said, "I can't go anywhere until five o'clock."

"But that's too late, the bank will be closed," I whined.

"For another thing," Andrea continued. "I already told you, I'm not investing a dime in North Dakota."

"This is the only way to go," I stated. "You need the training before we move on to the big time."

"I'm a very quick learner."

"Andrea." I cleared my throat, and frowned. Felt like I tore off and swallowed my epiglottis. "If I don't get this store, there isn't going to be any Colorado." This was falling on deaf ears. "And I really really want to shove this thing down Mike McEwen's throat. I don't mind him covering his bases," I said bitterly, and it's hard to say how much was an act, "but he should have told me he was talking to Hernandes."

Andrea's ears were now working. She grew smug. "The McEwens aren't as holy as you thought, huh?"

"You were right."

I don't do sheepish very well, but it worked. Andrea was vindicated. And apparently that meant more to her than escaping North Dakota. We agreed to meet at the bank at four-thirty.

DANA'S FACE lit up when I walked into the shop a little after noon. I was on my cell with Kenny the Wells Fargo branch manager, confirming my ability to deposit funds to the Bluffs construction account.

Business that afternoon was terrible. I wished I could send Dana home, or at least not pay her for being there. She broke character and volunteered to scrub the floors, and I took her up on it.

'Round about two o'clock I forgot Bart Shock's name. It didn't bother him a bit—it's not unusual for me to call you Lady or What's-His-Face. When I greeted him with, "Hey…you", Bart figured it was part of my shtick. But I had no clue what his name was. Couldn't even put his face into context; felt like a big black gap where a whole lot of memories should be. I had a small nervous breakdown.

I DIDN'T see Andrea's pickup when I pulled into the bank parking lot at four-twenty-five, so I waited in my van. Time passed slowly. Even though I was tense, I had to struggle to stay awake. Getting up at five every morning, with or without cancer, meant that I couldn't sit down to read a book or watch television, or eat, for that matter. I got drowsy taking a dump, fell asleep jacking off. Coffeeshop owners do it on their feet.

At four-forty I left the van, sucked chilly air to dissolve the mental fog, and started across the lot. Mike McEwen fell into step beside me.

"What a coincidence," he said sarcastically. I kept walking, not looking at him. "Kenny told me you were coming," he said. "What are you doing?" He was bumping me, jostling me. I was ready to send him flying into the shrubbery when I realized he was limping badly and struggling to keep up.

I stopped. "Heard you broke your ass."

"Tailbone fracture," Mike grunted. Sweat beaded on his forehead.

"That's your coccyx." No clue whether my pronunciation was right. "Fifteen grand, right? That's the required earnest money."

Mike grimaced as he tried to stand comfortably. "I'm not here to talk money. You have no business trying to get back into this thing. It's too late."

"As far as getting back in…" I stopped. Mike shouldn't have gone to Hernandes behind my back, but I shouldn't have strung him along. We were even, and at this point all that mattered was our business arrangement. "We have a signed contract that calls for me to open a James River Valley shop at that site. The deadline for depositing the earnest money is the thirty-first. That's today." Who was I kidding, we weren't even, I had cancer. "And as far as I know, I was never out of this thing."

"That's a hell of an attitude." Mike kept a careful eye on the customers coming and going from the bank, timing his remarks, worried about making a scene. "I would have expected a little more gratitude from you."

"Mike, I am grateful. But I would have expected—"

"Save it." He chewed the inside of his cheek as he glared at me. "Can't believe you think that anything you're doing is acceptable."

"I'm just trying to stay afloat, Mike."

"Helluva way to stay afloat, by shoving my head under the water."

"You know I'm doing you a favor," I might or might not have bluffed. "You give that shop to Hernandes and you'll be looking for a new anchor tenant by Thanksgiving. I can't believe he even has the money to finish the store."

"Speaking of which, where are you getting it from?" Mike demanded.

On cue, Andrea pulled into the lot. "I have a partner."

"This deal was with you, exclusively."

"My partner is investing the money in me, not the store."

Andrea parked in the spot right in front of us. The bumper of her pickup stopped a foot from Mike's knee. Mike was choking on his own angry bile, oblivious to his surroundings. "Who the hell would loan you fifteen grand?"

A fair question, but with a week or two I could have pulled together that and more. Quite a few of my friends and acquaintances in Jamestown and back home had a naïve amount of faith in me. I just liked and respected them too much to lose their money. (Sorry, Andrea.)

I cut across the lawn as Andrea climbed out of her pickup. "I need to get inside before the bank closes."

"I already promised Edna Applejack this store," Mike barked at me.

I opened the vestibule door. "I'll talk to Edna tonight at the College ceremony. I'll explain everything to her."

Mike shook his finger at me. "She doesn't..." He wheeled as Andrea stepped onto the sidewalk behind him. Mike's leg gave out and he had to use the bug guard of her pickup for support. He thrust himself back to an awkward standing position. "What are you doing here?" From ten yards away I saw a globule of what could only be angry bile glistening at the corner of his lips.

"What?" snapped the Woman Without Fear. "I can't bank here?"

I hurried inside and jogged across the lobby into the warren of cubicles where the business bankers lived. Matt my banker was on the phone. He held up his hand, asking for a couple minutes' privacy. I plopped down in his guest chair and started massaging my cancer leg, grimacing.

Matt talked quietly into the phone with his back to me. I climbed on my chair to periscope my head above the cube partitions. There was Andrea, filling out a form at the customer workstand. And there was Mike under a big potted tree in the corner, on his cellphone and steaming. I ducked back down. Matt didn't notice a thing. I wondered if I shouldn't find a more observant banker. Decided a clueless lender was probably the right choice for me.

I pulled out my checkbook and filled out a deposit slip. Wandering the alleyways between the cubes, I flagged down Darlene, a tall investment advisor with huge cheekbones and a bouffant hairstyle, and asked her to take the deposit slip to Andrea. I described her vividly.

Darlene was puzzled by my request.

"I don't want Mike McEwen to see me," I explained.

Darlene gave me a knowing nod and hustled off. I felt like part of an underground resistance movement. I wasn't selfishly exploiting Mike's generosity, I was striking a blow against Jamestown's ruthless overlord who picked every winner, built every building, and always got a table at Olive Garden, the banker from It's a Wonderful Life and that dude up in Mordor all rolled into one. Once I got to know Edna better, I would take up a collection to pay her to strangle Mike, and then the sun would come out and we'd have a parade.

Standing on Matt's chair again and peeking over the tops of the cubes, I watched Darlene do my righteous bidding. When Matt finally hung up the phone, he chastised me. "That was a confidential customer call."

"Bull," I said. "That was Nancy," his wife. "You're just talking about what you're having for dinner tonight."

"It's still confidential, Brian," said Matt, smiling reluctantly.

"I won't tell anyone you're ordering pizza again tonight."

"I wish that was a joke," said Matt. "So what can I do you for?"

"I need to move fifteen grand from my James River Valley account into Mike McEwen's Bluffs construction account. Maybe Kenny told you?"

"I don't recall." Matt swiveled to his computer and started clicking. "For the new coffeeshop? I heard at roundtable—the business bankers have a roundtable every morning at seven—so much for banker's hours, huh?" Matt's a small guy with red-blonde hair and fuzzy sideburns. He has a wry style and a fatalistic outlook. Maybe he's taken too many corporate spankings for extending bad credit to struggling little businesses like mine. "I heard at the roundtable this morning—we always compare notes, you'd be surprised how many businesses have overlapping transactions or needs. I heard Bill Hernandes was going in there." He stopped clicking and got this faraway look in his eye. "And Edna Applejack."

It was amazing the spell she had on this town. She wasn't Salk or Gandhi. She wasn't even Travis Hafner. "She's a sweetheart, huh?"

Matt clicked through what must have been an e-labyrinth, judging by his intense concentration. "Brian, you don't have the funds…oop, something just popped in. A cash deposit, for fifteen thousand. Coincidentally."

"It's no coincidence. I have my own private genie."

"That's the fifteen grand you want to move, huh."

"Think of this as legal money laundering."

Matt had a limited range of facial expressions. He inclined his head a couple degrees to indicate he got the joke and that it was a good one, and scratched his cheek real slow-like to suggest that I never utter that phrase again. All with the same weary cynical look. "It can take up to two days for deposited funds to become available."

"Andrea Goldine—my genie—has an account here. You can see she has the funds to make the transaction."

Matt eyed me. I sounded and probably looked desperate. "I'll need to get manager approval."

"Kenny knows I'm doing it."

"Actually"—Matt checked his watch—"my business banking manager is in Fargo."

"It has to be today, or I don't want to do it. And if I don't do it, we might as well work out a plan to liquidate my shop and pay off as much of my loan as possible. Ten cents on the dollar is my guess."

Matt winked at me. "We'll make sure you stay in business long enough to pay it off, with interest."

"Then we need to move this money today."

Matt excused himself. I slumped in the chair, to conserve energy. Maybe I wouldn't attend the Edna ceremony tonight. I was exhausted. I closed my eyes for a moment.

It was 4:58 when Matt breezed back into his cube, into his chair, onto his computer, clickety-click-click. He stabbed a key with finality. "Done deal. You're no richer or poorer than you were a half-hour ago. Free money—that's a pretty fair way to capitalize a business."

I shook his hand. "It's not free, not by a long shot. I appreciate the quick action."

"I'm looking forward to that first cup of coffee from your new shop."

"I wish I could give it to you for free, but I know it's against your code of ethics."

Matt shook his head. "It's de minimis."

"Not to me."

The lobby was empty of customers. Darlene the investment advisor waited for me at the door, unlocking and then locking it behind me. Gave me a wink goodbye. No sign of Mike in the parking lot, but there was Andrea in her pickup, making busy with her checkbook. I rapped on her window. She did not startle.

"Thanks," I said when she rolled down the window.

"Sure." She smacked her gum and looked at me like I owed her something. "So we need to get together and talk business."

I wanted to bask in the glow of owning a new shop before starting to worry about how I was going to keep it. "I'm going to the Jamestown College basketball game tonight. They're retiring Edna Applejack's number."

"What's an enda applejack?"

"That's a basketball star who murdered her man with her bare hands."

"How nice." Andrea seemed impressed, intrigued.

"You wanna come? It would be good for you to start meeting people."

Andrea considered this the worst idea she had heard all day. "No, I don't think so. Why don't you swing by afterward."

"It'll be pretty late."

"Maybe some things are worth losing sleep over."

"Okay. Did you talk to Mike? Does he know you're helping me?"

Andrea smiled, smug and satisfied. "He was back and forth, in and out of the bank manager's office. And then he stormed out of there just before they closed. Yeah, I think he knows we're working together."

"You might want to get in the habit of checking your brakes before you get in the vehicle. I gotta run. Sure you don't want to come tonight?"

"Why are you going?" Andrea wanted to know.

"Edna might kill someone. I don't want to miss it."

On the way to the game I got a call from the hospital. "Brian, it's Dr. Bonilla. How are you?"

"Feeling pretty good, considering."

"That's good. Good to hear. Hey, so, I was taking another look at your MRI this afternoon, and there are a couple things I want to follow up on. Can you come in for additional pictures?"

"Follow up on…" I let that sink in. Follow up on… Anymore, my body was primed to overreact. I broke into a cold sweat and lost my peripheral vision. I had to pull over, into the Hardees parking lot at the busiest intersection in town, at the main bridge over the James. "How soon do you need to, uh, follow up on…it? Shouldn't I make an appointment?"

"Are you available to come in first thing in the morning?"

My fingers tingled. My arms went numb. My automatic life-support system was shutting down. I switched over to Manual, rocking back and forth to pump oxygen and blood. "'First thing', that definitely has an urgent ring to it."

"You know how we operate with this kind of stuff," said Dr. Bonilla. "We want to set everyone's mind at ease as quickly as possible."

"Dr. Bonilla, my mind hasn't been at ease since I met you. If you really care about my peace of mind, cure me already."

"You know we're doing everything we can…" He blathered his malpractice insurer's mandatory CYA spiel while Jeanie McDonald, a regular customer, pulled into the adjacent parking spot and jumped out of her car to say hi. I waved and let my head droop, questioning whether I had the energy or the pride to lean out of the van to puke. When I looked up, Jeanie was gone.

"…and sometimes additional tests turn out to be unnecessary," Dr. Bonilla wrapped up the required disclosure. "But it's always better safe than sorry."

"Why don't I come in tonight? Since I won't be sleeping anyway."

"I could probably make that work," said Dr. Bonilla after a short pause. "Let me make a couple calls."

"No." If eight a.m. was early enough for Dr. Bonilla and his malpractice insurer, it must be fine. "I really should attend the JC exhibition game tonight."

"They're retiring Edna's number," Dr. Bonilla gushed. "I'll be there too. She was incredible."

"It doesn't bother you she murdered her husband? With her bare hands?"

"I can't imagine what she must have endured up to that point. It must have been a horrible environment."

"How terrible could it be, living with a computer geek? Boring maybe."

Dr. Bonilla's voice flattened. "I didn't really know much about him."

"If it turns out that…"

"Mm? Brian?"

I was going to make a joke about how if it turned out I was terminal, I wanted to marry Edna and then bore her so badly she felt compelled to tear me apart with those beautiful hands of hers. But my lungs failed to provide enough oxygen to weave the scenario. "The MRI?" I managed to say. "You think it's bad?"

Dr. Bonilla paused. "I can't speculate, Brian. Come in tomorrow and let's get a good, all-over look at you."

"If it is—say it is bad. What then?"

"We have other therapeutics we haven't tried yet. Or we can get more aggressive with our current treatment plan."

I no longer salivated at the word aggressive. "Most of my organs were already dissolved by the chemo. If you get any more aggressive, the cancer won't have anything left to eat. Which is a form of a cure, I guess."

"We'll try to strike the right balance."

"Maybe I should try…" I made sure the unspoken name Dr. Bhani came through loud and clear. "…an alternative treatment." It was a bluff. I wanted Dr. Bonilla to take care of me. I was comfortable with him. He was calm and cool and professional, ninety percent of the time, and he was dedicated to curing me, within the bounds of reason if not my expectations. I wanted reassurance I was making the right choice.

"Yes, of course, other options do exist, as we discussed with your mother and your friend after your surgery." Dr. Bonilla labored through his least favorite subject. "There are many scientists, some reputable, others not as much, who are working hard to solve various forms of cancer. I monitor the journals closely, for treatments that have been confirmed effective over an extended period of time. If there were any miracle cures out there, I would have heard about it."

"I guess the pharmaceutical industry would be all over a real cure."

"There would definitely be some people ready to profit by any new treatments that are proven effective. And safe. Of course nothing moves very quickly in the world of drug development."

"Damned feds."

"Mm." Dr. Bonilla had no room for banter, he was working too hard forming his next thought. This was the one I would bank on. "I would feel professionally negligent if I encouraged you to spend time chasing treatments that are still in the unverified stage. I have seen, unfortunately, patients who dropped everything, their jobs, their relationships, everything that gave their lives meaning, to pursue a cure. It's admirable to take your health into your own hands. I'm an advocate of patients feeling responsible for their well-being. But there's a cost. Potentially a great one. Cancer research is incredibly complex and confusing. It makes physicians' heads spin. I feel sorry for laymen who feel compelled to enter that thicket."

"That's what I thought." My vision returned to normal, my grip strengthened on the wheel. The sweat had stunk up my clothing but cleansed my pores. I rolled down the window and gave a "Hey lady" to Jeanie returning to her car, waving as she munched French fries.

"If you want," said Dr. Bonilla, "I'll refer you to a website that publishes information on studies that might be looking for volunteers."

"I don't think that's necessary. I'd rather stay the tried and true course. I'll see you tomorrow morning."

"You'll see me tonight too. I'll be there cheering for Edna." My doctor was in love. "Goodbye Brian."

I'd rather have my doctor hang up on me, I decided, instead of telling me "goodbye". Just say "fuck you, Brian" and hang up. Doctors can't help but sound sinister when they say goodbye.

I PLAYED for Davis High, so I was familiar with the sound of a crowd that loves its team. I was too short and not quick enough to consistently get my shot off, which limited my playing time and meant I didn't get near enough opportunity to feed off the crowd's energy. I was envious to see the JC men doing just that, firing passes more crisply than usual, getting extra lift on their jump shots, aggressively driving to the hoop, looking more athletic than their norm. Holding their own against the superior Pan-Am team.

In the waning moments of the first half, the excitement level in the civic center peaked. And then rose higher above that false summit, until the roar became the frenzied single-note scream that only comes in the final seconds of a tight, meaningful game. With two ticks remaining on the clock, JC's Danny Bernstein came up with a loose ball in the corner and the fans erupted; when he launched a three-pointer as the horn blasted, the scream strangled silent while the ball looped to the hoop, and then resumed times ten when it went in.

The aural blast continued for some seconds, everyone's arms thrust in the air, delirious to the point of insanity. The public address man knew exactly why it was so and before the teams had even left the floor announced, "Ladies and gentlemen, I give you the greatest basketball player in North Dakota history—Edna...Applejack!" The screaming went ultrasonic.

"Nice," I shouted to council president Jasper and his wife Denise. We were crowded into the runway between the bleachers. "Now I have cancer and I'm deaf. I heard there's an eclipse next week. Think I'll look at the sun."

Jasper couldn't respond because of his fingers in his mouth, folding his tongue to channel a shrieking whistle.

Edna took a few long strides to reach center court, beating the man with the microphone. With that kind of speed in heels and a tight knee-length dress that was a wearable map of the state of North Dakota with a neckline star representing not the capital but Jamestown, how could anyone have stayed with her as she filled the lane on a fast break and jammed down another two of her twenty-five thousand three hundred eighty-one points?

"Thank you," said Edna, and then into the tardy microphone, "North Dakota, God bless you." The cheering couldn't get any louder, people must have been spitting throat blood. I know I was. "Jamestown, God bless you!"

A man carrying a glass-framed jersey strolled out to join her. "That's Jim Adelson," I was told by a stranger, a woman. "He's the most famous sportscaster in North Dakota. Ever." She had to lean in close to make herself heard. She had to rise up on her tippytoes to speak into my ear. She had to be one of the sweetest little numbers I had seen in a long time, glossy hair framing dark flashing eyes and a beautiful smile, with a body that was alive and fidgety with energy. This lady would have turned heads in any other crowd; she was unfortunate to be standing in a town where Edna Applejack walked free.

I nodded and elbowed her chest to get a better vantage point.

"We're here tonight to honor this woman," bellowed Adelson, seventyish, silver-haired and ruddy in a checkered sport coat. The crowd never took a breath and neither did he. "The greatest basketball player of either sex in the history of our state!" Banshee cries of group ecstasy punctuated each phrase. "Number twenty-one at Jamestown High and number twenty-one for the Jamestown College Jimmies, Edna Applejack, it was my honor to watch you then and retire your number now!"

I'm not kidding, people were dancing in the bleachers, they were falling off the ends, they were jumping and screaming and losing their minds. Edna hoisted the framed jersey, making the North Dakota plains shimmer and roll.

"Thank you North Dakota!" she shouted. "I love you!"

She came right for us with Adelson jogging to keep up. Like the next leg in a relay race Jasper, Denise and I started moving backward so that by the time Edna reached us we were at top walking speed alongside her, while Security sealed off the runway and kept at bay the surging screaming horde, gawking, clapping and shedding tears, whiffing in their attempts to pat Edna's back like defenders swiping futilely at the ball as Edna broke down their double team.

In no time we were inside the athletic director's office. The closing of the door vacuumed out the crowd sound. I stood there like everyone else coping with my deaf buzz. Adelson opened his arms and embraced Edna, his face nestled into the sharp crook of her neck.

Edna doled out hugs, five of them counting the athletic director, tall and crane-necked with acne scars on his jowls. He shook our hands, introducing himself as AD Guldseth. "Edna, that is unprecedented," he said. "Never before—not even when you were playing—has our house rocked like that."

"I don't know," said sportscaster Adelson. He had a puffed chest. "I remember a few games…the state class A high school tournament final against Bismarck Century in ninety-three."

"That was some game," said AD Guldseth. ADG struck a relaxed pose, one hand in his pocket and the other picking at his throat; but he was watching Edna like a hawk, every fiber tensioned to leap into service, if he could only anticipate what she might need. "Edna, you went off, if I remember right. Fifty-three points."

"It was only forty-eight," said Adelson. "Only. Phew."

"I was watching with the other Shanley varsity ballplayers," said ADG. "We had a great team that year…"

Adelson clapped him on the back, making ADG jab himself in the Adam's apple. "You were a fine ballplayer in your own right, Bobby. Edna, are you a little overwhelmed by all this?"

"A lot." Edna perused ADG's photo gallery. She was in half the pictures, either in action with her hair flying or posing smiling with various Most Valuable Player plaques. She had a real jumpshot, not a girlie ass-out-and-push-from-the-chest, judging by one framed photo prominently displayed to the left and ahead of ADG's desk where he could glance at it on a regular basis whenever he got tired of looking at the framed picture of his wife and kids beside his computer. Edna's release was high above and a little in front of her head. The ball was resting lightly on her finger pads, like it had been lowered on a string from the ceiling and placed there. She had long, tapered, cream-colored thighs.

Edna tapped the glass of one of her action photos. "Jasper, I forgot that I played with a girl from your hometown, Kulm. I know she's a little older, but did you know Tammy Akin? She was a great baller."

Denise snorted gaily. "It doesn't matter who you were going to say, we would know her. Kulm's so small, there's a good chance we're related."

"Denise and Jasper are cousins," I told everyone.

"We are not." Denise slapped my arm while Jasper chortled.

First, I mouthed to Adelson while absorbing increasingly firm slaps. Denise was a sizeable gal, a Farm Girl, and I had a bolt of fear she would bruise my bone and start fresh cancer. And she was scandalized over nothing, no one seemed the least bit disturbed.

"You look fabulous tonight, Edna," said ADG. "Not many people can pull off wearing our state."

Jasper stared at Edna's dress, the kind of blatant ogling that is illegal on some campuses. Denise started palm-striking his shoulder but couldn't dislodge his puzzled gaze.

Finally the light came on. "Ohh," said Jasper. He slapped his forehead and cackled like a crazy man. "That's North Dakota." And sure enough his gaze went straight to Lake Sacagawea, a reservoir stretching across Edna's stomach, a cool blue patch tastefully blended with the green prairie grass shoreline.

Denise moved to stand beside Edna and began pointing out areas of interest. "Do you see this, Jasper?" She indicated the sharp-pointed neckline. "This star is Jamestown. Here's Kulm," a couple inches below

Edna's left breast, "and that is Lake Sacagawea." She was the geography instructor of every horny teenage boy's fantasy.

"I see, I see." Jasper's laughter was high-pitched and high speed. "Where's the state capitol building?" he asked innocently, and then cackled again. I'm no expert in North Dakota landmarks, but I was pretty sure it would be a little south of the lake.

Denise threw up her hands and pleaded with the rest of us for sympathy, before putting her husband in an affectionate bear hug. "I can't believe you sometimes."

"You better believe it," said Jasper as they rocked back and forth.

ADG clapped once and hugged Edna with one ropy arm. "I am so pleased to give you this evening. It is so well deserved. You have meant so much to the state, to this city, to the College," ADG carried on. "And to me personally. If there is anything I can do for you—"

Adelson broke in before ADG could propose something unprofessional. "I know the administration here would love to have your name associated with the College, Edna. You might want to ask for a building to be named after you, while all this euphoria is still hanging in the air."

And that's when an idea, a particularly wonderful, dreadfully perfect idea hit me. While Edna mulled over which building would be best suited to bear the name Applejack, I plotted. And realized I had stumbled upon the answer to my prayers. I had made a connection. It involved stepping on more toes and breaking more promises, so I had to be careful.

I needed a way to get Edna Applejack alone, without starting any more rumors and soiling my reputation so dirty it would never come clean.

"Edna, you wanna get a beer with me? I have a proposition for you."

T-6

EDNA TOOK a raincheck in favor of a party the McEwens were throwing for her back at their pad. Maybe that's why everyone craved her, she was so good at playing hard to get. Or maybe it was because she was gorgeous and athletic and sexy and dangerous and convinced that North Dakota was paradise.

Edna was the thirty-six-year-old bomb. I wanted to picture her while they slid me shivering into the MRI tube the next morning. Instead I kept envisioning my cancer hiding from the camera, escaping detection by ducking behind my spleen, holding still in a kidney-like clump, masquerading as organs, playing dead, buying time until it could creep up my spine and infect my brain.

Then the MRI machine started clacking, not clickety-clack but CLACK-CLACK-CLACK, bone-jarring attack clacks meant to stun the cancer, disorient it while the computer took a good picture of the horde I feared was swarming my testicles and gobbling up the soft tissues in my gut.

Then again maybe it was the chemo doing the swarming and gobbling. In which case the MRI tech would present the incriminating photos of chemo molecules shredding my testes to confetti, pancreatic gore dripping off their chins—my doctors would nod and knuckle-knock each other and tell me everything was going according to plan.

Very soon I had to focus on pretending I wasn't stuffed in a small tube, like being shoved backwards into a zipped-up sleeping bag, which my best friend Ryan and I used to do to each other, the torturer holding the open end closed until the torturee had a panic attack. Which I didn't want to do there in the MRI tube, because we'd only have to start the whole process over again, meanwhile giving the cancer extra heads-up time to hide.

So I imagined myself lying in a grassy meadow, the non-itchy type of grass, gazing at the high clear blue sky, a gentle breeze caressing my face. This was fairly effective, although in my imagined meadow I had no explanation for the CLACKs.

After taking my picture, they pumped me full of my daily dose of poison and sent me packing. Driving to the shop I tried not to dwell on what the MRI results might reveal. That was the tough thing about having cancer—always working hard not to think about it. Any other problem, I would obsess on it until an action plan came to mind, and then attack it. Here, I might as well be agonizing over world hunger. I could ponder my cancer all day every day, and no action plan was going to take shape.

The same could be said for my descent into bankruptcy, of course. Look how long I had agonized over that one, and what good it did me. In the end it wasn't brainstorming that materialized a solution out of thin air, it was being in the right place (next to Edna Applejack) at the right time.

Should have been focusing on driving. We were having a late May storm, rain changing to sleet changing to ice on the streets as the temperature plummeted. North-facing street signs were caked white. The Y-shaped Hardees intersection just past the bridge was a five-vehicle accident scene, so I bypassed Main and crawled through the backstreets into downtown.

The shop was spunky for ten-thirty on a weekday. The bar chairs were all full, three of the six tables occupied. I worked the crowd on the way back to Terrence, in his corner writing. "So how's it going?"

He had a lot of scribbled-out slashed-out sentences on the journal page in front of him. "Not bad," he lied. "Yourself?"

"Oh, you know. Could be better." I thought about this for a couple seconds. "Could be worse." I rubbed my face, gently. Probably psychological, but I was sure the powerful MRI magnets had further scrambled my decaying epidermis. I imagined my fingers knocking loose some of the corrupted underlying layers—they would fall in chunks and collect under my chin, leaving behind the outer skin like a sheet of cellophane. I took my hand away from my face. "It's bill collecting day today. I'm not looking forward to lying to all my suppliers. I'm really not looking forward to them not believing me."

"That's crazy," said Terrence, surveying the temporarily-packed joint. "I can't see how this place isn't profitable. Everyone loves your shop."

"I know. But there's love, and then there's volume." I shifted my weight off the cancer leg and crunched coffee beans. I looked down at the beans scattered on the floor around Terrence.

"Spence was throwing beans at me," Terrence explained.

"You see beans. I see pennies."

I knuckle-knocked him and joined Charlotte and Spence behind the bar. "Grande skinny mocha," Charlotte told me.

Spence stepped away from the machine and started tidying up the bean buckets. I popped out the portafilter and knocked the old grounds into the trash hole, with authority. "How's things?"

"We had a fairly good morning," said Charlotte. "Maybe five hundred." Under her breath she asked, "Did you see Mr. and Mrs. Adultery?"

"Hard to miss them."

Bob Macafee is a State Farm insurance agent. He's been selling insurance for years, a highly visible face in the community—he smiles at you from a billboard at the south end of town, and seriously contemplates your insurance needs in one of the silent still-shot ads that run before every movie at the Buffalo Cinema Seven. Bob was recently divorced, again. Everyone knows he's a letch, except those to whom it matters most, his ladyfriend targets.

Greta Church had worked for the county for twenty years. Also very visible. But still married. They stood whispering by the Culligan water dispenser. Their lips were inches apart. Bob was stroking Greta's arm. Greta's forty-five year old hips were doing slow gyrations, tempting Bob's forty-eight year old penis. They pretended to be conducting confidential business—from time to time Bob would throw out an insurance term— but their puppy lust was obvious to anyone watching.

And we were all watching. Our little public peep show. Sometimes they would park in a secluded spot by the shop. (There wasn't really such a spot.) Then the gawking began, a constant parade of my customers and employees past their car. We were forced to walk closer and closer as the windows fogged over from all the dry humping.

Times like this, we were treated to an in-store heavy petting show. They would squeeze themselves into a corner. Thinking that their Klingon cloaking device was working, they would go to town. Bob was an unbelievable salesman, able to talk himself and his newest squeeze into precarious, ridiculous, adulterous situations.

"If they gotta be adulterers," I grumbled, "then I guess they gotta be. But do they have to do it in my shop?"

"I overheard a little bit of the conversation," said Spence. "I think they're debating which motel to check into."

"I hope they don't choose the Motel 6 again," Charlotte complained. "My sister hates it when she has to listen to Bob tell her the room is for an out-of-town client."

"That's where I conduct my insurance business," I said. "Out of town in a room at the Motel 6. Grande skinny mocha," I announced.

"Thanks Brian," said Cat Jefferies.

"Any time, lady."

"Oh yeah," said Charlotte, "and Liza is using all our paper again."

Liza sat at the display window table, scribbling furiously on my paper. I bought tower blocks of three-by-three-inch scrap paper, for us or our customers to jot down notes or reminders. "Liza", this woman with plastered black hair and clown makeup who reminded us of Liza Minnelli, would peel off big hunks of my paper, write for a couple hours, plowing through sheet after sheet and mumbling to herself all the while, and then push the heap of paper into her handbag and hurry out. Each tower cost me ten bucks. I was betting Liza had gone through three of them.

"That really burns me," I said. "Can't she bring her own paper? Charlotte, go tell her to stop."

Charlotte shook her head vehemently. "She's psycho. It's your shop. You go do something about it."

"How much did she take?"

"About two inches." Charlotte spread her thumb and forefinger to demonstrate. The gap was more like three. She raised her eyebrows, as fed up with my gutlessness as I was with Liza stealing my paper.

"Alright, I better go say something." I shuddered. "I wonder if I could write her a note and throw it on her table as I run by."

"It would just get lost in her pile," Charlotte pointed out. "Uh-oh." She nodded at the door. In walked Mr. Greta (Trent) Church, like a gunslinger into the saloon. "Ooh, this is going to be good."

Trent stood like he was a customer in line. I nudged Charlotte. "Ask him if he wants something to drink."

"Do we have whiskey?" she whispered.

That reminded me of the Kenny Rogers song where the big heartbroken farmer—and Trent Church was big, he was a mountain of a man—begs his wife Lucille not to leave. I actually had that song in the random CD loop. If we had a particularly rowdy morning crowd, I could lead a honky-tonk sing-along when it popped up. I hoped it wouldn't happen now.

Trent started forward. Bob Macafee saw him, gave Greta a little shove to create space between them. She had a hurt puzzled look on her face as her big husband bore down on them. Without the hard-on I'm sure Bob would have wet himself.

Seems Trent wasn't so much heartbroken as insanely angry. "What are you doing?!" he asked his wife. I think he was trying to keep his voice down, but it boomed through the shop. Cat Jefferies jumped a foot in the air.

Greta shook her head, looking at the floor. Bob raised a shaking hand and stepped forward. "Let's talk about this—"

Trent swatted his hand away. "Shut up Bob, and stay out of this."

"I think this concerns me," said Bob in a quavering voice.

Charlotte and I glanced at each other. Her eyebrows were way up there. Considering the weather I was wondering whether I should preemptively call 911 to give the ambulance a head start.

Into my shop walked Frannie the sign nazi, removing her hair scarf and shaking sleet on my floor. I decided I truly hated that woman. More than the city and its inconsistent rules. More than Bill Hernandes and his quest to put me out of business. More than ticks and crushing injuries.

Trent towered over Bob. "Step away from me. Right now."

"I can't do that." Bob mumbled, because his balls cuddled his larynx.

Nazi Frannie slithered toward me. As luck would have it, John Jones from the city council was in the house, having coffee with PK, Pastor Kyle. They were scooting their chairs to clear space for big Trent Church to operate. PK bumped Cat Jefferies, who spilled her drink and called for a rag. It was a busy day at the shop, my kind of atmosphere, minus the nazi.

Trent's hands were balled into fists the size of boxing gloves. He was leaning forward while Greta burrowed into his stomach, pushing him back. "You don't know what you're messing with," he snarled at Bob.

"You don't know what you've been doing to her," Bob squeaked.

As I came around the bar my cellphone was playing Funkytown on the counter. "Could you get that for me?" I asked Charlotte, doubting she could hear me over Trent and Bob.

"What I do with my wife is none of your damn business!"

"I'm making it my business…"

I tried to catch somebody's eye as I approached. "Hey you guys."

"…you need to listen to your wife."

"You don't tell me a sonofabitchin' thing about my wife!"

"Guys," I whispered like they were not yet making a scene.

"Gentlemen," said PK.

"Mr. Lawson," said nazi Frannie. The crazy hag was right behind me.

"Trent, Bob, Greta," I said sharply, getting their attention and pointing toward the door. "I like a good scrum as much as the next guy, but you have to take this outside."

"Brian, I apologize for this," said Bob, playing the grownup's role.

I wanted to punch him in the nose. I wished Trent would just get it over with. Maybe strike Frannie a glancing death blow. "Let's go." I ushered Trent into an about-face. He crossed the floor in five giant strides and blasted the door open. Greta hurried after him, looking at no one, while Bob apologized on Trent's behalf to anyone who made eye contact.

I kept him moving, out the door and into the blizzard. When I turned around there was Frannie, sticking a piece of paper in my face. I looked past her to see Charlotte beckoning me with my phone.

"Mr. Lawson—"

"Excuse me Frannie." I ducked around the nazi and caught a glimpse of Liza tearing a fresh sheet off the stack. My stack. "Hey." I leaned over the table and lowered my voice. "I'm really sorry, but I'm going to have to ask you not to use all our paper."

She blinked at me. Her mascara was clumped on her eyelashes, a little clinging to her pencil eyebrows. I wish I could say she didn't look like Liza Minnelli up close. "I'm writing letters," she said.

"I know." The shouting outside was distracting. "But it's expensive for me to supply you with paper all the time."

Liza laid her arms across the scattered pile of used sheets. "I have my own paper, you know."

"Then you should use it." I resisted grabbing my depleted stack of paper as I left her table. I put a hand in front of the nazi's face before she could speak. "Frannie, I have a phone call."

Frannie stayed right on my tail. Her thin raspy voice made my neck hair stand up. "It's Francesca, Mr. Lawson. And this bill is past due."

"If it makes you feel any better, that's not my only one."

"The fine is set to double tomorrow. I wanted to give you a grace period."

At least I think that's what she said. The argument outside my front door was loud. I admit that I was straining to hear what they were saying, which shouldn't count as eavesdropping. My customers looked uncomfortable. "PK," I said, "can't you break it up and counsel them through this?"

"Well I thought about it," said Pastor Kyle. "But I don't want to get punched out."

"Me neither," said Councilman Jones. "Brian, it is your shop."

"That's what Charlotte tells me." I looked down at Councilman Jones. "John, I'd really like you to see what you can do about this sandwich board fine." I put my forearm in the small of Frannie's skeletal back and nudged her forward. "Otherwise I'm going to mount big blinking neon signs on each side of my building. Really."

Councilman Jones tipped his chair back and looked at Frannie like she was a dentist with a big whirring drill.

"Can I call them back?" I asked Charlotte as I backpedaled toward the door and the cockfight cacophony outside.

Charlotte pointed at the phone. "It's your doctor."

I made a face and stuck my head outside. "Guys." Trent and Bob stopped in mid-argument, face to face tucked against the side of the building under my little awning. Why hadn't Trent killed him yet? "We can hear you in here. It's distracting for my customers." The sports fan in me wanted to watch, the business person knew better. Not much better, but a little. "You're going to have to take it further away."

Both men looked at the wall of sleet coming down sideways. Greta was already standing in it, white on one side. She took off walking across the street and Trent followed her. Bob hesitated and then started after them.

"Bob, I wouldn't." Not waiting to see his fateful decision, I hustled back across the floor. Councilman Jones and Frannie now occupied Macafee's make-out corner, John receiving a verbatim reading from the city code book. Conversational buzz resumed. I took the phone from Charlotte. "Hey doc."

Liza walked up to the bar across from me. She had a handful of loose three-by-three sheets. She waited until I looked at her and then threw them at me, flinging the little paper snowstorm right in my face.

"Brian, are you there?" said Dr. Bonilla. "I wanted to talk to you about…"

"I'm never coming back in here," said Liza.

"Good, because you can't," I told her. Liza sashayed out the door, with a certain savoir faire, a certain practiced grace, a touch of star quality. Holy cow, I thought, could it be?

I had to re-start Dr. Bonilla again. "I'm sorry doc, could you say that again? I'll listen this time."

"I'd like to have you come down and discuss your MRI results. Are you available…" He did his best to strip the urgency from his voice. "…now?"

"Right now?" I did my best not to sound scared shitless. "No. But I could be there in fifteen minutes."

"That's reasonable," said Dr. Bonilla. "Come up to my office on three."

I disconnected the call and set my hat on the counter so I could wipe away the sweat. "Aw cripes."

"What?" Charlotte was prepared for the worst. "What did he say?"

"He wants to see me. Not tomorrow. Not this afternoon. Now." I bent over the counter and looked at the ghostly reflection of my great big shiny forehead. "You know, sometimes I get a glimpse of myself and I just go, 'What am I thinking? How could I have left the house looking like this? Am I serious?' You know what I mean?"

"So you're strange looking," said Charlotte. "Nothing's changed."

"Yeah? Yeah, I suppose you're right. How do I get friends then? Why do people seem to like me?"

"It's the coffee," Charlotte said definitively.

Edna Applejack walked in. She was wearing a woolen scarf over her head, sunglasses, and a short denim jacket over a form-fitting lacy pink dress. Everyone stopped what they were doing and stared. Only when Edna peeled back the scarf and removed the sunglasses did the greetings fly and excitement buzz through the shop.

"That was a good disguise," I said. I was ignored. Charlotte forgot I had cancer and ran to the till.

"What can I get for you?" she asked before Edna was anywhere near the counter. She was talking and laughing gaily with Pastor Kyle. Councilman Jones practically threw Frannie aside to get back to the table before Edna moved on. Too late. She bypassed Charlotte and came to me.

"Lady."

"Mr. Brian. I've been thinking about your proposition all morning."

"What proposition?" Charlotte demanded.

"Edna can't answer that, because I haven't made it yet," I said.

"What is it?" Charlotte demanded.

"It's secret," I said. "I guess I have two propositions for you," I told Edna. "The first one is, you wanna come to the hospital with me?"

"Sure," she said, and quite a few people in the shop groaned. The crowd sank into a sullen state as I made two double-tall cappuccinos, some of my best work, and then slipped out the back with their precious Edna in tow.

My precious. "So here's the deal." I maneuvered the van out of the lot behind my building. Cancer privileges, I had started taking a spot. A spot-and-a-half, because I am a poor perpendicular parker. "There's only one place in this town where a coffeeshop is an automatic moneymaker," I told Edna. "The campus. And there's only one person in town or in the world who would be allowed to open a shop on campus."

"You," said Edna.

"No. Whoopsies, look out." Almost flattened a pedestrian crossing the alley with her head bowed against the storm. "But hold that thought for the next statement of fact. Which is, there's only one person in this town who knows how to run a successful coffeeshop."

"Bill Hernandes," said Edna.

While I was pretending to be offended while Edna pretended to be serious, I took a quick glance at her smooth egg-shaped kneecap. I could imagine the temporary paralysis when that kneecap speared my thigh as Edna took a power hop-step into the lane to establish position for a short deadly jumper. "The campus is the only sure thing I've ever seen. I've coveted it since the day I arrived. It's the best spot in town. Maybe the only spot."

Not only was the JC campus a retail goldmine, but it's a Christian college. I used to be pretty confident in my relationship with God, until cancer screwed with my head. Seemed straightforward that you believe in God and go to church and feel bad for your bad deeds, and you get into Heaven in the end. Now I wasn't sure at all whether my everlasting soul was in good hands. Assuming Jesus was a capitalist in favor of his minions making reasonable profits from other minions on sales of a quality product, partnering with a Christian school had to burnish my eternal résumé.

"Bill says the endcap at the Bluffs is the best place in town," Edna parroted with authority. "He says it's the hard corner."

"The hard corner, huh?" I steadied my cappuccino as we fishtailed onto Main. Brought the cup to my lips; but after fasting for the MRI, after the call from Dr. Bonilla, my stomach wasn't prepared to receive the tasty offering. "Bill's got the lingo down. But he doesn't know what he's talking about. For one thing, it's not a corner. It's a strip mall along a highway. And even if it was on a corner, there would need to be another couple thousand homes up there to make it a desirable location. Hard corner. Come on."

"Then why did you work so hard to steal it from him?"

"I made the required payment before the contractual deadline. So technically, it never was Bill's location. And when there's a contract involved, the technicalities matter."

"But originally you were only willing to put a store up here"—we were cresting the hill leading to the hospital and the Bluffs—"because Mike promised to finance the whole thing."

"If you want to get technical, yes."

"And then you had sex with his ex-daughter-in-law, so he offered it to Bill."

"While I have been schtupping Andrea for some time now, I believe Mike found out about it after giving Bill the Bluffs. Still, probably fair payback in Mike's eyes."

Edna fell silent while I pulled into a spot on the south edge of the hospital parking lot, closest to the Bluffs. "Crap," I said, counting at least five construction workers scurrying in and out of the new shop. "They're already spending my money over there."

"Mike is eager to get it done, regardless who owns it," said Edna, monotone, eyes fixed on the van's outdoor temperature gauge, which read 28°F—and then warmed up two degrees under her intense stare.

It was like waiting for my dad to make a decision. Their styles were similar—a deep retreat into their own thoughts, faces serene, one knee pistoning two strokes a second.

Edna's leg stopped jimmying. She turned her big blue eyes on me. "Did you know that a friend of mine at the state pen used to get your coffee and share it with me?"

"Kerry Bjornson."

"That's right," said Edna.

"She robbed a farmhouse outside of town, and then burned it down."

"The McGoogans. Snowbirds who were gone nine months a year. They tried to recruit me to play for Arizona State. I never cared for them. Kerry burned their house down by accident. She was a basket case in prison."

"Did you make her your bitch?"

"No."

"Good, because I slipped her a shiv in a pound of Guatemalan."

"Did you really?"

"No, but I always wanted to try, to see if I could get away with it."

With a smile Edna reached over and turned off my van. "I like you, Brian. Jamestown is lucky to have a guy like you. Let's get you healed."

WE EXITED the elevator on the third floor. "You don't mind doing this with me?" I asked.

"I'm not squeamish about cancer," said Edna.

"Me neither." We stopped outside Dr. Bonilla's open door. "I do have a big issue with dying though."

"It happens," said Edna. I had a flash vision of her long white fingers around my throat. There were worse ways to go. She linked her arm with mine, took my hand in both of hers, and we crossed the threshold together.

"Edna Applejack!" Dr. Bonilla exclaimed, launching out of his chair. "What a surprise! Hi Brian," he said as an afterthought.

"Hello doc. You two know each other?"

"Not exactly. I'm Paul doctor—Doctor Paul—I'm Paul. Bonilla. I'm a doctor." He wanted to shake Edna's hand, which meant she had to let go of mine, which I was reluctant to allow. "I'm an Edgeley boy," Dr. Bonilla plowed forward, mastering his tongue. "I followed your career closely."

"Where did you go to college, Paul?"

"UND. Both my undergrad and med school."

"You stayed in-state to get your MD," Edna approved. "I've heard the med school in Grand Forks does a fabulous job."

"I like to think so," said Dr. Bonilla.

"I like to hope so," I said.

"So…" Dr. Bonilla was uncertain what came next.

"Edna's not afraid of cancer," I told him, and became weak in the knees. "I am though. I'd like to sit down."

Dr. Bonilla guided me to a chair and Edna into the hall. "We'll be a little while, if you want to wait in the lounge." He stepped back into the room and closed the door. "That's pretty special that Edna came with you," he complimented, probably puzzling how a bald scarecrow had pulled it off.

I wondered the same thing. "It's just business," was the only explanation.

Dr. Bonilla nodded, not comprehending. "So, your results."

"I didn't expect to hear anything until tomorrow."

Dr. Bonilla perched on the corner of his desk, hands tucked under his armpits. "Unfortunately they didn't turn out as good as we had hoped. You have a more aggressive cancer than we thought. I've discussed—"

"It moved?" I croaked, trembling.

"It spread," Dr. Bonilla qualified, and the room tilted. "We're seeing signs of malignancy in the abdomen, and the pelvic area." He used his own body as a demonstration device, waving his hand over the areas where the cancer was currently going about killing me.

I had to stand up. I was compressing the cancer, squishing it, squirting it all over my insides. I would never sit down again.

Dr. Bonilla realized I was falling before I did. He slipped his arm around me while the floor tilted like the deck of the Titanic. I managed to turn away from him and threw up on his small gray filing cabinet. One of the drawers was partially open. My brain decided I was vomiting up my own cancer-ravaged stomach lining, which really freaked me out. I hurled with a vengeance, gasping and choking and trying to identify the chunks I was filing. An orderly put a towel to my face and we marched out of the office and down the hall, me coughing and crying and retching all the way.

I was in the bathroom so long that Bonilla probably tried to slip out for a drink with Edna. The brave young orderly stayed with me for the duration. I made a lot of noise in there. I should have been embarrassed to limp out and climb in the waiting wheelchair while nurses, doctors and Edna watched. But I was empty, no shame or Cream of Wheat or thoughts of seeing June.

I apologized to the orderly and then the nurse who helped me into a bed, and then Bonilla when he stood over me, not because I was sorry, only because it was the polite thing to do. I didn't want anyone thinking I went peacefully or willingly. I'd rather go down making a scene, kicking and screaming and spewing my guts everywhere. I wanted the spectators traumatized. Disturbed. Devastated, if I could help it.

I couldn't believe what I had heard. I didn't want to say a thing, or move a muscle; I wanted to listen and feel for the cancer inside, make self-confirmation that the doctors' interpretations of my MRI were correct. This was denial. It lasted a couple minutes. Then I started to cry.

"I want you to take some deep breaths," said Bonilla. "This is not out of the ordinary. I've been through similar developments before, and it is not as bleak as it sounds. We have more weapons we can use…"

Blah blah blah. I was a dead man. I looked past Bonilla—I would no longer call him doctor, unless it was Kevorkian, because doctors saved lives, and Bonilla was only hastening my demise. Edna stood in the doorway. I pulled the van keys out of my pocket. "Here you go. I shouldn't have dragged you down here."

Edna gave my hand a nice squeeze as she took the keys. "What should I do with your van?"

"Keep it."

She bent closer, assuming I hadn't the strength to finish my sentence. "Keep it where?"

"At your house. Or sell it if it's not your style. Whatever." Brian Lawson, master thespian of the overly dramatic, or the king of understatement. But this was no act. "I'm not going to need it any more."

"Brian, you need to slow down a little here." Bonilla sat on the bed and rested his hand on my good knee. "You are going to die someday, but it might be a few decades. What's happening inside you right now isn't good. But it isn't a death sentence."

"It spread," I filled Edna in. "All over me." I wept softly.

Bonilla continued addressing me. "We can see two nodules, one below the stomach and the other in your groin. Neither was big enough to detect during the physical exam I gave you prior to the MRI. That's a good thing. There are a few very small shadows in the surrounding digestive cavity that we'll need to follow up on—"

"Great," I sobbed. "More follow-up."

Bonilla raised his voice and talked over me. "—but that might not be anything. We get blips."

Blips and shadows, things a doctor doesn't have to take seriously. Never mind they always turned into tumors. Bonilla was more shook up by my despair than my cancer. Regardless the outcome, I got the feeling he would sleep well at night knowing he had followed standard procedure. Under Bonilla's interpretation of the Hippocratic Oath, the physician was graded not on healing but on strict adherence to the published guidelines.

"Wherever it is, Brian, you have to fight it." Edna dropped into a crouch and rested her pointy chin on the mattress. "You're a lucky guy, actually. You have yourself a partner who can pick up the slack while you're in treatment."

Andrea? I was thinking, wanting to cry more.

"You and I will carry each other through the tough times," said Edna.

She was going to partner with me. I sniffled and dried my tears.

"Did I miss the engagement notice?" Bonilla asked. A married man, he still seemed crestfallen Edna might be off the market. Another reason for him not to risk pulling a mental muscle straining to find a way to beat my cancer.

Edna kissed my forehead and stood. "It's a business partnership. But that doesn't mean we aren't going to break some hearts." She left the room, with my keys. Bonilla stared after her, thinking about me, thinking about Edna, I don't know.

He sighed. "Brian, the way I see it, you have two treatment options." I didn't want choices. I wanted Bonilla to tell me how he was going to cure me. "I could point you to a grief counseling group. We have ten or so terminal patients and their loved ones that get together regularly."

"Ten, or so?"

"The membership fluctuates."

"Nice to see you haven't lost your sense of humor."

"I got that one from one of the members of the group. You'd be amazed at how they come to grips with their mortality. It can be a little shocking at first."

I closed my eyes. "Maybe I should attend. I should probably get to the point where I'm not so afraid of dying that I go out crying and puking."

"It's a heckuva deal, isn't it?" Bonilla studied me. "You can pretend there's nothing wrong, nothing to be afraid of, and then get blindsided at the end.

Or you can spend all your time adjusting to the possibility you could die, preparing for death and beyond. Either seems like a strange way to live."

"What's my second option?"

"You can decide you're going to live, and we can hit this thing even harder." Bonilla climbed all the way onto the bed. His thin arm was beside my head, his skin radiating a powerful clean, like he had scrubbed, dried and deodorized each hair individually. "We'll use a different chemotherapy cocktail, at a more aggressive dosage. We'll go after anything living. We'll knock out what's left of your hair, stop your fingernails from growing, make everything inside and out sore. And kill the cancer."

"I like that part." Sniffing a man's arm, feeling comforted by the heat of his hand on my stomach. Only in a hospital. "And you could spend the next couple weeks researching what's out there, in case other doctors are having luck with new treatments, or new breakthrough drugs."

"I know exactly what to use. It's well documented in the literature." Bonilla rubbed my tummy and slid off the bed. "We'll discontinue the last two days of this cycle and start the new dose Monday. Ordinarily I'd wait a couple weeks for your body to recover. But that means the cancer recovers too. We're not going to allow that."

He threw a right hook to my jaw to affirm his tenacity. Bonilla was going to cure me by the force of his determination. The chemo was nothing but a backup. Probably a placebo. Might have worked if I had any faith left in him.

"I'll still point you to the grief group if you'd like."

"I'd have us drinking Guyana-flavored Kool-Aid by the third meeting."

Two candy stripers came in and scrubbed the vomit off my shirt sleeve. Bonilla winked at me. "You hang in there Brian. I'll see you Monday."

THE SHIRT was damp, clinging to my chest and making me shiver as Edna drove me back to the shop. "Maybe you should wear pants," she suggested.

"It's almost June. I can't wear pants in the summer." My teeth chattered. "Even if it is snowing."

"You feeling better?"

"I'm not going to throw up again anyway."

"Was it the chemo drugs that made you toss your cookies?"

"And bawl? No, it was fear. I'm pretty sure I'm going to die soon."

"I think you're in great hands. Dr. Bonilla seems very talented."

"You only think so because he got his MD in North Dakota," I said. Edna's face clouded and I received a displeased look. I decided to move along. "I don't think Bonilla likes my chances. He's been hitting it with surgery and radiation and every chemo drug in the book, and the cancer keeps coming."

"You seem like the kind of guy who can beat long odds." Edna squeezed my knee. The other knee. "How are your parents handling it?"

"Not great. They keep asking me to move home. I don't plan on telling them about today."

"You have to be honest with your folks, and trust they can handle it," said Edna. "If they're anything like you, they can."

"If they're like me, they'll throw up on the phone and start wailing. Actually," I admitted, "they're a couple of the toughest people I know. And you're right. When this wave of despair wears off, I'll be ready to beat this thing."

Edna gave me what looked like a flirtatious smile. That couldn't have been Evolution talking. Guys riddled with cancer and full of pluck were inspirational, but didn't offer the best odds at perpetuating your bloodline. "While you were recuperating I talked to Bobby Guldseth, the AD at the College." Edna drove with one hand down the slick slushy hill into downtown. The brake lights of the cars ahead flashed, trying to warn us. "He's going to set up a meeting with Terry Lovold, the head of Student Affairs."

"Did you get a sense whether Bobby thinks a campus shop is possible?"

Edna laughed. "I got a sense alright."

Ahead of us a little pickup fishtailed and then lost it, occupying most of both lanes as it drifted sideways downhill. I felt the thump and heard the frictional whirr of brakes locking all around us. Edna slipped the van into Neutral and guided us to the left, squeezing between the meridian and the bumper of the sliding pickup. I nodded to the driver, Kip Carlson, who was looking over his shoulder, pretending to steer. We eased past him. I looked back and watched Kip spin another ninety degrees to face downhill again, and then drive straight into the steep ditch, taking a little Honda economy car with him. No need to call 911; we glided through a bottleneck created by a tow truck, an ambulance and two police cars already assisting at another accident scene at the bottom of the hill.

Edna shifted back into Drive and tucked a loose tendril of kinky blonde hair behind her ear. "That's a tricky hill." North Dakota was right. This woman was special. She would be good at anything. NASCAR, B-ball, tiddlywinks… coffee. "By the time I was done talking to Bobby," she continued her story, "he was begging me to put a coffeeshop on campus."

I was dazed, unable to comprehend the speed with which we had become partners. One thing was for sure: Edna was my goldmine. Assuming I lived to see the new year, I was going to get a shop in the promised land. "So when's the meeting with Terry Lovold?"

"I don't know yet. Do me a favor though. We need to swing a good deal on rent, so don't seem too eager when we talk to Terry."

"I don't think that'll be a problem."

I had dealt with Terry Lovold when I first moved to Jamestown. With five thousand students rich enough to afford the pricey tuition, stranded on a campus isolated by the river, I knew where I needed to be.

When I couldn't get an appointment with Terry, I had driven onto campus, admiring the old New England style buildings with fresh paint on the wood and ivy clinging to the brick, and pretty coeds strolling along the riverwalk under some of the only trees in the state. The administration building had a clock tower and a spire with a cross.

I had walked up to Terry Lovold's secretary and asked to see her. Terry heard my voice and walked out of her office. "Mr. Lawson, I was going to return your calls. There was no need to come in."

"Hi. I'm Brian." I had turned on the charm, until it became obvious it would get me nowhere.

"You're interested in putting one of your shops on campus."

"I thought it might be a win-win—"

"The College has a strict policy against allowing commercial interests to locate on campus. So I'm sorry."

"Is that a religious decision? Because I'm very…"

Terry shook her head so hard I couldn't keep talking. "It's campus policy."

"How about right next to campus?" At this point I already hated her. "I mean right next door. With a big sign the kids can see from the other side of campus. I could call it God's Brew."

"You'll find out that the College owns most of the land adjacent to the campus." Terry is structurally attractive, thick glossy hair and smooth golden skin, with the face and style of television's 1950's mom. But with every word she looked more like Disney's wicked stepmother. "I'll give you a tip. There's a retail development in process across the river. A company owned by a gentleman by the name of Mike McEwen is refurbishing an old newspaper building. You should look into opening a shop there. Okay?"

"Thanks for the tip."

My wicked stepmom wouldn't let me go to the ball. But everyone knows what happened when Cinderella got herself a powerful goddess.

T-5

WEDNESDAY NIGHT Edna cooked for me. She lived in a brick house in the ritzy end of town, north of the Bluffs retail center and with approximately the same square footage. In her marble kitchen, in her Wolf oven, Edna broiled a herb-crusted flank steak that I couldn't stop eating, because of a certain spice that drove me wild, until it was gone, at least a pound of meat, by far the most I'd eaten since the diagnosis.

I chased the steak with a cup of green tea and two shots of ouzo, which aided my digestion as the Greeks promised, a miracle given that yogurt shakes were the only protein my stomach had been contending with during the current round of chemo.

It came as quite a surprise, that Edna might be hot for me. My head was shaved but my hair was still obviously thin, and patchy, my skin pasty. I limped from the pain in my leg, which made me appear not two but three inches shorter than her. And I had cyclophosphamide breath. And yet she stood close to me. She squeezed my thigh a good six inches above the knee when she left the couch to grab the ouzo bottle. She said suggestive things, like, "How drunk do I have to be to get you to put me to bed before you leave?" Like Charlotte said, it must be the coffee.

We didn't really talk strategy for the next day's meeting. Edna just went on about how excited she was to work with me, how she was looking forward to being back on campus again, how we were going to make a boatload of money—and would we be able to turn the shops over to our employees for a week at a time so we could take vacations together? Listening to her I could believe I had a long life ahead of me.

She was different at home, just the two of us. She spoke more softly. She looked me in the eye for extended periods. She operated inside my personal space, the space many men dreamed of sharing with Edna Applejack. I was touched by the care she put into cooking and making me comfortable; and I was surprised at the sad shadow across her face when she made an offhand reference to the time lost in prison. Had I assumed she lived life to the fullest in the slammer? That life was good for Edna Applejack regardless whether fate put her behind bars, or burka-bagged her for some Taliban freak, or decreed a windswept rural existence? Yes. So I might have overreacted to her vulnerability that night, and I was probably overly flattered that she allowed me to see it, hoping that she couldn't help it because she was so deeply smitten with me. I wanted Edna in deep smit, because I sure was.

WHEN WE met Thursday afternoon in the JC parking lot, Edna hurried over to me and grabbed my hand and pressed against me. When my first girlfriend on our first date slid across the bench seat of my folks' Cutlass Sierra to sit hip to hip with me, that's what it felt like.

"Pants and everything," Edna approved, giving me the once-over.

"Are you ready for this?" I could talk quietly, the only way my throat liked it anymore, because she walked so close to me.

"Let's go get us a campus coffeeshop," said Edna. This was the trigger for a rapid transformation back to her public persona. She was calling out to administration old-timers from her glory days and smiling at star-struck students practically creaming in their pants as we crossed the lobby and walked into the office of the VP of Student Affairs without knocking.

Terry Lovold hurried around her desk. "Edna! It's so good to see you again!" A sizeable gentleman with dark Brylcreemed hair abandoned his guest chair in time to avoid a midget's-eye view of Terry's breast as she hugged Edna. Terry wore her blouse and skirt tight, but it didn't feel like a bid for sex appeal. From my impression of her, she was punishing her big tits and sweet childbearing hips for making her look soft and feminine and would have worn a suit and tie like Mr. Brylcreem if she could have gotten away with it. Maybe the answer was simpler, she was ready to move up a size.

"You know Brian Lawson?" Edna introduced me.

Terry pretended not to as she shook my hand. "Hi. Terry Lovold."

"We've met," I said.

"Glen." Edna saved up a big hug and kiss for Mr. Glen Brylcreem. "Long time no see."

"Edna," Glen purred. "You are a sight for sore eyes." He hugged her like he meant it, enveloping her, bending her backward, getting grease on her face. If he hadn't been the president of the College, I would have had to challenge him. Snap my depleted twig of an arm on his square jaw.

"Brian Lawson," I announced. "I own James River Valley Coffee."

"Great little establishment you have there," said Glen. He must have been talking about the exterior because I knew for a fact he had never set foot in my shop. "Jamestown is lucky to have you."

"Isn't there another coffeeshop," Terry wondered, "closer to campus?"

"There is a coffeeshop across the river," I said. "And he calls it Campus Coffee. But it's actually a little further."

Terry frowned and nodded in the general direction of Hernandes' shop. "But it's right across the river."

"It would be closer, you're right," I said, "if you had a boat. It is closer as the crow flies. Supposing you were a crow."

"I still think it's closer," said Terry.

"Excluding sailors and crows, I'm closer by almost two hundred yards."

"Sounds like you've already stepped off the distances," Glen joked.

"I get upset when a competitor resorts to false advertising. That's all."

Edna threw me a warning look and indicated that everyone should take their seats. "So let's talk about a real campus coffeeshop." She remained standing, waiting for everyone else to sit. Gentleman Glen was determined to wait for Edna. They ended up sitting down together, synchronized sitters, foreplay for Glen from the way he licked his lips as he gazed upon her.

I worried whether they had something going on. A steamy affair would guarantee us a campus shop; I was ready to give up coffee and sell Mary Kay to keep Edna to myself.

"Bobby tells us you'd like to open a coffeeshop here." Glen spoke to Edna. He had to lean forward and look past me to do so. His voice was deep and confident. The hair on his temple was a vividly etched curve sprinkled with a touch of gray, perfect sidewalls. He crossed his legs like a girl and still looked like a man. "Terry and I have discussed it. It's an interesting concept."

"It's a concept we can make a reality before the leaves start to fall," I said. "Which is early August around here, am I right?"

Glen humored me with a polite smile, and then got back to ignoring me. "We feel you're the key to this idea, Edna. You would be the draw. The reason why kids come in."

"I've never done a study to back this up," I said, "but the key to a successful coffeeshop has to be the quality of the coffee. You bring in Bill Hernandes to run things, and you'll be out of business in two years. No offense to Bill; but he doesn't know jack about coffee."

Edna eyeballed me like I was dangerous. To avoid having you draw any more unflattering conclusions about me, I probably should have skipped this detailed description of the meeting and just reported to you that everything went fine and we got the shop. But I'm not ashamed to say I'm a little competitive. I'm accustomed to being the first and last one talking. Not an easy transition to fourth wheel on the trike.

And my mental state, it wasn't all that stable. I was three days gone from a death sentence, three days away from starting a really aggressive round of chemo that Bonilla promised would destroy every living thing inside me. And still leave me alive? Only if I was somehow more than the sum of my dead parts. If I had any dependents to provide for, I would have started trafficking my innards on e-bay while they were still functioning. Do some self-surgery. Start a bidding war among research institutions specializing in deformed organs.

"Edna is an important part of this deal," I said. "But you need to know that I have a great track record running coffeeshops here and in California."

"We'll be sure to check your references before we decide on anything," Glen promised. "So Edna, tell me." He uncrossed his legs and shifted onto one buttock, tilting toward Edna, getting intimate with her through me. "Can we expect to see you here morning, noon and night?"

"Do you think you could keep me away?" Edna rose and spun around her chair, gliding behind me. She was taking over the meeting and I had no ability to contain her. I could imagine similar frustration from defenders back in the day when Edna made an unexpected backdoor cut to the hoop for an alley-oop slam. She gave me a disciplinary pat on the back, continuing on behind Glen, laying a softer hand on him. She perched on the corner of the desk. "I have missed our school so much. Having the opportunity to come back is so exciting for me. I have many opportunities in Jamestown, as I'm sure you can imagine. But I want to be here with you. At the College." Edna clasped her hands to her chest. "It's where my heart is."

"We are so excited to have you," said Terry. "The students would be thrilled to have a living legend on campus."

"You would be a powerful recruiting tool," said Glen. "And not just for athletics."

"Your name means excellence," said Terry. "Period."

"That's why I believe Edna is the perfect partner for James River Valley Coffee," I said. "We both stand for excellence."

"Brian's coffee is wonderful," Edna testified, staring at me, a frozen smile on her face, willing me to shut up. "He has a great reputation in the community that will carry over to our campus shop. Brian could go anywhere in town—anywhere, period. And he chose me and the College."

"The town has any number of very fine retailers," said Terry. "I can't tell you how many times we've had to regretfully reject proposals to partner with the College. Everyone wants to be on our campus."

"It's your students," I said. "They're rich."

Edna cleared her throat to reclaim Glen and Terry's attention. "The sophistication of the JC student base makes this an attractive coffeehouse market. This is really win-win, you guys." She got chatty, and Glen and Terry ate it up. "The shop will be profitable. And you get to offer an amenity that a lot of the top schools are providing to their students."

"Which brings us to our preferred plan," said Terry. "We'll own the shop, so that the College retains control over the hours, the menu, the staffing. Edna, you'll manage the store. Brian, we'll pay you a licensing and consulting fee for your business model and expertise." She was unaffected by my head wagging back and forth. "The name will have to be closely linked to the College, with a possible religious theme. Eternal Brew, something along those lines."

"No, no, no," I said.

This was mild compared to Edna's reaction. She blew past Glen, picked up her handbag, and said sharply, "We're singing from different hymnals. Brian has no interest in selling his management style, and I don't care to be your figurehead." She gave me a nod and I jumped to my feet. "Thank you for your time, Glen. Good luck here. I hope you can come up with a workable plan to give these students a quality coffeeshop."

Glen clutched Edna's hand. "We want you in here." Belatedly he took a step back and spread his arms. "We want you both. Brian," he said solemnly, sincerely, "we know you have a great product. And Edna...you know how much we love you. How much you mean to the College. We'll work this out."

"I love what you're saying," said Edna. "But the only things to work out are where we're going to build it, and when we can start."

"Agreed," said Glen.

AND THAT was that. Ten minutes later we walked out with a handshake deal to open a James River Valley coffeeshop next to the student union.

"That went unbelievably well," I said at Edna's car. "I can't wait to get together to start mapping out the steps to opening day."

"We'll start now, by breaking the good news to Bill," said Edna.

"Mm?"

"Let's go tell Bill he gets the Bluffs site after all."

"I guess...yeah, I guess that is good news." I'm not a procrastinator. I like to move at high speed. My speed. Edna's pace made my head spin. "We're sure this is a done deal?"

"I can guarantee it, sweetie." Edna hugged me hard. A lesser man would have yelped, because I had a severe neck ache, like a knife in the spine. When Edna hugged me that knife jabbed up into my brain. I was already convinced that chunks of my cancer could be jarred loose from their relatively harmless locations and end up sticking somewhere vital. This knife-in-the-noggin sensation only fed my compulsion to remain perfectly still at all times.

Edna tipped her head back and soaked up the weak sun. "I can't wait to tell that SOB we have a campus location."

Just like that, Bill Hernandes was Edna's enemy too. "We should wait a little longer to tell him," I cautioned. Man I hated being the conservative one, the passenger along for the ride. "Just in case."

"Glen won't dare back out on me." Edna waved to a group of girls loitering on the front walk of the library in the distance, watching us. You know how sometimes it seems like your life is being recorded, how even when you're alone you're under observation, maybe by God, maybe by some other monitoring committee, and this keeps you from being completely uninhibited or gross or uncool? For Edna the sensation would be accurate.

"This is an earthquaking development for Jamestown. We shouldn't waste our big announcement on Hernandes."

"We won't mention this shop," she acquiesced. "But I'm going to let him know his partnership with me is over. And you need to sell him your investment in the Bluffs."

This did sound more enjoyable than getting a refund from Mike. "Alright. You want to ride with me?"

"No," said Edna. "I'll race you there."

EDNA TURNED into the parking lot first, but I beat her to the door. I pointed up at the Campus Coffeehouse sign. "I see another name change in Billy-boy's future."

"He can just cover the sign with a Going Out of Business banner."

Bill must have had a video surveillance camera out front, because he was jogging toward us before we were through the front door. "Edna Applejack!" Everyone in the shop stopped what they were doing, even the dude playing folk guitar on the temporary stage under the velvet Dylan poster. Bill hugged Edna and rubbed her back. "What a pleasant...pleasure. And Brian. Looking for a good cup of joe? Ha-ha! Come on in." With Edna pinned to his hip, Bill walked the aisle waving like a star at a world premier. A few people clapped.

Bill gave a high sign to one of his employees sitting with her girlfriends. They all jumped up, grabbed their drinks and swept crumbs off the table, and retreated to stand against the wall. We sat down. "I really pack them in with this music," said Bill. "Brian, you ought to try it."

"My customers are obligated to laugh at my jokes. That's enough punishment."

Edna laughed, loud and sparkly. Only great athletes have the natural ability to sound good whooping. She gave me a high-five. She was out of the loop, didn't know about the knuckle-knock. Felt good to have something to teach her. Edna needed me. "I knew we were going to make a great team," she said. Hernandes's face fell, and I gave her a sharp look. She patted me on the chest, not too hard thank goodness. "Bill, I'm pulling out of the Bluffs. Sorry. But there's good news. Brian is here to sell you his interest in the site." She turned a blind eye to Bill's state of alarm. "How much, Brian?"

"Maybe we should give Bill a minute to absorb."

Edna took Bill's hand and placed it atop the table, under hers. "Bill can absorb the dollar figure at the same time."

"I put down fifteen thousand." I crossed my legs and tapped the table, my best high-roller impersonation.

Bill nodded. He probably knew that already. Good thing I hadn't tried to turn a quick profit. He squirmed and scowled at the folk singer. When he finally spoke, his accent returned so thick I thought I could understand Portuguese. "Well that is good news. What a good site. So close to the hospital."

"In case your customers have a reaction," I said. "Milk allergies and what-not."

Bill's upper lip trembled. "I, I guess I'll need to think about your offer."

"There's no time," said Edna. She pinched the inside of Bill's elbow, claiming his attention. He looked at her with touching sadness. Edna smiled, and over time Bill's expression mirrored hers. "I know you had financing lined up before Brian decided to invest in the Bluffs. You need to tap it and get in that store ASAP." She was mesmerizing. "I've heard Starbucks has been scouting Jamestown. And you know Mike is the guy they would be talking to. The Bluffs is a natural fit for Starbucks. Or for you. Everything needs to be in place by the end of day tomorrow."

"Tomorrow," said Bill with sluggish tongue. "That could be difficult."

Edna shook her head. "Brian starts another round of chemo Monday. I don't want him burdened financially. You and I will sit down tomorrow morning with Mike and work this out. If you're not sure about the Bluffs, Brian will just revert his interest back to Mike, to be resold to the highest bidder."

"Let's not loop in Mike yet," said Bill. "I do want to be there. We can get this done. I'm ninety percent certain...I'm sure I can get you the money tomorrow morning. I'd...yeah, I'd like to get this done. Today, if possible."

"Great," said Edna. The woman possessed Jedi mind-control powers. Why was I surprised? She released Bill from her grip, if not her spell. "I'm going to act as Brian's proxy. Finances get him all worked up." She winked at me. "What he really needs to concentrate on is getting well."

"He looks like hell." Bill willed me to keel over dead. Bill was not a Jedi.

"Brian's a warrior," said Edna. "He'll be back." She said this with such authority I straightened up and believed it.

"Edna…" Bill's eyes got misty. "I was looking forward to working with you."

"I know," she said sweetly, sadly.

"That's what you're saying isn't it? That we can't work together? That you won't be my partner?" He reached his manicured hand toward her.

Edna's hand was no longer on the table. "Timing is everything, honey. We were that close." She held up a tightly-spaced thumb and forefinger.

We walked away. I looked back and Bill still hadn't blinked, the image of that narrow gap burned on his retinas. "So that's that," said Edna, outside. She gave me a kiss on the cheek that sent warm tingles down my side. "I'll have your money in hand by tomorrow noon."

"You're like Sherman marching to the sea. Nothing stands in your way."

"Aren't you glad you're Union?"

"Yep. Wow. This is really going to happen. Assuming I stay alive."

"It'll happen anyway." Edna laughed gaily. "But that would be best. Can I interest you in stopping by later for celebratory drink?"

"Can't. I have a dinner date. With Andrea."

Edna chortled and said, "Okay," giving me permission. "Watch out for that one, though, okay?"

CLEARLY I should have backed out on dinner with Andrea. But on the phone she had sounded lonely and needy and maybe a little too small to survive on her own. I couldn't see how Rick had been able to abandon her. I, a man who could physically protect no one, had stepped into the role of her guardian.

Andrea opened the door in a light pink blouse and calf-length pants, a defenseless outfit if there ever was one. Her childlike arms dangled from the loose sleeves. How could those arms push a lawnmower or shovel snow or even tighten a loose screw on the toilet paper holder? Andrea would be an apartment dweller until someone married her.

Which seemed like contributing to the delinquency of a minor. Maybe that was part of her appeal, forbidden jailbait fruit. Maybe it was that smug look that told me how highly she thought of herself and how confident she was I was going to kiss her hello and hope for more later. I wasn't sure if I was attracted to her for the child she wasn't, or the woman she thought she was. I threw my ballcap to the floor, stepped in close and lowered a kiss to her upturned lips.

"Mm. Well. That was nice."

"Likewise." I produced a bouquet of imported wildflowers from behind my back. "Vase?"

"Flowers. Hmm." We strolled into the kitchen. "Top cupboard."

On tiptoes I selected a glazed earthen vase decorated with Aztec symbols. "You couldn't have reached this with a step ladder on top of the counter."

"Rick put them up there when he helped me move in."

"Has he no respect for your dwarfism?"

"Ha ha. What made you decide to bring me flowers?"

Because I felt like celebrating.

I was high on the adrenaline rush of success. Gone was all the frustration—eight years in Davis, five in Jamestown, each time growing the business for three years and then watching sales flatten and expenses fatten, knowing I had a great product with a sweet delivery and yet no way to serve more than a couple thousand customers a year. Dried up was the puddle of blood, sweat and tears that had reflected the heartbreaking fact that success was impossible no matter how hard I worked—that the golden confluence of passion, decent (not great) margins, ample disposable incomes, and an addictive product meant absolutely nothing.

Success...I was one of the last to figure it out, so I'm sure this is no new news to report: it isn't what but who you know. Terrence yearning to get published, and Theresa desperate to get into pharmacy school—like me they had talent and a great product. We had all three labored under the false assumption that while success may be far off in the distance, we were progressing toward it, each failure a stepping stone to eventual triumph. In fact the gap had never shrunk. Like me, Terrence and Theresa were worshipping the false idol of perseverance. Unlike me, they didn't have Edna Applejack.

This campus shop was going to be huge. We were going to crush Bill Hernandes within the year, and hold our own against Starbucks. Edna was the biggest name in North Dakota; we could set up shop on every campus in the state. I had stumbled onto a frigging franchise. Andrea was welcome to come along for the ride.

I ran water in the vase and arranged the flowers to the best of my ability. "I bought these flowers, because they're pretty like you."

"Yeah, well." Andrea pretended not to buy this line, then spent a little extra time arranging the flowers. They weren't the prettiest flowers in the world, so I moved the conversation forward.

"Thanks for having me over. I smell something."

"It's lasagna. I hope you like lasagna."

"I'm probably not going to do it justice. My stomach is all messed up."
Along with my mouth, my throat, my intestine and my anus. I believe that's
the alimentary canal, and mine must have looked like a four-thousand year
old pockmarked Venetian street.

"Fine." Andrea was girlishly snitty. "I don't need you to eat like a real
man. So you remember Thor and his grandmother Rebecca?"

"Sure do." The cancer kid from Bhani's lab. Skinny and reserved with
blonde hair in his eyes.

"He had the treatment," said Andrea. She maneuvered the lasagna pan
to the edge of the oven rack, preparing to lift it.

I hurried over. "Let me help you with that. So?"

Andrea gladly relinquished the potholders and retrieved a manila envelope
from the counter. "You need to see these." I received an MRI negative.
Andrea said somberly, "This is Thor's scapula before the treatment."

I held the negative up to the light. We were in the presence of a demon,
a shocking photo of the bogeyman, a glimpse of a child-eating monster at
the margin of the videotape that prickles the pores on your back. Andrea
pointed unnecessarily at the cottony amoeba mold growing on the bone.

"Fuck. Sorry." I pushed the picture back at Andrea. "Quick show me
the good news."

Like those before-and-after weight loss photos, I swear the lighting was better
in this one; Thor must have been standing straighter; he had been drinking his
milk. The bone was bigger and brighter, knock your socks off better. Maybe
it was the lack of a thunderstorm-gray cottonball creature that improved the
subject's attractiveness the way a few missing pounds never could.

"Come on. This is someone else's scapula."

"Thor's cancer is dead," said Andrea. "It melted away."

"Doesn't that seem a little too good to be true? Did Bhani use those words
when he talked to Thor? I hope he sprinkled his magic talk with lots of maybe's."

Andrea stared at me, hands on her hips. "After all this time, you still
don't believe it works, do you? How many cures have I told you about?"

"Yeah, but…" Cures I heard about second- or third-hand were easier to
believe (or dismiss) than one I was witnessing myself. "You know I don't
believe most of what you tell me."

Andrea whacked me on the back. I really wished she wouldn't do that. "Hey," she said, "I have a surprise for you." From the pantry she produced a copper-plated la Pavoni espresso machine and set it carefully on the countertop. "Look what I bought."

I crossed the kitchen to caress the sleek Italian beauty. "This is topnotch, lady. You shouldn't have."

"Shouldn't have what?"

"Bought it for me."

"Yeah, right. This is for me. I need to become an espresso connoisseur."

"How come?"

She frowned at me. "So I can run the new store with you."

"Right, right."

"I need you to teach me how to use this thing. But not tonight. Right now I just want you to make us a cappuccino."

"Us, including you? You're part of 'us'?"

"I'm going to learn to tolerate coffee."

"For one thing, we're going to make espresso, not coffee. It's the difference between Canadian whiskey and single malt scotch." I filled the reservoir and switched on the pressurizer. "For another, nobody tolerates my espresso. I'm going to make you fall in love with it."

"We'll see about that. After the lasagna."

"I'm too excited to put this bad boy through the paces. Two double espressos coming up."

Andrea produced a pound of James River Valley beans. I poured three scoops into the hopper in the back of the espresso machine. "Check this out. Built-in burr grinder."

"You're not proud I bought your beans?" Andrea demanded.

"Very proud." In no time I had created two double-shots of espresso. "Get 'em while they're hot."

Andrea warily accepted her cup. "No cream and sugar for me? I must be sweet enough already."

I shook my head. I sipped. "Oh yeah," I cooed. "That's a good machine."

Andrea sniffed her espresso and wrinkled her nose. "Maybe you'll own it after all." She sipped once, and again. "It's different than I thought."

"Different…?"

"In a good way. That's not the way I remember coffee tasting."

"That's because it's not coffee," I said through clenched teeth. "Gol. Gee."

"Calm down over there." Andrea drank some more. And repeat. She finished hers before I did. The first sign of trouble.

"So tell me more about Thor's treatment."

"He got real sick," said Andrea, "just the way he was supposed to. Dr. Bhani's injection inspires a huge response from your immune system. It thinks it's fighting a flu bug, but it's really attacking your cancer." She licked her lips. "Since we're just standing around talking, why don't you make us another one. They're so small."

"They do pack a wallop."

"My grandma swears she can't drink caffeine after nine a.m. But my mom was adopted, so I don't think it'll affect me the same way."

Unless late-morning coffee turned Granny into a horny devil-cat, she was right about that.

I filled the portafilter. "So what are my chances of being cured by Bhani? Or of even surviving the treatment? I'm not as young and hardy as Thor."

"Your chances of survival are almost one hundred percent," said Andrea.

"It's the 'almost' that gets me."

"Brian, do you know the mortality statistics of your cancer, when they use the standard chemo treatment?"

"Honestly, I don't. I haven't wanted to look it up."

Andrea caressed my back as I pulled another couple shots. "You basically have the same cancer Thor did. In every study we've seen, these types of sarcomas have very little long-term response to chemotherapy and radiation." She slipped under my shirt and scraped the waistband of my underwear with what I knew to be a long shapely fingernail.

"But my tumor did shrink."

"False hope," said Andrea. "They trick you into thinking that a reduction in tumor size or slowing the growth rate means progress. It doesn't. It only delays the inevitable." She explored my back, stabbing me with a fingernail, producing a blossom of electrical currents and possibly drawing blood. Sort of a cross between S&M and necrophilia, she was seductively abusing me while discussing my certain demise. "And in the meantime chemotherapy causes permanent damage to just about everything except the cancer."

"Is Bhani's procedure covered by insurance?" I asked over the roar of the espresso machine bludgeoning the ground coffee with hot water. "Because the chemo is fully covered."

"It's free," said Andrea. She caressed the base of my spine while I lovingly worked the la Pavoni. I had an erection, but I wasn't sure which one of them deserved the credit. "Dr. Bhani is still working off a couple grants, so he doesn't need your money. He needs your data to submit to the regulators."

"I'm not looking forward to more chemo," I admitted. "I'm still feeling the effects of the last round. I start another three-week protocol on Monday."

"Don't do it." Andrea pounded her shot of espresso. "A strong immune response is crucial to Dr. Bhani's treatment. If your immune system is depressed from the chemo, Dr. Bhani would wait at least a month before treating you." She beamed up at me, a weird light in her dark eyes. I heard Sumatran natives whisper-chanting to a primitive drumbeat somewhere in the far reaches of her caffeine-addled brain, as she towed me into the living room.

"Just so you know, I'm seriously thinking about Bhani's treatment."

"I think it's time for you to stop thinking," Andrea rasped, pulling me onto the couch, leaning into the sloped armrest. "You might have something better to do right now. Hm?"

I was more than a little ready myself. Bhani was going to cure me, I was suddenly a believer. By itself, that faith would have simply left me relieved. Coupled with my business partnership with the official state goddess, and I was pumped. Felt more alive at that moment than any time in the past few years.

Twenty seconds into kissing and Andrea was already moaning, more like grumbling, as our heads sank into the corner of the couch. Submerged in grumbles and slobber, I lost track of time and space. Visual snippets of the sweat on her stomach and the wetness between her legs flashed into our secluded world. When she put her hand on me, an aggressive act for Andrea, I realized I was way ahead of what I liked to think of as my marathon pace, too far along to slow things down. In a hurry I shucked our pants.

The orgasm came soon after. It was troubling. I'm accustomed to a seemingly infinite flood of energy and what-not leaving my body. This one never really got going. It kind of jammed inside me. I kept thrusting, hoping I was about to be blessed with a mystical, multi-stage, escalating orgasm.

My penis squished out. I smushed it up against her a couple times, got no response from either of us, and laid still.

"Well," said Andrea. "That was something."

I grabbed my pants and made for the bathroom. Tough luck for Andrea, but my psyche was in no condition to pick up with my fingers where my limp dick had left off. My plumbing had me worried.

In the bathroom mirror my once-impressive legs were skinnier than ever. Thin legs did make my dick look fatter, anyway.

Pride in my relatively impressive penis evaporated as I examined my body. My ribs showed, but I still had a bike tire of fat low on my stomach. My skin was mottled—from the sex or the chemo or the cancer? I touched around my belly button and regretted it—tenderness on the outside, pain on the inside. My forehead was slimed with cold sweat. Not the way a healthy body looked and felt. Not even a sick body putting up a good fight. I was dying.

The gray specter of death shadowing my face confirmed it. Maybe that was the effect of two burned-out light bulbs above the mirror, I don't know.

It was all I could do to kiss Andrea goodbye and pretend I was basking in the afterglow of great sex. I had to fend her off, she was wired and ready for more. I should have kindly informed her that if she did have the insatiable caffeine-driven urge to go out and get a little more, I hadn't much polluted her with jizm.

I drove home agonizing over what had gone wrong. Either my tank had been empty from the get-go, or I had a blockage. Even though it would entail more medications, more procedures, more pain, I preferred the blockage explanation.

I really would rather not analyze my semen, here or in general. But sex and semen are so central to what it means to be alive. That's not just my personal credo. From what I understand, once the genes realize your seed-spreading days are over, the body's defense systems give up. Everything's geared toward copying oneself into the next generation. Once that's no longer possible, once the sperm-manufacturing process is mothballed, the body sees no sense continuing to take up earthly space.

Back home I attempted to jack off, unsuccessfully. I selected Edna, which was a big mistake. Even with complete fantasy control, I was intimidated by her. First I made her sex-starved and begging for it, which turned out to be too implausible. It was up to me to turn her on. When I couldn't even imagine such an achievement, I forced myself on her, staying just on the bad-boy side of the rapist line. Edna punched me in the face and threw me out of the toilet stall. Finally I was the one pleading for it, all the while my dick begging me to stop.

I stunk of desperation. I went from trying to trick my body to trying to motivate it, to convince it there was a reason to put up a fight and live, even if it was in the sad state of the eunuch.

"Body, goddammit, sex isn't everything. Does it really matter whether I can get jiggy with it right now? I'm not married, so it's not even appropriate. Jesus frowns on it, and for crying out loud, let's hope Darwin did too. In the meantime I'm contributing to building a rich and vibrant society. As I'm sure you're aware, Body, it's tough to propagate the species if society is breaking down. And your fixation with ejaculation is a bit old-fashioned. Thanks to medical technology, I don't have to copulate to reproduce. The final five-to-eight inches of piping are irrelevant. Get with the times, will you? And p.s., please don't give up on those final five-to-eight inches."

Was my body paying attention? Who knows. Andrea called while I was indisposed, and left a message:

"I just want you to know you made a big mistake leaving early tonight. The thoughts running through my mind, well," she had chuckled, "they're probably not even legal. If this is what caffeine does to me, I'd say you're going to be in for a treat when we're working late together at our coffeeshop in Denver. Of course, if you decide to go home early like tonight, it'll have to be some lucky customer or employee. Let's hire a lot of cute young boys, just in case. If you get this and decide you're not really that tired, I'll be up for awhile yet. Quite awhile. Feel free to come over. Okay then, I guess I'll hang up. Bye."

With all this still fresh in your mind, let's skip ahead twenty hours, to Friday night. It explains a lot of what would happen in the weeks to come.

"You're back so soon," Andrea greeted me at the door to her apartment. "So soon, but way too late. Unfortunately for you, the caffeine has worn off. And I won't be drinking any in the near future, because it left me with a really bad headache that I'm just now getting over."

"Can I come in?"

"Sure," she said, like she was being magnanimous after the way I had treated her. Like I was there for one thing and one thing only, and she wanted to make sure I knew she knew it. I think psychologists call that projecting. "Can I get you something to drink? Something decaffeinated?"

"Naw. I should get to the point, since we'll probably be discussing it for awhile. Hopefully discussing, and not arguing."

"Wow." Andrea stood behind the couch and crossed her arms. "What?"

I dug a bank receipt out of my pocket. "Bill Hernandes wired fifteen grand into your account today."

"Why?" Andrea asked with a sharp, suspicious edge.

"I had him buy out your investment in the Bluffs shop."

"Why did you do…" Andrea couldn't finish the sentence, her voice mechanisms collapsed.

I set the receipt on the end table. "I'm backing out. That location is a loser." This had nothing to do with the Bluffs and everything to do with Edna and the campus location; but the more I thought about that site, the more I believed what I was saying. "We would have lost our money, sooner than later. Don't ask me why Bill is so eager to get in there. Well, I do know. He's an idiot." Andrea shrank while I talked. She uncrossed her arms, searched for something for her hands to do, and finally let them dangle at her sides. "You can find a much more profitable way to invest your money," I told her.

Andrea's head quivered like she had Parkinson's. "So we're not going to run a coffeeshop together?"

"Nope." I tried to be blasé, but I'm pretty sure I was brusque. Maybe downright rude. Andrea was jeopardizing my prospects with Edna, I had decided. "It won't work."

"Not anywhere? Colorado or California?"

"I don't plan to move any time soon."

"Suddenly you like it here?" she snapped. If she were any bigger I would have been scared. "Suddenly North Dakota is the greatest place in the world?"

"That might be stretching it." I gave her a little chuckle, to convince her we were still on the same team. At least until I was out that door. "But the prospects have definitely improved over the past couple weeks."

"Oh. Oh. And me?" She wanted to give me a snotty look, but couldn't bring her eyes up to mine. "You don't give a crap about me, is that right?"

"No. I mean it's not right."

"You don't care about me, and what my plans are."

"If they coincided with mine it would be great—"

"No." Andrea did me a favor cutting me off—that explanation was heading in an exceptionally tactless direction. "You don't give a shit about me. It's all about you, isn't it? Are you thinking about me at all? No." It didn't really matter what I had to say, she was perfectly capable of conducting both sides of the conversation. "Who are you thinking of? The McEwens? I'm sure that's it. They got to you, didn't they?"

"Not at all. Mike probably won't like this any more than you do."

"Then why?" Andrea's voice cracked. "Why?"

"Andrea, don't over-think this. A different opportunity came up, that's all. A different opportunity that makes the Bluffs unworkable. I wish I could have thought of a gentler way to tell you this. But we know each other well enough, we can be honest with each other and avoid spending a lot of time—"

"Are you opening a different shop?"

"I don't feel comfortable discussing it. From a business perspective, I mean. There are confidentiality issues."

"You're working with someone else. Why?" Now Andrea looked me in the eye, pleading with me, not for an explanation but for a change of heart.

I needed to calm her down, she was borderline hyperventilating. "It's not about you. This is a unique opportunity that only works with this person." I kept my voice low, purring the way I would like to hear from my mother if I was a lion cub and men with guns were hunting nearby. Actually I would want to hear the men screaming as my mother tore them to shreds. Andrea was going to have to settle for purring. "The Bluffs would have dragged us all under. By switching gears to this new opportunity, I'm actually looking out for everyone's best interests."

"Who is it?"

"Edna Applejack."

For a second Andrea seemed to be thinking, Oh, that makes sense. Then her body quivered. "You are a bastard. I can't believe you're doing this to me."

"I'm not doing anything to you."

"No. No. Yes you are. Yes you are. You are and you don't care."

"Come on now." I moved forward and she turned her back on me.

"Go." She pointed at the door. "I want you to leave. You don't care enough about me to treat me with respect, so I don't want you here. Go."

If I was the sort of guy who's comfortable walking up behind an angry woman and wrapping her in his arms, this would have been the perfect opportunity. There must be dairy farming in my genes, because approaching an agitated female from behind was instinctively wrong. Plus there was nothing I was going to whisper in Andrea's ear that would improve her disposition.

"I'll call you. Later." For no one's benefit I pointed at the receipt curled up on the end table. "Don't forget to verify that the wire went through."

Andrea was crying. It was real hard to leave her like that. She looked so defenseless. She looked so small, even in that little apartment. I would have felt a lot less guilty leaving her crying in an efficiency.

T-4

ON TUESDAY Edna came to the shop at the right time, minutes after the morning rush became the midday lull. We talked at a table while Charlotte ogled her and wiped down the bar in preparation for what would hopefully be a busy afternoon.

Business had picked up. No doubt due to Edna's constant presence, the past week we had averaged an additional $125 a day. That's close to four grand a month—not striking it rich, but a nice start.

"We're looking good at JC," said Edna. She was looking good, slacks and a soft blazer over a silky blouse that exposed a sweet V of breastbone. She was skinny, wow. Her crossed legs were off to the side, but that didn't mean she sat sideways. In my book that's flexibility. I've heard that world-class athletes excel at keeping their core centered. That's what was happening there—her core remained comfortably balanced on the chair while her legs played over there. How do you defend against that? You don't.

Edna knocked on the table, accustomed to corralling a man's straying focus. "We're going to be kicking Bill's ass by September first. I want to have our grand opening on the Saturday after the first week of classes."

"Pretty aggressive."

"I've already cleared it with Rick."

I choked on my coffee. "McEwen?"

"They'll be ready to start whenever we say Go."

I held a napkin to my mouth and coughed coffee out of my lungs. "That's not such a good idea. My relationship with the McEwens is rocky."

"Rocky" was being positive. I heard through the grapevine they were saying uncharitable things about me. I was getting a lot of hang-up calls—which was actually a relief, when it wasn't the hospital with more "follow-up" items. If I didn't pick up, someone was leaving messages. The first few were heavy breathing, Nurse Nancy, I assumed, trying to get me to come join them in Dennis's apartment. Then there was the occasional muttered slander like "ingrate" and "bad beans". At least that's what it sounded like through all the clicking and static I was getting on my cellphone, which led me to believe it was tapped. Also, Dennis was watching me all the time, either sitting at my counter or in the rocking chair at his front window. I knew if I challenged him, he'd claim that was the way he always behaved, and I couldn't argue with that.

"I don't want you to give the construction another thought," said Edna. "I can deliver Rick. And whatever ill will Mike might be harboring for you, he loves me."

"I think you're underestimating Mike's ability to hold and avenge a grudge. I'd really like to explore other options."

"Brian." Charlotte was standing right beside me with the phone in her hand. "Phone for you."

I looked up at her, keeping my hands on my coffee mug. "Are you sure? I didn't hear it ring."

"You didn't even hear me walk over here."

"Of course I did. What, you want me to say hello every time our paths cross?" I waited for Charlotte to sass me, but she was watching Edna stroking the back of my hand with a finger. Charlotte forced the phone on me. She was still staring at that finger as she left our table. "Hello?"

"Brian? This is Tami down at Dr. Bonilla's office."

"Shoot, I was hoping it was a crank call. Or a bill collector."

"Oh, ha-ha. Dr. Bonilla was wondering whether you were planning to come in today?"

"Tami, I'm sorry. I'm not. I forgot to call you."

"That's okay. Should we set up an appointment for tomorrow? We could squeeze you in the afternoon. I know afternoons are better for you."

"No."

"No good? Let's try Thursday. Friday at the very latest. We really need to get you in here." You would have thought Tami was working on commission.

"I'm going to explore another option. I honestly don't know if I could survive any more chemo."

"Dr. Bonilla would be happy to talk about modifying your treatment plan," said Tami. "This decision shouldn't be made hastily."

"I'm sorry," I told Tami. "I've decided to go in a different direction."

"I'm going to have to let Dr. Bonilla know," said Tami with the same tone the playground monitor had used as she headed into the school to tell my 4th-grade teacher I had kicked dog crap into Michelle Bazzalla's hair. "I'm sure he'll want to talk to you."

"If you have to. Do me a favor? I need a refill prescription for the immune system booster I've been taking. Can you have the doc write it for me?"

"I'll see what I can do." If I was unwilling to let Bonilla keep shrinking my testes with his chemo ray gun, Tami didn't sound inclined to do me any favors.

Edna had waited impatiently. "What other option?"

The smart person would have played something this controversial close to the vest. Don't think for a second that I don't know what smart persons do. "I'm sure you heard about Brent McEwen while you were in the slammer. He had a similar cancer to mine. He received this experimental treatment from a researcher named Dr. Bhani, and it sounds like it cured his cancer."

Edna was up to speed. "Brent died of an infection from the treatment."

"Per the McEwens. Dr. Bhani says his treatment had nothing to do with it. He says it was an infection a lot of people get in the hospital."

"What else was he going to say? My bad?"

"Good point. But he's had some amazing successes. I met one of them, a young kid who had bone cancer, too. Dr. Bhani's treatment completely wiped out his tumors. I know there's some risk, but right now I'd try a witch doctor's potion instead of going through another round of chemo. I wasn't kidding on the phone. The drugs are killing me faster than the cancer."

Edna pushed my coffee cup aside and slipped her hands inside mine. "I'm sure a miracle like Bhani is promising is attractive. But honestly, isn't chemo the only tried and true weapon against cancer?"

"Get this. I was reading a book someone gave me. Alright, it was my girlfriend, Andrea." Not a flinch from Edna. In fact she squeezed my hand, which I interpreted as Enjoy it until I make you stop. "I didn't think I'd like it, but I read the whole thing this weekend. I couldn't put it down, it had me so excited. It was written by a guy named Neil Ruzic, who was diagnosed with cancer. He was encouraged by his doctor to start aggressive chemo and radiation therapy immediately. He knew what chemo was going to do to his body, so he went looking for other opinions. He's a rich guy, he could afford to fly all over the country and consult topnotch oncologists. He heard the same thing from every other doctor he talked to—chemo is the recommended treatment."

My voice quavered. In the span of a weekend I had grown attached to Neil Ruzic and his battle. His incredible research effort—years' worth—was stunning to read, and the heroic lengths he went to, to beat cancer and then write the book to educate the rest of us, put me to shame. The deeper I read into the book, the more I was pulling for him. The more I listened to his optimism and love of life (and unpreparedness for the afterlife), the harder it became to separate our stories. After the first few chapters I stopped trying.

Neil's cure came from an experimental cocktail that starved his tumors of their blood supply. This is what drugs like Celebrex do for a living. Neil recommended them highly. Gerry Olson the pharmacist had slipped me two weeks' worth of Celebrex samples, and in a couple days I would be begging him for more.

To my chagrin, Neil never explored the idea of using deadly bacteria to stimulate the immune system. But Dr. Bhani was exactly the type of maverick researcher Neil worshipped and recommended.

"Instead of blindly following his doctor's orders, Neil did a ton of research on the effectiveness of chemo," I told Edna. "And he discovered it does a lot more harm than good. A lot more. Chemo does postpone death—but only for a few years. Five-year survival rates are basically the same with or without chemo, for most cancers. Including his and including mine."

"Then why do all the doctors recommend it?"

"Maybe they're too busy to read the journals about the new research out there. And a lot of them specialize in chemo. They know it well, so that's what they prescribe. And, it's what insurance companies pay for."

"But chemo really doesn't work?"

"No." I was getting worked up. "And it's insane what it does to your body. Worse than I thought. The effects Neil described, I'm experiencing them all. Organ damage, ulcers, gum bleeding…" And loss of mental abilities? I was pretty sure. But I couldn't bring myself to tell Edna that her business partner was in mid-stage senility. "Neil had friends die on chemo, friends he made after he was diagnosed. Friends he couldn't convince to stop the chemo and try one of the new therapies. It tore him apart, and it was awful to read. His book convinced me to stop the chemo. If I'm going to die anyway, I would like it to be without a shriveled penis."

Edna's big football-shaped eyes glowed. "Do you feel like Dr. Bhani's treatment is your last chance?"

"I haven't explored every avenue out there. No avenues, really. Mostly because Bonilla frowned on it. But I would imagine that if this fails, with all the time it would take to figure out what else is out there, and get signed up for a different protocol…" I was hip to the vernacular after reading Neil's book. "…it would be too late."

"I want to hear more about this."

"I have write-ups on Dr. Bhani's treatment results, and descriptions of the procedure, back at my apartment."

"We'll go get them when we're done here," said Edna. "If it looks good, we're going to get your treatment started immediately."

"Well, okay, I guess. I mean, I'm—"

"If it looks promising, we're not waiting," said Edna. "We're going to assault your cancer. Massive counter-attack. You are being attacked, right?"

"Sure feels that way."

"Then you have to return fire." It was halftime of the conference championship and Edna was not going to allow her team to lose. "You have to know you can beat it." Edna tapped her forehead. Then she picked up my hand and pulled it to her lips. She kissed two of my knuckles, individually; I heard Charlotte moan and then cover it with a cough. "We'll beat it together," said Edna, lips brushing my knuckles.

"I get the feeling you could beat my cancer without my help," I said.

Edna winked. "Let's finish our discussion on the campus shop. I have some ideas about hiring. Even though we won't be open for a couple months, I want our team on board as soon as possible, so they can hit the ground at full steam on Day One."

I struggled to switch gears. "We'll have to post for applicants soon. There are four or five kids who periodically check with me about a job. We can start—"

"Hold that thought." Edna rose as Jolene Crause and Butch Johnson chugged to our table, and laid hugs on both of them.

"We heard you were back in town!" Jolene was sixtyish. She rubbed Edna's upper arms fast enough to throw sparks. "You are looking so good!"

"Thank you," Edna said sincerely.

"I'm Jolene. This is Butch," she introduced the beaming retired farmer.

"Butch and Jolene are an item," I informed Edna. "Everybody's waiting for them to set a date."

Butch pointed the toe of his boot to the sky and swayed back and forth, his burnt brown cheeks reddening. Jolene spared me a polite smile. "So, Edna, we were just talking about what a thrill it was to watch you play basketball!"

"Well thank you. I loved playing in front of Jamestown crowds. No one appreciates basketball like North Dakota fans."

"It's so true," gushed Jolene.

"I've heard Indiana has the second-best fans," I said.

This was ignored. "So, you got any eligibility left?" farmer Butch asked with a tobacco-stained leer.

"I'm afraid not." Edna leaned in and spoke very close to Butch's grizzled face. "And then there's that little matter of my murder conviction that the NCAA might have trouble with."

Butch hooted until he choked and coughed and produced a hanky to catch a grain dust lung biscuit. My dad runs a crop insurance agency, I might have mentioned. I had worked autumns adjusting crop losses and yields. I knew what grain dust smelled like.

"What are you doing now then?" Jolene inquired, gripping Edna's hand and staring up into her face, head cocked like a puppy at its master.

"Believe it or not…" Edna put a finger to her lips. "…opening a coffeeshop on the JC campus."

"Oh, my! No! You are? Well that will be our new favorite coffeeshop," Jolene pretty much screamed. She remembered me. "Oh, Brian, I'm sorry."

"We're going to own it together," I said.

"Oh wonderful!" Jolene squealed. "Then we won't have to feel guilty!"

"You still should," I said. Guilty that they were ready to choose a famous personality over the best coffee they'd ever had (not to mention an equally compelling personality). I was bitter over this flaw of human nature, and excited to start exploiting it.

"We'll be open September first," Edna proclaimed.

"We'll be your first customers!" Jolene yelled.

"Yep," Butch agreed.

"It's still sort of a secret, though," I cautioned.

Charlotte cleared her throat. I excused myself and met her at the end of the counter. "What's going on? Are you opening a new store?"

"With Edna," I confirmed.

"Ohhh…"

"Breathe, Charlotte. Breathe, girl!"

Charlotte warded off my hands. "I don't need chest compressions. Ohmygosh. You're serious. You and Edna…. That is going to be huge. Where?"

"On campus. It's still a secret, though. Sort of."

Charlotte shivered with anticipation. "I'm so excited I can't tell you."

"So I see."

"I want to work in that store," said Charlotte as she returned to her post.

I sat down again with Edna and nodded toward Jolene and Butch, whispering excitedly to each other. "Looks like we have our first two lifetime customers. Not that it's a huge commitment at their age."

"I can pull 'em in," said Edna, bringing her famous face close to mine. Her skin showed some age, a few lines and a slight loss of suppleness. But it still wasn't normal skin. Those weren't mortal muscles moving her mouth, not mortal bones underneath it all. Her head didn't glow and it didn't crackle with electricity, but it was something like that. Her face was inches away and simultaneously projected on the big screen. A thousand pairs of eyes looked on Edna's face with mine. "But I can't keep 'em all by myself. Neither can you. We need great employees."

"It's crucial," I agreed. "It was my biggest challenge when I opened a second shop in the past. We need to hire employees who really want to work. Kids who need money more than they need to party. Kids who show up when they're scheduled, and take pride in—"

"We need mature employees," said Edna. "We need professional retail salespeople who thrive on commissions and dream of opening their own coffeeshops. We need adults."

I blinked at her. Given that I had fifteen years behind the bar, compared to her fifteen minutes, I was dumbfounded Edna felt comfortable running the show and instructing me on the perfect coffeeshop employee.

But what was I going to argue? No, I'm a firm believer that scantily-clad girls are the key to success. I could see how one might draw that conclusion, but the truth, Edna would soon learn, was no one older than twenty-five would work for what we could pay them. And removing sleeves and shedding a layer was the only way for youngsters to make a decent wage. Sex might not sell coffee, but it did increase the tips. For the females. The male employees were left with having to be friendly to the customers.

"We'll put out a statewide casting call," said Edna. "Newspapers, the Internet, flyers. We'll hold auditions and hire them as soon as possible, and then have them hit the streets and work the community and the campus to drum up anticipation. We'll teach them to pull the best shots this town or any other has ever seen. Our customer service is going to blow everyone away."

"It's a crock."

"Ouch." Edna laid her fingers to my neck. "That sounded rough."

"I wasn't clearing my throat, I was commenting on customer service. I hate it."

Edna withdrew her hand. "Most people would agree customer service is the key to business success," she suggested.

With hiring, I could afford to let Edna live and learn. On the topic of customer service, there must be no mistake. "The concept of customer service has single-handedly set American business back twenty years," I informed her. "It's been translated to mean 'The customer is always right.' 'Serve the customer when they want, where they want, how they want.' Nails on the chalkboard. Who's the expert here, me or the customer? I've never asked a customer how she wants to be served in my life. I'm betting you never asked the crowd how you should play defense, or whether you should pull up for the J or drive the lane."

"Don't believe I did," said Edna.

Across the room Butch toasted that sentiment with hoisted cup.

I leaned forward and lowered my voice. "Every suggestion a customer has ever made was bunk. 'You need to stay open later.' 'You need to turn down your music.' 'You need to stop serving me regular when I ask for decaf.' 'You need to clean your pastry case.' 'You need to sell soup and sandwiches.' I will never sell a sandwich or an appetizing pastry as long as I live. It might please the customer, but I'm not in business to please customers. I'm here to make money, pure and simple."

"Amen, brother," said Edna.

"Some of my customers would be pleased if I offered waffles in the morning and sandwiches at lunch. And pastries that are fresh, and attractively displayed. But I don't want to buy waffle equipment. I don't want to clean syrup off my chairs. I don't want to contract with a prepackaged sandwich company and pretend to be grateful for the pathetic margin and hold my temper at the spoilage I have to eat. I don't like food, and I'm not selling it. I can picture the scene, a customer walking back up to the counter. 'My cappuccino tastes weird.' 'That's because you just ate a smoked turkey sandwich with horseradish mayo on tomato'n'herb focaccia.'"

I took a breath. "I don't want to have to hurt anyone. I'm here to make money. To serve the best damn mug of coffee and itty-bitty cup of espresso I can. With a story thrown in here and there."

"That's beautiful," said Edna.

"Our business plan should be to charge each customer individually based on whether we like them or not. 'I'll have a brewed coffee.' 'That'll be a buck.' Next customer. 'Brewed coffee, if you please. And could you clean off that table over there? It's got crumbs on it.' 'Six dollars.' 'What? But that guy only paid a dollar.' 'I like that guy. I don't care much for you. Six-fifty.'"

Edna beamed. "Our coffee is so good, and our shop is going to be so kick-ass, he'd pay it."

"It would cut down on all those helpful suggestions real quick. Don't you ever take a customer survey," I told her. "I haven't met a customer who knows better than I do. The great retail chains don't ask customers what they want. They tell them. And then it becomes true. What the customer thought he wanted is irrelevant." I sipped my coffee. "Just my opinion."

"No it's not," said Edna. "It's our business model. It's also going to be the make-or-break question for our prospective employees." Edna laughed. I entertained her, if nothing else. I wouldn't get much fulfillment out of being a full-time comic, but I do like to put a smile on your coffee-slurping lips.

"I can't tell you how excited I am for these interviews," said Edna. "We're going to have such a strong team by Opening Day, we'll already be planning our next campus shops in Bismarck and Valley City." She was staring at the bar—at Charlotte or the espresso machine, I couldn't tell. "We're going to rock this world, Brian."

For the first time in quite a while, I felt like a rocker.

Edna stood. "Let's go have a look at Dr. Bhani's credentials, shall we?"

Charlotte stretched across the counter to hand me two standard envelopes and a large manila one. "You got some personal mail here." I cringed at Charlotte's farm girl vernacular, as Edna seemed to size her up.

The wind beat on us as we stepped outside. "I'll drive so you can open your mail," Edna volunteered. I eagerly accepted. She had a Talon. I was smitten with those cars, knowing full well that five years from now it would be considered the mullet and the mesh tanktop of its generation.

Jamestown had been without rain or snow long enough to dry out the street grime, powder it to a fine grit, and send it airborne. We crossed Main with heads bowed, squinting, lips pressed tight. In North Dakota, which way does the wind blow? In your face.

I settled into the passenger seat and groaned. "Something wrong?" Edna asked.

"No, that's normal." I tucked the bills beside the seat in hopes I would forget them there, and opened the manila envelope. "Huh. Pictures…"

I thought they were of torture victims, shot from above and from low angles, the victims lying on their backs and on their stomachs. "Disturbing stuff. Jeez." Naked, bloated, bruised all over. Open sores on the groin and in the armpits. Gaping oozing wounds with blackened pus-crusted edges.

And then I realized the pictures were of the same person; and the person, even with his face swollen, and his throat and cheek…eaten, was Brent McEwen. "Oh man."

Edna tried to look while she drove us through downtown's noon rush. I held one of the pics for her to see. She blanched and put her eyes back on the street. "No. I don't want to see that."

Comprehension continued to come in stages. "Holy hell." Comprehension, accompanied by chills. "It's the infection," I realized. "It's Bhani's cure."

"What? What do you mean?"

The pictures lay on my lap. I didn't want them touching me, the filthy fucking scary things. I piled them together with the back of my hand and pushed the lot onto the floor. "Maybe you should find a place to pull over. I may have to get a refund on that breakfast burrito."

I had eaten too much that morning, a whole burrito and a carton of yogurt, excited about Neil Ruzic's cure, about seeing Edna, about believing that in the near future I was going to have money to spend. Now the odds of being alive to love Edna and make and enjoy that money were miniscule. The bottom had dropped out and I was falling.

Edna stopped the Talon on the gravel bed beside the railroad tracks. While the car rocked in the wind, I sat breathing and already missing my life so much it tied my ribs in knots. Edna was patient, and I was finally able to return to the moment. I tried to unkink my ribcage without really moving, willing the muscles to relax so I could speak without gasping. "I guess I don't have to puke. That's a first. But thanks for pulling over."

"Give me the story on those pictures."

"It's Brent McEwen. Probably in the morgue. Somebody wanted me to see what he looked like when he died."

Edna grabbed the envelope. "There's no return address. Who sent this?"

I swiveled my eyes to look at the envelope, careful not to let my better-than-average peripheral vision catch sight of the pictures. "I don't recognize the handwriting."

"Why did someone want you to see those?"

I thought talking about it might do me good. "It wasn't cancer that killed Brent. He died of an infection. I knew that, but...I had no idea." His purple and green face was contorted in a terrified snarl. Brent did not go quietly. "Maybe I should throw up." I opened the door and tumbled out. Tears streamed from my eyes and I gagged out a couple coughs before tossing creamed burrito in a yogurt sauce into the sharp gray rocks. Edna's door opened and I hollered, "I'm okay. It's over. Maybe a Kleenex."

She reached across and through the passenger door to hand me a moist towelette. I wiped my mouth and buried the soiled cloth in the rocks, and climbed back into the Talon. Edna squeezed the nape of my neck while examining the pictures, careful not to let me see. "It's like he was tortured to death. What kind of infection could do this?"

I closed my eyes. "A bad one? Ebola? Typhoid, black plague?"

"I have never seen anything like that." Now Edna couldn't get enough of the grim pics. "Dr. Bhani said it was an ordinary hospital infection? That doesn't look ordinary."

"No. Huh-uh. Nope."

"I want to see Bhani's treatment results," said Edna. We peeled out of there, throwing jagged rocks at the deserted Burlington Northern shed. "Then we're going to pay him a visit."

—

Best I could gather while lying face down on my couch, Edna was impressed by what she read. She called Bhani but couldn't reach him or Andrea. So she went looking for him, and mercifully took the pictures with her.

I'm not going to belabor the dread I felt. Chemo was out of the question, but there was no way I was going to die like Brent. Bhani would not be filling me full of his bugs. And seeing as how Neil Ruzic and I had very different cancers, it was a very long longshot to expect the researcher who had cured him to do the same for me—not that it would even be possible to get accepted into what was now undoubtedly an extremely popular protocol. Even for Neil, it had taken all his time, energy, money and connections. I was a little short on all those. So I would continue the over-the-counter version of his miracle cure. And that's about it.

I planned to remain face down all evening and night, wallowing in the depths of self-pity and trying my best to sink ever lower. But around five o'clock it really hit me: when the secret formula for coffeeshop success had finally become known to me—perhaps in the form of the girl of my dreams, who could say?—I was going to die. That's the kind of irony that makes a man thirsty. I decided to go buy something expensive to drink.

Watching me function at a high level the rest of the evening and over the next few days, you might draw the conclusion I had somehow come to grips with the fatal nature of my disease. Not at all. Death and Nothingness and the disappearance of Brian Lawson from the face of the earth and from people's thoughts and my parents' lives—the utter lack of me in the future and how it really didn't impact anyone or anything in terms of their ability to carry on and laugh and love and vacation and work, how it didn't interfere with Time's ability to simply move on and cause all kinds of amazing things to happen without me ever knowing it—these were my constant companions then and in the coming days.

You forget that for the past five years I had operated under the near-certainty of business failure, or breakeven mediocrity at best. All that time no one could say I was depressed or lacking in vitality. Brother, that's why they come to my shop. I'm a happy person. I laugh, and I like to make others do the same. Now was no different. I'm intrigued by people and the amazing and unexpected events they cause to happen. I can't get enough of it all. That's why I don't want to die.

T-3

IT HAD been three weeks since my last chemo treatment, since Edna and I made our pact to take the coffee world by storm. We were holding interviews, in one of the College's conference rooms. By the time I arrived, Edna had arranged the space to her liking. The fifteen-foot marble table with its supporting pedestals was somehow pushed into the corner. Four chairs formed a tight square in the middle of the floor, with tablets and pens for Edna and me. We had interviewed twenty-some candidates, and I hadn't taken many notes.

I was distracted, though no fault of my own. I had tried to find spiritual peace beforehand, before I polluted our prospective employees with my fear of dying.

The night before had been the worst yet. I hadn't slept a wink—that's a lie whenever someone claims it, but it's as good as true in this case. Every time I woke up from dozing off, the silent oppression of my empty apartment and the vastly unpopulated state of North Dakota beat down on me, a low bass wobble of the funeral organ, long shallow sound waves without the sound, a sample of what death would feel like.

Of course death would have no feel, not even the dull hopelessness of eternal silence. That thought smacked me so hard I lost a few degrees' body heat—I would have gone insane except for some mental deficiency that prevented me from grasping and holding the Nothingness concept for very long.

Edna had been encouraging me to stay over. If she persisted, eventually I'd get over my reluctance to spend the night in her bed blubbering with fears of death, or blubbering in her extra bedroom after she spurned my unwanted advances. Me with one foot in the grave, pawing at Edna's boobs. Pretty sad.

I spent two hours that morning enduring full-body MRI and CAT scans. I would hear the results Monday and they would not be good. I wanted to be ready and reconciled to my ending, that I might die sad but at least not shrieking. Better yet of course would be a reason to wholeheartedly believe in the afterlife.

So I had visited Pastor Kyle in his office in an aging strip mall on the east side, sandwiched between Domino's Pizza and H&R Block. PK didn't have his own church—his congregation met in an abandoned Our Own Hardware. He had labored for years to grow membership to the point where a building fund was feasible. In advance of my visit, I had given PK an executive summary of what I was looking for: sort of a road map to Heaven. But when I arrived he spent the first twenty minutes talking about his own challenges, hoping to route my heavenly journey through a permanent home for his ministry.

I have pastors, priests and the like in my shop every day, and there's a good-natured but intense competition to sign me up. As PK complained how hardware store architects didn't know squat about acoustics, I was tempted to officially designate him my pastor, to get his highest quality counseling. But I didn't want him resting on his laurels. I wanted to keep PK's competitive fires stoked. Clergymen are the most competitive people I know. Far more than doctors, let me tell you. If preachers could earn credits for every soul saved, Hell's volume would slow to a trickle.

Unfortunately, they have to earn money instead. While I went on about how badly I wanted to be saved, PK keyed on the how. Next thing I knew he was talking customer service pledges and spitballing a new faith-series of books, while an unearthly fire burned in my knee and then my hip.

As I left, PK begged me to schedule a follow-up visit, practically clinging to my pant leg or whatever they call the shorts' version. Even though I had the feeling a lot was riding on keeping my butt in his chair and committing myself to the painstaking process of coming to grips with the means to salvation, I wasn't in the mood to brainstorm the lecture series that would make PK a Christian-secular crossover sensation. I figured if I walked out his door, shamed him a little and put the pressure on him, maybe he'd come up with the answer I needed, before it was too late. Pardon me for dying, but I needed a little personalized attention.

What I needed was a bolt of lightning. Burning bush, flood, pestilence. Something to make me believe. Not canned phrases; not customer service pledges. I needed answers. I needed Faith. Faith is hard. I understand that. But professionals should have the tools to make me believe. The doctors couldn't make me believe in their cures, and PK couldn't convince me it didn't matter.

I had a sinking feeling that if I hadn't yet developed a full-fledged case of Faith, regardless whether PK rose to the challenge and showed me The Way, it was too late. I was that pathetic soul desperate for a deathbed conversion; and God's no sucker, that much I know. You didn't come to Me when you had a good day at the office, or when your credit score hit 775. Now you're gasping your last breath, and suddenly you got religion? I don't think so.

That's where my head was, as Edna gave the bum's rush to our latest pair of interviewees. We saw them two by two. Contestants, Edna called them. They had come in all shapes and sizes, and truth be told, I would have hired most of them, even if my brain was calm enough to listen to what they said. Edna was cold to anyone under the age of thirty—and, I'm proud to say, anyone who used the term 'customer service' in a positive fashion.

Edna had been visually assessing my vitals for the past half-hour. Now she knelt beside me. "How you doing?"

"Oh, not good. How many more do we have waiting out there?" Edna had turned the adjoining conference room into a holding pen.

"A few. But I think we already found our managers." She was referring to a guy named Dennis and a gal named Patti, both well north of thirty, and coincidentally, both bankers, Dennis local and Patti from nearby Valley City. Not so coincidentally, not at all surprisingly, both were huge fans of Edna Applejack. "It's you I'm worried about."

"Yeah, I'm going downhill here." I was hungry, for calories to arrest the slow shutdown of my engine, and queasy, knowing that the digestive system would need to move fast to extract nutrients before my stomach sent the food back up the pipe.

Edna treated me to her incredibly expressive eyes, studying me while mulling something behind the scenes. "You should take Dr. Bhani's treatment," she finally said.

I shook my head. "I'm going to stick with the Neil Ruzic route. Popping Celebrex to reduce the blood flow to the tumors."

"And did Celebrex cure him? All by itself?"

"He was on heavier, experimental stuff, too. Same theory, though."

"Your doctor actually prescribed Celebrex for your cancer?"

"Not exactly."

"Then how did you get it?"

"I have my connections." Gerry the pharmacist had run out of free samples, but Charlotte's mom works for an orthodontist, and somehow she's able to get any meds I've ever needed, in exchange for free drinks. Lucky for me she's not into pricey specialty drinks—she's a traditional brewed coffee drinker, and not a heavy one at that. My kind of prescription drug plan.

"Why stop with Celebrex?" Edna challenged. "Why not take the experimental drugs this Neil guy did?"

"I would actually need a doctor's recommendation for the heavy artillery. Bonilla has more faith in chemo than experimental procedures. I could start shopping my cancer around, try to get into a protocol, but it doesn't sound like my chances are good. And I'd have to do a lot of research to find a promising one."

"You're not being very proactive," Edna scolded.

I got defensive. "I thought I was. I don't have the time or money to devote my life to a cure."

"Sure, it's only your life. No time to save it."

"Wouldn't be much of a life to save if all I did was work on saving it."

"Then you should have taken Dr. Bhani's treatment a long time ago," said Edna. "And if you're so worried about money, we'll find a way to get more."

"I don't think I can raise any more money in good conscience. But I really did appreciate the golf tournament."

Edna smiled. "Eleven thousand bucks for your treatments."

"I wouldn't be feeling so guilty if my foursome hadn't won. And it felt strange calling it the First Annual Brian Lawson Memorial Golf Tournament."

"I'm already thinking about the First Annual Brian Lawson Memorial Bowling Tournament."

"So you can pop out of another cake in that Wonder Woman costume."

"You should see me as Catwoman."

I squirmed in the chair. "Not to be a party planner pooper, but…"

Edna rested her cool hand on my forehead. "You have a fever, honey."

I suddenly felt like crying. "I don't want to continually lay my troubles on you…but I have a bad feeling about what's going on inside me. This past week I've been having pain I've never felt before. It's scaring the shit out of me. I'm dreading the results of my tests from this morning."

"From now on, I want you to stay away from the hospital," said Edna. "From what Dr. Bhani told me—"

"You talked to him?"

"I told him I'm researching alternative treatments for you. He gave me copies of all his research publications and excerpts from his case files. I've called him a few times since then to get clarification on a few things. We're pretty chummy."

"You're amazing."

Edna winked. "He's certain Brent McEwen died from an infection he caught in the hospital. The bacterial strain Dr. Bhani uses is very similar to what Brent caught—that's what makes it so hard to prove it wasn't his."

I fought back images of Brent's death photos. "So what killed Brent?"

"S. pyogenes."

"What does that mean?"

"That's the bacteria that killed Brent."

"I know, but what the hell is S. pyogenes?"

"S. pyogenes." Edna's voice sharpened. "That's what it's called."

"Alright, sorry, I guess neither of us are doctors."

"That's true, but at least one of us has spent the time to do some research."

"And I really appreciate it."

"I don't want your gratitude, honey. I want you cured. And I've studied Dr. Bhani's materials long enough that you need to believe what I'm telling you. I've also spent time surveying other alternative treatments out there, and the reactions from the medical community. I wanted to know how Dr. Bhani stacks up, and what his peers have said about him." Edna's long fingers played with the hairs on my arm. Felt good. "Dr. Bhani's method is extreme. That's why he's not getting any favorable press. And other doctors have had some trouble replicating his results."

"Why?"

"The other doctors are scared to apply his treatment to the extreme that Dr. Bhani recommends. Making you violently sick in order to make you better sounds medieval. Suffice it to say a lot of people think he's a crackpot."

"That's why I'm more afraid of his treatment than I am of the cancer."

Edna's nostrils flared and her eyes grew bigger yet, from footballs to rugby balls. "Who sent those God-damn pictures to you?"

"I'd tell you if I knew. I'd have to guess one of the McEwens. They're the only ones who would have had access to the pictures. And hate me."

Edna gave me her hand, and together we stood. "You're coming with me tonight," she decided, "to the July Chicken Fry. I was invited to go with the McEwens, but you're my date. We're going to find out tonight who sent you those pictures."

"I'm not sure it matters—"

"It matters," said Edna. "It matters to me."

I nodded at the door to the adjoining conference room where the rest of our applicants waited. "What about them?"

"They'll have to come back later. We're worth it."

EDNA PICKED me up at six in the Talon. Yeah, she was the man in this relationship. Edna had a way of taking charge without making me feel threatened. Besides Charlotte, she was the only person I felt comfortable talking for me. And I didn't even agree with a lot of what she said. "I was thinking," Edna told me as I dropped into the Talon, "maybe that heavy-set guy, the one getting his MBA from UND by correspondence, wouldn't be a bad choice. He had some interesting marketing ideas."

"Wasn't his name Brian?"

"That's the one."

"We can't have two Brians."

Edna laughed. "He couldn't tell whether you were joking about that."

"That's because I was pretending to be pretending to be serious."

"It's not the name," said Edna, "it's the way that you use it. When people say 'Brian', it'll be obvious who they're talking about."

"Did you mean me or him?"

"Well, both."

"See?" I said. "Confusion already."

Edna frowned. "Okay," she decided. "He's out."

Felt good. So maybe I wasn't completely ready to hand over the reins.

"Did you get some rest?" Edna asked.

"Yes," I lied. I had gone into work, to will my customers to choose me over Hernandes's first day at the Bluffs.

"You look good," said Edna.

Probably also a lie. Although some of my hair had grown out a half-inch. If my medicine cabinet and handheld mirrors could be trusted, an illusion of decent coverage had been created, allowing me to shuck the ballcap. "I am ready to party all night."

From Edna's tight smile, she could tell this was a bluff, thankfully.

"We probably shouldn't make a scene tonight," I recommended. "No matter what we find out about the pictures."

Edna put her hand on my leg. "There's no occasion so sacrosanct that evildoers should enjoy immunity from prosecution."

"Sure, that's one of my rules of thumb, too. I just thought tonight, a community event, in a church…"

"Complacency kills. Churches understand that better than anyone. Life without strife and struggle is empty of significance."

I was dating a revolutionary. "Speaking of struggles…I drove through the campus yesterday, and there is absolutely nothing happening at our site. No way we can be open by September first, right?"

Edna shook her head. "Rick has committed to me. But if it makes you feel better, we'll corner Mike and get him to do the same."

"Before or after we accuse his family of using their son's horrific death to scare me away from a potential cure?"

There was the grim smile again.

"The pictures really aren't the deciding factor in my decision not to use Bhani's treatment," I assured her. I was in no mood for a confrontation with the McEwens. "I was freaked out by the idea already. And I want to give Celebrex a chance to work. Honestly. I'm not foolin'. You're not listening to me. At least not closely. Hey, look, the Bluffs is almost deserted." I spotted no more than ten cars in the lot as we drove by. "That's a shame."

"Bill closed early for the July Chicken Fry," said Edna.

"Oh. How, uh, how did you know that?"

"I stopped in after our interviews."

"Checking out the competition?"

"That's right."

"You didn't make a cameo appearance behind Billy's bar, did you?"

"No."

"Was he busy?"

"Fairly."

"How many customers would you say he had? Ten? Less than twenty?"

"Doesn't matter," said Edna. The Assembly of God church parking lot was full, and yet she drove to the front row and found an open spot. "Things will be different the day we open."

I had no doubt that was true. But I wanted to be kicking Hernandes's ass all by myself, without Edna's star power.

Bill Hernandes, the first person we saw as we descended into the church basement. The air was heavy with chicken-flavored carbon dioxide, a hundred people laughing and chewing and talking, crammed onto folding chairs at long tables. A couple guys yelled my name, and a few more shouted for Edna. My vision was blurry, I couldn't make out who was calling to me, so I smiled and waved like a float queen. It must have been a hundred degrees in there.

A puff of air down the stairwell parted what felt like some longer-than-acceptable strands of hair on the back of my head. As I reached up to pat down my scraggly 'do, Hernandes grabbed for my hand, so I gripped his right hand with my left.

"Pleased to meet you, Bob Dole," Hernandes quipped, holding our unconventional handshake aloft for everyone to see. "And Edna!" He was on top of the world. He ruled the joint. He owned the town. "Thank you for stopping by at our grand opening today, Edna. That meant so much to me." The room rapidly quieted down. Parents shushed their kids in order to tune in their conversation. Hernandes clung to Edna's arm. "It stamps your seal of approval on the new location, do you know?"

Edna wiggled fingers at her admirers. "Was business good then?"

"It was crazy," said Hernandes. "The place was buzzing after you and Rick left. I swear they must have been calling their friends and telling them to come down. We became even busier."

"You went with Rick?" I asked her. "McEwen?"

"And speak of the devil," said Hernandes.

Rick sauntered over from the line to join us. "Brian." He stood uncomfortably close and gave me a serious, caring stare. "How are you, man?"

Rick hadn't been in my shop for months. Maybe it was the fatigue, but seeing him brought on a melancholy nostalgia. "I'm good. You know. It's really good to see you."

He gave me a quick head bob and gripped my shoulder. "I know I haven't stopped in lately, but we've been thinking about you a lot."

Considering everything that had transpired with Andrea and Mike, this gesture meant a lot to me. Tears filled my eyes. I nodded to Tyler, following his dad and towing his mother with him. "Hey kiddo. Hey lady."

Andrea wouldn't look at me. "Tyler had his last basketball game today and scored ten points," Rick reported.

I tousled that young-un's hair. "I think he's grown a couple inches since I saw him last. Is he as tall for his age as you are?" Rick was around six-three with broad shoulders that carried a couple more pounds each time I saw him, experience adding gravitas to his frame, making it easier and easier to picture him stepping into Mike's shoes to run the company.

"A couple girls on his team are taller than he is," said Rick.

"What, cheerleaders?" Hernandes blurted. And then he looked at Edna and almost started crying.

Rick was a space invader as it was. But he was really standing in Hernandes's wheelhouse when he said, "It's coed. Nerf league. They started it when Edna was playing at JC. Because every kid in diapers wanted to be like her."

"Now they'll all want to be coffeeshop owners," I said.

With Hernandes frowning over that one, Edna took hold of Rick's forearm. "After we're done eating, Brian and I want to talk about the construction schedule. Among other things." She let go and left fingernail imprints.

Hernandes was slight and small-boned. He looked up at Rick and then Edna, back and forth, a child trying to catch Daddy's and Mommy's eyes. "What construction schedule?"

"You haven't heard?" I said nonchalantly. "Edna and I are opening a coffeeshop on campus."

"Whoa," said Hernandes. "Really. Wow. The two of you? That's great!" He pumped Edna's hand. "Congratulations!"

Not the reaction I was hoping for. I wanted tears. "We're not sure what we'll name it, since 'Campus Coffee' is already taken. Maybe 'On Campus Coffee', huh?"

"That's a good one, man," said Rick.

Pastor Kyle had been eyeballing us since we walked in. He was pinned against the dirty dishes cart by an older lady attempting to lay her heavy burden upon him. "Looky there, it's Brian and Edna!" He pretended to notice us for the first time. "Excuse me for a moment, Agnes." PK broke her grip and fled. "Two of our biggest stars! I am so glad you came!" He shook everyone's hand, some for the second time I'm sure.

The minor commotion inspired council prez Jasper to stand at the farthest table and beller, "Hey! Get yourselves over here!" He pointed in a commanding way at two empty seats.

"No!" I yelled back.

"Lawson," Jasper growled. He headed for us while Denise shielded her eyes in embarrassment, peeking to enjoy the spectacle her husband loved to create.

"That Jasper," PK said with affection. "What are we going to do with him?" He put a hand on my shoulder. "Listen Brian, I feel terrible about how our conversation ended this morning. Maybe we can sit down and eat together? Did you bring a big appetite?"

"I think I can do a little damage."

PK surveyed the masses. "For our inaugural year I'd say we're doing all right, don't you think?"

Jasper plowed into us and shook PK like a rag doll, making his Charlie Brown head float side-to-side like a Macy's Thanksgiving Day parade balloon. "Jasper," said PK, "I've been having back problems, and I promised my wife I wouldn't overdo it tonight, carrying around the big tubs of chicken." He arched his back and groaned. "Now she's going to think I lied to her."

Jasper just grinned.

"Still, I'm glad you're here. I was telling Brian how pleased I am by the turnout. It's a combined effort of four churches," PK told me, "and Jasper volunteered a lot of his time distributing flyers."

"Almost as busy as the Catholic fish fry," I congratulated them.

PK leaned into our group and said in a conspiratorial whisper, "That's what we're aiming for. We're considering going head to head next year."

"Throw in a raffle, and you could put the Catholics out of business. Speaking of which, did you hear Edna and I are opening a new shop on campus?"

PK nodded approvingly. "Let me tell you, I think that could be a real moneymaker."

"You think so?" I stole a glance at Hernandes. Were those teardrops forming in the corners of his bulging chinchilla eyeballs? They always glistened so it was hard to be sure. I urged PK to go on. "You think people will dig us?"

"I would think that between the two of you," PK obliged me, "you'll land every coffee drinker in town. And create a few new coffee lovers on campus."

"Coffee is a great study aid," I mumbled. The heat and the nostril-clogging grease were getting to me. I wanted Edna to take me home, but she was grilling Rick about the construction schedule. Hernandes drifted near them, pretending to be included, downcast and probably wondering whether it was too late to get his old job back. It served the dumb sonofabitch right, thinking he could waltz into my town and start a shop. Who did he think he was? Hernandes could build a bridge to the campus and it wouldn't matter. Hire an Edna Applejack impersonator—"Watch the North Dakota legend throttle a city boy with one hand and whip up a skim-milk latté with the other!"—and we'd still be kicking his ass...

My mind stumbled down its own ranting road. And then I realized I really had stumbled. I suddenly had a fever, a few thousand BTUs escaping out the top of my head, leaving me dizzy and weak and covered in a sheen of cold sweat. I looked for a nearby chair, empty or otherwise.

"I'm going to get Brian's sign-off on our store plans," Edna told Rick, the sound ebbing and flowing, "and then we'll want you to start pronto." Her voice was hypnotic like the ocean. I wished for seasickness pills.

Rick rubbed at his jaw, as if his sparse blonde stubble was a genuine five o'clock shadow. "I was taking a look at our schedule today. It's going to be tough to get started until after Labor Day."

"Maybe we should be working with Redd Vapp," I named the McEwens' only competitor, playing the part of the tough negotiator while pawing for the wall. I slid for a few feet along the circa 1970s paneling before getting my sea legs under me. No one seemed to notice, or care, that I was fading fast.

"Rick will handle this," said Edna, deciding the issue.

I was wrong, my slow fainting spell hadn't gone unnoticed. Valerie McEwen was beside me, her warm hands in the small of my back. "Brian, you need to sit down."

"Or I could just fall down here," I offered, teetering, knees shaking. It was going to take more than one little McEwen to keep me on my feet.

"When we talked earlier, I wasn't aware Dad made a couple late season commitments," Rick explained to Edna. "They're rigid."

"That's something for you to work out internally," Edna said firmly.

Rick shook his head. "I'd like to…"

"Andrea," Valerie called. "Andrea," she snapped, "could you help me?"

Andrea debated coming to my aid, slowly approaching, disgusted.

"As long as you're in the mood to disappoint me," said Edna sharply, glaring at Rick and pointing at me. "Why don't you tell us why your family sent Brian those pictures?"

"Oh boy," I said as the room faded.

"What are you talking about?" I heard Rick ask.

"You know damn well," said Edna. "The pictures of Brent."

My sparkles cleared in time to see the color drain from Rick's face. "What pictures?" he said.

Edna had the decency to tone down her reply. "His autopsy shots."

Rick wasn't an expressive man. He had two faces, a police interrogation face and a softer hint-of-a-smile police interrogation face. Nothing new now, except he fixed his no-nonsense stare on an imaginary block of wood that he chopped with an axe-like hand. "I never saw any pictures." Air whistled through Rick's nose. "After Brent got sick, I never saw him, period."

Mike wandered into the conversation like a dazed accident victim. His coccyx must not have been healing properly, because he walked with a limp and a cane. "What did you see?" he hissed at Edna as Valerie abandoned me to cling to Edna's arm.

My tall gorgeous partner dared the McEwens to meet her fierce gaze. "Someone used the pictures as a scare tactic to frighten Brian away from Dr. Bhani's treatment. It was a cheap, sniveling, gutless—"

"What pictures?" Mike demanded.

"I did it," said Andrea. She too left my side, to stand beside her ex, hugging Tyler in front of her.

"What pictures?" Mike demanded, this time of Andrea. He had chicken grease smeared on his chin. It was really obvious. Pastor Kyle was looking at it. We were the highlight of the dinner now, bigger than Jesus, and more than a couple folks were staring at Mike's greasy chin. I was pissed at Valerie for not wiping it off. Mike was going to need all the dignity he could get. "You have pictures?" He advanced on Andrea. Valerie closed from the other side, until I could no longer see the little woman. "I want to see them. I never saw him. I never saw my son."

So it was Andrea. Maybe she was looking out for me, I theorized. Maybe she was having second thoughts about Bhani's treatment—she was too ethical to publicly criticize her boss, but determined to do the right thing and warn me of the danger.

Man I'm a good person, I decided, unable to control my meandering brain. Look at me giving Andrea the benefit of the doubt, when everyone knows she's nothing more than a vindictive bitch.

Rick wedged between his parents and Andrea. I thought his folks were the least of his worries. Edna was circling behind Andrea, who was clueless, counting on that old adage, that Jesus looks out for the child-like, the self-righteous, the smug, the guilt-free.

"The hospital wouldn't let us into the room." Mike was having a reminiscence of sorts as he struggled pathetically to get past Rick. "They said it was too contagious. They wouldn't let us see his body."

Edna had Andrea in her sights. She and Mike would simultaneously lay hands on the little woman and a tug of war would ensue, until someone got the lion's share of the wishbone.

They say there's never a cop around when you need one, but we had the next best thing, pastors, four of them. PK, Pastor Brad, John the Baptist minister, and Reverend Sergio converged on the scene. If everyone had ducked, I think they would have banged heads.

"I want to see those pictures," Mike babbled. Valerie was clawing at her son, going to claw right through him to get to Andrea.

Who was now in Edna's possession. As long as I wasn't going to pass out, I needed to save her. I lurched from the wall and was bumped by PK. Yes he's a solid guy, but at my normal weight and without a fast-moving fever playing havoc with my professional-grade equilibrium, I wouldn't have gone down.

I fought it—shouldn't have—and careened forward. Looked like I dove, Jasper told me later, into Mike McEwen's knees. His cane snapped like a twig and he buckled. I looked up to see Valerie's sexy but tasteful underwear, and Edna lifting Andrea off the ground so abruptly that Andrea's head snapped back. "God!" Her yelp had a Doppler effect, like she was whipping past on a roller coaster. Instead of pleading for her life, or even struggling a little, Andrea was indignant and inert, confident justice would prevail and the men in her life would soon have this maniac in restraints.

"You nasty little bitch." Edna put Andrea down and squeezed her cheeks, no doubt infuriated by the smug look that would not come off. "What you did was goddamned wicked." Any second now Edna was going to pop Andrea's head like a grape, and Rick knew it, working quickly to pry away Edna's fingers, assisted by Jasper and John the Baptist minister. A rush of diners left their seats and overran PK and Pastor Brad's peacekeeping positions. The first few were careful not to step on me and Mike, but chaos was building in the shouting, jostling rugby scrum above us.

"You need to knock this shit off right now!"

"Some son of a bitch just bit me!"

"You are fucking psycho."

"Everyone now…hey, hey, hey…God damn it, you need to settle down!"

Don't worry about the tender ears of the men of God. They're the most intense guys I know. Besides golfers out on the course, preachers in casual conversation are the most likely folks to let fly with a cuss word. They get credit for two of the quotes above.

We needed to get off the floor. I crawled to Mike and helped him to his feet. He lurched past me before I could ask him if he was okay. Edna was screaming, and everyone was shouting for her to settle down, except Andrea, who was scowling and checking her puffy blouse for damage as Rick led her away from the fray. "You are screwing with Brian's life!" Edna raged after her.

"If Andrea managed to scare Brian away from that fruitcake Bhani," Valerie said with a quavering voice, "then she saved his life!"

"Valerie, listen to me." Edna shook off John the Baptist minister. She was free for the moment. "What happened to Brent was just terrible misfortune."

Mike waved his hands to ward off what he saw as Edna's temporary demonic possession. "You don't know. Edna, you weren't there to see what that man did to my boy. How sick Brent got when Bhani injected him with those toxins. Even though he seemed like he was getting better afterward, we should have known. We should have seen that he wasn't okay…"

While PK and John the Baptist minister were captivated by the family drama, this was too public for Pastor Brad. "Mike, Mike," he said in an urgent hush, "come on, let's take this somewhere private."

But Mike only had eyes for Edna, and now they were locked up, gripping each other's forearms and speaking, loudly, face to face.

"It wasn't Bhani's treatment!" Edna insisted.

"You weren't there!" said Mike.

"I've done the research!" said Edna. "What Bhani is doing is right!"

"No-no-no! He's experimenting, on helpless people! It's not right!"

"He is curing people! Terribly sick people who would die without him!"

It was whips-and-chains sensuous, the way they were arguing right into each other's mouths. Valerie must have thought so too, because she wormed her way into the middle, forcing them apart. I almost pulled her back.

"Don't you tell me what I'm supposed to feel about my son," Mike pleaded with Edna.

"And don't you presume to know what's right for Brian," Edna retorted.

"Edna!" Bobby Guldseth the College's athletic director barreled down the stairs and grabbed Edna from behind, wrapping her up tightly and pulling her backward. Because they were the same height and because of Bobby's crane neck, their heads were side by side like Siamese twins. This combined entity rocked back and forth, the Edna head growling and the Bobby head saying, "Take it easy, baby," in a soothing purr.

"Bobby, it's okay," said PK, as uncomfortable as the rest of us with this scene. "Edna's okay."

Looking perplexed, Bobby disentangled from Edna. "I didn't want you to do anything to jeopardize your parole."

"I'm not on parole," said Edna.

"Probation," Bobby corrected.

"Nope," said Edna.

Mike turned on me, wincing and unsteady on his feet. "Whatever you do, don't let that Bhani bastard get ahold of you."

This we agreed on. I grabbed a napkin from the condiments table and handed it to Mike, indicating his chin. When he didn't understand, I took the napkin back and wiped up the chicken grease myself.

"That is such a beautiful sight," said Valerie.

"That grease was driving me crazy."

"The bastard almost killed me," said Mike, clutching at his back and limping away.

Edna knifed through the gaggle of peacekeepers and took me by the arm. I threw a goodbye wave at the crowd and was marched upstairs.

"Elvis has let the building!" I heard Jasper announce.

Edna was silent en route to our front-row parking spot. I jabbered, riding an adrenaline boost. "I'd be worried that little scuffle tarnished our rep and ruined our chances with the campus location, except I think Bobby gets turned on when you get feisty. I thought you were going to break Andrea's face. I broke Mike's cane. And maybe his back."

We dropped into the Talon and Edna turned to me. She tucked gossamer hair behind her ear and took my hand. "I want you to move in with me. Right away. When Dr. Bhani administers his treatment, it's going to be rough, and I want to be there to pull you through."

"I appreciate the offer, but..." It was hard to disagree with Edna. And hard not to be suspicious that she fully expected major complications from Bhani's treatment, hoped for them almost, so that she could be my savior. It wouldn't be Bhani proving the McEwens wrong, it would be Edna. "I'm not planning to go to Dr. Bhani."

She shook her head. "I know it's a big decision, and you need more time to prepare yourself, mentally." Edna touched my cheek. "Either way, you and I are partners. I want us to be as close as possible."

"You really want me to live with you?"

"I do."

"Well..." This was obviously a big decision, but I skipped right past the pros and cons list. "...okay." What Edna wants, Edna gets. Who was I kidding, there was no need for her to waste time arguing with me over Bhani's treatment. She knew she would get her way.

Something whacked my window, making me spasm so hard my seatbelt locked. Andrea stood beside the Talon, fuming. Edna made to jump out but I grabbed her wrist and held her in place. Andrea's men had now saved her life twice that night. I pushed the door open. "What's up?" I said casually.

Andrea's voice was snottier than ever. "I wanted to tell you something. That book I gave you? The guy who found his own cure for cancer?"

"Neil Ruzic," I said.

"Yeah, well, it turns out he died last year. Of cancer."

"What?"

Andrea soaked in the shock registering on my face. "Just wanted to let you know." She turned on her heel and marched off.

"Holy...shit." I let the door pinch against my cancer leg.

"What's going on?" Edna demanded.

Tears ran down my face, and I didn't know how to tell her why. Why I was crying for a complete stranger, who had died a year ago.

EDNA COULDN'T understand, and didn't really try. She was still boiling over Andrea's manipulation. At least she didn't argue when I said I needed to be alone. She left me on her couch and went to bed. First night living together and we slept alone. I could marry a woman like that.

I wouldn't have been able to find the composure or the words to explain my grief over Neil's passing. As I read his saga, his battle had become a proxy for mine. I had been pulling for him, because I knew deep down that if he could figure out a way to win, I would too—his way, my way, some way, the cancer didn't stand a chance. No matter how bleak things got, I would be holding this certainty as my ace in the hole.

And so maybe my depression over the cancer's relentlessness had been some sort of affectation—a lot of reality, sure, but perhaps a fair amount of subconscious theater, acting the way a terminal patient should, looking for sympathy, all the while just as subconsciously certain I was going to win the battle. All that existential gnashing of the teeth and beating on my breast over the existence of God, convinced I had sunk into uncharted depths of despair—to a certain extent, I had been fooling myself.

Because this was deeper, this was worse. Underneath the depression was now a gaping hole where that ace must have been. Three years ago Neil Ruzic had declared himself cured. Two years later he was dead. I was dead. Cancer didn't give a shit who I was or what I had done, how much time and effort I spent on a cure, or how passionately I wanted to live. Cancer was unstoppable.

I cried some more, a mess on Edna's couch. Take away the future, and your past disappears too. I had truly become meaningless. The sounds of the grandfather clock ticking and car engines running outside, the feel of my pulse in my shin, the vague memories of happier times...all of it floated in the black goo swirling around me, random bits of meaningless data embedded in the vortex.

My mind must have finally grasped the certainty of my pending annihilation, for a virtual PK appeared, floating above me, soothingly reciting a touched-up timeline of my life, reminding me Jesus was waiting, administering a last rites home version. I choked and wailed at the utter lack of comfort and almost died right then and there. I think I came that close.

T-2

THE NOTHINGNESS in my head left me open to detailed observations I don't normally make, as I sat in the exam room Monday morning. The sanitary paper was crinkled where it stretched over the end of the padded exam table, creased by someone's sweaty behind. The stirrups' mounting rods were coated with dirty grease, a schmear of active cultures. The Danger—Explosives! sign was two-thirds missing on the oxygen tank, which leaned heavily against the flimsy cart's restraining strap.

The healthcare profession has done a helluva sales job convincing us they have it all under control. American hospitals are viewed as sanctuaries of healing and revitalization, and we trust American doctors to give us the best treatments. Yet here were all these warts, these signs of harried, overworked staff too tired or careless to keep the germs away. I wished for a rag and a jug of bleach so I could do a quick disinfect.

What did it say about the doctors? Were they taking time-saving shortcuts too, choosing whatever the pharmaceutical companies told them was best and pretending to be experts? After a long day studying charts and listening to endless complaints, were they willing to spend a couple hours at home absorbing the latest research reports and treatment efficacy studies?

Some. That was as good as it ever got. Some aides and orderlies disinfected all the way into the corners and the crevices, and some doctors picked up the Journal of the American Medical Association at ten p.m. Some.

"Brian." Bonilla was inside with the door closed before I registered his presence. He reached down to shake my hand. "How are you today?" His eyes were on my leg. I hiked my shorts to give him a clear view up to my knee. "Hm." Bonilla lowered his roller stool to put him on level with my knee. He didn't ask me to hop up on the table, because he probably doubted I could. He squished the puffy bruised area below the knee, exactly like I wished he wouldn't. "You didn't bump this over the weekend?"

"It's gotten worse, hasn't it?"

"Since Saturday." Bonilla rolled to the countertop to retrieve my file, pretending to study it while he perfected the message he had to deliver. He closed the file, crossed his legs, and hooked a knee. "From what we see on your scans, the cancer is aggressive." Remember when I used to like that word? "We would now type it Stage Four. There is some movement into your abdomen and possibly your chest. Small enough that we feel confident we can have success with another round of chemo and targeted radiation. These past three weeks we lost some time and some of the advantage we had gained, to be honest with you. I fully respect your decision not to have undergone another round so soon after the last one. I appreciate what you're going through. But if we're going to stop these nodes from further proliferation...."

I nodded through the whole spiel, first trying to recall what had possessed me to have stopped my treatments for three weeks, then reminding myself it wouldn't have mattered anyway. "You know what, doc, I don't care one way or the other. I'm ready to do whatever you recommend."

Bonilla frowned. "You need to hear the rest before you make any decisions. I've been struggling with this...but seeing your leg now..."

I was amazed he could even look at my leg. But he leaned forward and continued to examine it, probing above the knee. I have sweet quads, teardrops on both sides of the kneecap, thighs made for the short-shorts I had always done my best to keep in style. So he had to get past some muscle, just not as much as a few months ago.

"I don't have confidence that chemo and radiation can reduce this tumor or even stop it from growing," said Bonilla.

I was suddenly sure he was going to refer me to Dr. Bhani.

"This is tough to say and much tougher to hear," said Bonilla.

"It's okay, doc. I can handle it."

"We need to remove your leg at the hip."

I stood and then fell back into the chair, making it slide and squeal. Bonilla reached out to steady me. I started to convulse across my midsection, shaking hard and losing control of my arms and legs.

"Come here." Bonilla bent me forward into his lap and rubbed my back, telling me to breathe. Obviously I know implicitly the importance of breathing, yet it helped to be coached.

"Oh no," I said, and then repeated it, again and again, slower and more softly until Bonilla made me stop.

He sat me up straight and scooted in tight, putting stabilizing hands on my hips. "Brian, you're right, this is serious and it's traumatic. But it isn't the end of the world. It isn't the end of anything."

I nodded. He probably thought I was agreeing with him. I rocked back and forth, fighting back the rising bile. There was no hurl pail at the ready, quite an oversight given my history.

"I want you to calm yourself," said Bonilla. "Don't think of anything but a future without cancer. Okay? Stay in this room as long as you like. In fact I'd like you to stay here for a couple hours. I have other patients to see, and then I'll stop back in. In the meantime I'm going to ask one of our counselors to come see you." He gave me a final steadying squeeze before rolling away to stand. "Dr. Carter is a psy-D with a lot of experience with folks who have made it through similar circumstances. And you will make it through.

"Remember…" Bonilla patted his own chest in a soothing way. "Life without cancer is going to be wonderful."

I waited long enough for him to move down the hall to his next patient, and then abandoned the room and ran limping to the elevator. I escaped the hospital without being challenged and drove to Edna's. Maybe I wouldn't even go back to my apartment, ever again. I didn't want to die there.

I WAS shocked to wake up and find I had slept, curled up at the foot of Edna's bed. It was dark, after ten. There was no sign Edna had been home. With numb lips I ate a handful of mixed nuts and a package of ramen. I sat there for awhile, at Edna's kitchen bar, doing my best not to think of anything. And then all of a sudden I was ready to call Mom and Dad.

No answer. What a message to leave—but I had to say it, I couldn't wait any longer for them to know. "Had another doctor's appointment today. A follow-up from the tests on Saturday. Not good news. It's spreading. They think they can wipe out the new spots with more chemo and radiation, but the leg with the original tumor really worries them. My doctor wants to amputate my leg. All the way up to my hip." My throat tightened; only by picturing my mom sobbing as she listened could I act brave. "I'm not a big fan of that idea. I'll let you guys know as soon as I decide. So…I don't know, maybe I'll even fly back home. Let Charlotte run the shop for awhile. Edna would probably be happy to do it, too. We'll see. Not sure of anything right now.

"Hey Dad, I just remembered you're having that dinner meeting with the ASCS office tonight. You'll have to let me know how it went. I'm up late tonight—I think I've done all the sleeping I'm going to for awhile. So give me a call when you get home. I'm at Edna's. She's been great…."

I wrapped it up before the warning beep, not bad considering how comforting it was to talk to my parents' machine.

I sat, I walked around the house. I bounced up and down. I did the stairs, three times. Sometimes the leg didn't hurt at all. There was still a lot of good left in that leg.

When Edna wasn't home by midnight, I curled up on her couch and stared through the big front window at the night air drifting down the street and eddying through the trees, keeping the few remaining houselights at bay. I savored the memory of walking through that air. When I was in it, I didn't need alcohol; the smell of it was enough to make me giddy and horny and deliriously happy to be alive. Not creative, not inspired to do great things. I'll work from sun-up until the sun goes down, but not a second later. Night is the time to spend a little money and convince her to stay out past a responsible bedtime, to enjoy the fruits of my hard work, to take pride in all those great accomplishments and hope she felt it too. I prayed to be allowed to experience the night air again; and not just one last time.

WEDNESDAY MORNING behind the bar I wore my grungiest look in a long time. Ball cap. A bad bum's scraggly beard. A pair of worn pajama pants that fit easily and comfortably over my knee, and under my apron an old long-sleeve Cal-Davis practice jersey I've had since I was sixteen, when Ryan and I conned homely little Bev Dalrymple to violate her sacred student manager duties and cop a couple for us. Now it fit me again.

We were midway through the morning rush, the shop crowded, Charlotte and Sara by my side. Terrence was making a rare appearance with the regulars at the counter. While making drinks I told Charlotte how I had spent the other night waiting up for Edna by rifling through her files on Dr. Bhani's treatment. Everyone else was free to listen in.

"Doc by the name of Hotchkiss tried to replicate Bhani's results. So yesterday I called him. At the Mayo Clinic. I couldn't believe he took my call. I told his secretary who I was and why I was calling, and she put me right through to him."

"Maybe he heard you're dating Edna Applejack," Terrence suggested.

I wasn't sure I liked him with a quick wit. Charlotte didn't, judging by her unhappy snort. "I told his secretary I was dying. Next thing I know, I'm talking to him. From what I hear, mostly from reading Edna's research file, this Hotchkiss is well-known for his research on the immune system…"

"What'd he say?" Bart Shock prompted.

I smiled the way storytellers do. "You don't think I know how to tell a story, do you?"

"I could tell you were stumbling," said Bart.

"Whatever, man." I put a drink on the pickup shelf. "Skinny no-foam latté." Being around my favorite customers, and my favorite employee Charlotte, almost, almost was enough to make me enjoy the morning or at least the minute without sinking into a mental coma. "So I told him about my situation…" I stopped, drawing a blank on the drink I was preparing. I looked at Charlotte.

"Decaf americano, room for cream," she said.

"Thanks. I told Dr. Hotchkiss I was contemplating going with Dr. Bhani's treatment, and the next thing I know he goes into a rant."

"He wasn't encouraging?" Charlotte asked as she retrieved another gallon of whole milk.

"You could say that. He said he tried it on five patients, and none responded. 'Flat-out', that's the phrase he used. 'Those goddamn toxins flat-out don't work.' Bhani's Toxins, that's what the other scientists are calling them. Hotchkiss said Bhani has no credibility. So there."

"Did you believe him?" asked Donna.

"Bart threw off my rhythm, so I'm not sure if I mentioned that Dr. Hotchkiss is a world-renowned cancer researcher. So yeah, seems like a good idea to listen to him."

"Maybe he's in competition with Dr. Bhani," Bart countered. "Working on a similar cancer cure."

"I wasn't really looking for anyone to play devil's advocate, Bart."

"That's the only reason this Hotchkiss would have been chosen to verify Dr. Bhani's results," said Bart. "Because he's familiar with the field, and probably doing similar things."

"From what I've heard, Bhani is off on his own rogue path," I said.

"The peer review system is flawed," Bart declared, a little put-out I wasn't agreeing with everything he said, because his wife is a pediatrician after all.

"Flat-out doesn't work," Terrence quoted my quote. "It would be hard to imagine…" He paused, humped over in his chair. "It would be hard to imagine a peer feeling comfortable making that sort of allegation, unless…" Terrence gave a slothlike look toward the front door. Everyone waited. We were a patient audience that day. "…unless he had rock-solid proof to back it up." He looked for agreement with a raised eyebrow. Terrence has thick, expressive eyebrows, with plenty of room on his forehead for those beetles to run.

I knuckleknocked him above Bart's coffee cup. "That's what I'm saying."

"What did Edna say?" Sara asked, smiling. I was surprised, not about the smile, about the fact that she had been paying attention earlier when I related how high Edna was on Bhani. Not to brag, but when I told a story, people listened. Not to be a downer, but when I was gone, someone would no doubt step into my role, or not, and life would easily go on.

"I haven't told her yet. Decaf americano on the bar. Cal," I greeted the Ford dealership owner. "I don't feel like arguing about it with Edna," I told Sara. "I'd rather—"

Charlotte interrupted. "You and Edna are like an old married couple now? Arguing with each other, reading the paper over breakfast without saying a word to each other, that sort of thing?"

Through the door waltzed Kenny, the Wells Fargo manager. "Well, look who's back," I greeted him.

Kenny gave me a goofy smile. "What? Brian, I haven't seen you for awhile. We must be on different schedules. Work has been crazy lately. Going gangbusters, can't even draw a breath. You probably don't even remember my regular drink anymore," he babbled on.

"I remember."

"Brian has a long memory," Charlotte informed him. I had told her about finding Kenny and Laurie in Hernandes's shop, twice, and seeing his car parked at the wrong end of the Bluffs strip mall, more than a couple times.

"A good memory comes in handy," said Kenny. "Wish I had a better one."

"So you could remember where my shop is?"

Kenny stood awkwardly in front of the bar while the regulars looked him up and down. "I'd never forget the best coffee in town," he said.

I let him believe he was off the hook. "I was just telling these guys about my conversation with Edna the other night. She came home—"

"I heard Edna's your new partner here," said Kenny, all sparkly-eyed. "Is she in on a regular basis?"

"Here?" I played dumb. The sonofabitch was here to see Edna, not to patronize my establishment. He was counting out his money. "That'll be six-fifty," I told him. It didn't register. "Six-fifty for your drink, Kenny."

He gave me a blank stupid smile.

"I raised the price today. For you."

"But…" He mumbled a few words. Charlotte stared at him with outstretched hand. "Ha-ha," said Kenny, digging in his pocket. He pulled out three more dollars and gave them to Charlotte. "It's worth it for your coffee."

"Good, because that's your minimum price from now on."

I was feeling eyes on me, and now I spotted their owner, Liza Minnelli, standing forlornly beside what used to be her usual table in the window, before I banned her.

"So," said Kenny, "is Edna—"

"Edna doesn't have anything to do with this shop," I cut him off. "She and I are partnering on a new store on the campus that will be open with or without me on September first."

"You should know that, Kenny," said Bart, prickly on my behalf. My customers were a loyal bunch. I was a lucky man. Kind of. "You're probably financing the construction loan."

"Maybe Kenny can only lend to one coffeeshop at a time," I suggested. "That would be Bill Hernandes's shop at the Bluffs."

"Ha-ha," said Kenny, an onomatopoeia of a laugh.

"Is Bill making enough money to stay current on his payments?" I asked. "I figured that's why I see your car in his parking lot all the time. You're keeping an eye on your bad debt."

"Ho-ho!" said Kenny, startling the Red Hat ladies at the big table. "Not all the time. You don't see me there all the time. It's just very convenient to our branch on the north end."

Charlotte breezed past. "I drive by his shop." She was back and forth, doing it all, ringing up and chatting up the customers, filling bean orders, swapping out the empty pots, and keeping close tabs on the conversation. "I've even peeked my head in the door. That's all the closer I can stand to be. He's not very busy."

Liza inched toward the counter, on pace to arrive early that afternoon.

"So anyway," I resumed my story, "I had just finished ransacking Edna's office when she stumbles in around two a.m. Turns out she was wining and dining Rick McEwen."

Cal was goggle-eyed. "Rick is making it with Edna?"

"It's business," I explained. "No, really. This woman is all business."

"Listen to this guy," said Charlotte. "A month ago he didn't even know who Edna was. And now he's the Edna expert."

"Are you jealous?" Cal asked.

"Hell no."

"I think you're jealous," said Terrence.

"Bye Kenny," I called as he tried to slip away unnoticed. He raised his cup and ducked out the door.

"Maybe we're all a little jealous about Edna," said Cal. "But who should we be jealous of?" he asked me. "You or Rick?"

"Since Rick's got more than a year to live, I'd pick him."

"Get outta here," said Cal. "You ain't goin' nowhere. I don't know a lot—I never finished high school, d'I ever tell you that? Started at the Massey Ferguson shop as a mechanic."

Everyone got restless. "You may have mentioned it," said Bart with a grin.

"Alright, alright," said Cal. "I won't bore you fine gentlemen with all the details." I handed him a coffee spiked with espresso. "Thanks. I'm just here to tell you, I wouldn't be where I am today without knowing how to read people. And let me tell you, Brian Lawson, you'll be around after most of these fellas here are long gone."

"I wouldn't bet the dealership on it."

"You're gonna die an old grandpa," said Cal.

"I guess we'll see about that."

"Yes we will."

"Yes we will." This was a stupid argument.

Liza Minnelli cleared her throat.

"So what was Edna's business purpose for screwing Rick all night?" Bart asked, quietly enough to be considered discreet. "And can she take a deduction for that?"

"Honestly, it's not that sort of thing," I said.

"Maybe you don't get Edna all to yourself after all," said Charlotte.

"Go take care of Liza," I ordered under my breath. Charlotte gave me a cold look but did as told. "Rick's building our campus shop," I finally neared the end of my story. "We need the shop finished by late August. Which I guess would be speedy."

"Supersonic," said Cal. "Brian, this is North Dakota. Construction firms have six months to make a year's worth of income. I know for a fact McEwen has two huge projects to finish before the snow flies. One down in Kulm, the other outside of town here. If Rick's taking time from those moneymakers to build your little shop…"

"She slept with him," Bart decided.

"No way," I scoffed. "You know what, Edna is Edna. She doesn't need to resort to sex to get her way."

"Maybe she even likes it," Cal suggested.

"Brian," Charlotte called me over.

"One way or the other," I told them as I backed toward the till, "we'll be up and running by September first."

"Are you closing this store then?" Bart asked.

"No," I whined, exasperated. "No, Bart. No. That's not the plan." I was ready to explain how this was finally my opportunity to grow, to expand and prove I was ambitious and capable of bigger things— California or North Dakota, it didn't matter, I could make money, I could be a success by any measure. But then I remembered it didn't really matter anymore. "This shop will stay open." I turned on Liza. "Lady. I told you September first."

The elfin woman with the plastered black hair shifted foot to foot like she had to pee. She cocked her head, staring at the countertop. "I'm sorry for throwing the papers at you."

"I know. You already apologized on the phone. Twice."

"So I'm forgiven?" She made a half-turn toward her table. "I can come back…now?"

"September first."

Charlotte huffed and walked off. "Oh, oh," Liza squeaked, "I can't take not coming in here. I haven't written a letter, not since you kicked me out. I'm so far behind. I need to be in here." She presented a loose stack of papers and then yanked them back. "I brought my own paper."

I sighed. "Okay."

"Oh good! Coffee, large, please." Liza ran to the table to drop off her pen and all that paper, then hurried back.

I had her coffee ready. "That'll be five dollars."

"Hm? Huh? No. It's one dollar ninety cents." She reached for the steaming cup of coffee.

I pulled it back. "Until September first, five dollars."

"Brian," Charlotte hissed.

I sighed. "Okay. Two dollars."

Liza counted change in her palm, mumbling and shaking her head.

"Look out." Charlotte hip-checked me toward the counter crowd. "I'll ring her up."

Cal had left. Bart was humming. Terrence grimaced uncomfortably. Sara shook her head, almost not smiling, unwilling to look at me. "Tomorrow I'm going to charge Kenny seven bucks for his drink," I declared.

This cheered Terrence. "So your campus shop will be open by Labor Day?"

"A few days earlier, hopefully."

Bart whistled. "She's good."

"Brian," said Charlotte, on her way to the little office, "can you come in here when you get a minute?"

Bart shook his head. "She's not supposed to be able to order you in there."

I acted disgusted. Terrence stopped me as I headed for the office. "Amber and I want to have you over for dinner. Can you make it tonight?"

"Sure. Can I bring something?"

"Some manners," said Terrence. He may or may not have been referring to the way my hand was grabbing at my crotch. The inseam on my pj's was goofy. I decided henceforth to wear sweats instead.

"Shut the door," Charlotte ordered when I entered. I did so. "Brian…" She was going to cry. I had found that if I pretended she wasn't, she wouldn't. "I'm really upset about your hiring for the new store. Isn't it going to be James River Valley Coffee?"

"It is." I sensed where she was going with this, and I was embarrassed I hadn't addressed it proactively. "It'll probably be called The Blessed Cup or something like that. But it's going to be part of our chain."

"It's going to be a chain." This was worse news for Charlotte. "Great. So…how come I'm not interviewing for store manager?"

"Who says you're not?"

"Brian, I know you already hired a manager. I talked to Carissa, my friend at First Bank, and she said you hired her boss, Dennis. She said he told her you're only hiring 'adults'."

"I don't know if that's necessarily true," I said. "And you're twenty-two."

"Obviously you don't consider me an adult."

"Aw, come on," I said gently. "You're the best employee I've ever had."

"Well? Then why didn't you…" She angrily swabbed at the tears sparkling in her eyes. Before I could respond she said, "Craig is pissed, too. He doesn't understand why you didn't offer him a job. Assistant manager or whatever."

"He shouldn't have gone to work for Hernandes."

"You fired him."

"I'd call it laid off."

"Brian, don't be an ass right now."

"It's hard to turn it on and off."

"Just turn it off and leave it off." She was going to cry again.

"Char-lotte!" I bellowed so that everyone in the shop could hear. That always got a chuckle. This time it got me a sore throat and a disappointed scowl from Charlotte. I shook her shoulders and when her body relaxed, hugged her. Slapped her hard on the back. "Come on now! Here's what I can tell you," I used my indoor voice. "Edna has a firm opinion of the hires we need to make. I don't know if she's right, I don't know if she's wrong. I haven't taken the time to think about it. She wants a strong sales background. She wants people who have a long-term goal to manage multiple stores."

"That's me. That's me, Brian."

"I know. And older. She wants you to be older."

"See! I knew it! Brian, that's age discrimination."

"I don't believe North Dakota has laws against it."

"I'm not talking about suing you." Charlotte sounded too weary to sue anyone. She was weary for her age. "I'm talking about what's right."

"Maybe you're right. Time will tell. But for now, this is the direction we're going. Plus," I tried to soften the blow, "I need you here."

She held her arms tight to her body and lowered her head, composing herself. "So what about this shop? Will Edna make you go the same direction?"

"No. This is my shop, and mine alone. I'm very happy with the staff I have. Everyone does a great job. Everyone except Dana."

This prompted a weak smile. "Every store has to have someone to pick on and talk about behind their back," she said.

"I need to remember to tell Edna that. Come on now, cheer up. I love the job you do for me. You know I'd pay you more if I could. We would have gone under a couple months ago without you."

"What will the manager make at the campus shop?" Charlotte demanded.

Both our eyes went to the leaning tower of bills. "Let's just say this: they're going to be sorely disappointed if they expect to make as much as they did at the bank. Or the zoo, or the convenience store, or wherever they're coming from. This is a gamble on their part."

Charlotte waited for a better answer. For all I knew, Edna was paying them six figures with full bennies, bonus and profit-sharing. I wasn't going to admit how little control I had over the process. Charlotte left the office unhappy, and left work early complaining of a migraine.

I LEFT work at three and caught Edna on her cell. I invited her to Terrence and Amber's for dinner, but she had a meeting with Rick and the College's facilities manager, to agree on the exact site location, the square footage, the orientation of the front door. They would decide on the number and location of parking spots. Architectural style and color. Signage.

Things were moving forward. All I had to do was stay out of the way, stay alive, and Edna would take care of everything. I would have loved to oversee this design phase, but there was no portion of my mind available for future thought. I would try to plan something—creative new drink names for the campus shop, a round of golf, what to eat for lunch—and suddenly the gears would stop turning with an audible clunk, and a gray blanket would descend, a heavy numbing shroud laying upon my brain, unfurling to cover more and more of my body. Maybe it was a mental representation of my cancer. Maybe it was the cancer itself.

Edna wanted me to move all of my things to her house, and make it official. Her motivation was unclear. But whether it was affection or infatuation, to help me fight for life or to be my hospice caregiver, any rationale was fine with me. I liked the attention, and I had no guilt over subjecting her to the mental toll of living with a terminal patient—without a doubt, Edna was strong enough to watch me die and then move on.

When I mentally traveled down this road, the word legacy came to mind. If anyone could guarantee my legacy, it was Edna. I believed she would be committed to ensuring the Brian Lawson Coffeeshop Experience lived on. Maybe even a Brian Lawson, Jr., if I could get her drunk enough. I guess I was still capable of some future thought.

An older gentleman was sitting on the stoop of my apartment building. He rose as I shuffled along the sidewalk, and became my dad.

"So I did have the right building," he called out. My dad has a ragged, airy voice. Even before my own diagnosis, I was always afraid he was developing throat cancer. "There aren't any names on the mailboxes. And I've only been here once, when you first moved out here. How long has it been?"

"Five years," I said, legs weakening as I moved up the walk.

"Why the hell haven't you bought a house? Paying rent is just throwing money down a rat hole."

"I know." I stopped a couple feet in front of him. "Dad, wow…"

"Well here then." Dad stepped forward and hugged me. I got two quick pats on the back. And then as we separated, he hugged me some more. Dad is short, but that's not how I'm going to describe him. He has an enormous center of gravity—it covers his entire torso and extends halfway out his limbs, generating amazing leverage. Dad could have picked me off the ground and carried me inside, even thirty pounds ago.

After the hug he kept his hand on my shoulder. His eyes darted down to my leg. "Are you doing okay then?"

"Yeah. You know. You want to come inside?"

"Sure. I should grab my stuff."

"You flew here by yourself?" This I knew because grabbing his stuff was Mom's job.

"Your mother and I figured we could take turns staying with you for awhile. Till you get over it."

"You'd leave and then come back? You'd fly here more than once?"

"That's what we were thinking."

"Wow. I suppose I should tell you that you don't need to do that. But I'm glad you're here. I would have dressed nicer if I knew you were coming."

Dad fingered the sleeve of my Cal-Davis jersey. "I remember this shirt." He cocked his head and squinted up at me. "I really want to be here with you, Brian."

I looked into his eyes and nodded. "We better get your stuff and get inside before my waterworks start."

Dad chuckled and squeezed my shoulder. "You have room for me?"

"Sure. You're going to stay with me, for...?" I didn't want to assume; knowing Dad, he could have a return flight booked for that night.

"I thought two or three days, if you'll have me."

We cut across the lawn to the parking lot. "By tomorrow afternoon you're going to be going crazy thinking about work."

"Probably. But that's okay. Work can wait."

I wished he would stop saying things like that. The lump in my throat kept thickening. There was never any doubt Dad loved me and would do anything for me. But he is totally devoted to his job. He thinks about his crop insurance office every waking minute. This dedication is a little overboard—crop insurance isn't the NORAD situation room—but his workaholism isn't an escape mechanism. It's the way he was raised to be. It's just the way he is. Dad loves his family, but unless there's an emergency, work has to come first. This was the first emergency.

"Our financial guys are really worked up about our capital levels right now," Dad was saying as he carried his suitcase into the building's foyer. "It shouldn't have anything to do with me. But I'm constantly answering their questions about the expected losses in California..."

We talked about his job while he dropped his suitcase in the spare room, while I made us coffee.

"Coffee? No fancy lattés?"

"My espresso machine is at Edna's. I've never seen you drink anything but coffee."

"I just like to give you a hard time. This place looks deserted," Dad commented accurately. "Where's all your stuff?"

"I'm moving in with Edna."

"Is she a nurse?"

"A nurse...?" He got a chuckle out of me. "I don't look so good, do I?"

"Naw, you look fine. You have lost a lot of weight."

"I had some to lose. Not the muscle, though. That really bums me out. I haven't been active at all. No Taekwondo. No basketball. Not even golfing much this summer. I did play in my own memorial tournament. Won it." I sat down and started telling him the story.

"You told me about that. Pretty funny."

"I already told you that story...? Sorry about that. They say the chemo messes with your brain. It might have taken my IQ down a notch. I probably don't want to know."

Dad ran his fingers through his curly silver hair. "So this Edna wants to live with you even without muscles and a fully functioning brain." He winked. "She must really like you."

"I think so. You'll have to meet her. Edna is unique. She's a basketball legend in North Dakota."

"Right up your alley. I always thought you could have been really good if you had grown a few more inches."

"I asked, but your genes said no."

"We should have moved here. You could have been a North Dakota legend too."

"The hoops quality isn't as bad as you'd think. They take their b-ball pretty seriously around here."

Dad wasn't buying it. "You were fun to watch. I never saw anyone go for the ball like you did. I remember that time you stole the rebound from the center for Sacramento East and put it back in to send the game into overtime."

"I loved doing that to the big guys."

"I know you did." Dad stared at me. "So. They want to take away your leg, huh?"

"Yeah."

"You thinking about letting them?"

"I don't know. It feels really permanent."

"Yep."

"Permanent things scare me right now."

"Everything's permanent, you know. Getting older, losing abilities. Just make a decision one way or the other. Things'll work out the way they're supposed to. In the grand scheme of things, losing a leg's not really a big deal."

"I know. I know it's true. I'd probably approach it that way, if I thought... I mean, I'm feeling like, either way..." I'm fucked, Dad, I wanted to say. "Edna wants me to try an experimental therapy."

"So?"

"It's experimental. Edna's been researching it, and she thinks it's a miracle cure. But it's the same treatment a local guy received, and that didn't end so well."

"Mm," Dad vibrated his grim lips. "There's nothing foolproof out there. Maybe you should do it."

I was startled. Dad's a conventional guy. I wondered if Edna had been talking to him, brainwashing him. Maybe she threatened to kill him.

"You can't wait around until they get it all figured out," Dad said. "Because it'll never happen. I've seen people die from cancer. I've seen a few live. You have a pretty bad one it sounds like." He cocked his head and squinted at me. "But you always struck me as the kind of guy who would try the risky thing if you thought it was worth it." He chuckled. "I remember you about twelve years old, climbing that crack at Yosemite so you could see the bighorn sheep babies."

"Oh man, I had forgotten about that…"

"That was way up there. Scared your mother to death. Your buddy Ryan wouldn't do it. He was scared shitless. You never bragged about climbing that crack. But you talked about those baby sheep. For a month."

"I can't believe you remember that."

"I remember the important things," said Dad.

He has unforgiving gray eyes, but I like them. "Those crazy little babies," I recalled, "they let me pet them, touch their little horns. I stayed up there with them for a long time. I knew I was worrying Mom, but I didn't want to come down. That's what started me rock climbing. That feeling of being in a place no one else could reach."

"Of course I did have to go get the park rangers to get you down."

"Sorry about that."

Dad winked. "It was worth it."

"If I hadn't torn my bicep climbing at the indoor gym, I think I would have been pretty good. Quite a few of the kids I climbed with went on to do competitions. They got their pictures in the climbing magazines."

"You had a job," said Dad. "They didn't. You were always a hardworking kid. Your mom and I were impressed. Always have been."

That would sound great in my eulogy, but Dad lived by the credo that hard work paid off. My lack of accomplishment was staring us both in the face.

"Then how do you explain this, right?" Gesturing at my lame-ass abode helped push the words through my constricted throat. "Fruits of my labor."

"Huh? You have a good thing going here."

"One little shop. In North Dakota. That's not much." I was going to choke up if my sentences were any longer.

"Hey, Brian…"

"I wasn't trying to avoid going to college, or getting a real job. I didn't see this as the easy path." My chest heaved as I swallowed back the breakdown. "I've worked as hard as I could."

Dad reached across the corner of the table and put his gnarled bony hand on mine. "You're worrying about the wrong things, Brian. Don't think about what you haven't accomplished. Think about what you're going to do. Plan your next move, and then do it. Then plan the next one. That's the only way it works. That's what leads to success."

"That's probably the next Nike ad campaign, but clearly it's not true, or I'd be a coffee mogul—"

"Aw, that's bullshit." He got up and grabbed the coffee pot, refilling our cups. "I'm not going to listen to that. Let's change the topic a little here. Let's talk about work. Tell me what you've been doing at your shop lately."

Dad didn't get it. He was never understanding enough to let me feel sorry for myself, even when it was perfectly appropriate. I considered tipping my cup and spilling coffee all over the table, to see if it mattered. "Mostly I've been talking to pastors and friends with strong faith. Trying to convince myself there's an afterlife, some kind of heaven where I'm still me. I think that'll go a long way toward settling me down. I don't want to be afraid, you know?"

Dad squirmed in his chair, readjusting his jeans. "Maybe…" He cleared his throat. "Maybe we should get something to eat."

I had pushed beyond Dad's ability to cope, and it was time to let him off the hook. I had set the record straight, accomplished what I needed to, and felt awful for it. "It's dinner time. I know you're not a fan of eating out, but…. Might be some 'Nilla Wafers in the cupboard…"

The phone rang. It was Terrence. "I'm making sure you're still coming to dinner."

"Whoops. Holy crow. My dad just got into town, unexpectedly. So…"

"Bring him along," said Terrence. "He's not completely like you, is he?"

"He's a little smarter than me," I reported. "Maybe not quite as funny. A lot nicer."

"Then yeah, bring him. Amber is making plenty."

"That won't be an issue. Dad's not a big eater. We'll be lucky to eat a full serving between us."

"Even better," said Terrence. "We'll see you in a few minutes?"

"Okay homey." I hung up. "You're okay with eating over at a friend's house? Terrence and Amber are really good people."

"Sounds fine," said Dad. His voice had degraded from raspy to hoarse with fatigue. Probably the last thing he wanted to do, but he agreed.

HE WAS quiet as we climbed in my van. Silent as we skirted downtown, other than a couple wheezy replies to my inquiries about Mom, her housecleaning business, her hammer toe. Dinner guest etiquette demanded I draw him out of his moodiness before we went inside. Get his mind off me.

"Terrence and Amber are worried about making their house payment," I said as we pulled up in front of their house. "Terrence just found out the firm he works for is discontinuing profit-sharing bonuses. He thinks it's a bad sign. Amber spent months building a natural products pyramid only to find out the company's founder has developed a phobia of supplements. Thinks his own products gave him cancer. Meanwhile she's being sued by the next-door neighbor for stealing her Longaberger basket pyramid."

When Dad spoke, it wasn't in reply to my gossipy dossier on our dinner hosts. "I was thinking," he said, "how I never had to tell you that life is hard." He sat small on the seat, hands folded in his lap. "I never had to use that concept to motivate you. I've given that speech to your mother from time to time, to remind her why I have to work so much. And I've given it to your Uncle Verlyle, more than once." He looked over at me. "But I never gave it to you. Sometimes I thought I should give you the opposite speech. Your mom was always afraid you took life too seriously. That you worked too much."

It dawned on me that Dad was doing a very difficult thing. He was trying to admit he had been wrong about his core philosophy. Hard work doesn't always pay off. I wanted to make it easy on him.

"There's a customer who comes into the shop, a housewife who's been taking science and math classes for three years, prepping to get into a pharmacy program. She gets almost all A's. And yet her application was rejected."

I shut off the van. The cessation of the engine's vibration beneath us was a punctuation between my examples. "And then of course there's Terrence here. He writes every day for two hours, on top of his regular job. He's been doing it for years, his writing is excellent, and yet he can't get his novels published. It's not much consolation—none, actually—but I'm definitely not the only one who's failed at his dream."

Dad pinched his brow and shook his head. "I don't know about these other people you're talking about." He pinched harder, and then his voice cracked, became smoother somehow, as the tears came. "But you are not a failure. You're only thirty-two years old and you own a business. Working for a company, that's the easy way out. You're a risk taker. You never even considered working for somebody else. That's incredible, okay?"

The high-pitched note of anguish in his voice made me choke up. "I didn't know you felt that way."

"I didn't understand that you didn't know it," he said. "Everybody that you've met, you've touched. Mom and I saw it in you as you grew up. Everybody wanted to be around you. People are drawn to you. We hear it all the time. We think you're incredibly successful."

And now some real blubbering began. Not many tears, maybe due to the desiccating effects of age, but Dad's body shook. I started bawling right along with him…while simultaneously, implausibly, a little magically, experiencing a strong current of electricity coursing through my brain. It was weird, and wonderful, crying and feeling excited at the same time.

Terrence knocked on the window. I keyed the ignition to lower the window, not bothering to wipe away the tears. "I'm sorry man," I told him. "We got talking out here, and the next thing you know, we're weeping."

Terrence was solemn. "Take your time."

"Terrence," I snuffled, "this is my dad."

"Hi Mr. Lawson. You both take your time out here. No rush." Terrence walked back to the house. He paused to look up at the backyard cottonwood towering over his roof. I stared at it too. I was struck by the soothing rustle of the leaves in the evening breeze. North Dakota trees huddle close to the few rivers that struggle across the windblown prairie in hopes of trickling across the border. The town has a number of big mature trees, providing the only shade for a hundred miles, beckoning to travelers and field-weary farmers, blocking the wind. Jamestown was an oasis, I realized.

Terrence called from his stoop. "Brian, don't feel like you're obligated…"

"I'm actually feeling better," I called to him. "Dad and I'll be in soon."

T-1

"SO THANKS for dinner last night," I called to Terrence, in his nook, pretending to be capable of ignoring me. Dad sat on a stool at the counter, flanked by regulars, Oscar, Cal, Bart and Donna "It was good, wasn't it Dad?"

"It was," said Dad.

"I'm making an announcement this morning," I told the counter crowd. The zest in my voice kept startling people. "Two of them, actually."

"Oh Lord," said Charlotte. She was running around, doing whatever it was she did. Agitated. "I don't think I'm ready to hear this."

"It's good stuff," I assured her.

"Oh I'm sure it is. Dana, could you please clean up the corner table? It's been messy for awhile now."

Dana studied the table, trying to decide if messy was the right description.

"Or not," said Charlotte.

"I got it," said Dana. She hummed sinister organ music on her way to the table. Working in a coffeeshop for Dana means making drinks, and nothing else. She's clueless as soon as she steps away from the espresso machine. With her black-rimmed eyes and S&M wardrobe, I expected my customers to scatter whenever she came near. But more than a few consider Dana my best employee. She makes great drinks; and they figure that anybody dressed that way is surely headed for stardom. Conservative, Christian North Dakota has so few celebrities, they're ready to embrace the second coming of Ozzy Osbourne as long as the world acknowledges which state spawned her.

"You might need a rag," Charlotte called from her crouch behind the bar while rummaging for a fresh bottle of vanilla syrup.

"Okay," said Dana. Charlotte growled softly into the low cupboard.

"What a team I have!" I bellowed. "I have a couple announcements to make, don't I Dad?"

"I guess so."

"Why don't you just tell us?" Charlotte suggested, no longer sure my insanity was an act.

"PK!" I called to Pastor Kyle before both his feet were in the shop. "You're just in time for my announcement." I had seen him coming, already had his americano ready.

"Have you ever considered Pastor Kyle might not like to be called PK?" Charlotte asked me. It never crossed my mind.

"Coming from someone else, well I might take offense," said PK, like a cowboy without the drawl. "Coming from Brian, it's clearly a sign of affection."

"See?" I said to Charlotte.

"Whatever." Charlotte started to quote PK his price, then turned to me. "How much am I charging Pastor Kyle for his americano today?"

"Normal price," I said.

PK looked back and forth. "You mean I could have had a discount?"

"Not likely," I said. Maybe if he was working harder to save my soul. "I've implemented a flexible pricing structure. But rarely does it flex down."

"So I guess I better start minding my p's and q's," said PK.

"You gotta take risks."

"So what's the announcement?" PK asked.

I turned up my volume. "Okay everybody—do you want the big news first, or the really big news?"

I heard "big" and I heard "really big". "I'm going with the big news," I decided. Everyone in the place had stopped talking except for Judy Wellstone at the table directly across from me. Her current man-friend Tommy pinched her, but Judy kept on talking. "Okay, here it is. I'm opening a new store."

It was big, but not exactly news. Once everyone realized that was it, I received a nice round of applause. Someone said the actual word "hurrah". Judy Wellstone looked around, mouth open in mid-word, and then continued her story. I pointed at Dad. I gave credit to my number one homey, laying a stone-cold cocked-bow straight-arm point on his ass. Dad nodded.

"Congratulations, Brian," said Oscar. To humor me he asked, "Where's the new shop going to be?"

"On the campus."

"Hey, that's wonderful."

"Thank you. I'm really excited about it."

"You left out the biggest part of your big news," said Charlotte.

"No I didn't."

Charlotte's irritation was either part of our standard act, or it was real. "Tell them the rest," she ordered.

"I already told them the important part."

"Brian."

"Okay." Everybody quieted down again. Judy was not a member of the set of Everybody. Judy was Judy, and she was cackling over something she had just told her soon-to-be-former man-friend Tommy. "I left out one small piece of information. I'm opening the store September first…with a partner…whose name is…Edna Applejack."

The applause was louder this time, it's true. There was some actual cheering. Also some horny hooting from Bart.

"Unfortunately none of you can go to that store," I killed their joy. "It's going to get plenty of new customers, so I need you all to keep coming here."

There were grumbles and there was muttering amongst the assembled.

"Will Edna work here too?" Cal asked.

"She'll make an occasional appearance," I conceded, to appease the people.

"That's not good enough," Terrence tried to throw his voice.

"How about if I let you see her right now?" I offered.

"It's a start," said Bart.

I motioned toward the back hallway. "There she is." On perfect cue Edna appeared. Chairs squealed and banged to the floor as everyone jumped to their feet and clapped and cheered. Edna walked to me and kissed me on the lips. We faced the crowd together, her arm around my shoulders instead of my waist where I believe the woman's arm belongs. I saw that Dad noticed.

Edna thrust her fist in the air, clipping the menu board hanging above us, rocking the hundred-pound slab of lumber and glass on its little bitty hooks. "Don't you think it's about time we had a coffeeshop on that campus?!"

The crowd roared its approval.

"Alright," I shouted, disconnecting from Edna, "are you ready for my next announcement?" Customers walked in. I turned to Charlotte. "Fix Bruce and Lydia their drinks, would you?" I would have asked Dana, but she had taken a seat at the table she was cleaning.

"This is my favorite of the two announcements," said Edna.

"Mine too," I agreed. "Although I'm not sure I'd be as excited about this one, without the first one. Okay, so I think everyone knows by now that I have bone cancer."

"Yeah," everyone said, real soft like, soft murmurs, soft eyes.

"And I've taken two rounds of chemo and radiation, and it's killed everything but the cancer."

Everyone acknowledged this unfortunate fact. "Why do they even recommend it?" Charlotte wanted to know.

"We won't get into that," I said. "But it's because the doctors own shares in mobile radiation labs, and because they receive free trips to Hawaii from the pharmaceutical companies that make the chemo drugs, and because they're too lazy to research other options that definitely exist."

The crowd was mine now, laughing a little, cringing a little, looking around to see whether any docs were in the room, but in all cases very attuned to what came next.

"So I've decided to stop the chemo and radiation, and go with a radical treatment that should cure me."

This started a hubbub. I heard "Brent" and "McEwen" on more than a couple lips. Good guess. "Dr. Bhani," Edna confirmed, loud enough for everyone's benefit. "It's Dr. Bhani's treatment."

"Good for Brian," said Bart emphatically.

"It's dangerous," I announced, in case anyone thought they could stop pitying me, and to stop Edna from taking over both of my announcements. "It's painful. It's not guaranteed. I hope it's free. And if it doesn't cure me, and assuming I don't die from it, they're going to have to saw my leg off."

Gasps were exactly what I was going for. I limped around the counter, out onto the floor. It was the Chernobyl version of the Willy Wonka scene: pity builds as Brian Wonka Lawson hobbles front and center; then instead of relieving the tension with a backflip, I lift my pajama pantleg and point to my tibia tumor.

"Oh Brian, good Lord," said PK. With everyone else recoiling, he bent to touch the knobby misshapen mass growing like a black tree fungus under my knee. Bruce and Lydia's little girl started crying, and then shrieking.

"My God, Brian, I had no clue," said Donna, recovering to step around PK and stroke my cheek. Oscar couldn't look; he turned away, cuddling his Lake Tahoe mug. Terrence couldn't speak—this was no pause, there was absolutely nothing going on behind the scenes.

"Dr. Bhani's toxins can cure even that," Edna pitched some snake oil. "You are not going to be able to believe the difference."

She was generally ignored. A first. "Brian I am so sorry," said Lydia.

"Don't be. If I have to lose the leg, I'm okay with it. I realized I'll be like any other war veteran. Damned lucky to have a good leg, and to be alive." I winked at Dad; not sure if he knew I was paying watered-down homage to the dead soldier mindset, but he winked back.

Abort

I CAN'T spring this on you any faster than it was sprung on me. I woke six days ago with a lump in my crotch, in the hollow between my balls and my thigh. I touched it as soon as I came to, like my hand had been waiting for me to wake up, watching for my eyes to open, and then going straight to the lump. It's why my pants had been so uncomfortable. It's another tumor.

Each day it's grown bigger. Now I'd call it tennis ball size. I don't want to walk, for the physical pain and much worse the psychic terror of bursting or dislodging it. Don't ask me why this is what terrorizes me. Maybe it's because I don't truly comprehend how cancer works. The tumors just sit there and kill me. I'm so revolted and horrified to have them inside me. I can't believe I'm allowing them to sit there, and do whatever they want.

Three days ago, a lump formed in my lower back. On Wednesday it was a tightness, Thursday a thickness, Friday a lump. Now it's bigger too. Dr. Bonilla thinks it's pressing on my stomach, because now it hurts to eat. It hurts like unbelievable hell to swallow, and it's excruciating when food reaches my stomach. I haven't eaten solid food for two days.

My shin and my knee and my crotch ache and ache and ache. Maybe I can find a position that pleases one, but not all three.

This is the end. Each stage in the cancer's progression over the past few months must have been preparing me, because the sickening fear of death is no longer with me. Maybe it's the pain—I can't catch a breath big enough to relax long enough to worry. It's hitting me so hard and so fast, I only picture one thought over and over. Misery.

I'm in Edna's house, her bed. When Dr. Bonilla was here yesterday and Edna stepped out of the room, I told him I was ready for the amputation. Partly I just wanted to be anesthetized against the pain.

Bonilla knelt beside the bed. I smelled my own stink, my rancid breath and sour body reflecting off his freshness. He put his hand on my stomach and pushed around gently while telling me that I was probably too weak to handle the surgery. My cancer is spreading too fast for the amputation to do any good, he said. He said "not now" to the surgery, when he meant "not any longer."

He ratcheted up the pain meds. I don't think they've reduced the pain, I think I just don't care as much now. Still that one word, when Edna asks me how I'm feeling, and when I ask myself the same question. Misery.

Edna told me groundbreaking for our new shop took place at a small ceremony involving only the college administration and a few special invitees, including the Jamestown College music director and his senior leaders singing chorals. The College's music program is nationally recognized. Edna and the administration want to discourage the perception that the shop will be a jock hangout.

They've poured the foundation. The skeletal structure will be up in a week. Edna and Rick are debating whether customers should queue from the right or the left when they enter the store. I'm sure it's a great question. Edna is conducting evening training sessions for new employees, after-hours at my shop. She started them Thursday. She's not asking Charlotte to assist her. Charlotte was in to see me yesterday, but she didn't bring it up.

"Tell me about the shop," I had croaked to her. The scans on Wednesday didn't show it, but I know I have a tumor growing in my throat too.

Charlotte sat there, swallowing.

"You're terrible at one-sided conversations," I told her. In normal circumstances she's great at them. She can go for an hour on nothing but nods and mm-hm's. She just couldn't do it with me in Edna's bed looking like a corpse. She cussed some, cried some, and hugged me goodbye. She left behind flowers and a giant get-well card from all my employees and regular customers.

Edna pokes her head in. "Are you up for company?" Sure. In walks Kenny and Laurie, Steve and Melissa, Tim, Caitlyn, Terrence and Amber.

"Looking forward to having you back on your feet," says Steve. Pretty stupid fucking thing to say, I suppose, but I tell him I appreciate it.

"You're looking pretty good," says Melissa, topping her husband. She wiggles my big toe under the sheet. She's a sweetheart.

"Thanks," I rasp.

"The shop's not the same without you down there," says Tim.

There's a long pause, everyone struggling to come up with something uplifting. This is perfect conversational rhythm for Terrence. "You're losing customers like crazy," he says with a sad smile. "You better get back down there."

"I will, homey."

"I see they broke ground on your new place," says Kenny. "When will you open?"

Edna tells him. She has the McEwens on task, on time, on budget. Everyone discusses the new shop for awhile. I do nothing more than nod at the appropriate times, and it still wears me out. Edna sees it. "I'd like Brian to get some rest now, if you all don't mind."

I get a knuckle-knock from Terrence, a quick hug from Amber, another toe wiggle from Melissa, and waves from everyone else. I'd be afraid to get too close to me, too.

Edna comes back in after they've gone, with a fresh glass of water and a hot cup of tea. "God-dammit, I can't get ahold of that sonofabitch," she rages, referring to Dr. Bhani. "I had to talk to Andrea again. I don't know why he didn't fire that bitch after I told him about her scheme to scare you away," she rants. "She's worthless. She's not sure where Bhani is. Sounds like he caught wind of a JAMA article coming out, that doesn't sound favorable. Here, drink this, it might help your throat."

"I hate tea."

"Drink it."

"Okay." The tea hurts like everything else I pour down there. Drinking is no longer accompanied by mental pictures of the coffee or Mountain Dew or water. Now it's silver razor blades.

"Do you want to take a walk with me? It's beautiful outside."

"Maybe later."

"I'll be gone most of the evening," says Edna. "We have a construction progress meeting. I really wish you could be there." She sounds sincere, but she really doesn't need me there, sick or healthy.

"You have it under control," I whisper. I don't want to talk anymore.

And so Edna leaves me alone, and I do my best to sleep. I thrash in slow motion for a long time.

"Okay, okay," I say when it's dark, to an empty house. "I'll take the toxins."

I'M IN a lazy fetal position with the sheet knotted around my good leg, face down into the mattress but no drool pooled, mouth so dry I can't wet my tongue to say "toxins" when Edna kisses my cheek. She undresses in the dark, down to nothing, a beautiful silhouette to go along with the perfume lingering on my cheek. She pulls on a long sleeping shirt and leaves the room, and now I can't tell if it's perfume or cologne I'm smelling.

TWO DAYS later. I'm having a good period, the painkillers doing the trick. It's possible the tumors are doing the trick—all three are bigger, with what seems to be a new one in my armpit. I imagine that at some point the brain gets tired of receiving pain signals, sticks its fingers in its ears and says la-la-la-la-la real loud. It's giving me a window of opportunity to concentrate, so I call the shop. "It's Brian. Brian Lawson. The owner of that coffeeshop."

"I know," says Dana. "Hi Brian."

"I'm calling to see how things are going down there."

"Here, I'll let you talk to Charlotte."

Dana couldn't wait to get off the phone. Now I'm feeling the same way. I try to think of a reason for my call other than to tell Charlotte I'm dying.

"Hi Brian."

"Hey." I like to put the emphasis on the last syllable.

"Things are fine here," says Charlotte. "Everyone's asking how you're doing. I think Edna is telling people you're too sick for visitors."

"It's probably true. I like the sound of the espresso machine running and people talking in the background. Sounds busy."

"It's not too bad. For as hot as it's been, business has been okay."

"I was thinking about our bean inventory, and how the checking account is probably pretty low."

"Kenny increased our credit limit. I didn't even ask him."

"Wow. I didn't know he still cared. Normal price for his drinks from now on. Oh yeah, some credit card company with no business acumen sent me another card we can max out, too."

"Okay. Should I...do you want me to stop by and get it?"

"I'll have Edna drop it off."

Charlotte tells Dana to take the till. I can tell she's walking to the office, for privacy. "So...when do you think you'll be back?"

A knot of sadness clogs my throat. "I don't know how to answer that," I finally say. She has almost asked if I'm dying. I've almost told her. "Edna's trying to get a treatment scheduled for me."

"That's good. Is it that same treatment you were talking about when you made your big announcements? I wasn't sure you were going to do it."

"Yep."

"She's been in here a couple times lately. We've been trying to figure out how much coffee she'll need for her first week."

"Probably twice our average, to be safe."

"That's what we thought." Charlotte has shifted to business mode. It's a good thing I called, she needs me, to make a few decisions. "Do you mind if I ask Craig to come in after hours and roast?"

"That's a good idea." All of a sudden it's difficult to focus again. I feel like my blood pressure and temperature suddenly plummeted. "Let him know that with two shops, you'll probably need a full-time roaster in the near future."

"Yeah but, so will that Hernandes."

"He'll be out of business soon."

"Good. I hate him."

"Me too." I can conjure up no such feeling. "You like working with Edna?"

"Sure."

"Make yourself indispensable," I tell her. "I have a list started on my desk, with all the things she'll need to think about in the couple weeks before and after she opens. You should finish it and make it your own, and take it to her."

"Okay." Long pause while Charlotte fights her emotions. "You don't plan on coming back any time soon, do you?"

"Not soon. I told Edna you're a smart, organized, hardworking person."

"You told her I'm smart?"

"Aren't you?"

"Well, sometimes."

"You're smarter than me, that's all I know for sure. You should aim for being Edna's personal business manager. She's going to have a lot of irons in the fire, knowing her."

"Yeah?" Charlotte gets excited. "You think I could do it, with no degree?"

"Definitely. It wouldn't hurt for you to start taking classes, though."

"At JC? Do you know what tuition is there?"

"I'll talk to Edna. I'll bet she could get you enrolled for free."

"No way. You think so? It wouldn't have to be free."

"Maybe Edna could create the Edna Applejack Scholarship program for James River Valley Coffee employees. Make you the first full-ride recipient."

"God would that be wonderful." Weary cynicism won't let her be too hopeful.

I wish I had treated Charlotte better. If it's the last thing I do, I'd like to accomplish this much for her. "I'll see what I can do. Anything else? Otherwise I think I'll stop talking for awhile."

"That's it. There's nothing to worry about down here. Get better, okay? Are your folks there?"

"They get here Friday."

"That's good. Everybody says hi. And we want to come see you, as soon as you're ready."

"I'll let you know. Talk to you later."

Edna steps into the bedroom. "Strong enough for a visitor?"

My head is swimming and my lips are numb. I feel like I'm sinking deeper into the mattress. It's a comfortable feeling, actually. "Okay."

Edna stands aside and in walks Andrea. Half Edna's height. Homely in comparison. Maybe it's the sneer. "God," says Andrea.

"That bad?" I ask.

"It's not good," she says, maintaining the haughty look until her upper lip trembles. "It's not good. God." She forces herself to my bedside. "How are you feeling?" After resting her hand on the blanket, she folds her arms. "Not good, I suppose."

"This has been a helluva week."

"Yeah, well…. I haven't seen you for awhile."

"How's work?"

Edna interrupts. "I wanted Andrea to see you. I want her to understand we need to move forward with Dr. Bhani's treatment. Soon."

"Sooner is better," I agree. I imagine that Edna picked Andrea up and carried her here, complaining all the way. "I'm probably down to my last option."

"Okay," says Andrea without sounding like she's agreeing to anything. Edna leaves, closing the door behind her. "So." The knowing, sarcastic touch returns. "How are you?"

"Dying."

"Really."

"Want to see?" I pull the blankets aside to expose my leg. Andrea only glances. "I won't show you my groin. Or my back. Or my armpit."

She nods, looking at the headboard. "I'm sorry, okay? I'm sorry."

"It's okay."

Andrea uses the length of her finger to wipe away her tears, trying not to smudge her mascara. "No it's not. We should have got you in."

"You tried to convince me, for the first few months."

"Yes I did. So why didn't you tell me things are getting so much worse?"

"It's been all of a sudden."

"Mm." Andrea does a good job keeping her composure. "I'll do what I can. Dr. Bhani's research assistant is in town for a few days. His name is Dr. Sawyer. He's great. Maybe he can do it. Dr. Bhani has been going crazy defending himself from the state and federal regulators. I guess I have been too, pulling his results for everyone, trying to prove what they don't want to hear. I don't get it at all. He's cured so many people."

"Then I appreciate anything you can do for me."

"I'll try." Andrea brightens. "I have some news. I probably won't be around to see you recuperate. Rick and I are moving back to Colorado."

"Together?"

"We're going to get married again. This weekend. We're not going to tell anybody until it's done. He says he hasn't been happy since we divorced." By the smug look on Andrea's face, she had clearly told him so. "One of their foremen is going to take a bigger role in the business. That way Rick can start a company in Denver, the way we planned before his brother got sick."

"Congratulations."

"Since you weren't available."

"Right."

She puts her hand on my arm, the blanket between us. "I'm glad I got to know you." A goodbye on two levels.

"Anything you can do for me before you leave, I'd really appreciate it."

"Okay. Bye." Andrea crawls halfway onto the bed to kiss me on the forehead, then leaves. I wait for Edna to come back in. I should get up and go tell her the news, such juicy gossip, but I haven't felt this comfortable and pain-free in quite awhile. I think I'll sleep.

"GET UP Brian. We're going to Fort Yates."

"That's on the Indian reservation."

"Correct."

"I'm glad you got me an appointment with a medicine man."

"With Dr. Bhani. Our hospital won't let him perform the procedure, because of the injunction request from the McEwens," Edna explained. "Basically, it's not going to happen in the U.S. So it has to be the rez." She's at her dresser pulling out underwear, a tanktop, shorts, jeans. "We're driving there now with Dr. Bhani's assistant. Dr. Bhani is going to fly into Bismarck and meet us there. We'll have to spend a couple days at least, so pack accordingly."

"Wow. Okay. I'm so freaking tired."

"I guess you'll get moving if you want to live."

It's a major debate. A car ride sounds awful. Lying in bed, wonderful. Not sure I can sit up.

Edna leaves the bedroom. I stand staring at my clothes; I own the right half of Edna's dresser. I take a few items out; put a couple back in; take out a few more, some of them for the second time. Shove them in a duffel bag Edna left on the bed for me. I really have no idea what I grabbed—some blue stuff, a yellow…something else, and a hat?

Edna's in the doorway. "Ready? I asked Bobby Guldseth and Rick to come with us."

"Why?"

"Extra security. The rez isn't known for law and order. Which is why we're going there, of course."

"I'd rather bring Terrence then."

Edna mulls it over. "Okay. I can ask one of them to stay behind."

"Both. One Terrence is all we need." I don't want Bobby or Rick along. Bobby Guldseth tonguing Edna's ear to help her through the grief, that's not going to be the last thing I see before I die. And Rick…he's probably married and living in Colorado by now. What day is it?

"Fine," says Edna. "Call Terrence. Right now, Brian. We need to get going."

I SIT sideways in the Talon's passenger seat, so I don't put pressure on the tumor in my back. Every bump and shimmy makes me moan. Every muscle in my body feels torn, the ruptured fibers pushing their way through my skin. My gut is on fire, like I've been swallowing batteries and chasing them with Easy-Off oven cleaner. I'm sweating from the exertion, of not dying.

"You okay?" Edna asks as we swing into the hospital parking lot.

"I'm having reservations about my reservation reservation."

Edna parks in a visitor space. "You said that already."

"I'll wait in the car," I say.

"Marvcus wants you to come down to the lab," says Edna. I stare blankly. "Marvcus is Dr. Bhani's assistant. Dr. Sawyer."

"Why do I have to come? Do you know why? Go ask him, I'll wait here."

Edna comes around to my side of the car, opens my door, holds out her hand. "You can do it." I rally the energy and commit to reaching the front entrance. Our progress is slow. Then Edna redirects me, and making the course correction, overcoming the inertia, is overwhelming. I stop until the shaking in my leg subsides. The pace is again sssslllooowwww.

An orderly is waiting at a side door. He's about my age, stocky with a shaved bullet head. He stares lovingly at Edna.

"Hi Curtis. This is Brian."

"Hey," says Curtis without looking at me. "Dr. Sawyer is waiting for you. I found an exam room you can use."

"We don't have to go to the basement?" I ask.

"Dr. Bhani was evicted," says Edna.

"Bad press," says Curtis. We follow him way too fast down the hall.

"It's not far I hope. It's not upstairs I hope."

"Brian's not feeling too well," Edna explains.

"Dying, really," I clarify.

"Hence Dr. Sawyer," says Curtis. He looks where he's going only often enough to avoid dinner carts and wheelchairs and shuffling patients, otherwise trying to maintain eye contact with Edna. "So have you been playing any hoops since, you know, lately?"

"No time for basketball," says Edna. "Brian and I are starting a coffeeshop on campus. You'll have to come."

"I'm not a coffee drinker. Will you have anything else? Like fountain drinks or sandwiches or smoothies?"

"No," I say.

"I'll still come," Curtis tells Edna. "Here we are." They stand aside so I can go in first. I nod my thanks to Curtis. "Some of us get together to play ball every Sunday night at the high school," he says quietly to Edna. "If you want to come down, around seven, that would be cool. I know Grimke, the girls' head coach," he name-drops.

A petite man in a starched gray button shirt and slacks waves me forward. "Come on in. You're Brian, I'm betting. I'm Dr. Sawyer." He shakes my hand and beckons me to the exam table. He would be good looking except for his stature. Unfortunately there is a size threshold men have to exceed in order to be attractive. I feel bad for him. I mean, he is damned handsome, Rob Lowe-like. But no woman is going to want a mini Rob Lowe.

I climb up on the paper sheet. "I have to warn you, I have a bad habit of throwing up in exam rooms."

"If you blow chunks, we'll just call Curtis back," says Dr. Sawyer.

"There won't be any chunks," I tell him.

Edna strides in. "Marvcus."

"The v is silent," says Dr. Sawyer. "You're Edna. Thanks," he dismisses Curtis, who is watching the movements of Edna's skirt. "We'll call you if Brian pukes." He shuts the door in Curtis's face, proving that boners don't make good door-stops. "Let's have a look at you." Dr. Sawyer helps me take off my shirt. "Edna, it's up to you if you want to stay."

"It's naughty," says Edna, "but I'm enjoying watching you undress him."

"Dr. Sawyer is aggressive but surprisingly gentle," I tell her, my pajama pants around my ankles.

"You have a lot of activity here," says Dr. Sawyer, poking and measuring my "activity", recording the data in a little black book. "I don't have access to your file, so I can't get a feel for the progression rate of your cancer."

"I'd call it fast. I'd call it fucking fast, if I wasn't afraid of offending you. Given that you're my last hope and all." Dr. Sawyer continues feeling me up, so I keep talking. "I didn't have the tumor on my back or the one between my legs a week or so ago. I'm pretty sure a new one's coming in my armpit."

Dr. Sawyer prods me there. "Definitely." He's a tiny, crisp-talking Rob Lowe. "So you're metastasizing rapidly. I understand the original diagnosis was Ewing's sarcoma. When was it made?"

"April eighth at eleven-forty-three a.m. Approximately."

"Other symptoms?"

"I feel like shit."

"Can you be more specific?"

"Really shitty. And exhausted, if I forgot to mention that."

"Brian has had a headache since yesterday," Edna reports. "He can't eat, because of pain in his throat and stomach. He's lost at least ten pounds in the past few days, on top of the thirty he says he lost over the last few months. He didn't want to get out of bed to come here, and then he didn't want to get out of the car in the parking lot."

"I'm going downhill fast."

"Fucking fast," says Dr. Sawyer. We stare at each other. He's pondering whether I'm worth the effort.

"Where's Dr. Bhani?" I ask.

"He'll be meeting us in Fort Yates."

"Oh yeah. Edna told me."

Dr. Sawyer moves in tight and pushes two fingers against the inside of my thigh. He nods rhythmically.

"How's this for you?" I ask Edna.

Edna smiles. "Not bad."

"We'll need an ambulance to transport Brian," says Dr. Sawyer, stepping back and looking me over. "I don't want to take any chances. Your vitals aren't great."

I'm not upset to hear this. More vindicated—I'm a little p.o.'d at Edna for dragging me out of bed.

"Maybe we should talk outside," says Edna to Dr. Sawyer.

"He's not telling me anything I don't already know," I tell her. "There's really not much you can do at this point, is there Doc?"

"Sure there is. But I am concerned about the stress of the trip."

"My mom and dad are flying here Friday. I don't want to go to Fort Yates unless you're sure we can be back by tomorrow afternoon. At the latest."

Edna frowns at me. "Brian…" She turns to Dr. Sawyer. "He's been saying things like that today. I feel like he's suddenly giving up."

"It happens to some people," says Dr. Sawyer.

Not me, I'm a warrior, I say to myself, at the same time thinking how beautiful it would be to take a long, pain-free nap in Edna's bed. Or here on the exam table.

Pain is a great motivator, I remind myself. No pain no gain. Pain means I'm alive. And if nothing else, I gotta remember that pain is something that can be controlled. It's not real, it's just the brain's representation of the information it's receiving from the body. An information representation, that's all pain is.

Feels like my bones are liquefying. A moan escapes my lips, turns into a sob. "I'm really hurting…"

"We'll see if we can get you something additional for the pain," says Dr. Sawyer. He pulls out his cellphone, talking to Edna while he pushes buttons. "Any way we can rustle up an ambulance?"

"Curtis will do it for me," says Edna.

"Tell him to make it snappy. I'm going to update Dr. Bhani."

I should clothe my hideous body, but the best I can do is use my shirt like a blanket and curl up on my side on the table.

I HAVE only a vague understanding that we're leaving…

…semi-conscious glimpses of a gurney and the back of an ambulance...

…turning corners at high speed with Edna's hand on me. An occasional bump in the road.

"EDNA." MY voice rattles through the dried-out flesh inside my mouth and the corridor of pus-spewing sores that is my throat. "Where are we?"

"Halfway there," says Edna, looking down on me. She's sitting on a folding chair. I'm lying on a mattress on the floor. Edna steadies an IV bag lurching over my head on a flimsy stand. An oxygen tank is bungeed to the wall, clanking metal on metal.

"This is a horseshit ambulance."

"It's your van," says Edna, distracted, listening to Dr. Sawyer, on the phone behind me. Edna doesn't seem to like what she's hearing. She makes an effort to give me her full attention. "We couldn't get an ambulance. Curtis went to the trouble to outfit your van for us."

"That Curtis is all right," I whisper.

Edna presses her lips to my forehead and forgets them there while eavesdropping on Dr. Sawyer. Fine by me. "Terrence's here," she tells me. "He's up front with Curtis."

"They should hit it off pretty well, huh?" I gently clear my throat, bringing up bloody pus to wet my mouth. "What's up with the doc?"

"I'm here, Brian." Dr. Sawyer scoots a folding chair into view and pockets his phone.

"Hey doc. I feel really dehydrated."

"We have an IV going, so you'll be okay."

"Could I just drink it instead?"

Dr. Sawyer pats my chest. "We have some powerful painkillers mixed in. You wouldn't like the taste. It might be best if you napped a while more."

"Sounds like a plan. How's Dr. Bhani?"

"That's a great question," says Edna, scowling.

Dr. Sawyer is uncomfortable. "That was him. A few things happened while you slept," he tells me. "I'm going to handle your treatment. No big deal. I've done a couple myself, and assisted on many more. It's not a complicated procedure, as you'll see. So not to worry."

Edna stares at Dr. Sawyer so fiercely the hairs on his temple curl. I prop myself up on an elbow. "What happened?"

"Dr. Bhani got cold feet." Edna dares Dr. Sawyer to dispute it.

"Considering everything he's been through, that's not fair," says Dr. Sawyer. "You have to understand the pressure Dr. Bhani is getting from all sides."

"And that's why he needs a successful treatment," Edna argues, voice rising. "Brian is perfect timing."

"Dr. Bhani doesn't see it that way. But," Dr. Sawyer cuts off Edna's protest, "I'm going to be honest with you. I'm a little surprised at his decision."

"A little surprised?" says Edna. "You sounded floored on the phone. I could hear both sides of the argument."

"There was yelling?" I ask.

"Dr. Bhani yelled," Edna reports, "and Marvcus took it."

"Dr. Bhani doesn't want me to have his treatment, huh?"

Dr. Sawyer grimaces. "We'll be okay." He turns away from Edna, trying to keep this between the two of us. "Dr. Bhani has hit upon an incredible cure. But he's feeling a little picked on. Most of the patients he receives, especially lately, are very far along."

"Their cancer, you mean."

Dr. Sawyer nods. "And they've already been subjected to months, or years, of chemotherapy and radiation. Their immune systems are compromised. Sounds like you've gone through a fair amount of chemotherapy."

Seeing as how I'm just snapping out of a dreamlike haze, I have no real ability to read the situation or gauge Dr. Sawyer's mindset. But I'd say he's on the fence, considering calling it off. Could be wrong, maybe it's solely Edna's agitation creating tension. She seems ready to hijack my van and put a gun to the doc's head and demand treatment for me.

I do know for certain-sure that I want the treatment. In my stupor I think I dreamed about dying. It left a very unpleasant sensation in my brain. "I haven't had any treatments for a month," I tell him. "They wanted to put me through another round of chemo, but I wouldn't let them."

"Good," says Dr. Sawyer. He scoots closer. "You have to understand I owe everything to Dr. Bhani. He's brilliant, and one of the bravest researchers out there. Few people have the strength and conviction to persevere with everyone aligned against them. But unfortunately I think he's been reduced to calculating the impact of any given treatment on his career. He's afraid to make a mistake with you."

Now I see it in his eyes. Marvcus is going to save me. "You're not afraid."

"To be fair," says Marvcus, "I have nothing to lose. I'm still free to operate the way Dr. Bhani used to. I can make every decision based on what's best for the patient."

"And this treatment is definitely the best thing for me?"

"Without a doubt. Dr. Bhani hasn't made you a convert?"

"I tried my best to convince Brian," says Edna.

"It sounds a little crazy, you have to admit."

"The concept of germ-inspired healing isn't out of the blue," says Marvcus. "Before medicine became the structured, regulated business it is today, doctors were known to infect their patients with a deadly disease in order to cure them of a deadlier one. They used malaria and gangrene to cure cancer. And syphilis to keep it from coming back."

"That one might be a toss-up," I say.

Marvcus flashes a tight smile. "If a patient had an open wound or sore, doctors would deliberately soil the dressing. Make sure it was thick with infectious agents."

"Bhani should use that one in his marketing literature."

Not too long ago I was certain I had long since passed the point of no return. Now I'm getting excited about the possibility of living some more. Amazing what good drugs can do for your mood. "Hey, I remember Andrea requesting a sample of the original tumor that they removed from my tibia. She said Dr. Bhani wanted to make a personalized vaccine for me."

Marvcus wrinkles his nose. "That was for show. Cancer vaccines are all the rage, so Dr. Bhani throws one in to placate the medical review boards."

Mom sniffed that one out from a mile away.

My parents are showing up soon. I love them, love sitting around and shooting the shit with them. I like bumping along a choppy state road, lurching around when Curtis floors it into the passing lane. I like Edna. Maybe I really like her. She's bizarre like a movie star, but I could be a movie star's man. I love making coffee for people, making them happy. There would be a hole in the world if I was gone—mostly a hole in my own life, admittedly, but in other people's too.

And I want to golf more. Jasper has been golfing his whole life, but I know I can beat him eventually.

Wow do I like the concept of eventually. Eventually, with all its anticipation; and all the life that comes between now and then. I love eventually.

Marvcus's phone rings. "There's the hospital... Hello, Dr. Sawyer speaking. ...yes...yes—yes I saw it. ...yes. ...uh-huh. We're almost there...uh-huh.... yes. ...yes. ...okay." He snaps his phone shut and disconnects the call. "Fort Yates read the medical journal editorial on Dr. Bhani."

"I wouldn't have guessed they had a subscription," I say.

"They're turning us away," says Marvcus. "We lost our hospital."

Edna screeches and starts pounding the back door. We grind to a stop on the graveled roadside. Fast-moving feet crunch outside, and the back doors open. Curtis jumps in and gives me the once-over. "You okay?"

"I'm good. Hey Terrence."

Terrence hovers in the doorway. "Brian. How are you?"

"Been better I suppose. I really appreciate you coming. Looks like our trip is being cancelled, though."

"The goddamn reservation won't take us!" Edna yells.

"We lost our reservation reservation," I say.

"It's not funny!" Edna yells at me. "It's not fucking funny! Who do these punks at the Journal of Medicine think they are?" This is directed more at Marvcus. "They're messing with people's lives! How dare they? God dammit!" She hurdles Terrence and bounds down into the ditch to throw curses at the amber field of grain waving in the wind.

Terrence stares at me. "You look relaxed, considering."

Marvcus and Curtis glance at me, then wait for Edna for direction.

She trudges up from the ditch. "I'm sorry. I don't know what to do."

It's obvious to me. "We go back to your place, and Marvcus here gives me the treatment."

Marvcus harrumphs. "That's just not going to be possible."

"Oh you're going to give me the toxins alright. Curtis, turn this mother around."

Terrence claps his hands. "Let's move."

NOW WE'RE humming along in the opposite direction, back home. "The shop's been running smooth," Terrence reports. He gave up his front seat to Marvcus, who was looking a little pale.

"Charlotte is good."

Terrence spends some time on his next statement. "She misses you." He puts his hand on my stomach, preparing to say something nice and comforting. Nothing comes out of his mouth, his hand remains on my stomach, and it's nice and comforting.

We ride like this for a few minutes. I use Terrence's ample biceps for leverage to shift onto my side, to take pressure off my aching back. The pressure doesn't change one bit. If I was being more accurate in my descriptions, I'd call it excruciating pain. The IV drip is no longer doing the trick. It's time to jab a straw into a major artery and empty that bag. "By the way," I say, "did you hear Andrea and Rick are back together?"

Terrence stares at me, expressionless. Maybe this is old news. I'm a little fuzzy on timelines at the moment. Maybe they're already remarried.

Edna rustles in the corner where she crouches. "What did you say?"

"Rick and Andrea are remarrying and moving back to Colorado."

"No they're not," Edna vetoes the idea.

"I'm just going by what Andrea told me."

Edna's feet slip out from under her, plopping her into a sitting position. "I dated Andrea for awhile, you know."

"I'm aware of that," says Terrence.

"She's a bizarre human."

"We all thought the same thing about you," says Terrence.

Edna sits silent and crumpled while we banter. I realize she's crying. I don't say anything, because Terrence seems oblivious.

After a few minutes the crying stops. For the rest of the ride Edna rocks back and forth, knees tight to her chest, silent even when Terrence and I discuss the new campus coffeeshop. Edna is in full-out anguish, and it takes my plodding brain a while to come up with the obvious answer. Damn chemo.

I'M PLEASANTLY surprised. Marvcus was a busy beaver during the drive to Edna's house. A home-health crew is already loading their truck, having finished a quick sterilization of Edna's bedroom.

We enter Edna's expansive foyer. I'm the only one not carrying anything. "Smells hospital-fresh in here. I thought I was trying to catch an infection."

"Nope," says Marvcus, following Edna into the main floor guest bedroom, pointing Curtis where to set up the monitoring equipment. "We only want your immune system to think you have an infection. In the state you'll be in, a real infection could do damage—or at least distract from your immune system's real mission, destroying the cancer. By the way Edna, besides taking the liberty of having your bedroom disinfected..." He stops talking when it's obvious Edna isn't paying attention.

"How did you know the address?" Terrence wants to know.

"The home health crew didn't need any direction. When I said Edna, they said 'Applejack? We'll be right over.'"

I take a seat on the bed. "They probably drive past this house a couple times a day. Hoping to catch a glimpse of Edna."

"I know I do," says Curtis.

Maybe he's hoping that remark scores points, but Edna is in her own world, absentmindedly shuffling the few items the cleanup crew left sitting on her dresser, a bag of cotton balls, a tissue box, a picture of her in her JC uniform flanked by her proud parents. She stares at herself in the mirror, becoming more distraught before leaving the room and heading upstairs.

Terrence and I exchange looks. "What do you make of that?" I ask him. He shrugs, no intention of going on record. I'm not so reluctant. "I think she has a thing for Rick McEwen. I don't doubt they've been meeting every night to discuss coffeeshop construction, like Edna claims. I'm just saying they adjourn each meeting with a kiss. A long wet one."

Marvcus ignores me, laying out syringes and needles and little bottles of what I assume are the toxins, on a white cloth on Edna's vanity on the other side of the bed. Curtis is all ears as he sets up the IV station left behind by the home health crew.

Terrence stares blankly at me, as if unaware I've already spoken. Finally, "How does that make you feel?"

"If I live through this treatment, I'll throw a hissy fit."

"Keep your mouth shut and count you blessings, dog," says Curtis.

"I'm with you, dog."

"You are on the inside, Holmes. It's where we all long to be, dog."

"Doggie gotta lay down now." I'm trembling through a hot flash of gut-sizzling nausea. I do a half-ass job of propping Edna's pillows before collapsing into the soft comforter. My heart races; at the same time I can feel a pulse in my shin, beating slow and steady. The tumor is in great shape.

I can't remember whether it's today or tomorrow. I lay still, trying to reconstruct the day's, or days', events. How long were we in my van? "Are Mom and Dad here?"

Terrence blinks. "I thought you said they're coming Friday?"

"Yeah, that's right. Sorry." Nobody says anything for awhile. They all assume (correctly) that I'm losing my mind. "I'm really feeling like shit." I feel like crying about it, a mixture of extreme discomfort and hopelessness. The cancer is taking over my general operations. Taking me over and doing a horrible job running things. I'm trying to teach myself how to swallow, before I choke on the saliva pooling in my mouth. I should just spit it on the floor, because I think the cancer is now running the show in my stomach and there's no sense making its life any easier.

"Time for me to fly," says Curtis. "You're all ready to rumble, doc."

"Thanks for everything." Marvcus pats my foot. "I'm waiting for a call from Dr. Bhani," he informs me. "Then we'll start."

"Okay. Where's…" Holy shit, I was going to ask for my mom again. "…uh, where's…Edna?"

"Still upstairs," says Curtis, gazing up at the ceiling. He loses himself in thought for a moment, and then leaves.

WE WAIT. Me in misery. I smack my lips, a horrible awful deathbed sound. "How long has it been? Maybe we should just do it."

"It's only been an hour," says Terrence, sitting beside me. "You okay?"

"I've been better. You know."

Marvcus checks his watch, eyeballs my vital signs. "Okay. Let's do it. Shit, didn't Curtis get the IV going? Crap. I guess…I guess I can do it."

"You're a doctor, right?" Terrence verifies.

"It's just been awhile," says Marvcus. "And tapping veins was never my strong suit." He hesitates, looking at my arm. It's covered by the sleeve of one of my all-time favorite shirts, an Arkansas Razorbacks jersey a friend sent me after his family moved to Fayetteville. I was never a Razorbacks fan, but I loved the shirt, up until my sophomore year when I grew out of it. "I didn't think to bring a gown for you," says Marvcus.

"I can take this off." I do so. Terrence backs up, stricken by what he sees. "Hey, I'm sorry you have to be here for this. Why don't you go get something to eat, and we'll call you when it's over."

Terrence shakes his head. "I'm not going anywhere."

If Terrence was a painting, the doorway would be an inadequate frame. "Thanks homey," I said. "I really appreciate it." Good friends are priceless; at crunch time, big friends are even better.

Marvcus rubber-straps my upper arm and does eeny-meeny-miny-moe to select a vein. He punctures it. "Hope that wasn't too bad. I almost didn't make it through residency for botching these things." Marvcus adjusts the drip rate on my bag of juices.

"What's in there? Good drugs, I hope."

"Sorry. Saline. I want you lucid and all systems fully functional. We need you hydrated, because before too long you'll be bringing up a lot of liquid."

"You mean he'll be puking his guts out," Terrence confirms. "'Bringing up a lot of liquid', that's a good euphemism. I like that. I think I'll use it."

"When everybody asks you how this went, tell them I was bringing it. 'You should have seen it. Brian was bringing it for hours.' I'll come off sounding pretty good."

"First step is to scarify the sites," Marvcus informs.

Terrence and I look at each other. "I'm sure it's nowhere near as painful as it sounds," he says to me.

"We just rough up the skin a bit," says Marvcus. "It's the optimal way to apply the treatment. We'll scarify and inoculate the original tumor and three additional lymph sites, behind the knee, the lower back, and the right armpit. Fifty cc's each, with another twenty-five-cc booster in five hours. And then we'll play it by ear."

From his bundle of tools Marvcus produces a cheese grater. "The scaryfier?" I ask.

"Scarifier," says Marvcus. "We scuff the surface to get a clean interface with the solution. We'll give you a topical first, to numb the sites."

"Nurse Nancy said Brian has been a bad patient and doesn't deserve any anesthetic," says Terrence.

"Shut up, Terrence," I tell him. Marvcus has already swabbed and stabbed my shin, keeps stabbing it with an anesthetic needle projecting from a paper packet. He taps my arm and I raise it, and he swabs at my pit hair before deciding to grab a scissor and a razor. After cleaning out the undergrowth he repeatedly stabs my armpit. Hurts. I hope it feels the same for the tumor. Raise its pulse a bit.

"Flip over," says Marvcus. Terrence plays orderly and helps me roll over onto my stomach. Marvcus gives it to me in the back. Each stab of the needle prickles my scalp. A whole lot of weariness pushes down on me. "How does this feel?" I'm asked.

How does what feel? I wonder....

I'm pretty sure I dozed off, because I open my eyes to find that I'm lying on my back again.

"I'd say we're ready," says Marvcus. In his hand the cheese grater. The scaryfier.

"I think someone's calling for Edna," says Terrence, leaving the room while Marvcus grates away on my shin like a prep cook.

Preceded by a wave of huffing and rustling, Mike McEwen bursts into the bedroom and beelines to my bedside. "That's enough," says Mike. "Stop what you're doing."

Marvcus stops.

"Mike." I shake my head at him.

He's ready to cry. "I can't let you do this, Brian. I'm sorry."

I know why he's here. I see the grief—for himself, for his son, for me. He's being tortured by a terrible case of déjà vu—with a rare hero's opportunity to change the past.

Empathy passes quickly. Hero my ass. Mike's a meddler, here to salve his soul. By derailing my treatment, he'll finally be able to lay Brent to rest, to leave Edna's house content that this time he did the right thing. My fate is really irrelevant to him.

I give Marvcus the green light, and he resumes roughing up my already raw shin. Mike tries to grab the grating tool.

"Sir," Marvcus barks. "This is a sterile site. You are jeopardizing this man's health."

"No, you are!" Mike must have worked himself into a lather on the way here, because he's already at full steam. "You're the one killing Brian! And I won't allow it!" He tries to pull the blanket over me, tuck me in, for a long, long snooze.

"Mike!" I produce enough volume to make him pause. "Come on," I cajole. "You can't decide for me. I want this."

"It's illegal, Brian." The three of us wrestle for control of my bedding. "There's an injunction against Bhani."

"Mike, please."

"I'm sorry, Brian."

I take hold of Mike's wrist and squeeze, until he takes a breath. "How about we get Edna and have a group discussion."

"There's nothing to discuss." Mike twists out of my grip and stumbles against the bed, betrayed by his effed-up coccyx.

"Honey," Valerie frets in the doorway, pretty sure her husband will be on his ass again soon. "Mike," she implores, "honey, let Dennis handle this."

I didn't see him come in—why didn't someone lock the front door?—but sure enough Dennis is now ambling toward Marvcus. Dennis is stocky, with a helmet head and a stout neck under his long silky middle-parted hair. He was a wrestler in college, and belongs to three different martial arts schools in town. Like I've said, no one knows how he earns a living. The morning counter crowd likes to play a game called "Who Did Dennis Kill Now?", where they scan the news and obits for high profile deaths in the cities Dennis visits on his frequent "business" trips. During his recent visit to Spokane, the city sanitation director died in a car accident. Coincidence, not Dennis's m.o.

"I'm sorry," says Dennis, his serenity soothing the McEwens' angst and doubling the room's tension, "but you're going to have to stop what you're doing." He spreads his arms like muscular Jesus. Marvcus is his flock. He's about to get herded.

"Dennis." Terrence has taken it all in quietly, pushed into the corner by the latecomers to my bacteria party. Terrence is the funhouse mirror version of Dennis. He moves with a similar easy style. His voice is just as calm. He has the same blunt projectile head, except it rides a foot higher off the floor. His shoulders are as broad if not as deep as Dennis's. Terrence actually has a waist. "You need to let the doctor do his thing. Brian needs this treatment. He has a real chance at a cure, if you'll stand aside." Terrence must have spent his time in the corner scripting this speech, because there are no pauses.

They square off. "I'm afraid I can't do that," says Dennis. "Terrence, you know the Hippocratic Oath. First do no harm." Dennis takes hold of Terrence's shoulder. "C'mon, think about it. Do you think Dr. Bhani and his little helper are following that creed?"

Terrence removes Dennis's hand. He doesn't let go, because that hand plans on returning to his shoulder. Terrence twists that hand a bit. Dennis acts as if it doesn't hurt. Neither shows it on his face or in his voice, but they are Indian wrestling. "The doctors who put Brian through chemo are the ones who broke the Hippocratic Oath," says Terrence. "Dr. Bhani's cure is Brian's only hope." Whether he believes it or not, Terrence has the company line down pat.

"That's the wrong way to look at it," Dennis advises, lip quivering from the exertion.

"There is no other way to look at it." Terrence throws down Dennis's hand. It stays down. Terrence's hands are fists at his waist. "I'm getting angry," says Terrence, this so calmly that I think Dennis misses the significance. Terrence doesn't like to share his feelings. It takes an extreme situation for him to self-report what's going on inside. "I'm getting angry thinking about what you and the McEwens will be saying when Brian dies. You'll be telling everyone that at least his suffering is over. And at least he died with his friends around him."

This is a little hard to hear, but I still like Terrence better without the pauses.

"Maybe you think you're doing the right thing," Terrence says quietly. Marvcus, the McEwens, they're all leaning forward to listen. "But this isn't a question of right or wrong. This is life or death. And Brian doesn't want to die."

Dennis widens his stance and puts some flex in his knees. "We don't always get the choice. It's not easy to accept."

"You don't get the choice," says Terrence, eerily calm. "This is Edna's house. She calls the shots, not you." Terrence points at Mike. "Not him."

"Murder's still murder," says Dennis. "Can't let it happen."

"'Fraid you're gonna have to."

They're using gunfighter stances and syntax now. Things are about to get crazy. I sit up and swing my legs over the bed. "Guys—"

Marvcus pushes me back down and holds me there. He picks up my bad leg and grates some more cheese. Blood seeps through the tool's perforations.

Dennis does a double-take. "Hey now, I told you to stop." He lays his hands on Marvcus, and Terrence lays his hands on Dennis.

Dennis backhands Terrence's palm. Terrence takes a half-step closer and glares down at Dennis. His shirt is more like second skin now.

"Folks, break it up." Officer Jay Pilsson pushes past the McEwens and squeezes between Terrence and Dennis. Officer Pilsson is five-ten and a hundred eighty pounds, so it's a brave move even with a gun. "No-no, move back, both of you," he barks the order, enforced by two other officers, one wearing a hazmat suit complete with helmet, which he tosses to the floor. He shadows Terrence while his partner, Zach, I think, beckons Dennis to join him at the door.

Terrence and Dennis reluctantly give ground. Through it all Marvcus does his job on the other side of the bed, mopping blood off my knee and readying the syringe. Officer Pilsson notices. "That means you as well."

"Thank God," says Mike.

"Are you Dr. Sawyer?" Officer Pilsson asks Marvcus.

"I am."

"You should know there's an injunction issued to stop these treatments."

"I believe the injunction only applies to Dr. Bhani," says Marvcus.

"No sir," says Officer Pilsson. "That's not the way it works. Please put everything down. We'll need to put everything here under our control."

"Well, officer," says Marvcus, flustered, "I would need to see some paperwork before I allow you to do that."

Officer Pilsson shrugs this off. "You'll see the paperwork soon enough."

Mr. Hazmat appraises Terrence's threat to interfere. He decides the possibility exists and points him into the corner. Terrence's Superman act only goes so far. He complies, and Mr. Hazmat heads for Marvcus.

I'm going to be denied. "Officer Pilsson, let them treat me." My voice quavers. "Honestly man, this is my only chance."

"I'm sorry, Brian."

I've always loved having Officer Pilsson come into my shop. Two years before the Columbine shootings in Colorado, Jamestown high school had a similar situation. A kid with an assault rifle took the basketball team hostage during an after-school practice. Officer Pilsson was the first to arrive. Before backup could get there, a shot was fired. Officer Pilsson ran inside, hurried downstairs to the weight room, ordered everyone down on the floor and charged the snot-nosed punk with the gun. The kid took a shot at one of the basketball players and missed, and then it was lights out for him. From the disturbing writings they found after, the kid definitely meant to off a few jocks. Officer Pilsson was a hero.

When I was in school, I called my teachers by their first names. I use acronyms for pastors. Doctors variously earn and lose their titles of respect. But it'll always be Officer Pilsson, for everything he's done for Jamestown.

Still I hate him. I hate him with everything I have left.

"I don't have any choice on this," he says.

I let out a howl. This can't be happening, when I am this close, when the cure is right there in Marvcus's hand.

"It's the right thing, Brian," says Valerie, making me growl.

"That's enough, Mrs. McEwen," Officer Pilsson warns. "Clear this room," he tells Officer Zach, who beckons Terrence and Dennis to precede him into the hall.

Edna wanders into the room, stumbling into Zach's dragnet. She looks terrible, like she's been weeping. "What's going on?" She moves quickly around Zach, bringing Mr. Hazmat back to alert mode.

"They're trying to stop Marvcus from curing me," I tell her.

"Edna, right there, stop." Officer Pilsson's voice cracks like a whip but Edna ignores him. She bears down on Mr. Hazmat, takes him by the arms, and drags him away from Marvcus.

"No one else comes in," Officer Pilsson barks at Zach and comes to Mr. Hazmat's rescue. "Edna, right now, this is over." He taps her shoulder, gets no response, and then peels her hand off his officer and puts it behind her back. Edna is flexible, he has to put it way up between her shoulder blades, her hand disappearing under her messy hair.

"No, no, no!" Edna screams, making Officer Pilsson's job difficult. Mr. Hazmat turns around and bumps into Marvcus, right behind him. Marvcus drops the syringe—it hits the tile floor and he says, "Uh-oh."

Mr. Hazmat runs up his commanding officer's back in his haste to get to his helmet. Officer Pilsson propels Edna out of the room, yelling, "We got a spill!" Officer Zach ducks out and slams the door behind him, leaving just the three of us. Mr. Hazmat is on his knees, fumbling to secure the helmet's seal.

"I got it," says Marvcus, also on his hands and knees on the far side of the bed. He comes up with a damp cloth. "I need a disposal bag, pronto."

Mr. Hazmat in his stiff gloves fumbles with the old-fashioned doorknob and then bolts from the room, slamming the door behind him. He's back in seconds with two canisters bearing the hazardous materials emblem. Marvcus holds the cloth at arm's length and deposits it in the smaller canister. Mr. Hazmat screws down the lid, twist after twist through a half-foot of threads. He drops this canister into the bigger one, likewise screws it down, and runs three revolutions of tape around the junction.

"Clear!" comes his modulated voice as he leaves the room.

Officer Pilsson pokes his head in the room, hand over his nose and mouth. "I need you both into the hazmat vehicle."

"It's not an airborne bacteria," Marvcus dismisses him. "There's absolutely no threat."

"We have to be sure."

"Even if it were communicable," Marvcus lectures while attending to my shin, "even if we were 'carriers', which we're not, the best option would be to stay in here and not spread it all over the house and neighborhood."

Officer Pilsson reluctantly enters the bedroom. "What are you doing?"

"I need to bandage Mr. Lawson's open wound." Marvcus folds a cloth across my scarified shin and secures it with a shiny bandage. "We had the tumor site prepared for the treatment. If you haven't noticed, this isn't exactly a sterile environment. I don't want Brian to catch something truly dangerous."

Officer Pilsson is beside himself. "What were you thinking?" he berates Marvcus. "Performing an illegal procedure in a private home? You'll have your license revoked."

"Oh I'm not a practicing physician." Marvcus is talking and acting a good game, but he's sweating.

Officer Pilsson sees it. "Dr. Sawyer, I'm going to see if I can't find a reason to take you in. I don't like what I've seen here one bit."

"Go ahead," Marvcus sasses. "I haven't done anything wrong."

"Do we live in the land of the free?" I mutter at Officer Pilsson. My head is ringing. I'm on the road to throwing up. "Can you really do this to me? If I want to try something that could save my life, and he wants to give it to me, why can you stop me? I don't get it. I don't fucking get it."

Officer Pilsson—let's just call him Pilsson from now on—puts his hand on my shoulder. He squeezes hard, to snap me out of my growing hysteria, I'm sure. It works, but he's only postponing the coming freak-out. "The judge issued an injunction for a reason, Brian. The McEwens have been down this road before, as you well know. It may not be obvious right now, but they did you a favor."

"Please don't say that."

The son of a bitch squeezes my shoulder like he's some sort of father figure, father knows best, this is a good lesson for you son, life is full of these tough lessons and you'll be a better man for it, of course you'll be dead soon, but that's beside the point.

"And please stop touching me."

Marvcus detaches me from the IV and I shuffle into the showcase foyer. Nurse Nancy is here, in quasi-professional duds and eyeing me with clinical pity, poised to spring into hospice mode. Officer Zach monitors Terrence and Dennis having an intense conversation on the front lawn. Mr. Hazmat, helmet on, reenters the bedroom to confiscate any remaining toxins, probably the last batch in existence, to be flushed down the toilet or shot into space or locked and forgotten in a biohazard vault at the CDC.

Edna sits at the bottom of the winding staircase, legs splayed and her head bowed. Somehow I thought she'd be able to make this happen. She's Edna Applejack, Queen of North Dakota, and yet she can't lay down the law in her own home.

Valerie runs at me, face filled with awful pity. "Brian, I'm so sorry." She holds my cheeks in her hands, obstructing my oxygen intake channels. I turn my head and she pulls me into a hug. I'm dizzy and nauseous and this close to screaming. Mr. Hazmat passes by with the goods in a cooler equipped with a handy carrying strap.

"Brian, my boy," says Mike, hands in his pockets, looking mournful. "I am so sorry. This has been a terrible day. I can't imagine how you're feeling. I'm sure Bhani had you thinking it was a cure. We understand, we've been through this before. The worst thing is to be misled…"

He's choked up; he's remembering his son, and I could care less about that prick. Brent was a cocky motherfucker. Mike wants to commiserate and pretend we're in the same boat. I've got news for him. There's a difference between losing a loved one, and dying yourself. One of us gets to wake up tomorrow to a brand new sparkling clear day, the other's a dead man walking.

Mike is so emotional, poor poor Mike, that Valerie has to hold and comfort him and be the one to tell me about a Fargo doctor running an FDA-approved cancer drug trial. Being such important North Dakotans with such powerful North Dakota connections, maybe they can get me in.

"It's too late, but I appreciate the info."

"No, no, Brian honey, it's never too late, please don't think that way."

"Okay, whatever the McEwens think is best, right? The McEwens have it all figured out."

"That's uncalled for," says Valerie. "You know that isn't fair. We love you."

"You love me to death."

"How can you say that, Brian?" says Mike, voice quavering. "Can't you see what this is doing to our family?"

Edna advances on him. "Are you insane? You just signed Brian's death warrant!"

"There's an injunction," Valerie moans.

Edna shrieks. When Edna shrieks, people stop breathing. Pilsson stops thumbing through his notepad and catches Officer Zach's eye, silently putting him on red alert.

Edna's eyes are red-rimmed, the normally brilliant blue streaked black as if her pupils were leaking. "Don't push me," she hisses at the McEwens. "You have no idea where I'm at right now."

I should let that go, but I can't. "Sorry to put you through this. Don't worry, I'll be out of your way soon."

Edna's teeth grind. She reaches for my hand. I reject it, and she screams again and storms upstairs; the officers downgrade the threat condition to orange.

"Excuse me, Brian, can I see you?" It's Marvcus, exiting the bedroom, lugging his oversized supply case, doing his best to look dignified. Mr. Hazmat follows, carrying my rolled-up bedding and still wearing his helmet. They both instinctively give wide berth to the smoldering heat trace Edna left behind in the middle of her grand foyer.

Mike maneuvers between me and Marvcus. "There's nothing more for you to do or say here. Tell your boss this will be included in our lawsuit. If I have my way, there'll be criminal charges filed against both of you." Mike looks to Nurse Nancy and receives validation in her clucking and nodding.

Marvcus focuses on me. "I want you within shouting distance of the hospital. If you have any issues, get there pronto."

"My leg burns," I tell him. "I think the bandage is irritating my skin."

"Leave it on," says Marvcus. "It's important—we really scraped you up, and I'm afraid of infection. We shouldn't have done this outside an antiseptic environment."

"You stupid bastard, you just don't get it," says Mike, blotchy-cheeked and spoiling for a fight. "You shouldn't have done it, period."

Marvcus stares at my leg, something like wistfulness on his face. So close, he must be thinking. He heads for the door. "Just promise me you'll get to the hospital if you get sick."

"Sure." The Davis, California hospital.

"Tell your boss he screwed up big time!" Mike yells after him.

Burning up and shaky, I collapse onto the bottom stair and take my best shot at the McEwens. "Are Rick and Andrea registered anywhere? I have no idea what to get them."

"Rick is fucking insane," says Mike. "Just completely off his rocker. I'm going out of my mind about it."

"We're wondering if Andrea got herself pregnant," says Valerie. "She might be blackmailing him."

"We were so sure Rick and Edna were finally going to be a couple," says Mike.

"They've loved each other for a long time," says Valerie, sighing. "Since high school. Poor Edna, I think she's devastated."

I'm squirming, sweating, vision smeared with streaks of light. Oh shit I feel terrible. "I think I'm crashing."

No one responds. I said it too quietly, maybe no one heard. Maybe no one believes I can actually die. I focus on the center of a marble tile, everything a kaleidoscope around this square of fudge revel swirl.

Valerie's hand is on my cheek. "You're burning up. Do you want to lie down?"

"Brian should get back to bed," Nurse Nancy suggests, from far far away.

"Mike, help Nancy get Brian back to bed," says Valerie. "I'm going to make sure Edna's okay, and let her know we're leaving." She heads upstairs.

Pilsson crouches beside me. "Brian, you okay? Should we get you to the hospital? You don't look so good, buddy. Is this normal?"

"I'm going to throw up. That's not unusual."

They guide me into Edna's guest bathroom in the nick of time. A Jamestown College throw rug gets caught up in my shuffling slide to the toilet, bunched between my legs, supporting me while I retch. I stand up with a pounding headache. The pain fills my head, my eyes, my skull, my teeth. I'm shivering, my teeth actually chattering.

"Mike," Valerie calls from above, sounding concerned. "I can't find Edna anywhere. I think she left down the back staircase."

Mike deserts me, but Terrence's powerful arm is there to support me as I rinse my face in the sink. I look into the mirror. Terrence shakes his head. "You look rough, brother."

"Feel rough. I don't care whether it's Edna's bed, or mine, or the hospital's, I need to lie down." We shuffle together into the front entryway.

Mike hobbles from the kitchen. "Edna's car is gone."

From out of the blue I have a vivid, fever-enhanced, Technicolor image of the indigo hatred in Edna's eyes. "Uh-oh." I've never seen that much darkness in someone's face. I'll bet Edna was wearing the same look fifteen years ago, right before she killed her husband. "I think Edna is going to murder Andrea."

Takes a moment for this to sink in. Pilsson touches his shoulder walkie-talkie and clears his throat. He looks at Mike and Valerie. "Does that sound possible to you?"

Valerie moans. She holds her own cheeks with trembling hands. "Yes. Yes it's possible."

"Do you know where Andrea is?" Pilsson asks.

Valerie stammers. "She said, Andrea said, she was going to get things ready to move today." Her eyes flutter wider. "I think she's already had the phone disconnected."

"Cell phone?"

Valerie looks at Mike. "We deleted it from our address books."

Pilsson talks into his shoulder. "Kerry, I need a car, ready to move." He releases the Send button. "Do we have a last name and an address for Andrea?"

"Goldine," I tell him when no one speaks up. "The Briarcourt apartments on Fifteenth Street. Number sixteen." Everyone stares. I shrug.

Pilsson relays the info to Officer Kerry. "I'm going to run over there," he tells us, on his way out the door. "Please everybody, stay put. Somebody take Brian to the hospital. Call 911 if necessary."

"Holy hell," says Mike. Valerie tries Rick's cell and gets voicemail. "Call our house," says Mike, hovering. "I asked him to level the new pool table for me today."

With a shaking finger Valerie quick-dials her house, has to leave a message.

"Let's go," says Dennis. "I'll drive you to Andrea's place. Come with us?" he asks Terrence. "We might need you, buddy." A horde of cops, a gaggle of family members, an assassin, and still they need additional backup to bring down Edna. Seems prudent.

Terrence looks at me as he backpedals. He's in crisis mode and loving it. "You'll get Brian to the hospital?" he asks Nurse Nancy.

"He's in good hands," is her reply.

I wave Terrence out the door. "Go, go." As soon as everyone's gone, I make another run for the bathroom. Me and the JC rug embrace the porcelain crapper together.

My head is diving and dancing. My lips are hot and cracked, with no saliva left to swallow. "You gotta get me there," I tell Nancy. "Hospital. Dehydrated."

"Did they leave the IV equipment behind?" she wonders, tapping the cottonball Marvcus had taped to the crook of my arm. "We can get you resting comfortably—"

"I don't want to be comfortable," I do my best to shout. "I want to get better."

Nancy seems to be humoring me as we head for her Camry. She restricts me to a maddening snail's pace, lowers me like a paraplegic into the passenger seat. She gasps. "Your leg! What's going on?"

I straighten my leg enough to see my shin. I have to blink rapidly, recruiting my last micro-ounce of moisture to melt the blur coating my eyeballs. My shin and knee are flame red around the bandage. The flesh is raised with what look like infected goosebumps, throbbing with my heartbeat.

I hike up my pajama shorts. The inflamed pulsing rash runs up my thigh to my crotch.

"Good thing we're going to the hospital," Nancy coos. "You have an infection."

That's when it hits me. "Oh boy."

"What?"

I point at the rash. "It's not an infection. That's not what's happening." Hard to talk while Nancy strokes my cheek. "It's the treatment. It's Bhani's toxins. Marvcus put them on my bandage."

"No!" Nancy yelps. "Oh God…" She claws at the bandage.

"Let go! Nancy, stop! Leave it!"

"Get it off, Brian!" Nancy kneels into the gutter, wailing, as we struggle. "It's killing you!"

"Yes! Yes! That's a good thing! God-dammit, stop!" I grab her wrists and pull her into the car on top of me, face to face. "Nancy, listen. You have to get me to the hospital."

She's senseless, not comprehending, near hysterics, committed to me dying on the McEwens' terms. "Get it off, Brian, please…you don't know what I saw with Brent."

"That isn't this. This is the way it's supposed to work…"

"No, no, no…"

"…but I'm going to die of dehydration if you don't get me to the hospital." My mouth makes hideous crackling noises, a dual stream of English and African clicks. "Move."

Nancy cries her way around to the driver's seat. We take off with a short squeal of rubber on the hot asphalt. I can't take my eyes off the bandage. "This is the cloth Marvcus used to wipe up the toxin spill. He pulled the old switcheroo on Pilsson. Unbelievable. Marvcus told me how doctors in the early days would deliberately soil a patient's dressing to cause an infection. This rash is a good thing." I work to convince both of us as my leg grows more inflamed by the second. "It's a good thing. It means my immune system is attacking the tumors…"

I suddenly have my third consecutive moment of crisis-inspired clarity. "Uh-oh."

"What?" Nancy jerks the wheel. We nick a parked car and carom left.

"It's Edna." Ordinarily, even with a raging fever caused by a mad scientist's medieval medicine, I would have reacted to Nancy's bumper car routine. "Oh boy. Edna. Oh fuck."

"Brian, what?!" Nancy avoids a head-on with a gravel truck, overcorrecting to the right. We buzz the curb along an empty stretch of the street.

"Brake."

Firmly, Nancy does. We screech to a stop, straddling the yellow center line. "Drive, slower."

She's like the computer prototype of a voice-controlled car, not yet fully debugged. After weaving back and forth for another twenty yards the car straightens out. "What's wrong?" she asks, rightly full of dread.

"Don't freak out, okay?"

Deep breath, shuddering release. "Okay," she says.

"Let's drive to the McEwens' house," I suggest.

"Why?" Nancy screams this question.

"That's it. Pull over. I'll drive. I mean it. I'm feeling better." And I am, thanks to a triple-shot of adrenaline.

Nancy obeys. I drag my sorry ass around the front of the Camry while she scoots over and collapses into the passenger seat. I accelerate away from the curb and we're nearly bashed by a pickup I didn't have the time to look for. It's a soundless near-accident. No one uses their horns in North Dakota, except to say hello.

"Brian," Nancy moans, "what is it? What's wrong?"

"Edna's not going to kill Andrea. She's going to kill Rick. I'd bet on it."

"What? What? Rick?" Nancy's shrieking, now with rage. "Go! Go! Go!"

She calls Rick's cell and then the McEwen house. Nancy has all the right numbers, but no luck. We round the corner squealing onto the McEwens' street, and she reaches Valerie. "Val, what happened at Andrea's? Did you find Edna?"

Long pause. "What, what?" I demand.

Nancy shakes her head while struggling to hear. "Andrea's there...? She's okay? Edna—no Edna? Is Rick there? Val—Valerie, listen, Brian thinks—oh no," she moans, "there's Edna's car. She's here," Nancy gurgles, her voicebox turned to jello. "Get the police to your house now!"

We run up the sidewalk and Nancy trips over her flared-leg slacks. I have to catch her. Something in my cancer knee pops as I support the extra buck-fifty. No pain, but now the leg doesn't work so well.

Front door's locked. Nancy kicks it, not like SWAT, and then we retreat and hurry down the embankment along the side of the house. My downhill leg (cancer, possible ACL rupture) buckles repeatedly. I'm still as fast as Nancy, who puts a lot of shoulders into it, runs like a doll with a few pins missing.

Under the deck she tries the sliding walk-out basement door. It joggles back and forth with some play in the locking mechanism.

"Here." One, two, I rock the door back and forth and then yank hard and the lock snaps. The rollers are sticky so the door doesn't open all the way before Nancy barges through and knocks the door half off the runner.

"Careful," I try to caution, but there are screams from inside and Nancy charges forward and up the basement stairs. She puts some distance between us...I'm half the flight behind her, and now she's screaming too.

When my head clears the top step I see Nancy, clutching her mouth, knees stuck in the buckled position. I exit the stairwell door, to a grotesque freeze frame. Rick stands beside the wet bar, legs spread wide and making a broad triangle against the bright bay window. Edna is astride his back, atop his shoulders, wrapped around his head. She's looking at us. Her fingernails are sunk into Rick's bloody shredded face. Can't tell with the gore, looks like he's missing his eyes and crying at the same time.

Nancy lurches forward. "Oh God..."

Edna slides off Rick and points a knife, stopping Nancy. I limp forward, fixated on the hunting knife's serrated edge. Rick wavers on his feet, a zombie.

"The police are coming!" Nancy screams at Edna. "You drop it! You stop it!"

And there are sirens, sure enough. "Edna, come on," I cajole. "Let's talk. Leave him. You've done enough."

"He's evil. You don't let evil live." Edna pastes her hair to the side with blood. "Rick is an evil piece of shit. I'm killing him."

"Edna, Edna…he's just a guy. Don't do this. Let me—whoa." She swipes at me, almost gets me. Could have, if she had wanted to.

Sirens are much closer, turning onto the McEwens' street, almost here. Nancy hyperventilates, working up the nerve to charge.

"Edna," I sharpen my tone, "don't. Our coffeeshop—come on, think about it—what about our partnership?"

"Sorry." Edna blinks. A droplet of blood bubbles on her eyelid where a chunk of eyelashes have been torn off.

"You're the biggest thing in North Dakota," I tell her. "Let's enjoy it. We can enjoy everything we've both earned. We can enjoy it, together."

"Life without conflict isn't life at all," Edna murmurs, grabbing ahold of Rick's fine blonde hair and shifting the knife to a backhand clutch grip.

"Edna, no, no." She's gathering herself to strike. "Hey—I thought you were a barehands killer."

Edna pauses. I wait. Rather not charge her if I don't have to. Nancy is frozen like Rick. The cops break down the front door.

"This still counts," says Edna, and jams the knife into Rick's face.

"Get down!" a policeman yells, and we do; we all four head for the floor.

Rick had thrown up his hand to block the attack. On his knees now, his severed ring finger falls off and his maimed hand drops to his side. The knife is buried to the hilt, at an angle through his nose. Gotta be dead when he hits the floor, crashing against Nancy who I think fainted. Edna sits down and the cops still tackle her. I crumple to my side and start vomiting again.

Post Mortem

Not dead. Not even close, far as I can tell. This is post mortem's other definition: the after-the-fact analysis of what went wrong, and what might be instructional. I'd like to think we can all learn something from the exercise. At a minimum we should get the satisfaction that I've been taught a good lesson.

Before we get into all that, let me say that my new shop is a beauty. Edna and Rick did a great job designing it without me. Two hundred seventy degrees of curved bar with windows to match, like a space-age diner. As I stand at the espresso machine, the sink, freezer and refrigerator are right there, all the essentials at my fingertips. I've put back fifteen of the pounds I lost to cancer, thanks in part to this efficient setup.

"Kayla, Miranda, hey." I'm having to learn the new generation of names. "Kip. What can I get you three?"

"Iced javas," says Kayla, including Miranda in the order, "half-decaf, with a shot of sugar-free vanilla syrup and a dollop of whipped cream." She leers. "How's that for an order?"

"It's still rock'n'roll to me, sister."

The girls laugh. Kip grows more serious, frowning at the menu board. He's definitely the grownup here.

"Brian, your hair's hot today," says Kayla, nineteen, devilishly cute, tanktop.

"Imagine if I combed it." It's not a hair-care strategy I endorse, but something, either the chemo or the radiation or the cancer or the toxins, something inspired epic hair growth. I wasn't bad before, but I don't mind looking better.

"How do you get a comb through that 'do?" asks Miranda, leggy and freckly.

"Oh I could."

"It's so thick."

"It's luscious," I agree. I tilt my head to give them a better look.

"I'll take the grande-sized mattina," Kip orders.

"Grande mattina!" I yell, to me. I sing along a few bars with Squeeze. "Now she's gone, and I'm out with a friend, with lips full of passion, and coffee-not-decaf-baby in bed."

"Who is that?" Miranda asks.

"That is Squeeze."

"God I like their stuff."

"Squeeze got it goin' on."

"Yeah," says Kip, laying down two seconds of a two-finger percussion track on my pickup shelf. "We put a lot more work into our hair than they'll ever know, don't we Brian?"

"They'll never know," I concur. "You'll never know," I tell the girls.

"It's a mess up there," Charlotte reports, lugging a tray of dirty cups from upstairs. "Again." We have an upstairs, where couches and easy chairs await the customer, along with a view through the curved two-story windows, of the chapel and the river beyond. It's early October and the snow is flying, right on schedule.

"Damn college kids," Kip assumes.

"Mothers with their little kids," says Charlotte.

"Why do mothers even come in here?" Kip tries to strike up a conversation with the ever-elusive Charlotte.

"Because they like coffee?" Charlotte suggests. The kid will get no play with her.

"Ladies, your drinks. And Kip."

A forty-year-old guy in dress shirt and slacks has been wandering around the shop. He leaves without ordering. "What was up with him?" says Charlotte.

"Another pilgrim visiting the shrine. It's going to take more than two murders for Edna to fall completely off her pedestal."

"I'm telling you, we need to serve an Applejack latté or a White Edna Mocha," says Charlotte. "At least then the pilgrims would buy something."

"Bye, Brian," the girls bid me adieu.

"Later my man," says Kip. "Have a good one."

"You can't stop me."

The girls laugh. Charlotte puts her hands on her hips and stares at me. "Doesn't that ever get old for you?"

"I'm pretty sure it gets better with age."

Charlotte nods at a tall shaggy-haired dude walking in and asks me, "What's your guess, pilgrim or paying customer…Sam!" Charlotte abandons our central command post to run to hug our ex-employee, squealing all the way.

"Your dad said we might see you today," I greet Sam.

"You've changed!" Charlotte marvels. "Sam used to work for us," she tells Professor Adams, working at a nearby window chair and surreptitiously plugging his ears. "He went to Alaska for the summer to work."

"I know Sam," says the Prof. "Welcome back. I've heard working in Alaska can be lucrative."

"Now he's going to blow it all on one semester at JC," I lament. "Maybe you could get him a basketball scholarship. The Jimmies could use a tall guy like Sam, huh?"

"I'm sure they could," says the Prof.

Sam gives us his big goofy grin. Correction: now that he's thirty pounds lighter, I'm betting it's a sexy grin. "I don't play basketball."

"Can you believe it?" I ask the Prof. "What a shame, huh?"

"Maybe he has a brain instead," says the Prof, suggesting an inverse relationship between athletic ability and IQ.

"You have changed!" Charlotte repeats herself.

"Any fool can grow hair," I say.

"I can do it in my sleep," Sam says with a grin.

Charlotte links arms with Sam and escorts him around the bar. "It's more than that. But your hair does look great. And I think you're taller."

"How tall now?" I demand.

"Uh, I don't know, six-eight."

"No way. That's a lie. Don't lie about your height, okay? Okay? Jeez."

"Sorry." Sam grins. So sexy. "So how are things here?"

"Oh, same ol' same old," I say. "You know about Edna Applejack, right?"

Sam gives me a quizzical look.

"No? Your folks never told you?"

"We were on the boat or the island all summer," Sam defends himself. "There's no phone out there. We didn't get mail until the last day. I have a whole pack of letters I need to read."

"Let's see if we can get you caught up." A throng of coeds stream into my shop. "Hang on."

"You want some help back there?" Sam volunteers.

"Of course we do," says Charlotte. "You're going to work here for the school year, aren't you?"

Sam ambles around the end of the bar, admiring our setup. "There's no way I'm missing the chance to work in the coffeeshop of the future." After we make enough headway on the orders streaming in, Sam nudges me. "So...?"

"So...let's see, where did you leave off? I had cancer when you left for Alaska, right?"

"Had?"

"Had. Three-shot, two-percent, no-soy cappuccino on the bar!" I yell, way too loud for the circumstances.

The young coed customer doesn't notice, like her friends captivated by tall, lean, tanned, shaggy-headed Sam.

"So I had cancer," I repeat, and Sam doesn't push for more explanation, because he knows it's on its way, in due time. "Had Edna and I decided to open this shop together?"

"I don't think so."

"Grande Applejack mocha!" I announce, as I spot Terry Lovold, VP of Student Affairs, marching toward my shop in high heels, swinging her briefcase. I know what's in there.

My customer stares uncertainly at the Applejack mocha.

"Sorry. It's a skinny white chocolate mocha."

"That should be the Edna," Charlotte concurs.

"Last I knew," says Sam, filling a pitcher for me, "you were going to open a shop in the new retail strip by the hospital."

"Isn't that nice, having the milk right there? You're right, I was going to open a shop in the Bluffs. I partnered with Andrea—you remember Andrea, Rick McEwen's ex? She and Rick got back together, you heard that? You didn't? You probably didn't know Edna murdered Rick then?"

Sam drops the pitcher. It clanks to the staging shelf, sending a geyser of milk straight up, and straight back down into the pitcher.

"Careful there. Extra large iced decaf coffee. Next time it's double for decaf," I tell the girl. "I'm serious." I am. "Hey, we got ourselves a Veep in the house. Lady, what can I get you?"

"How about a private office," says Terry Lovold, "where we can talk?"

Three more kids come in. Perfect timing. "I'm pretty busy right now." I kick Sam before he can volunteer to spell me. "Can I give you a call?"

"I'll wait." Terry turns a window chair around to face me and mounts it, somehow crossing her legs inside the cozy confines of her overstuffed skirt without being indecent.

"Okay. Where was I? Let's back up. Andrea was begging to be my partner, business and personal. She was saying all the right things, talking about how we could open all these branches in California and Colorado, with her running the business aspect and me without a real role, spending a lot of time at each shop, guest-hosting behind the bar, keeping the customers happy. At the time it seemed like the only way I was ever going to be able to build my coffee empire, you know?"

"Sure," says Sam.

"Andrea was gung-ho to drop everything and move to Denver. But even with all the dollar signs dancing in my head, I was pretty sure she was more committed to escaping North Dakota than to running a coffeeshop. So I played it safe and convinced her that we had to get our feet under us here first."

"Conservative stance," Sam compliments.

"Except I procrastinated so long that Mike gave the Bluffs to Billy-boy. Pissed me off. So at the last second Andrea and I stole it back, right out from under Billy-boy's nose."

"Radical move," Sam praises me. "Who's Billy-boy?"

"Work with me here, Sam. You remember Bill Hernandes? 'Campus' Coffee? Just to bring you up to date, he closed that shop across the river three weeks ago, after we opened here. Not to jump too far ahead, but he's selling the Bluffs to Starbucks."

"Starbucks? Starbucks is coming?"

"Can you believe it?" says Charlotte.

"It was inevitable," I say.

"You're not worried?" Sam asks.

"Damn right I'm worried. I wouldn't be, so much, if…" I sneak a peek at Terry Lovold, stabbing buttons on her Blackberry, giving some poor bastard hell. I sigh. "Terry," I call out, "you're sure I can't get you anything? Water? Take-out from somewhere? Something to read? No? Okay."

"So," Sam wants clarification, "you and Andrea…?"

"You mean…?" I wiggle my eyebrows suggestively. "I guess we were dating, kind of. I mean, I had cancer pretty bad, and with all the chemo and radiation, I was barely human."

"Nurse Nancy never seemed to mind," said Charlotte, somewhat uncharitably. "You shouldn't have dropped her."

"I might have reconsidered, but she started seeing Dennis. I mean immediately, within the hour. Not the Dennis who works for me. Assassin Dennis. By the way, where is the Dennis who works for me?"

"I sent him to Sam's Club for supplies," says Charlotte, a little dismissive.

"And Patti's at the downtown shop? Right?"

"As far as I know," says Charlotte, a touch snotty.

"I can't believe you have two stores," says Sam. "How in the world did you get a shop on campus? I thought it was impossible."

"It was all Edna." I nod at Terry Lovold while turning up the house music—the control console is right at my fingertips, how convenient is that? "That's why what's-her-name is here. Now that Edna's doing thirty-to-life, the College wants to renege on our contract and take possession of this shop. I can't blame them for trying—they paid for most of the construction, and the whole deal was based on Edna generating all this goodwill and publicity. Their high-powered legal team will probably convince the judge to rule in their favor. I need to hire an attorney, but all I can afford is a lawyer."

"An attorney or a lawyer, what's the difference?" Charlotte asks.

"A zero in the price tag." I put up the last two drinks and turn the music back down. "I've been here fourteen hours a day since we opened. I'm making some money, but sure enough, just like I feared, I'm losing business at the downtown shop."

"I'm sure some of it is coming here," says Sam.

"Like Terrence." I nod at my resident writer tucked in the nook beyond the wraparound window. He thinks I had the nook designed especially for him, because that's what I told him.

"I'm trying to eavesdrop on your story, I hope you don't mind," Terrence calls to me.

"Come on over, pull up a chair."

"How's the writing coming?" Sam asks Terrence as he joins us.

"Still plugging away."

Terrence wrote an article about the federal farm program's effect on Jamestown-area farmers. It was as good as anything else I read in magazines or newspapers. He submitted it to a few magazines, unsuccessfully. "He still can't find an agent or a publisher with a clue," I say.

"I'm sorry," says Sam.

"I'm not giving up," says Terrence. "One of these times I'm going to hit the right topic, at the right time."

"So where was I?"

"You were telling us about your relationship with Andrea," says Sam.

"You were talking about why you gave up on the Bluffs," says Terrence.

"No," says Charlotte, "you were finally getting to what happened with Edna."

"I think what I was about to say was, I'm a little heavy at the manager position. I'm going to need to fire at least one in the very near future."

Sam nods at Charlotte. "Her?"

"Just try it, and see what happens to these stores," Charlotte threatens.

Edna probably had the right idea paying extra for professional managers like Dennis and Patti, to facilitate rapid expansion. Now that contraction seems to be the direction I'm heading, I'm going to have to go cheap. Charlotte.

"Back to the story," I say.

"I'd call it a disjointed collection of scrambled thoughts," says Charlotte.

"I'm still recovering from the effects of the chemo. It destroys brain cells, you know, so cut me some slack. So, about the time I partnered with Andrea to open the Bluffs shop, I started my second round of chemo. Which I'd still be taking if it was up to that hack Bonilla."

"Dr. Bonilla is my godfather," says Sam.

"You might want to reconsider, if it isn't too late. I'm not sure he's even qualified for godfather duties. So I was feeling awful. And my hair was falling out. I have to admit that got to me a little."

"It looks great now," says Sam.

"Please," says Charlotte. "We've already spent way too much time on that topic today."

"Probably true. Terry?" I call over to the Veep. "I'm sorry, but this story is running long. We'll have to meet some other time."

Terry taps her briefcase. "We have to do this." What does she have in there? An attractive buyout agreement? A picture of Edna she'd like autographed? A free pass to Heaven? Make me an offer I can't refuse, Terry.

"Call me," I tell her. "Call Charlotte here, and set up an appointment."

Terry slides off the high chair and tugs at her skirt. That sucker doesn't budge. "I'm sorry we can't do this now, Mr. Lawson. It's only going to get more difficult if we need to involve our attorneys."

"I don't have an attorney. I have a lawyer."

Terry debates whether I'm a stupid jackass or a wily smartass. She hooks a curved fingernail under the lid of an empty cup abandoned on the table in front of her, and like a crane operator pivots to drop it in the trash can. "Take care of our building in the meantime, okay?"

I watch her sashay out the door and down the walk, trying to hate her. "I suppose I'm going to have to give this place up."

"No!" Charlotte yelps. Two girls come through the door and Charlotte dials down her outrage. "You're not giving this up," she growls from the till.

I nod at the kids and whisper, "You don't even like them, do you?"

She checks to make sure the girls aren't listening. "No," she hisses.

"Well?"

"So?"

"I'll make these drinks," says Sam. "You keep telling the story."

"Thanks homey. Alright, so I'm fading fast. And thanks to the cancer, the chemo and the radiation, I'm running low on the spite I need to get the Bluffs up and running. Things are bleak. And that's when Edna Applejack—you know, the famous basketball player and manslayer, that Edna Applejack—she comes to me with a proposition to open a JRV on campus. And then on campuses all across the state. I'm not the savviest businessman, I've proved that a few times in the past. But it sounded like a good idea. So I sold the Bluffs location to Billy-boy, ditched Andrea, and moved in with Edna. Can you believe that?"

"Impressive."

"I thought so. Turns out she was seeing Rick McEwen the whole time. Daytime friends and nighttime lovers. They were high school sweethearts."

"Wow," Sam marvels. "Incredible."

"They did a good job keeping it secret. I sure didn't have a clue. Did you know?" I ask Charlotte.

"Nope."

"And Charlotte was Edna's number one groupie, so—yes you were. Probably still are. Charlotte, just admit it. But as it turns out, Rick and Andrea kept their love an even bigger secret."

Charlotte shakes her head. "I don't get that. He could have had Edna, and he chose Andrea. I will never get that."

"It's Small Woman Syndrome," I explain. Everyone looks confused. "It's like toxic shock syndrome. No one believes it, but it's all too real."

Charlotte glares at me. "Brian. No."

"Okay. It's like Shaken Baby Syndrome." Charlotte doesn't like this one either, but I'm getting a favorable response from Sam. "Small Woman Syndrome. It needs to be eradicated. I'd rank it ahead of adult illiteracy on the national priority list. The government needs an informational campaign to teach men that small women are people too, and they can make it on their own. Men need to learn that it's okay to break it off with a small woman. Before we have more tragedies like this one."

Sam chuckles. "So when did Andrea and Rick break the news?"

"I was on my deathbed. In Edna's bed. Andrea came over to tell me they were tying the knot again and moving back to Colorado. So of course I told Edna."

"She took it poorly," says Terrence.

"Speaking of which," I take us back one step in time, "I should explain how I got into that deathbed. The second round of chemo almost killed me, but not the cancer. It was back in my shin again. I go in for another checkup, and Dr. Zhivago tells me he'll have to amputate my leg."

"Oh no," says Sam. Then he chortles despite the horror. "Dr. Zhivago."

"Get the connection? Neither of them are real doctors. I was a little bummed to hear about the need to hack off my leg, to say the least." I hike my shorts to an inappropriate height to demonstrate the proposed cut line, at the hip. Sam and Terrence wince, although there's really nothing to see now. My shin is almost the same size as the other one, a little puffy and slightly discolored. It doesn't hurt a bit.

"That's when Brian stopped coming in to work," says Charlotte.

"I was really sick, and really depressed. Charlotte, what's the one thing I hate to do, more than anything else?"

"Die," says world-weary Charlotte.

"Close. Die, with only one leg. Andrea had been working on me to go with her boss's treatment. Which is, using deadly bacteria to make you so sick that your immune system attacks anything in sight, including the cancer. It sounded a little medieval to me."

"That's the treatment Brent McEwen tried, isn't it?" says Terrence, the storyteller's straight man, supplying the occasional key fact in the form of a question to create a faux conversational feel, never interrupting the flow or forcing the story in an unscripted direction, careful not to ruin the punch line.

"Correct. When I was finally desperate and brave enough to take the treatment, Andrea anonymously sends me gruesome pictures of Brent's autopsy."

"If it was anonymous," says Sam, "how did you know who sent them?"

"That's where you benefit by hearing this story two months late. All the loose ends have been tied up."

"Check," says Sam.

"The pictures were unbelievably hideous. Brent died of flesh-eating bacteria. Which, as it turns out, is basically the same bacteria Dr. Bhani uses for his cure. Scared the shit out of me. Edna was livid that Andrea tried to spook me, when she knew how successful this treatment could be. I thought Edna was ready to kill her. Keep that in mind, by the way, for later in the story."

"Why did Andrea send you the pictures?" Sam asks.

"Spite, for dumping her. I was her ticket out of North Dakota. She made it out now, back to Colorado with her son, but you'd have to call it the hard way. So anyway, I'm freaked out by the pictures, and then I read all these articles about how other researchers think Dr. Bhani is a mad scientist. How his toxin treatment doesn't work. How dangerous it is. So, of course, I decide to take the treatment."

Sam pauses, about to hit the blender switch for a batch of raspberry mango smoothies for two cute coeds. "Why?"

"Partly because I was growing tumors in my back and my groin and my throat and my armpit, and probably a few other places they hadn't caught yet. Mostly because I wanted to live to fulfill my dream of running a chain of campus coffeeshops with Edna."

"That's not why you took Dr. Bhani's treatment," says Charlotte. "Tell the real reason."

I nod to Sam and he hits the switch. There can be no conversation during the running of the blender.

Prematurely, before all the ice has been pulverized, Sam turns off the blender and looks at me. "Are you crying?"

"Maybe." I tried blinking the tears away, and now I have to wipe them from my cheeks. "You got a problem with that?"

Sam snorts a happy "no", finishes the job, and hands the girls their drinks.

"Brian always gets emotional at this point in the story," says Charlotte.

"Charlotte knows I'm going to cry, that's why she has me tell this part." This, what I would call a secular salvation testimonial, is part of the story, by now scripted almost word for word. It's way too personal for a place of business, but I really want the people I care about to know, and that's the way it works in my shop. "Aaa. Hang on. Okay. After I got the amputation news, and the toxin treatment looked like a sham, I was really down. It was way beyond a depression. I was in a deep hole with a lid on top. I knew I was going to die soon, and I was scared shitless. Most people acquire a strong faith in God right about then. But I went the opposite way. My faith had always been kind of fuzzy. And now it deserted me completely."

I can't describe it without feeling it. I'm back there again, right now, a couple inches, a few days, a missed heartbeat from slipping into Nothingness, that unimaginable world where there is a complete lack of Brian.

"And then," Charlotte prompts.

"And then, all of a sudden, Dad shows up." My voice shakes. "Just Dad. He never travels alone, without Mom. He's committed to his job, hates to leave it. But here he was." I'm wiping tears as I talk. "Dad tells me he's going to hang out with me for a few days. And then…hang on, I'm sorry."

Sam squeezes my arm. "It's okay, Bri."

"Okay. There. Sorry. So…alright, here's the really emotional part. Huh, Charlotte?" I look over and she's crying too. She nods. "I'm telling Dad how sorry I am that I was a failure in the coffee business. I'm confessing that I'm incapable of running more than one little shop…and he looks at me…and he tells me how proud he is of me."

I'm crying way too hard for the tissue to keep up. Customers are coming in, but there's nowhere to hide in this theater-in-the-round setup.

Terrence turns away to hide his tears from the gawking college kids. "Brian, I'll never forgive you for this."

"You're going to have to stop telling this here at the shop," says Charlotte. "I think I've cried every day this week." She turns her back on the till to wipe her eyes, then faces the customers. "What can we get for you?"

The pause for the drink orders is the breather in needed. "Maybe Dad was trying to soothe my soul so I could die in peace, without any regrets." I encourage Sam to add more foam to the extra-dry cappuccino. "But that's not the way I took it. I believed he expected to see me do something incredible and pull through. Dad made me feel so good about myself...honestly, the thought of dying just disappeared. From that point forward, I knew I was going to live."

"But not without a last-second save from our heroic, injunction-bucking doctor," says Terrence.

"Bhani," says Sam.

"At least you didn't guess Bonilla. Bhani benched himself at the last second for a pinch-hitter. Our hero was Dr. Sawyer. Brave, and handsome. Like a young and really small Rob Lowe. Charlotte should move to Minneapolis and contract an incurable disease and let Dr. Sawyer cure her. It would be a beautiful love story."

"I just might," says Charlotte, out on the floor retrieving dirty coffee cups. "Assuming he doesn't go to prison."

"I'm guessing there was an injunction against Dr. Bhani's treatment," says Sam, demonstrating excellent powers of listening and comprehension.

"That's what Mike McEwen was screaming, when he barged in to stop us." Sam is incredulous. "At the hospital?"

"Edna's bedroom. Because the Indian reservation didn't work out."

"Of course," says Sam, making me wonder whether he's paying attention.

"Mike brought Dennis—not our Dennis; Dennis the Assassin."

"The enforcer," says Charlotte.

"Luckily I had one too." I nod at Terrence.

"Oooh." Sam gets ready to hear about a rumble.

"They were this close to duking it out. I mean they were bumping chests and jockeying for position."

"I'd pay money to see that one."

"All posturing," says Terrence. "All for show."

I give Sam a quick shake of the head to let him know Terrence is posturing on the posturing. "Meanwhile Doc Sawyer pushes ahead. He roughs up the skin on my shin, makes it bleed real good, in preparation for the injection of Bhani's toxins. He's about to stick it to me, when the cops burst in. Officer Pilsson and his boys. They pry apart Dennis and Terrence, and tell the Doc to drop the needle. So he does."

"He dropped it?" Sam verifies.

"He literally dropped it," Terrence confirms.

"He pretends it's an accident. One of the cops is in a hazmat suit, because the McEwens had them freaked out about these killer bacteria. Everybody runs screaming from Edna's bedroom, certain that the flesh-eating bacteria is coming for them. Doc Sawyer wipes up the spill—with a cloth—and properly disposes of it in a hazmat container. Then he bandages my wound—with a cloth. The cops cart him away, and I start getting really sick. I'm sure I'm in my cancer death throes, puking my guts out, mostly in the can, some on the floor, a little on the walls. Edna doesn't care, because she's distraught about Rick and Andrea, completely wigged out. Hey, look who's here."

Dennis (the Assassin) enters and hails Sam. "Look who's back! How was Alaska?"

"Great." Sam nods at me. "We're at the part where Brian is throwing up."

"Which time?" Terrence quips.

"In Edna's house," I clarify.

"Oh, oh," says Dennis, "this is my favorite part. Okay, go on."

"So you two put down the gloves and made up," Sam correctly evaluates the lack of animosity between Terrence and Dennis.

"Tensions were high that day, what can I say," says Dennis.

"How about when we all realized Edna is a homicidal maniac?" I ask.

"Thanks to your hunch," says Terrence.

"Too bad my hunch was a little less than perfect. So Edna disappears. During the time I knew her, she got mad at me a couple times, and I would pretend to be afraid she was going to kill me. Suddenly it hits me that it's no joke. I'm sure she's going to kill Andrea. The cops and a citizen posse take off for Andrea's apartment, while Nurse Nancy drives me to the hospital. That's when we notice that the skin around my bandage, my whole leg, is burning red. The worst looking rash you've ever seen."

"Oh boy," says Sam.

"And it dawns on me: Doc Sawyer wrapped my scuffed skin with the toxin clean-up rag. He pulled the old switcheroo."

"No way," says Sam.

"I was undergoing treatment without anyone knowing it. Nurse Nancy freaked out and tried to tear off the bandage. I didn't let her."

"And she's hard to resist," Dennis testifies.

"I'll bet," says Charlotte, disgusted.

"Nancy is driving like a maniac to the hospital, when it hits me: Edna doesn't murder women. She's a man-killer. We turn the car around and head for the McEwens…"

"I'm leaving for this part," says Charlotte. "I don't ever want to hear this description again. I have nightmares just from hearing about it."

"You're coming back down here if we get customers," I call after her as she heads upstairs. I take a pull from my water bottle. "I don't blame her."

For once Sam isn't smiling. "Pretty bad, huh?"

"I knew she murdered her husband with her bare hands, but I had no clue. The cops said this was similar to her first go-around. Except for the knife, which as I pointed out to her at the time, was sort-of cheating. But, academic at this point." Sam's eyes are wide. Terrence studies me. "The cops tackled Edna so hard they fractured her back. She's in a wheelchair in prison."

"I hope they put that cunt in SuperMax," says Dennis, adding extra color to the sentiments I've heard from a lot of people. Jamestown can forgive one cold-blooded murder; two is crossing the line. "Put that bitch in a hole and throw away the key."

"Mike and Valerie are a mess," I report. "It's really hard to accept that Rick's dead."

"I'd like to shoot that bitch between the eyes," says Dennis. He must have decided Edna got off easy in his first fantasy scenario. "I'd like to hunt her with my Bowie knife. I'd like to jump down out of a tree"—Dennis acts out his fantasy—"and land on her shoulders, and start stabbing. That's what the bitch deserves."

We all nod. "So let me see where your tumors were," says Sam. "I heard they just melted away."

"Hey…I thought you hadn't heard anything?"

"I lied," says Sam. "Mom called me every day for awhile there. I even caught a couple of your interviews on TV. I just wanted to hear you tell it."

"Amen, brother." We knuckle-knock. "It was downright miraculous. Your godfather Dr. Seuss couldn't believe what he was seeing. My immune system went ape shit, turned into a cancer blender. I guess they were draining dead tumor soup out of me for a few days. I wish I had been awake for it."

"I heard it got pretty bad," says Sam.

"Practically everybody in town came to see Brian," said Terrence. "You couldn't find any flowers to buy, the stores ran out. People were picking them from Amber's garden."

"A few of us tried to keep 'round-the-clock vigils in Brian's room," says Dennis. "The nurses were getting cranky. It was amazing. It was like when Donna Bennamin's cat had that calico kitten with Lawrence Welk's face on its belly. People were waiting in line to go see Brian. The hospital gave everyone numbers in the lobby, and then took groups every half-hour up to his room."

I shrug. "What can I say? I'm as big as the Bennamin kitten."

"Poor thing got pneumonia from all the draftiness, having the door open all day," Dennis reports. "It died."

"Pussy. Although I shouldn't talk, because the cure almost killed me. Basically put me in a coma. I actually preferred the coma. Spared me from feeling violently ill for three days. When I came to, I felt great. And the tumors were just about gone." It had taken me a day to straighten out my thoughts, and separate wild coma dreams from equally wild reality.

"What does Bonilla think about Dr. Bhani's treatment now?" says Terrence.

I shake my head. "He doesn't. He's treating it like a miracle. From what I can tell, my cure hasn't changed anything. Everyone still thinks Bhani is a fraud. Doc Sawyer is in trouble for violating the injunction. I'm giving a deposition tomorrow. Dr. Bhani called me from a payphone, asking me to play ignorant about what may or may not have been on that cloth bandage. Since he's not going to benefit anyway. Doc Sawyer might avoid jail time if no one can prove that I had the toxins in me."

"Didn't they take blood tests?" says Dennis.

"They did. But that's the beauty and the curse of Bhani's toxins. They're hard to distinguish from infections people pick up in hospitals all the time. That's the story Bhani and Doc Sawyer are going to stick to. It shouldn't be hard to get them off the hook. Mom and Dad, the McEwens and half the town are convinced I somehow saved myself. With a big helping hand from God."

Sam grins. "But you think differently, don't you?"

"I know I owe Bhani and Doc Sawyer my life. Without a doubt."

At the end of the story, I always get tearful hugs from the women and heartfelt handshakes and the occasional hug from the men. This time is no different.

Charlotte descends the stairs. "Is the gross part over?"

"The coast is clear," says Sam.

"You missed the hugs, though," says Dennis.

"I've hugged Brian enough lately."

"Amen."

Charlotte slugs me in passing.

"Makes all this trouble with the College seem trivial, doesn't it?" says Dennis. "All that really matters is, you're alive."

I've heard comments like Dennis's a hundred times in the last few weeks, and said it to myself a few more. No matter what life throws at me from this point forward, no matter how little success I have, regardless how little money I make, I should be deliriously and unconditionally happy. Simply delighted to be here.

And I am delighted. I am thankful to Dr. Bhani and Doc Sawyer. They single-handedly saved my life. For Doc Sawyer, at great risk to his career. He's the bravest guy I know. In the Single Moment of Outstanding Bravery category, the award goes to Doc Sawyer.

But I'm a conditional man. I may be delighted, but I'm not going to be happy unless I've earned it, unless I succeed to the level I'm capable of. I'll tell you what, I'm going to be hard to live with, if another fifteen years go by and I'm still treading water, still scraping to get by. Dad, thank you for your love and your pride, but I'm afraid you're still selling me short. Getting to where I am now—which is basically where I was ten years ago—isn't anything exceptional. It's not enough. Here comes Starbucks, to prove it.

Of course maybe I'll mellow as the years go by, finally settling down with the realization that the world is viciously competitive, regardless whether you live in San Fran or Jamestown, and this is as high as most of us can get. What are a few equivalents to owning your own coffeeshop? Middle manager at a bank? Regional head of a crop insurance agency? Probably. Salesman of the year for a drug company? That would be ten times the money, with ten times the demons—so as far as success goes, equivalent. Most people top out somewhere in the middle. Most small businessmen are just that. Small, with no franchise-able growth in the cards. So I might not be in such bad shape; just too young yet to realize it.

Dennis and Sam leave as the Period Four flock descends upon us. "Thanks for stopping in," I tell them.

"This is the only way we get to see you anymore," says Dennis.

"Not to mention wall-to-wall college girls," says Terrence; and then he pauses, out of order, costing him an honest admission. "In any case," he says quickly, "we're glad you're here. The College would be crazy to lose you."

"Amen," says Sam.

I knuckleknock 'em. "I appreciate it, homies."

The first wave of students hits the till. Terrence asks me, "How many Edna interviews have you done, since that day?"

"Five. I have a guy from The Atlantic magazine coming tomorrow. We have six hours blocked off, and then more the next few days if he needs it."

"Don't give the interview."

"Okay."

"Seriously." Terrence is agitated. "I want it. I'm sitting on a gold mine. Edna Applejack…her story's got movie rights written all over it."

"It's true, people are crazy for info on her. And not just North Dakotans."

"Two mocha coolers and a berry smoothie," Charlotte relays an order.

"Two chilly chocolates and a bloody Maggie! Stat!"

Charlotte sighs and apologizes to the customers.

"I would love for you to write this tale," I tell Terrence. "I know you'd do a great job. But when you get right down to it, it's really my story."

"True. True."

"So…let's write it together. You and me, fifty-fifty, everything down the middle. We'll even split my acting income when they cast me in the role of Brian Lawson."

"You'd be great in that role."

"I'd nail it."

"Can you write?"

"I can tell a good story. Should we find out if they're the same thing?"

"Brian, you can't write," says Charlotte. "Terrence is our writer, not you."

"I might need a little help with the grammar."

"Editing is my forte," says Terrence. "You just write wild and free, and I'll clean up after you."

"You know," I start dreaming, "we might have something here."

"This could be our springboard to the big time," says Terrence. "Can I drink for free during the collaboration period?"

"No, but maybe you can tax deduct it."

Terrence types into his laptop. He looks up at me. "Okay. Our story has begun. I can see already that there's one question we have to answer. One question everybody wants to know. With everything Edna had going for her, all the basketball success, all the love from the people here and around the state—why did she do it?"

"Of course I've asked myself that question a few times. I even asked her, when she pulled the knife."

Charlotte covers her ears. "You said you were done talking about that."

"Do you mind? We're working here. We're talking character motivation."

"Sor-ry."

"I can recall Edna babbling something about life needing conflict. We could work with that angle. I can craft some pretty impressive theories. Do you have any trouble with me making some things up?"

"Not at all," says Terrence.

"Nice," says Charlotte. "Can I get a grande iced chai and a tall skinny mocha, light whip?"

"You forgot to say 'or else'."

"You know the 'or else'."

"You are not going to come off flatteringly in our book," I warn.

"Flatteringly?" says Charlotte. "Terrence, is that a word?"

"I think so."

"Not a good one. I'd think twice about writing a book with Brian."

"I think we're sitting on a gold mine," says Terrence.

"You think so?" My heart beats faster. "You think we could make some money? You don't think a movie deal is out of the question?"

"This story has it all," says Terrence. "Murder and athletics."

"Sex, drugs and rock'n'roll, baby. Hey mister," I greet Spence as he arrives for his three o'clock shift. "Take over for me, would you? That's the mocha, that's the decaf caramel macchiato." I lean over the counter across from Terrence. "How far back do you think we should go?"

"Let's start with Edna's first murder and work forward, her prison time, her release, her relationship with you, with flashbacks to her playing days."

Charlotte clears her throat. "Brian…" The queue of kids waiting to order and the cluster awaiting drinks have both grown.

"We can interview the JC athletic director," I tell Terrence. "And I'm sure we can track down a few high school and college teammates. In fact, Patti, one of my new managers, used to play against Edna back in college."

"That's good stuff," says Terrence.

"Which means Dennis draws the short straw," I muse.

"Brian," Charlotte's voice is sharper now. "Help, please."

"Damn customers," I mutter. "I gotta go to work."

Acknowledgments

AS THIS book took shape, our writing partnership was still brand new. It was an exciting time—we loved telling this tale in Brian's words, while discovering our own unique voice. But cancer plays a starring, nefarious role here, and meanwhile we had family and friends suffering through chemo and radiation treatments. Their trials demanded that fictional or not, Brian's experience be true. Writing *Java Man* was an emotional process; oftentimes what carried us through was the potential for a cure.

And so we give thanks to the researchers, and the writers who cover them. Of the latter, Stephen Hall is a master. (Even the fictional editorialist at the beginning of this book thinks so.) Hall's recounting of William Coley's heroic efforts a century ago captivated us. Siddhartha Mukherjee's *The Emperor of All Maladies* also stands out—in particular, for exposing the incredible, malevolent genius of cancer. We all owe a huge debt and gratitude to the scientists dedicated to finding not just a cure, but preventions and early interventions as well.

Half of Harris Gray tried to close here with an exhaustive list of everyone we want to thank, for the time, inspiration and sacrifice they gave us to write, and their assistance getting this story to you. The other half did what he does best, saving everyone from being exhausted, ending it right there. With the exception of one final thank you. People may consider us a couple, but our real partners are our wives. Julie and Kathryn, we couldn't have done it without you.

Also by Harris Gray

Vampire Vic

(Book 1 in the VV Trilogy)

WOULD YOU give up donuts…for blood? Fat, balding accountant Victor Thetherson hoped becoming a vampire would turn his life around. But Victor can't stomach confrontation and gets queasy at the sight of blood. Instead he gets it from the blood bank, diluted in bloody Bloody Marys. The result: a vampire who doesn't bite, and a man who gets no respect.

Victor's slacking staff mockingly calls him Vampire Vic. Victor's boss amuses his wife by intimidating Victor on video. His ex makes him stay out late while she entertains boyfriends in the house she insists they continue to share. One night it finally boils over, and Victor bites someone. And then another…and very soon, he's no longer visiting the blood bank.

Muscle replaces fat, and his comb-forward widow's peak takes root. Victor basks in newfound attention and respect, at the office and at home. But real vampires get hunted, and as the transformation reaches the tipping point, Victor must decide how much he's willing to sacrifice for the power of the vampire.

Available at Amazon.com.

Book Two in the VV trilogy coming Spring 2014!

About the Authors

IN THE nook seat of Jason's coffeeshop, Allan wrote. And eavesdropped, as Jason told stories. One day Allan found waiting for him a little yellow notepad, crammed to the margins with Jason's tales. Allan typed them, touched them up, and called it good. Jason had other ideas.

A collaboration began. The writer and the storyteller. As their tales converged and became inseparable, as they were fused by the stories they told…all the king's horses & men can't un-make Harris Gray again.

VISIT HARRIS GRAY: harrisgray.com
FOLLOW HARRIS GRAY: twitter.com/harrisandgray
LIKE HARRIS GRAY: facebook.com/HarrisGrayAuthor

NOW THAT you have finished our book, won't you please consider writing a review? Reviews are the best way readers discover great new books. We would truly appreciate it.

www.ingramcontent.com/pod-product-compliance
Lightning Source LLC
Chambersburg PA
CBHW070208260626
47160CB00002B/486